About the Author

Martin Patrick was born in London. His education includes, BA Hons, MA, PGCHE and Ph.D. research in Film, Drama, Race and Gender in Cultural Studies. He has written five plays, including *Where To Now,* which won him the London Playwright's Co-op 1988 Best New Playwright award. His third play, *Give It Up Mum,* was selected by The Independent Newspaper for the Second Phase prize. He was Senior Lecturer in Drama and Film Studies. Now he teaches aspiring LGBT, Black and Asian authors at greatnewwriters.com, and he lives in London.

Dedication

DWL

A million words cannot describe how much
I've loved you.

Martin Patrick

LOVE BOTH WAYS

AUSTIN MACAULEY
PUBLISHERS LTD.

A CIP catalogue record for this title is available from the British Library.

ISBN 9781786297327 (Paperback)
ISBN 9781786297334 (Hardback)
ISBN 9781786297341 (eBook)

www.austinmacauley.com

First Published (2017)
Austin Macauley Publishers Ltd.
25 Canada Square
Canary Wharf
London
E14 5LQ

Acknowledgments

Oscar Wilde: one of the few virtuosos in narrative history.
James Baldwin: the author who assured me that I had the right to write.
E.M. Forster: your cool yet steaming heart gave us *Maurice*. Thanks
Pedro Almodovar: a storyteller whose work has inspired me from the 1980s to the present day.
Jean Genet: a truly great writer. Thanks for *Prisoner of Love*.
Frantz Fanon: *Black Skin, White Mask* has had a profound impact on my psyche from 1980 to the present.
Ralph Ellison: The *Invisible Man* changed my perspective concerning Black men's lives across the diaspora.
Peter Abrahams: *The View From Coyaba* inspired me to become a Black British author writing today!
Jacqueline Suzanne: whose novels I read as a teenager and adored!
Armistead Maupin: I cannot thank you enough for the sheer joy of reading *Tales of the City* and the *Baby Cakes* novels
Prof Stuart Hall: *Critical Dialogues in Cultural Studies*. From the day I met you at my debut play in 1988 to the day I meet you again, I thank you for your guidance, scholarship, your academic advice and counsel researching Black British Cultural Studies. R.I.P with my admiration and love.
To my visual consultant, who worked with me from the concept of designing the book cover, to his creation of *Love Both Ways* digital artwork, Wilson Ramires-Galucho: Thank you for everything!
Finally, to Mr. Dan Wright MA. A man who is no author, he is just one of the greatest friends I could ever have made at this stage in my life. Dan, you were the first person to read this novel and tell me how much you admired it. Our existential conversations compelled me to stop working for bloodsuckers and strike out on my own as an entrepreneurial novelist. February 2015 was the time when you helped me to change my life. For this and all the laughter; I extend my Love and Respect to you, your wife, and son. I wish you love and money for all the years to come.

Book One – Fear

CHAPTER ONE

July 1st 2014

A frisson shot through David's body which made him smile because whenever he saw his son, Adrian, that sense of joy was always there. He glanced in the rear view mirror to see how the emotion affected him. He liked the look on his face even though he wasn't happy with his looks. He did, however, love his exotic funky dreads that smelt as beautiful as they looked. Consequently, his hyperconscious state of *Being* gave him a glow that shone in his skin, his straight white teeth and his bright eyes.

It was one of those rare days in London; the weather was perfect. Driving from Islington in North London, with its middle-class families, and its arts and media neurotic singles, who lived in overpriced flats; to the racially diverse, fashion conscious, and highly desirable Borough of Hackney was a journey he'd made most of his life. He took the back streets because London traffic jams were a justifiable defense for road rage. His scarlet red Triumph GT6 MK3 Rotoflex caught the sunlight as he zigzagged through the streets with *Born To Do It* playing on his car stereo. The Craig David 'Garage' classic CD always reminded him of being at University in 2000. His nod was distinctly iconic of an Afro-Caribbean London raised Black guy.

He wasted twenty minutes trying to park and so had to walk for ten minutes to get to the house. On his way there several people waved and gestured at him because they'd lived there all their lives and knew him on sight since he walked with the pride his father had drilled into him as a boy. It was a neighborhood made up of family homes: mostly renovated WW2 terrace houses on a modest looking road with street lamps but no trees. Among all the black, green and brown doors on the street, only one house had a bright purple door with brilliant white window frames and a gray tiled roof.

David shouted across the road to a badly dressed elderly Caribbean woman.

"Why is the dirt still on the streets?" he asked with a refined Nigerian elegant London accent. She told him the dustmen were late and kissed her teeth. He waved her off pleasantly and turned into the garden path and up to the high purple door. After he knocked and waited, he adjusted his shirt and belt and stood tall.

Grace came to the door and let him in. She was a woman in her prime years, her thirties, and her face didn't show it. She was fine-looking. Wannabe teenage divas who fancied themselves as the next top model had nothing on Grace because she had true character and people knew that by her earth mother body language and psychology.

To avoid the police profiling him, David dressed in designer casuals, and his classic smart attire suited him. Grace looked him over, and he eyed her staring at him. He noticed that she had copper colored decorative beads in her shiny narrow funky dreads, and her hair was tied back with the same material as her dress. Her hazel brown complexion, green eye shadow, and red lips made her look even better than usual.

"You're spending too much time in the gym – look at you, fit as fuck!" Even though she wasn't born in Jamaica, she loved the patois dialect, and depending on whose company she was in, she leaned either toward Cockney with British and Europeans or patois with other Caribbean people and Africans. He kissed her cheek and said hello. His son Adrian came dashing downstairs into the hallway, and he threw his arms around his father. He was dressed in trainers that had a red flash on the sides, white shirt and jeans that fit him properly because David and Grace loudly expressed their disgust about guys who wore jeans that exposed their underwear or buttocks. Eyeing his parents, Adrian looked as happy as he felt which made him all the more handsome.

"Son, Happy Birthday."

"Dad for some reason I've been jittery all day." Adrian's diction was refined and colored with traces of his heritage. "Last night I just couldn't get to sleep."

"Well you're off to University in a few weeks' time, and you're nineteen. I'm not surprised you're excited." Looking at his parents, Adrian was so happy he was overcome. Tears threatened him, and he felt as some people do when they stand up too quickly and have to take a moment to re-compose themselves. David took Grace and Adrian's hands and walked them into the living room. They briefly formed a chain and entered the room in single file with David in the middle. Grace led, and Adrian moved in close holding onto his father's hand. There were hanging decorations and a table full of treats, presents, and candles, with a cake in the middle.

14

The mid-size room was decorated with plants, countless framed photos of Black heroes and leading spokeswomen of Black Politics; such as Oprah Winfrey, Diane Abbott and Baroness Doreen Lawrence, Grace's personal heroine. There were also images of the Rt. Hon Paul Boateng MP, Dr. King, Malcolm X, and Marcus Garvey. The room and the entire house were spotlessly clean. The furniture was old-fashioned, but most people saw it as a retro homage to Caribbean living rooms in the 1960s-70s that showcased chintz and kitsch. The lovely aroma of sandalwood drifted through the room from scented candles.

"Sit down," Adrian said. "I'll serve." David pulled a funny face at Grace as they watched their son bring treats from the dining table to them.

David observed. "He seems more like a boy doing that than a man – don't you think?" Grace took David's hand and nodded in agreement.

They sat for an hour engaged in small talk which compelled Adrian to say, "Dad, taking time off work for this: don't feel obliged. Are you bored?"

"What's more important than your birthday? Growing up, your grandfather..."

"Gramps is coming at five o'clock. He told me he had 'an opening' and so he's coming by and..."

"I'm not in the mood for him today," David interjected.

"You two..." Grace began. "Underneath it all, he's very proud of you David."

In a pitch-perfect tone of voice, David replied with a spiky Nigerian accent. "I don't have time for this excavation or analysis." Open mouthed, Adrian pulled a face rather shocked at how well David could mimic and rebuke his own father.

"Dad, he's not that bad."

"That's because I never allowed him to beat *you* up."

"Know what," Grace said to dispel the tension. "Let's open some presents."

David took an envelope from inside his shirt and gave it to his son. "Happy birthday."

Adrian looked at it for a time, and Grace watched the two of them. Finally, Adrian opened the envelope and took out the cheque.

"Fifty thousand pounds!"

"That's your University fees and lodgings paid for. Give the cheque to your mother." He ogled it and wouldn't hand it over. Mischief covered

Adrian's face for a while. Grace started laughing first and then David began to chuckle watching him.

Grace said, "Gimme the cheque!" But Adrian wouldn't let go which really made David laugh, so Grace gave him a threatening look that Black men read as a warning. Adrian handed over the money, and she walked away, fanning the room with her hips in provocative triumph. "You haven't told your father thank you."

"Thanks, Dad."

"You know what; let's go out to Victoria Park and have a drink…"

"We'll miss your father if we do," she said naïvely.

"Yes… so let's get a move on."

"No, I'm not gonna support this. I like your mum too much to upset her. You know Solomon will say we checked out to avoid him; he knows you'll be here."

David interrupted by telling her. "I can't eat anymore. I'm on a skinny day."

"Are you kidding me? What weight can *you* lose: with your 1% body fat and special organic micro-whatever diet and gym regime? You look as fit as Adrian."

"I'm kidding about going. Don't you know me by now? Besides, robbing my father of my son's life is really fucked up; I don't know what kind of person does that." He studied Adrian and noted his son's recognition of what honorable behavior means. At that moment David saw what truly made Adrian attractive; it wasn't that he'd inherited his mother's fine features. Adrian had never disgraced the family with any kind of 'immoral conduct'. The police never knocked on their door, nor did strangers come to their house to shout about some girl Adrian had 'knocked up'.

David dipped his hand back inside his shirt and took out a birthday card that he held aloft for Adrian, who got up and went to him for it. Grace left the room to get them drinks and Adrian took the card from his father and read it.

'Son – *happy birthday; you're twice the man I was at your age. Your intelligence and compassion are your greatest virtue. Because of you, I've learned what each generation can teach one other. No amount of money is greater than me giving life to you: your devoted father, David'*.

Adrian was overwhelmed, so he embraced his father shaking with pent-up emotion. In Yoruba, he said, "Daddy I pray for you all the time. No one else in the family understands what you mean to me. I don't look to

16

strangers for heroes; you're here." David's heart was so full because his son spoke to him in his father's language. He had achieved his goal to be a hero to his son. The intensity of their emotions was so penetrating; Grace felt their energy from the other side of the room and studied them. Deep inside her soul knew she'd never love any other men more than them.

The doorbell rang, and she quickly moved to welcome people in. Her lifelong friend and confidant, Amy, came in with her daughter, Suzanne. Amy was a sensuous looking, rich ginger redhead and her seventeen-year-old daughter was a very pretty strawberry blonde who resembled her mother. They were both tall and lean, and Amy watched Suzanne dash into the living room to see Adrian.

Amy said, "Hi! She saw David arrive, and I had a job keeping her in the house." Her Dublin accent sang out. "I told her we had to wait and give them some privacy, but she was nagging me to come over; everything alright?" Grace nodded, but Amy saw that she was emotionally taxed.

Reluctantly Grace said, "You know how moody and hostile Adrian gets if I go out with a bloke; and there he is with his Dad, like – like perfect!" Amy touched her dreads and then placed her hand on her shoulder comfortingly.

"Oh I know," Grace told herself impatiently. "I know. Find a man and get on with my life." Amy nodded in a manner that acknowledged how familiar they were with the subject, after the twenty years of confessions they shared as lifelong friends. Amy winked at her, and that made Grace feel so good she snapped out of it.

Half a minute later, David's father, Solomon, came up the garden path carrying a bag from Harrods, dressed in an immaculate azure blue Ozwald Boateng suit, pink shirt and handmade English brogues. He was a six foot tall, stern looking man with dark lips and perfect white teeth. Like his son and grandson, his thick eyebrows sat in a semicircle above his eyes. "Hello Grace; Amy," he said as he quickly rushed by them. "Where are my sons?" Amy looked heavenward and kissed her teeth; a characteristic Afro-Caribbean skill she had mastered with the help and instruction from Grace.

When Grace and Amy re-entered the living room, Solomon was talking to David and Adrian in Yoruba with exuberance and great gestures. He shook Adrian's hand and then gave him the bag. Solomon gave David a cocky glance that Grace found silly. Amy poked her, knowing the weary

17

expression on her face all too well. Adrian opened the box and threw out the tissue until he came to the Moschino brown leather jacket.

"Gramps, this is lovely, thank you," Adrian gratefully told him in Yoruba.

"What did you get him?" Solomon chivied.

"I gave him some money…"

"Money?" Solomon interrupted. "How can that be a present showing love?" he asked rhetorically. David glanced at Grace and Adrian.

Grace said, "Can we get this in English, please? If you're talking about gifts, David just paid for Adrian's University fees and lodgings."

Solomon quickly bowed to her. "Ok, I stand corrected. That's good."

Suzanne said, "Open my present Adrian!" The doorbell rang again, and they waited as Amy went and opened it. It was Tanya, a femme fatal of her own creation who gave men a hard-on and high blood pressure at the sight of her.

In her slinky outfit, she made Suzanne feel unappealing in her summer dress. Adrian went over to her, and almost everybody knew they'd lost his attention. David walked right up to Tanya and pulled Adrian away.

"Suzanne gave you a gift: you haven't opened it yet," he said in a scolding tone of voice. He pushed Adrian back into the room, and Tanya gave him a nasty look.

"Eyeball me like that again and see if you stay in this house two seconds longer." Solomon found Tanya as alluring as most men everywhere, so he smiled at her and tried to move David away from her.

David said, "You're not in court now so rest yourself, OK." Solomon didn't like his tone of voice, but he promised himself to exercise restraint no matter what.

Amy detested Tanya because her overripe obvious sexual allure made her feel old at thirty-eight, and she hated the fact that Suzanne became sullen whenever she knew Adrian saw Tanya.

Suzanne was a very pretty teenager who didn't have to use the amount of make-up that Tanya wore to be attractive. However, Tanya had a 38 inch bust with a deep cleavage. Added to that was the floral skintight pants she wore which overstated everything. Under her clothes was her voluptuous toffee brown body that excited men faster than an FA Cup winning goal. David walked up to Amy and gave her a protective look, and she gave him a subtle nod only Grace could see which added to her love for David. Grace eyed David's shiny perfectly kept funky dreads sitting on his shoulders. She couldn't resist touching them so she did and he turned sharply.

"Oh!"

"Relax, it's only me."

"You know I don't like people touching my hair."

Tanya moved in and said, "Are they real?" David gave her a high voltage look fueled with disdain. Tanya had the ability to dismiss most things she didn't like, but David's lion eyes really hurt. "I thought they were extensions," she replied as a matter of fact.

Grace said, "We go to 'Afro Natural'. You better not say shit like that when David's mother gets here."

In a tone of voice that only the best British Black folks can master, David told Tanya. "Please don't hear that the wrong way, my mother won't talk to you. The minute she sees this horse tail you're wearing on your head, she'll keep her mouth shut."

"This is *my* hair. I bought it," she announced glaring with attitude.

"And my hair is natural. I've grown it." He moved away as though she stank. Grace gave Tanya a dirty look because she considered her to be a 'ghetto bitch' unworthy of her son who went to church and spoke properly. Grace joined David, and he looked at her with such tenderness, Grace blushed, which compelled him to kiss her.

****

Michael sat on the sofa, beside his wife, smiling radiantly watching the end of Fellini's *Amarcord*. To some extent he looked like one of the characters in a Fellini film. "I love this finale," he told Lola in Italian even though she was Jamaican. There was no mistaking his Roman dialect even though he'd lived in Muswell Hill, North London for twenty-five years. His beard was graying and hid too much of his face, but that didn't matter to Lola because a lot of his mystery and good looks came from the light in his eyes which often sparkled like a topaz. Lola always thought a steady look from him revealed so much. She was wearing an embroidered cream colored kaftan, and he had on white linen slacks and an orange colored shirt. Reclining next to him she felt him breathe quicker as the music played out. He smelled of cloves that he carried in his pocket, which reminded him of his mother's gifts to console him from the poverty of their life in Rome during his childhood. As Nino Rota's score played out,

19

Michael pulled Lola in tight, and she loved it. In his arms, she often felt life was almost perfect.

His eyes flit from canvas to canvas all around the spacious room. There were many paintings leaning against walls, all for a client who loved modern art. The red velvet curtains were drawn, but the light from down the long hallway came into the room but stopped a foot away from the door due to the setting sun. It was a well-furnished room, decorated exclusively from Heals of London. However, the bric-a-brac came from his trips around the world, and every vase and lamp had been positioned by Lola.

He got up to stretch, and she noticed he was somewhat aroused. He was too big not to be noticed, and even though he was overweight, his barrel chest, broad shoulders and masculine demeanor still sustained his appeal. "Are you going to give me that for your birthday or am I going to give you a birthday treat?" she asked him in Italian. He became bashful, so she got up and embraced him.

"You're in a very good mood today," she said in English. "I'm glad because I've been very worried. I think you're working too hard darling," she added in Italian.

"It's not so much that. I don't want to be fifty," he replied in English.

"Is that why we couldn't have a party? I wanted to throw a big bash for you."

"No please, not that!" He pulled away, but she pulled him back, caressed him and touched him intimately. He purred like a leopard as she pressed herself closer to him and soon the smile she hadn't seen in so long spread across his face.

"Shall we..." she asked with a glorious expression, "Before we go out?"

"I don't want to rush, but later tonight..." he kissed her, and she loved it. "Although I love Shirley Bassey, *you* are real, mine for life." Delighted by him, she left. Michael sank back into the sofa and tried to focus on the evening to come. A few minutes into his thoughts the song he and Lola loved came on and he listened and then sang in Italian to duet with Shirley Bassey. He harmonized with her very well as she said *Never Never Never* and he sang the original Italian lyric. Soon Lola appeared, and she gestured like a grand diva in her full-length kaftan. Her black shoulder length hair styled into gypsy-like loose curls was most becoming. Michael moved toward her, and they came together as though they are a famous couple on stage. They filled the room with the magic of their passion. Her honey brown skin and his caramel complexion complemented each other.

His chestnut brown graying hair was disheveled, but he felt more at ease when he was less groomed, which Lola had grown to accept. Due to his good looks he never seemed unkempt, and he often surprised wealthy dunderheads and sophisticated idiots with his exceptional knowledge of Art and Classical culture.

As he and Lola sung about making each other laugh and cry they each drew on their life together and as he eyed her, he knew he could never love *any* other woman. He wanted everything to stay as it once was, but he knew things had changed. He wasn't the young man he used to be. Facing his lost youth, even as he sang to her, it filled him with regret and his heart hurt, so he poured more of his love for her into the song, and she couldn't resist him. She felt the greatest desire in her flesh and bones. Almost immediately she stopped acting, and her spirit exposed her true heart, so she sang to him in agony. He hadn't been this romantic in ages. He stopped singing and eyed her, then grabbed her and they moved back to the sofa to make love.

She pulled at his shirt, and he tugged her kaftan. This continued for more than a minute until they began laughing and they got some of their clothes off. Gazing at her breasts worked wonders, and soon he moved back so she could see him. One kiss led to everything else and before long his hands reminded her that foreplay was a necessity no woman should sacrifice. Michael was able to arouse her as she hadn't been all year.

He made love to her the way he liked. She knew it because as a couple they spoke about everything. He stopped and told her, without a word, to take what she wanted, and she kept him there and found the pleasure he seemed to have denied her for months. When Lola reached her climax, her nervous system ricocheted. He carefully eased her back and kissed her pink flesh deeply. Pins and needles broke out of her, and she echoed as no soprano could. She spoke to God until she lost her voice and only heard her own body.

Forty minutes later, Michael walked back into the lounge in his white linen trousers and bare chest, carrying two dishes of Italian ice-cream from his favorite supplier in London. He approached Lola, and she got up to put on her kaftan. Standing in the nude, every curve and arabesque of her body fascinate him, and this made her feel powerful. She was a proud woman who was glad she began yoga ten years earlier. Not many women aged forty-nine looked so good, because *they* used the wrong products, but her Caribbean genes also helped. Lola's silky skin was walnut brown, without any wrinkles. The blood that filled him up jutted against his trousers, and she took a breath with a smile. He put the ice-cream down and adjusted himself.

"Almost a year nothing; and now – Voilà!"

"You like," he stated in his Roman tone of voice which she adored.

"A virile man is good to find, especially a husband with a young spirit."

"And you; no one believes you're forty-nine with three sons and a daughter. Your body has not suffered. You are still more beautiful than other women to me."

"Happy birthday darling, I do love you."

"Come we eat this and..." the phone rang. Lola picked up her ice cream, and he got the phone. "Michael De Farenzino speaking." He listened and soon went into a speedy flourish of Italian. "Ok! In English... Yes, I know we are bloody well living in London and not Roma." He told Lola he was speaking to Cesare and then listened. "No, I didn't check my mobile. What text message? I'm here with your mother relaxing." He looked heavenward and then at Lola, who rolled her eyes and shook her head. "What is the text message?" He listened again, and the light went out of his face. Within seconds, everything sank in him, and he gritted his teeth.

"No, if you are too busy then don't come."

"What is it?" Lola asked.

"Cesare cannot come to my birthday."

She kissed her teeth, got up and took the phone from him. "Boy what is this nonsense you're talking about," she said with an irritated tone in her voice that revealed she really was Jamaican. "I don't care if its work. Tell your boss your father is fifty today and you have to get home to..." She listened. "But it's Papa's birthday."

Michael grabbed the phone. "You know what Cesare, do what you want." He hung up. "So we were going to eat ice cream?" He slowly made a move, she touched his back and he shirked, crossed the room and sat in a side chair, silent and withdrawn.

****

The room was now crowded with Adrian's family and his friends who were racially diverse middle-class boys and girls from his school and social life. David put his arm around his father's shoulder and asked him, "How are you, Daddy?"

Solomon took a look at him and replied, "Very well, I am especially pleased to see you looking so good and happy with Adrian. You should have let me give him the money for University. How did you get so much just like that?"

"I sold a band's contract to an American agent. They're going to be big. I'm glad to get rid of them. They make me sick."

"This doesn't make sense. If they are going to be big why didn't you continue to manage them?"

"I couldn't listen to one more second of their homophobic nonsense about who they'd kill if a man ever tried it on. Or..." he had to take a breath to regulate his tone. "The lead singer suspects some guy is trying to 'get to him'."

"Homosexuality is unnatural, and any Black man has the right to speak about that. We fear being corrupted and it..."

"I'm a Black man, and I don't fear it. For a QC, I don't know how you live with the contradictions. There are laws to protect human rights; we discussed this at length when we re-drafted my client's contracts."

"Are we going to fight today as well? It's my opinion I speak of. If someone killed a homosexual, I would prosecute him."

"You're a defense QC. Listen, all I want is a great day with my son. I need that right now."

Solomon studied him, and he could see that something deep down was troubling David. Because of their history and the tactic each of them engaged in over the years, he could read David's fear and distress accurately. "What troubles you?"

"I wasn't going to say anything to you, but I really could use your advice." David walked Solomon away from the family and into the garden. Grace saw them and discreetly followed to stand at the kitchen door and listen to them outside. In the garden, that was well tended by Grace's natural ability to grow and maintain life, the grass and vibrant colors of summer flowers shielded her home from the urban reality of city life. David was about to speak, but he put a finger to his lips and slyly looked around the corner of the door and caught Grace standing dead still with her head cocked, listening. He gave her a scolding look, so she left rather embarrassed.

David's survival instincts had always served him well, so he went back outside smugly, and Solomon resented and yet admired that about him. David began weighing up how much he wanted to say, and Solomon knew better than to force him to speak before he was ready. David ran his fingers up the lapel of Solomon's jacket and then looked his father dead in the eyes and said, "It's my wife; I'm sure she's cheating on me." The snarl and tightening of David's lip, along with the flare of his nostrils did not escape Solomon's attention because he had years of studying and cross-examining people from all walks of life.

"You think so, or you're sure?" Solomon's Nigerian accent overtook his English, and he continued in their native dialect. "If you want to get rid of her, I have no problem. You married her to spite me, and you see what she's done." He gestured as only elite and powerful Nigerian men do. "I am not surprised; she's dirty, ignorant; a slut who would do anything." He looked down and muttered for a while then held David in a challenging stare. "What are you going to do about her?"

"I'm going to disgrace her and then get rid of her."

The look of absolute pleasure and anticipation to hear more wrote itself large across Solomon's face. "How?"

"I'm going to get the dirt on her and then divorce her."

Solomon was clearly disappointed. "Is that all? Whores must be punished."

"She's an adulteress, not a whore."

"How can you defend something like that?"

"You're still too emotional. How you keep cool in court is amazing to me."

"Those people are not my family." Solomon's reply resonated with David because he knew almost everything confidential and important about his father.

"Dad, I understand her psychology; I know how to make her feel ashamed of the skin she lives in. I know everything nice and nasty about her."

"You like that kind of power."

"Look what it's done for us." David's words clearly made Solomon nervous. "Don't look so worried. I would never mention a thing about *that*." Solomon looked more ill at ease. "I'd get no pleasure from hurting you. You *know*...cruelty punishing. That's why I forgave you years ago."

With a heavy heart, Solomon embraced David and repeatedly told him. "Sorry."

CHAPTER TWO

Michael studied the text on his mobile and kept shaking his head. Lola came back into the living room with two cocktails, and she observed the shape and state of his body and found herself helpless. He seemed to have returned to the state of vacancy he had occupied all year. "Darling, what is it?"

"The twins can't make it. I have a text from Fabio to say Maria called him to deal with her boyfriend. She had some kind of argument or situation and Fabio has gone to deal with her boyfriend."

"I cannot believe them. They know what day this is. Forget inconsiderate, it's just plain rude to act like this on such an important day."

"Maybe it's all a joke?" he asked with hope. Lola's heart hurt because she knew he was a devoted father.

She could not answer him because she had no explanation to account for her daughter and sons' neglect. She gave him the cocktail, but he didn't drink it. He sat there staring into space and when she moved to him, he got up and left the room. She stood up to go to him but flopped into the side chair and cast her mind back over the last year and couldn't make sense of it, especially considering the lovely day they'd had started with breakfast in bed. She made it for him with loving intent and then everything came back to life throughout the day.

She pulled herself up and slowly walked out of the tastefully decorated room and into Michael's library. It was filled with books on Art history and the evolution of Art from ancient Greece and Rome, the Renaissance, European and Russian periods of history. There was also an entire wall filled with books on African Art and Civilization. She moved towards the section on Caribbean Art and history. Her father introduced Michael to Caribbean history and discussed the subject at length because he was a renowned Professor of Caribbean History at the University of the West Indies. When the mobile in her kaftan pocket rang, Lola answered. "Hello, darling... yes! I'm still at home." She listened and shouted, "Of course you can, Papa will be so happy!"

Lola dashed out into the hall and rushed up the stairs into the bedroom where Michael was lying on the bed in a fetal position, and she stopped and watched him for a moment. Very gently, she lay next to him and gave him the mobile. "It's Roberto. He's calling from Rome to wish you happy birthday."

He sat up and the relief he felt generated energy throughout his body. He took the phone and Lola moved closer. Through Michael's eyes, the primrose and magenta colors of the bedroom decor blurred into vivid patterns. There were photographs of Michael and Lola hanging on the walls but no pictures of their children about the room. The lace curtains defused the light coming into the spacious and elegant room.

"Roberto, you remembered," he said in Italian and then proceeded to speak to his youngest son and listen closely. Hearing Roberto sounded like the comforting voice a man needs from a loving relative when he's afraid. To maintain equality between the children, Michael and Lola wouldn't admit to having a favorite child, but since Roberto had slept through the night without waking up and smiled at everyone he saw, the family thought of him as a little angel. Michael loved Cesare and Lola adored the twins, however, there was something about Roberto, and so when they baptized him they gave him the second name, Angelo, which delighted Lola and Michael's parents.

Michael told Roberto none of his brothers or his sister was coming home for his birthday and his son cursed in Italian down the phone which made Michael laugh. "Mama wants to talk to you but listen. You called at the right time, believe me." He listened. "I don't know what we're going to do…" He listened again. "Yes – perfect!"

Michael gave the phone to Lola and quickly dashed into the adjoining dressing room. "I have nothing to wear."

"Great idea," Lola replied. "We've always had good times there with your brothers and sister. What made you think of it?" She listened and then held the mobile with both hands tenderly. "We'll have a great dinner. I hope we can get a reservation." Even though she didn't intend to, she spent fifteen more minutes on the phone finding out how his film degree was going. Michael returned dressed in a summer suit. "Basta! Roberto, we are going out in five minutes, say goodbye to Mama."

"Alright, darling I'll call you on Sunday." Then two minutes later she hung up.

"Look at me – I'm not ready. Give me four minutes to dress and six minutes to fix my face." She ran to the closet, and as he watched her something stirred in the heart of his soul.

Taking a moment to reflect, he closed his eyes and placed his hands together.

'Dear God, thank you for that confirmation. I said I needed a sign. I don't know how I'll tell her it's over, but I must say it right. She'll be hurt, and I don't want to tear her asunder with what is true. Please help me'.

****

Adrian's home was now packed with people and Grace pushed her way through, and the sound of classic Motown, the feel of laughter, the smell of Caribbean food, along with the harmony of voices swayed from English to French Caribbean.

Suzanne held Adrian's arm, but Tanya led him away, upstairs into his bedroom and leaned against the door. There was no question of her allure. "It's gettin' mad down there. I was getting' a headache." He rushed her all at once and pinned her next to the door as he kissed her but then backed away to gaze at her. Tanya unhooked her top and revealed herself. He buried his face in her flesh and caressed her nipples.

Downstairs, Amy, Grace and David were in a deep conversation that eventually erupted in harmonious laughter. Grace's brother, Erwin, squeezed his way in and greeted the family scattered between the seventy-four other guests. Erwin was the kind of tough, handsome Black guy lots of girls wanted to marry. He pulled David aside.

"Listen David; let me bring some people by your office because you need to hear them. I'm not talking smart 'Grime' tunes. Some of the group can sing." David liked Erwin a lot. He was a hard working car mechanic who was plain speaking and trustworthy. In the Caribbean people would call them 'spars'. To Erwin, David wasn't just his best friend; he was his brother regardless of the common law. They often went out at weekends, and Erwin told David he had to watch his wife because she once came to the garage to have lunch with him, but he knew what she was after.

Most women were interested in Erwin because he was generous with his money, satisfied every woman he'd ever had and he always kept out of trouble. He learned that after years of dealing with his father being stopped and searched by the police: his dad was a classic 1960s Jamaican Rude Boy until his dying day in 2006.

"Let me check how I'm booked and get my PA to set it up."

"Nice! Where's Adrian?" David gestured, indicating he was somewhere around.

David's mother, Cynthia arrived, and everyone she passed gave her a bit of cheer. Heading toward David, people admired her silver gray cocktail dress. She embraced her son, and her joy transformed her skin and her face. The music changed to early 1960s Blue Beat Ska and all across the room people's faces turned to smiles. Solomon stopped talking for a minute to take in the sight of everything because he was aware that none of the Embassy parties he been invited to hosted such a diverse multicultural array of people who weren't in any way trying to impress each other; they were together because they loved his family. The house looked like the Commonwealth came to pay respect. He wondered what it would be like if his most famous son was also there.

"I couldn't get away before now... How is everything?" His joyful expression signified everything was right. Grace and Solomon quickly came to Cynthia.

"Mum!" She led Cynthia away. Solomon was used to fighting for her attention.

Upstairs, Adrian held Tanya by the arms. "No way, I'm not about to shag you with my family downstairs." Chaka Khan's *Move Me No Mountain* filled the room.

"So why you'd make me feel it?"

"Because you grabbed me. I didn't say touch my dick."

"What is the matter with you?" she asked utterly confused.

"R.E.S.P.E.C.T – learn from the best," he said pointing at her. I'm going to University." As a well-spoken graduate with top marks from a private school, he told her. "I'm not your dog."

"But you like me and playing..."

"Tanya – decency." She looked like she was about to cry and he watched her. From their first date he knew she was a fake, but he fancied her nonetheless. In the intervening seconds, she could feel his rejection, and that really upset her.

"Why've you been coming to me all this time?" she yelled accusingly.

"You're nice." She smiled. "But I don't think with my dick." She stopped smiling. "I want to go to University while you want to go shopping!"

"But you made me think..."

28

"That I was going to throw away my life for a shag-, please. Fix yourself and come downstairs or leave." He walked, but she stopped him on the way out.

"Just 'cause you got both parents looking after you, an' I haven't, and your family are some high and mighty name back in Africa you can't…"

"Go back to your ghetto heaven and find yourself a boy you can manage…"

"We're not trash in South London. Who do you think you are?"

"A Bankole. We're all famous, and I intend to follow in my father's footsteps. Now, goodbye or as they say on the streets; bounce." He walked out on her because he despised people who thought he was a vacant 'black' kid. She was only defeated because she banked on sex to get everything.

An hour earlier Michael and Lola entered *The Old Country*. It was the only 2 star Michelin Caribbean restaurant in Europe. Cynthia dedicated her working life to make it *the* top Caribbean and now it was London's elite West End spot on Great Portland Street near Regent's Park. Lola spoke to the *maître d'*, Fred, a handsome Algerian with a waxed mustache, Valentino brilliantine hair and taught deportment.

"We didn't book. It was all last minute," Lola began to explain. Cynthia came into the dining room carrying bags and rushing through, and she saw there was a slight problem, and so she stopped at the desk. She was wearing a gray and silver Roberto Cavalli cocktail dress.

"What is it, Fred?"

"Madam, they don't have a reservation and…"

"It's my husband's birthday. I love this place, so I prayed on the way here."

Cynthia admired Lola's red silk dinner dress and deep purple cashmere Indian shawl. She had on gold Christian Louboutin slingback high heels and Lola carried herself with great self-awareness. She glanced at Michael, and his eyes held her on the spot.

Michael confessed. "This is our favorite restaurant and my birthday has been almost a disaster, so we came here to salvage what remains."

"Italian, yes?"

"Yes, you have been to Italy?"

"Florence and Rome, *bella*! I love Italian food. And my husband understands and adores Opera!" Cynthia went behind the stand and looked at the evening's bookings. "Frank, set up the auxiliary table and place this couple at the VIP table. Give them a complimentary bottle of Veuve

Clicquot 1976; happy birthday." She asked what his name was in Italian, and he was delightfully surprised to hear her speak Italian.

"Michael…" Cynthia turned her eye to Lola, who also stated her name.

"Lola, enjoy your evening. *Ancora una volta* Michele, *buon compleanno*. It's my grandson's birthday today too, so I'm rushing. He's off to York University in a few weeks, so it's a big day for the whole family." She was so proud. "He's only nineteen, but he's still in boy…" Cynthia's smile was so heartfelt Lola reached out and gave her a kiss on the cheek.

"Really this is so nice of you for my husband…" Cynthia placed her hand on Michael's shoulder. Fred led them into the plush dining room, decorated in turquoise, cream, and sky blue colors with photographs of different Caribbean islands. There was not one stick of bamboo or a coconut motif anywhere because Cynthia loathed that kind of trashy cliché. Fred took them to the VIP table and gestured to waiters to come in and help.

At ten o'clock, Adrian's birthday was at its height. The house was packed with all his friends and family. Among the many African headdresses, Suzanne's face looked calm now that Adrian was sharing jokes and laughing exclusively with her.

David stood beside his mother, and they both watched the crowd. Cynthia spotted an African woman in a cheap, loud dress. "What is that woman is wearing?" David laughed heartily with his mother.

"That's Lagos meets Layton ghetto fabulous."

"She looks terrible. I'd rather get hit by a car than die in that dress."

"Oh, Mummy!" He laughed so hard no sound came out of his mouth which was the truest sign she knew he was hysterical. He finally caught his breath. "That is delicious. Those clothes are the reason she's single. I don't know one bloke who'd take her anywhere dressed like that." He managed to stop laughing.

"And so why didn't you bring your wife? She knows how to dress and she's pretty." He looked away for ten seconds and then back at her. David then turned his back to the crowd and faced his mother. "I hate her. I detest her so much I can barely stand the sight of her. When she tries to touch me, I want to vomit." The feeling raised bile in him, twisting his mouth and made the veins in his neck pop out.

David turned around and eyed everybody in sight, and all he could see was smiling faces, African headdresses, people eating and Adrian getting pats and kisses from just about everyone. All at once he felt desperate and miserable.

"She's been shagging some bloke, not one of us – one of her 'kinsman'. I'm going to mess him up." His mother grabbed his hand to help steady him.

"Don't touch him. We know when Black men end up in court on assault charges; nine times out of ten we end up in jail even if the CCTV footage shows us defending ourselves from unemployed, underachievers who think the world owes him what you've worked for. You're not going to end up in jail."

"I've been thinking if I should confront her or play fool until I have the evidence to get her off my back without her getting a penny of my money."

Cynthia took his arm and led him out through the crowd. She forced a smile and gestured as though everything was fine as she marched him out the front door past guests, down the garden and out into the street where she hooked her arm through his and spoke with her finger conducting all her major and minor key notes.

"She's a drug user and opportunist. That bitch killed both my grandchildren with her drug addiction. Why have you stayed married all this time? Why?"

"Because I didn't want to be gay. You know he'd kill me if he knew."

Cynthia embraced him, kissed his head and told him. "We've had enough of that. I know you've struggled, and I know… If he touched you, I'd… God forgive me – I'd knife him. The days when he'd beat you are done!"

"Mummy I know you'd keep him off me. And he has changed. But can you imagine what he'd do if I said my tendencies as a kid had now become…"

"But how can you be gay? You haven't been seeing anyone. You can't lie to me."

"No, I can't. I haven't done anything."

"So maybe that teenage thing has passed now. Quite frankly I expected you to go back to Grace. But you were more interested in punishing your father than enjoying your life, a life that would be so right with Grace. I love that girl."

"I know; I love her too. Aren't you shocked – disgusted about the gay thing?"

"I don't believe in enforced sexual laws when it comes to identity. We're all made as God made us. You're not a 'pervert' as bigots would condemn you. You're a man, possibly with overlapping desires."

"I should have come to you instead of going to a therapist."

"You've been to a therapist?"

"Of course, how the hell could I live with myself knowing what I was feeling?"

"This is the 21st century where men who love each other can marry. I have no time for that old world shit that justified reasons to kill somebody who doesn't share my sexual philosophy."

"You know for all his mighty laws and power, this is why I love you more than him. You're a humane person. He isn't."

"Hey – you gave him a punishing life lesson that affects him to this day. He's ashamed of what he used to be like, and he's changed."

"Yeah, well he also nearly killed me." She was saddened to have to hear or remember that period of their life. It marked her gentle face with age. She was only sixty, but the battles in the past felt like a day of remembrance. David put his arm around his mother and hummed her favorite song *At Last*. As they walked back, Solomon came down the street quickly toward them, and he could see she was upset.

"Darling, what is it?" He looked at David. "Have you distressed your mother?"

"Stop accusing me of things, fucking bastard!" Solomon lashed out and hit him in his face. Cynthia covered her face as David told him, "Drop dead, you savage." Solomon looked and felt like he's been stabbed. His son's judgment reminded him he had failed as a father and that fact haunted him.

****

Lola put down her brandy glass and eyed people in the restaurant to see if anyone saw what she felt, but couples at their separate tables didn't notice them. Michael watched her, and he understood the pain she felt. "You're going to leave me... a divorce?"

"I feel I have nothing more to give the family. They don't need me..."

"I need you," Lola interjected, panic-stricken.

"Darling you can live without me. All this year you have been living with a ghost. I've no substance to myself. And today with the kids' rejection, it's too much. If I didn't get the call from Roberto, unlike the last time, I would have killed myself."

Lola's hand shook as she covered her mouth. She bit her nails and tried her utmost not to cry. In Italian, she started several sentences but couldn't complete them because she was shocked and so she felt a chill under her skin.

"Of course I have no one else. How can I love another woman? Any other woman, you are the only woman I could want or have ever had."

"I know you don't cheat, have affairs with other women."

"Not once, never have I taken anyone else to bed since we've been married. When I say I have reached this point of existential truth, I know what I mean." He took her hand and she looked into his eyes and his pain and sadness looked greater than hers. "My history before we married was a fact I told you about on our third date. Now that I am no more use to my children, and I lived like a ghost, a somnambulist in our life, I must resurrect myself," he told her un-apologetically.

"Michael I need you." Those few words drew on a lifetime of her hope.

"I am no use to you. You are a very independent woman. You have made your own business. You have established the best reputation for health treatment to Black woman with issues concerning their hair. You have admirers and a great social life. I don't go anywhere these days. I have contributed nothing to our marriage all year because every day I feel worse and more dishonest."

"Is there someone?"

He gestured in a dismissive fashion. "No one; but I'd like to find my own happiness now that I'm fifty."

"How have I failed so badly to make you happy and deluded myself like this?"

"I've lied by omission and fear. I should have said I felt unfulfilled before."

"What kind of fulfillment do you need Michael?"

"I think... a life alone to be what I want, and no longer struggle to be the greatest father and perfect husband."

"And what should I do? Throw our life away? I can't walk out on the kids, our home, my work, my belief in you as the love of my life."

"You should let me go. All this year and most of last year... Tony, you have relied on him." His neutral tone sent a shockwave through her.

"Michael," she said after the full realization of his implied statement hit her. "There's been nothing... I have never touched the man."

"I believe you. I'm saying, Tony loves *you*, deeply and very different from me."

"I wouldn't know."

"Yes, you do. You know Tony loves you, and you have told him to find somebody else." She wondered how he knew they'd had that conversation. "There is twelve years of his feelings and trust between you." He looked into her as he held her attention.

"I don't love him," she stated.

"Not like *us* but you do have love for him. Forget me as the children have." She was on the verge of tears. He stood up and made his way to pay the bill. Lola got her things together and discreetly exited the restaurant. "That lady who got us the VIP table, she's the owner yes?" Frank said yes. Michael took out his card and gave it to Frank. "Tell her if ever she is looking for a painting, I'm a dealer and can get her almost anything she wants."

Michael exit and went to Lola and put his jacket over her shoulders. She took his arm. "I can't give up as though our life means nothing. We have a lot to live for. The depression you slipped into will pass if I try harder, and you work with me."

"I would rather die than go on living a lie. I've become boring and – useless which is why the kids have rejected me, and apart from today, you and I had nothing."

"What kind of lie are you living with?" They walked in silence for a block.

"I died as a normal husband last year when I realized what I wanted now was the love I told you about before we got married."

She walked away, and he followed, but she turned and said, "Please take a cab. I'll drive myself home." When she quickened her step and left him behind he used all his strength to control his tears because he was now deeply afraid of what was going to happen to his life.

****

David was at the gym dressed in his brown belt Judo Gi suit as he circled his Sensei/Judo trainer who was a full-bodied Japanese man, aged thirty. He yelled, "Come on!!" and David went for him with Taekwondo fury and got the best of his trainer. Keyi fell to the mat and was quickly got up again because he was all muscles and methodology as he yelled out instruction. "Now switch to Judo," and David adjusted his mind and body to the hip throws, hugging high lift, stomach punch with fingertips, lifting hip throws, leg wheels, and triangular strangle, using the legs, front crossing kick, and numerous other moves that Keyi physically went through with him.

"Now rest and quiet your mind. We will try the Karate momentarily." They sat facing each other and David took his cue from Keyi's breathing and settled his mind.

Keyi mimed the moves that David studied with the greatest concentration and ten minutes later, Keyi asked. "Again, why have we learned these lethal moves?"

"I must protect myself to live and love and preserve my dignity. I must not be a victim of pathological hatred."

"What has changed now? It's been one year since we spoke of the rage in your mind and the fears that brought you to the art of defense class and meditation. Do you still feel the same level of unrest?"

"No, I've been going to my Acupuncture doctor, and his Tiger Balm treatment, herb remedies, and teas have detoxed me. Sometimes I still want to smoke, but I'm winning against that urge. I see what drugs have done to my wife, and I know the dangers, so I've brought my alcohol level down even more." Keyi nodded. "I was previously angry at the thought of my wife's infidelity. Now I know it's true I have no love for her. She's a disgrace to herself. I sometimes have sex with her." He thought about it. "I don't know why. I don't like her anymore." David didn't notice that he was involuntarily shaking but his trainer, Keyi did.

"Veronika and I were great at the start. I studied the Japanese Shunga Art, Tantric sex, and Karma Sutra. It's blended with my African knowledge, and I stayed hard for hours. I liked that." David smiled at that fact. "The man she's fornicating with, he's vermin, and I'm going to stamp his balls into a bloody mess like a dead rat."

"Show me your judgment and sentence against him." David got to his feet and went to the heavy bag and battered it with Karate blows, Boxing and Taekwondo kicks.

"If you strike with that fury; you'll kill him. Find another way." David pulled off his belt, whipped it around the bag and yanked it into a strangulation tie.

CHAPTER THREE

August 2014

David and eight of his best friends built his house into a renovated double fronted home in Camden. He bought the house for next to nothing because it was derelict after the housing crash of 1991-92 and it wasn't in the fashionable part of Camden Borough so he took his hard earned savings and had bought it against the advice of his father in 2002.

The house was something of a maze. It had doors at the front and back with wrought iron steps leading from the garden up the walls and spreading into a spider web of small landings and steps that were lit at night in green, giving the house a distinctly creepy aura. Sitting in the garden, the back of the house looked enchanted with its red painted windows and black iron, but as night fell the scarlet and black house took on a rather different character.

Inside, the house paid homage to the *Fin de siècle* era and art nouveau in particular. Consequently, it looked rather like a theater set. Throughout the twelve years he'd lived there, David's house was replete with furniture, mirrors, screens, elaborate tables and chairs that looked incongruous with the 21st-century world outside his door. David hired someone to shop for period *objet d'art* which he took the time to discuss and if it was right he'd buy it. Almost everyone who came to the house wondered how he was able to do his worldwide multimedia business in there.

The art nouveau motif and its relationship with entomology were all around the house, and some people found it unsettling, but the colors and light in the house were rather like a kaleidoscope everywhere, and it often resulted in his guests spending the entire evening discussing design, architecture, and cubism from African history. David truly felt in his element on nights or days when that happened. There was, however, one room that was unlike the rest of the house. He never talked about it.

David came home early from his lawyers and the minute he entered and closed the front door he took off his shoes. Standing there in black socks and sapphire blue Ozwald Boateng suit with his primrose-colored shirt and lilac tie made him feel grand. He sat on the padded green and brown hall bench with its decorative interconnecting wood extensions reaching across the wall. "Dear God, thank you for my life today." He began a prayer and sat there for five minutes; and then arose. He walked through the pumpkin and mint green color-washed hall, up the curved wood steps with its wrought iron decorative railings until he vanished from sight.

In the circular bedroom the landscapes from Africa and the Caribbean were distinguishable in the wall of mosaic colored glass in forest green, desert sand, and magenta. Because the mosaic was fractured glass, it made anyone in the room look disembodied at certain angles. Within the splendid room, there was a high raised bed that had wood spires, like tentacles, which spread outward to hold up a printed cloth canopy of Egyptian men and women from the 19th century, making love. The lights from the bedside lamps and behind the bed made the images transparent. The bedside tables and lamps, the elongated shapely chest of drawers, the desk and chair; along with the art nouveau inspired chaise longue gave the room a delicate aura. Conversely, the replica statue of Frederic Leighton's *Athlete Wrestling with a Python*, in bronze, behind the door was a stark masculine force of eternal power.

David tossed his clothes onto the chaise longue that his school friend Kwame had made two years earlier. He pressed one of the spaces on the wall, and it opened into an en-suite bathroom. He quickly brushed his teeth, pulled on a black and brown robe with a cubist design and headed back into the bedroom. He went to his desk and took out two iPads and one other mobile tablet device. He placed one on his dresser facing the bed. Another on the chaise longue pointing left and then across the room he placed another on the top of his desk point right. He crossed the room and pressed another surface, and the mirrored wall opened out into a space containing a 50-inch flat screen television, AV Receiver, and a stereo system. He picked up three different mobile phones that he had put there earlier to recharge.

He placed one on the table next to the chaise, one on the bedside table and the third under the bed. He crossed the room once again and picked up his suit and took his favorite mobile out of his jacket pocket and a packet of cigarettes and lit one and inhaled. He coughed rather loudly and dialed a number and then waited and waited.

"Solly, thank God! Listen, I'm half way there. I can feel my heart, though." He listened. "The lawyer told me to get her to confess to everything. I've planned this; now I just have to do it." He listened and eventually smiled rather nervously. "I can do this! I'm a shrewd Nigerian and tough Jamaican. That makes me ten times smarter than racists figure. Those ideas about our inferiority will be re-written after I fix her."

He left the room, walked through the hall and into his office. The office wall had many photos of him and his younger brother Solomon Jr. There must have been fifty pictures of his brother when he was a star player for a London football club. He looked all over the walls, and his face shone with pride and no envy toward his brother.

"I feel like when we were kids, knowing we were going to do something bad, and we were thrilled and scared Dad would find out and beat the sin out of us."

"David, if you don't want to do this, don't. You're not a fucking player who can roll like a motherfucker; you're too much like Mum. I could do it because I learned some bad habits from my former teammates."

"Solly, that bitch isn't getting anything out of me. I worked part-time when I was a student. I dealt with the mess as a struggling DJ on Uni Radio for three years, and a pro; plus I've managed some roughnecks in London and Manchester so I'm doing this."

"Just make sure you look good and come across in a truthful fashion?"

"How you mean?" he asked in their native language.

"You're a hit maker with 27 club classics to your name. You're a scholar and fashionista. You're not 'Street'. So my brother, who's gonna run things?" he asked.

David replied, "Me!" Solly asked him again. "Me." And again. "ME!!"

"I gotta tell you something. I'm gay. I've been playing it straight, but I'm gay."

"I know. It's alright my man."

David caught his breath and did his best to steady himself. "Wait!" He went into the filing cabinet, fished out a bottle of rum and drank some. "I just took a swig."

"Nice?"

"Yes, how did you know?"

"When you were fifteen I saw you with him. Then I saw you and him again when you were sixteen."

38

"We were very discreet; how did you know?"

"You talk in your sleep. And you'd hump your mattress, saying... Gus."

David tried to remember; he thought intensely, and he began to choke up because he sacrificed a great deal to be what he was expected to be and he idolized his brother.

"David? Dave?" Solomon asked and kept asking. He spoke loudly in Yoruba, and eventually David focused his mind and spoke to his brother.

"Solly, I can't believe you knew I loved Gus, and you still care about me?"

"We're not all like Daddy. You're a Prince! Now fix your mind on what's good for you." Those simple words resonated in his mind, and he remembered that he had made his life what it was and he could change things for himself.

"When you come home we have to talk about this."

"I *am* at home."

"Lagos isn't home."

"Tell that to my wife and kids."

"Well it is, of course, but it's not the real place. I miss you."

"You Skype and Face Time me every other day so..."

"Shut up." They shared a laugh.

David took another drink. "I bought a pack of cigarettes..."

"Do not start that disgusting habit again! You stopped ten years ago. I mean it if you're going to take up smoking again... I have nothing to say to you!"

"I took a couple of puffs. It was horrible."

"Fucking right it's horrible! You cannot even visit me if you're smoking because not only will you stink! I can't have you around the kids corrupting them with that kind of nasty shit."

"Hey man, cool your jets. I was just getting myself ramped-up for tonight."

"Have a drink like a normal bloke and toss those cigarettes. Besides; you're fit and strong – just plant it and get it done, for fuck sake."

"Alright! '*Operation Done-it-All*' underway. Oh yeah, last week Adrian's birthday went well."

"Focus, Dave, Focus! Get rid of her."

"I'll bet no one else in London is going through this shitty mess."

****

At exactly the moment, Michael and Lola were stuck in the hall at the front door. His suitcase anchored him there. "I will be back when the movers come for my books."

"When can I come and see you?" Lola asked. "This is all so crazy, leaving home. Leaving… me, leaving…" Dressed in her gray suit and her hair neatly styled into a French pleat she looked alluring and helpless. Her heart hurt, but she did her best to shield her desperation, but his imminent departure made her lunge toward him, but then stop as she experienced real inertia. "Michael, sweetheart," she told him in Italian: "*io ti amo*," because she did love him.

Michael covered his mouth and the cry caught in his throat. He put his suitcase down, suddenly struck with anguish knowing he was leaving his home, and she surged toward him, and he kissed her. She returned his kiss until he took her in his arm and their embrace unified them, which explained their metaphysical connection. He wiped the tears from her eyes and she kissed his face and tasted his tears.

"Why? Why?" she asked.

"I haven't humiliated myself or insulted you with adultery." She stroked his face nodding, knowing his words were the truth. "I've given the kids what's best, but they don't care for me, except Roberto. I want something for myself that will make me truthful." Her tears felt hot on her face. "Maybe I am wrong to think it will come from a man who's lived as I have." He couldn't control himself or his own tears as he felt what she was going through listening to him. "The punishment for being gay is so dreadful many of us twist ourselves into something obscure. I have become this… a phantom." What lie ahead for him was so unknown, fear shot through him and he shivered. He looked away from her for half a minute and then faced her.

"For over a year I have tried to explain to myself why I must stop being here, loving you as I do but having no love for myself because I am afraid to displease you." His voice climbed two octaves and sorrow poured out of his eyes.

"My darling – my darling, stop," Lola said.

"Maybe all those years ago… when I loved Alexander… and told myself: to be a man I must love women. And at that time I met you and cured myself." He smiled solemnly. "I think, even if I find what I need for myself, I will always love you more. But right now – I have to stop detesting myself and tolerating my own weakness. I want to be happy in my soul, and I'm not. This is not something you can fix, or I can solve by loving you and the kids. To be humane you *must* love yourself. I have to achieve that."

"And the only way for you to achieve that is leaving me for a man you don't have? For a life, you don't have."

"If I sound ridiculous it's because I know something hollow in me is making me feel worse every day. Maybe I am crazy to believe I can love a man since I haven't had any homoerotic involvement since I was a teenager and happy with that: and no fantasies of that kind since our marriage." Lola looked slightly comforted by that statement; nevertheless, the vacant look in his eyes was disquieting.

"You have done everything for me. And I have given you everything. Now I have to give myself something. I won't try to kill myself again. Life is important so." He opened the door and Lola was paralyzed to stop him; she just felt as if something inside her ripped apart the stitches she had during their year of agony which she could not have survived without her sister and Tony. She closed the door so that she could scream privately.

****

Veronika entered the bedroom and abruptly stopped when she saw David holding up a Jimmy Choo bag for her. She was a dead ringer for a world class Grand Slam tennis champion. Her thick barley blonde hair, blue eyes and strong features gave her sexual power. If her face displeased a man, her figure did not. She was a size 12, standing 5foot 7inch with athletic beauty. Wearing a little black dress with a white collar of cuffs she looked chic, feminine and gorgeous.

Veronika eyed David with mixed emotions. Dressed in his gym gear, she still fancied him. She loved his thin dreads glistening with strands of silver gray in the black, and his muscular dark brown body. "What is this?" she asked with a distinctive Romanian accent, but her husky voice was creamy.

"It's your un-birthday present. I saw it and had to get it for you."

"My un-birthday?"

"I told you all about Lewis Carol and *Alice in Wonderland*. You remember."

"You know so much," she said sarcastically, "but you still did not get picked for the *University Challenge* team." Her Romanian tone echoed in phlegm.

"There were other issues involved, and… despite that, I did graduate with first class honors, and I have an MA. I bought and paid for this house. I have just paid my son's University fees, and I do run my own business," he told her with aggravated cool. "It's important to focus on one's achievements, and I have a few of those.

"You mean I have no such achievements because my family is poor."

"Do you want this or would you prefer an argument?"

She gave in and smiled and then moved towards him to collect her gift. He watched her cross the room to the bed and sit and open the present. When she saw the £562 'Lilyth' red Jimmy Choos, she was happy and clearly satisfied. She took off her sandals and put on the decorative red evening shoes. She flashed him when she opened and crossed her legs *a-la* Catherine Tramell in *Basic Instinct*.

"Are you cooling off or acting out?" She picked up her purse and took a cigarette. "Most ladies do wear panties." She played the mysterious femme fatale well.

When she stood up and walked she sashayed like a vamp. He watched her tease him.

'Come on David, smile and show her that you care.'

"My God you know me so well, my size and interests, my likes."

'Yes, I know all about your interests you adulterous bitch.'

"I want to go somewhere to wear them. Maybe out for dinner?"

"Anywhere you want."

She screamed just a little and rushed and kissed him. "You are good to me sometimes."

"Yes, sometimes."

He kissed her neck and moved his hands up and she yelled, "My hair! Fuckin' hell be careful!"

"Aren't you supposed to make yourself beautiful to excite me?"

"My pleasure is my responsibility not yours," she told him playfully. His face told her how much she irritated him. "David I'm not saying I don't like to look nice for you, but I have to be responsible for myself."

"Leave some room for me, though."

"Naturally," she replied, and sashayed away. He laughed, but she didn't feel he was unkind. "Why do you laugh in that way?"

"You – the way you say *that* word. It's still your favorite English word I think."

She gestured and said, "Naturally." Then laughed out loud and said 'naturally' again.

"It's so English. And the way it is said here. "Naturally… like one is royal. I love the way your father says it, not to be African, but English."

"Africa isn't a country; it's a Continent – as Europe is a Continuant."

"When will my lessons stop?" she asked a little exasperated.

"When you learn." He knew all the mobile devices were recording everything.

She marched up to him and put her hand inside his shorts and played with him. "You men think you know everything." Stooped in front of him seconds later, he liked what she was doing. She stood up and got a good grasp of his hard-on and led him over to the bed. "You really want me to play your guitar?" A broad smile came out of him because he loved her sexual dialogue. "Look at you. I want to feel that riff that keeps music alive." He was pulsating, and she loved the feel of him. She stripped and had him as she liked. When he was naked, she swallowed him and took charge.

Five minutes later he surprised her by not giving in but instead turning her face down ass up. She moaned into the pillow, and he varied everything to sustain his momentum and just when she was sure she was done, he stopped and moved between her. What followed was a climax she hadn't expected. As she lived through it, he licked her long legs and gently bit her knees. The pleasure rushed inside her. As if that wasn't enough, he turned her upside down, so she was hanging off the bed and then he stepped over her and started again. "I'm not going to come yet," he shouted. And she yelled and insisted he didn't.

They continued this balancing act for over fifteen minutes with him on the verge of letting go, but he was determined not to let go of anything. So, he pulled her up and placed her on the edge of the bed facing the wall. He knew she could not see him, but the recording devices could so he began talking to her. "Are you mine?"

"Yes," she murmured.

"I belong to you. Do you belong to me?"

"Yes I'm your wife," she declared.

"For richer or poorer."

She knew she had to answer him. "For richer or poorer."

"To have and to hold, on this day and the others to come."

"Fuck me," she begged.

"To have and to hold? Tell me."

"Yes, to have and to hold. Touch my pussy." He did and she felt good.

"In sickness and in health?"

"Yes, sickness and health. Right there, do it harder."

"To love and cherish."

"Yes, love and cherish. Every kind of fucking riff is in your guitar; do play my music, David. Cherish it and love me. Love me like you ought to. Love me for everything…" she began moaning low because she felt as though she was losing her thorns which life and time had instilled in her body. He caressed her knowing her body as well as he knew his own. And that pushed her to another level of ease and passion.

"You work so hard to keep yourself fit – I love that about you." She began shaking; he moved away, and she turned around afraid he was suddenly spent. He moved into the room and picked up her pink panties and hung it on his erection and went back to her. She started laughing, and he liked that so he jumped onto the bed and kissed her all over. David inserted her panties inside her, breathed onto the material and drove her into a frenzy as he turned the cloth and mouthed profanities into her. She collapsed into the bed as if there was a space where she'd be pulled in. In all the years of their marriage, this was the best sex they'd since the night she conceived her son.

"Looking at you I say again," he told her. "To have and to hold from this day forward, for better for worse, for richer or poorer, in sickness and in health, to love and to cherish, till death us do part."

She remembered, on their honeymoon when he made love to her for the second time in their relationship; he repeated his wedding vows during foreplay, and she liked it a lot. She liked it even more now because recently he'd treated her coldly.

He took her panties out of her lips and tied it around his ankle and then climbed onto her. "Achilles had a weak spot, and it killed him. All men have the same weak spot; I want to protect myself with your 'intimate veil'." Her eyes sparkled when he said that. "I want to conquer the never ending realm of pleasure commonly known as the pussy but better understood as the mystical vulva."

"David, why have you hidden this love from me? Yes, discover my Pizdă…" she replied laughing, knowing the vulgarity of her slang which he didn't. "Kiss it." He then had sex with her in ways that are never seen in online porn. He'd learned a lot about women from the stories he learned

44

in Classical Mythology and Asian culture. Consequently, he had her in his power, and he couldn't help but wonder, as he delicately kissed her succulent flesh, why he seldom exercised this power with her.

"Tell me what else you want?" he said. Determined to incite her, his seductive masquerade skillfully trumped other *agent provocateurs*. He wanted her to speak the profane according to the Catholic laws she was raised by. "Say it... name it and it's yours." He went back and kissed her open and closed skin. At the feel of his lips against hers; she spoke.

"Take me from behind," she pleaded.

"Not that," he told her, with a fraudulent expression of shock.

"Yes. I told you before; your cock is a fucking guitar..." She had to take a breath to stop panting. "Your fucking riff makes me sing." She badly sang *Atomic* by Blondie. Caught up in the sheets she was utterly mesmerizing as a Rock slut goddess. "I will send energy through your cock like *The Matrix* and the Force. Imagine that." He smiled at the prospect, and she was certain she had him. "Wait a minute; I'll get some lube, and some Brandy." She jumped out of bed and dashed out the room.

David quickly checked under the bed, and his mobile was still recording. He rushed over to the iPads and other devices, and they were recording perfectly.

"You're going to see and hear more from my wife," he said standing before the iPad and then moved to the art nouveau chaise lounge. He laid back and took a cigarette and then lit up. He was getting the buzz when she came back and saw him.

"Oh wow! You're smoking again."

"I needed something."

"I have it."

"No, I have it," he said pointing at his erection.

"You see what happens when we wait too long. You get a prolonged hard-on. And you must be as full as a bull now." The look he gave her was beguiling. "Sometimes I forget how handsome you are. How beautiful, brown and strong your body is." She touched his chest, and he leaned in and kissed her. Thousands of girls sent flirts to his website and 'boyz' hero praised him. With a slight variation, they were having a night that his fans had imagined. Veronika opened her eyes startled by the sight of the sculpture with his outstretched arm holding the python at bay.

"Really, I don't know why you have to have that in here."

"I love it."

"Yes and I know why," she smugly replied. Before she could speak, he turned her away from the statue so that she could only see him.

"What did you bring?"

"The lube, the brandy and this," she replied holding out some cocaine.

"I won't start doing cocaine, not even for you my love. I never do that."

"Maybe this once, to get in gear."

"I am in gear, can't you see."

"Yes, that hard-on is serious."

He took her in his arms. "And inspired by you."

"For months you don't touch me and look at you now. I should record this, wait, let me get my camcorder I love to watch us afterward."

"You've got enough videos of me already."

"But you've ignored me all these months."

"Two months. Bloody hell woman, I was going through a re-energizing training program. Can't you tell I'm re-energized?"

"I thought you lost interest in me."

"It was just a few weeks. And you know, those girls who've been kidnapped in Nigeria *is* upsetting. It's affected Adrian so much he's going to University to... Anyway, shouldn't we get started? I'd hate to lose interest."

"Really, I understand now, you say what's upset you. Of course, if you don't speak to me of these things I cannot know what is upsetting you."

"You're right."

"Of course I'm right. Now, back to business."

"Business?"

She covered her mouth and laughed behind her hand. "Not like hooker business. No... serious business in the bed."

"Just checking."

"I cannot charge for this. I'm too expensive."

"So let me see my priceless woman." She put the bottle and the lube on the table and held up her arms like a winner of a competition. There was no doubt about it; she was a highly maintained Rock goddess in the mode of Debbie Harry. Standing naked in the realm of the art nouveau room with its iconography and excess, Vernonika was at ease because she was high and unashamed of sexual reality. David's aroused corporeal dominance and dark skin mystery cast the perfect shadow of danger over her; not only because she was so fair, but he was so dark with exotic tribal

46

skin patterns. Her desires covered her with sin as instilled by her Catholic upbringing. She offered him a pinch of coke that she had in a silver ring on her right hand, and he declined. She wasn't bothered as her gesture showed. She looked him over, and he excited her as he did the first time she met him. She filled her nostrils with coke and then filled her mouth with his pulsating flesh, and he let out a short cry of pleasure.

Shortly afterward he lifted her and carried her to the bed. In the softly lit room, he gently got her ready and then performed the perfect sexual taboo. In under a minute, she lost her reason seemingly transformed into a sexual lunatic. He'd seen her pagan doppelgänger several times when they rejected respectable conventions. She cried and whispered in her language, and the thrill could have exposed his own demonic trauma, made all the more real at the hands of his father's power, but he remained stoic and reminded himself with every move, that he had captured the evidence he needed against her for the first phase of his plan.

Ten minutes later Veronika rolled across the bed and got two cigarettes. One fell on the floor, and she leaned over to get it and saw the mobile phone under the bed. "You've dropped your mobile. I hope you didn't break it." The look of sheer panic and fear on his face startled her. She was facing him from behind, so he pulled her up and rolled her to the other side to get his mobile. He picked it up, got up and strode across the room to his TV cupboard.

"It's not broken it's just dead. I have to re-charge it." He put it away and head back to her. "Some guys are heartless fucking dogs... knowing some of these pricks, I always tried to love you, so you never think I'm one of them."

"I love you too." The significance of that lie stopped him cold.

"What? You're suddenly frozen? Maybe this coke is kicking my ass." She laughed for a prolonged period of time. "Oh... why that look?"

"Your coke habit cost you two kids – two miscarriages is no joke." He went back to her, sat on the bed and stroked her hair.

"You hate me for that." She grabbed the sheet to cover up. He shook his head. "Your mother does. She hates me half as much as your father; he detests me."

"To hell with him. He has nothing to do with our life."

"Don't be crazy. He beat you so much as a child *I* had to nurse you, play for you. Learn bondage to cope with you."

"That was a long time ago, and now I'm no longer affected by him."

"Don't be funny." She spoke in Romanian for a minute, half determined and incoherent. "If he says just something horrible to you…" she thought about it. "You fall apart. Now I know he's hideous I don't give a shit about him. I used to but…"

"How much coke have you had?"

She laughed and stopped and then laughed until she giggled. "Who knows?"

"Have you taken anything else? You're all over the place."

"You made me very unhappy instead of being bad to me." She moved away.

"How, I don't beat you or cheat on you. I give you all the money you ask for."

"You ignore me! I've been so alone these weeks," she yelled accusingly.

"Did you find someone else to make you feel, nice?" He got another cigarette.

She had to focus and re-play what he said in her jumbled mind. "No, but don't think I couldn't find someone because you're not the only man in town."

"What other Black guy do you know who's more successful than me? I made half a million last year, and musicians come to me…"

"You're not so great Mr. Bankole. You couldn't make *me* a star."

"Darling you can't sing. You have enough presence to give Lady Gaga a run for her money, but you don't have the voice." She pulled the sheet up to cover her breasts. "I put your face and demo in front of everybody, and they didn't buy."

"You should have tried harder. You made a star of that cunt!"

"I don't like her either, but *she* has a voice…"

"Fuck you! She sounds like a drunk Beyoncé, and I've seen her come on to…"

"She's a loud mouth, wig wearing, harpy who…"

"What does 'harpy' mean?" She asked moving in to face him head on.

"It means I have no interest in her because she's a horrible person without any compassion for anyone. I dislike people like that. Don't you know me?"

"And what about that mixed race pretty girl that you talked about so much… How intelligent, how you went to the same University. How she is politically brave."

"I respect Lynette for her talent and her pride. I don't shag my clients. I've never been a pussy hound, and I've never even kissed another woman; we're married."

"I know you haven't been with other girls. You're very aloof. You don't give them any heat. I've watched you and checked online what's happening with you."

"Why do you check me out online?"

"Because you're very secretive and… blocked! What have I done to be ignored by you the way it's been this year?" She was strangely rather vulnerable all of a sudden.

"I buy you things and take you almost everywhere with me."

"But you didn't make me a star!!" she screamed and flopped onto the bed. "When we met you promised me everything."

"You have to have what the people want."

"Half of the cunts on the pop scene are rubbish. Look the TV shows *X-Factor* and the other shit," she stated through her teeth. "I have nothing important to do."

"If we had our two children that would be different," he replied deeply hurt. "And now you're back on the coke," he concluded disdainfully.

"You think *you* lost two kids. I carried them. They bled out of me. Die in me." Clearly, her miscarriages had left deep mental scars on her that she had not dealt with.

"Your family made me take coke." He looked at her scornfully. "You think it's easy dealing with your family! Your father's high and mighty arrogance, your famous football brother; and your mother… high priestess of Caribbean cuisine and winner of good food…" He stood up and his naked strength filled his muscular frame.

"Take your mouth off my mother because she works for a living and she's respected for her life. Her father and my uncle fought for Britain in the R.A.F at home. We came to Britain as dignified war veterans, and I've earned every penny I've got!"

"Why do we always end up fighting?"

"Because you're a cokehead. You expect me and everybody to hand you gifts as though you're entitled to it. You have to work for things. But no – I have to give you money, put up with your drug addiction – listen to your bullshit about why you put our children's life at risk because you just couldn't stop doing cocaine! And all the rest of the shit you take." Behind his naked exterior, she felt his naked interior rage.

"I don't have to listen to this shit; I can go to my room."

"Yeah right, you have your own bedroom where you can use your vibrator, watch our sex tapes and take as many drugs as you like. You say I've ignored *you*, but what about the months you've kept me in here, sex-starved so I'll come begging."

She jumped out of bed and yelled, "I'm not your bitch; don't put your shit on me." The force in her five foot seven inch toned up and strong body was formidable. And when she tossed her barley blonde hair and dug her nails into her small waist she looked ready to tear someone apart.

David laughed and pointed in her face. "Thank Madonna, but you misquoted. What you ought to learn is kindness, a quality you seriously lack; among other things." Even if they weren't stark naked, they still would have looked evenly matched.

"You better watch yourself because I know people who can kick your arse for the way you talk to me," she warned him jutting her chin out.

"You're threatening to have me beaten up by your former communist friends, now living here and doing all kinds of illegal shit. Like that ignorant low-class scum I suspect of human trafficking or some kind of prostitution ring?"

"Don't high and mighty me, bastard! That same guy you dis' could kill you if I say you humiliated me, so…"

"I can get the law to deal with him. I mean what's he doing with that undeclared fortune he's accumulated? Sending it back to the old country to fund terrorism?" She was shaking with rage.

"You wouldn't dare say that to his face."

"Oh no? My father drilled it into me year after year. Stay on the right side of the law and fight with God's fury to defeat the evil doers trying to bring you down. As I live in this Black body and by all that's sacred! No illegal, hustler…weak ass commie bitch can do anything to me!!"

She was startled because she'd never seen him like that before.

"Listen, listen…" She tried to force tears. "How did we get to this madness? I came in; we make love and fuck, everything sweet and now this."

He pointed at the door. "Go to your room, and don't come back until the coke has worn off." She left defeated and tired.

"Don't be violent to me. You've never been violent to me."

"I mean it, Missy, I'm sick of you spaced out. Decency for God's sake." She gave him the finger and walked, out half Venus half Vamp cursing him in Romanian.

CHAPTER FOUR

Michael sublet a flat on Hallam Street in one of the exclusive apartment buildings in the West End near Regent's Park. He got the flat from one of his clients who'd been transferred to Manhattan for a year. Michael had to put his books in storage, but he had 100 books he couldn't live without delivered to the flat. The 1960s G-Plan, which his friend considered retro chic wasn't to his liking. There was also a fair amount of chintz throughout the flat, but Michael told himself to ignore it because it wasn't his home, he was just in a state of transition, and it would do.

Michael entered the old fashioned 1980s kitchen and opened a bottle of Barolo. He sat down for a few minutes and looked around the place and then got up and walked through the flat. It had fitted carpets, double layer of curtains everywhere, embossed wallpaper and elaborate lights hanging from the ceiling.

"Just a postcode… a fancy stupid post code he muttered," as he walked through the flat. He sat himself down and in the lounge and picked up some free gay magazines, available in most gay cafes and pubs and began to flick through. They showed him a great deal about the current London gay scene. He read and looked at the pictures and his expression revealed how little he cared for the life on offer. There was one buffed naked man after another in all four magazines as he flicked them all. Eventually, he came to one man who was among many party people. He looked at the Caribbean guy and then quickly went to his books.

He unpacked a number of art books and found the one he wanted. He opened Paul Dahlquist catalog from his big show and flicked through until he came to the photo of the heroic African American male who Michael gazed at, studying the man's physique and his gallant face. He suddenly closed the book and dashed to get his iPad. He set it up, clicked record and sat in front of it.

He fixed his hair and straightened his face. "OK, I am doing this. Today is my first day alone, out of my home. I have officially separated from Lola." He had to take some time to adjust. "That's very hard for me because I adore her. No, I love her out of respect for her humanity and the

happiness she gifted to our family and me. I left because I've become...
conformist. My psyche is esoteric. I've made myself into a simulacrum, a
copy of other husbands. But... this year the deepest truth has converted
me. No priest or psychiatrist can change it." He thought for a moment. "I
have to study myself as Jung studied his condition. We lie to ourselves
most of our life, so I want to observe and study these recording to
examine my nature?"

On August Bank Holiday, Michael walked through Holland Park with
Tony, his best friend of fifteen years, a handsome macho Brazilian, and
Lola's business partner. As men in their fifties, they understood life and
each other, especially since they were confidantes. It was the Notting Hill
Carnival and all around them the air was filled with Reggae and Calypso
music. In his summer clothes, Michael looked distinctly Roman as so
many actors who've played Italian tried to be. He was much taller than
Tony who was colorfully dressed in Brazilian Carnival clothes. Countless
people in a variety of costumes rushed and strolled past them by the
minute. Tony fumbled for his packet of cigarettes and lit up as he walked
and paid attention to Michael.

"I had a crush on my best friend when I was a kid," Tony said. "I
remember when an American guy came to live in our neighborhood, and
Pedro paid more attention to him; I was so jealous. One day I told him if
you love the American so much then go and kiss his ass." They laughed
together. "Americans take everything they want, and that guy was taking
Pedro from me. I was so angry at Pedro I punched him, not his face
because he looked so great when he laughed." Michael nodded with
empathetic clarity, remembering Alexander. "Pedro said I was his best
friend, not the American, so I said prove it!" Michael was so intensely
hooked on Tony's story his suspense exaggerated his features as he
grunted 'ugh'. "He grabbed me and kissed me, on the mouth. Then he
slapped my face and told me not to be an asshole." Tony laughed out loud.
"For about two months after that..." Tony checked all around him. "I
goaded him, went back to the same subject and asked if he liked it when
he kissed me."

"You were what age?"

"Fourteen, he was fifteen. I kissed him one time and..." Tony
clammed up.

Michael slapped him on the back of the head. "What?" Tony finished
his cigarette and shrugged.

"You fucked didn't you?"

"Don't talk mad, no. We jerked off – separately, but we watched each other."

Tony walked in silence for about 50 yards. "I would have killed anyone for him and the same with him for me. If he didn't like a girlfriend of mine, I'd dump her. When he met his wife 'to be' I told him to stop fuckin' around like a pendejo and marry her. He did. I'm godfather to his three kids now."

"Did you... have another experience... like Pedro?" Tony shook his head no.

"But when my brother told us he was gay, I kicked my cousin's ass for trying to beat him up: it's so ridiculous this hatred. And the Church speaks against gays when so many Priests are fucking our kids. That hypocrisy makes me see red!"

"Don't get me started on Catholicism. The 'die now live later' philosophy of transcendence gives me a pain. I have no shame about my desires or fears for the possibility of carnal relations with a man."

"It's incredible to hear you say this. I've always thought you and Lola are so right for each other. I never thought you'd be interested... in a man."

"I shock you?"

"Yes... I've told you everything about me. You even know after the 7/7 attack when the bus blew up in front of me I couldn't get it up and lost my girlfriend then suffered depression. I couldn't tell any other man things like that." Tony stopped walking. "Or that my mum is mentally ill," he said quietly.

Michael said, "Or that you love my wife and have desires for her." Tony couldn't deny it. His light brown face blushed and turned dark with guilt and shame.

"I have never been indecent to her or interfered with her. You're my best..."

"Tony, I know the both of you have been honest."

"Michele, I swear; nothing," he said animated.

Michael said, "But you do love her. You do want her. She makes you happy and..."

Tony covered his face and turned away. People continually past them but one Jewish woman noticed Tony was distressed. She came over to help, and Michael said he'd deal with it. When she moved on, Michael said to Tony. "Look at me." He wouldn't. "Look at me. Slowly he turned around, and his expressive eyes were red and his handsome face became gaunt, except for his mouth that trembled slightly.

"Tony, help me. I don't want to rob Lola of happiness. She has love for you too. I am not accusing either of you; she is free to make another life. And you'd be the man she'd turn to because she trusts you. You work well together. You're a big part of her business life. When we've been out with you, or you come to dinner, she always speaks of you affectionately."

"But love me enough to marry and forget you're her love and father of her kids. She could never do that."

"That isn't the issue. I'm canceled, removed. We have been through a bad twelve month period, and it's clear to Lola and the kids I'm not what I used to be."

"What does that mean Michael?"

"I lost interest in living. Sleepwalking on auto-pilot with my senses disconnected. Maybe it started when I sent Roberto off to University and then I began giving the other kids everything they wanted, and they took it all believing they have the right to everything. They haven't had to struggle for anything because Lola and I give them everything. Only Roberto is smart enough to say, 'Papa – Italy today was remade by post-war struggle. I want to be like De Sica, Rossellini, De Santis, and the Neo-Realists'. Roberto has courage, the others have *will*, but it's not the same."

"Your kids love you, Michael. You're a wonderful father."

"No. I shouldn't have made them think everything comes easy. To be good takes struggle. What confuses me is that they're Italian Caribbean, and they've seen the racial struggle; I expected more of them, but you know what..." Tony put his arm around Michael's shoulder. "I think they're passing as European; if I find out they are doing that... I will severely punish them."

"Only the twins are light enough to do that. They'd never dishonor Lola."

"The new 'professionals' today will lie about everything to get what they want. I never told anyone except Lola I was in love with a guy when I was seventeen."

"You were?" Tony replied stunned because he considered Michael to be the substance and image of a man, based on his mental and physical conduct.

"Yes. It lasted a year. I told Lola about it on our third date." Michael told Tony about Alexander, and he listened because it was a liaison of epic youthful passion.

Tony asked. "Do you have any other secrets because that's some story?"

"No, Lola is like a chameleon; she's evolved and adapted to my changes, so I've never needed to hide. We've supported each other through our psychological and cultural growth." Michael touched Tony's chest. "Tell me what you like about her?"

Tony was reluctant to speak, but Michael didn't say anything; he simply waited and periodically looked at Tony to confide in him and speak the truth. It took almost three minutes of hesitant silence but eventually Tony said, "She has so much courage... and faith in people. Sometimes I want to slap the shit out of the suppliers, and she'll tell them: 'if I have to disappoint my clients again because of you, you're finished'. No cursing and screaming. With all she knows about biogenetic African hair and styles. She just trusts me to take care of her." Tony felt nervous but compelled to continue because he'd never find a better moment to speak.

He looked off into the distance. "On the nights we've gone to the opera and she is dressed, very dramatic, in white with the gold scarf wrapping her hair... incredibly beautiful!" He looked back at Michael and saw recognition but no anger. "My God, the day she caught that stylist stealing and Lola said 'Either I call the police, or I deal with you'. Helena said, please don't call the police. Lola took off her shoe and beat her on the spot calling her a thief! Ask her why she did that when both of you provided Helena with home and family care. Helena was shamed. I liked Lola's fury; it reminded me of the women at home in Rio. It aroused me to see that side of her.

"I remember Lola cried, couldn't sleep; she was so hurt Helena stole money we had taken her into the family."

"These days women try to be everything and it makes some of them schizo, but Lola is at her best when she has back-up. I've seen it hundreds of times..." Michael nodded knowing Lola better than himself because his mood swings oscillated between euphoric and desperate.

"My God what have you been making me say?"

"Nothing, I just want you to be honest." A handsome young Mediterranean guy barely dressed even in his vest and tight shorts slowly made his way pass and Michael caught sight of him. The man felt the connection and told him in Italian to ogle someone else, more his age and Michael told him to fuck off in Italian and the guy yelled he was a pillow biter.

"Go home and smell your mother's knickers, boy!" Michael yelled.

The young man rushed at him and Tony raised a hand like a stop sign.

"Are you crazy? This man could be your father."

"Oh is he your 'Daddy', bitch?" Tony spat full-on in his face, and the guy was horrified and stunned.

"Don't make me hurt you, boy," Michael said. "Go clean yourself and enjoy the day. There doesn't have to be bloodshed, but if you say more shit to me, I will cut you."

The youth wiped his face and left because he couldn't take them on nor did he want to risk getting cut. He'd come to the carnival, and he'd had enough already, so he left.

"What made that guy behave like that? Suspecting you want him? How does this gay mindset you've come to, reach out and connect like that?" Tony was distinctly puzzled. "I mean... men our age don't do life changes so good. But that guy sensed you wanted him. How is that? Is it... wait! You have no interest in women anymore?"

"Calm yourself." Tony was disturbed to have to question their relationship.

"I did give him a look. Not so much for desire but curiosity. He was half naked in that vest and pants, his bells and whistle exposed. I wondered if I could ever do that. If that is the method to attract men, as a woman with her tits barely covered."

"If you walk around showing your dick, don't expect me to walk with you. Answer me. Have you lost all interest in women?"

"It's hard to say because I've never lusted after another woman; Lola was all women to me. Yes, Penelope Cruz and Shirley Bassey give me a hard-on. But since Lola is like Shirley but much more, I've never lusted after other women."

"This doesn't explain your desire to change. Is there a guy you secretly fancy? Because we all fancy football players." Michael slowed down as attractive Carnival seekers ran, skipped and danced past them as the joyous Calypso music increased its volume. From the uniformity of their red and green costumes, ten dancers rushed past.

"There must be someone?" Michael shook his head no, but Tony studied him.

"Don't lie to me because who else are you gonna tell. What happened to push you in this direction?" The undulating rhythm of the music rose up.

"Do you fully understand the Notting Hill Carnival? What it's based on?" Tony said no so Michael gave him a history lesson explaining the racial violence, murders, police history, 'no Blacks, Irish or dogs' which marked the immigration experience of Blacks in Britain in the late fifties and early sixties. "Black people are amazing to me. The women have faith in compassion and fair social policy as I've never experienced anywhere. The men are tough as only enslavement can transform the mind and body of a man. They're so heroic and also flawed by the legacy of prejudice and pathological resistance. This culture seldom rewards masculinity of that kind. Their fierce beauty keeps them strong and young. I was in Tanzania not that long ago. I spoke to an elder man – his wisdom really impressed me. In Barbados I spoke to a young athlete who was studying art and I was so impressed with his knowledge of human history and what he wanted to do in life to fulfill his dreams."

"You've always been attracted to Black women, do you fancy Black men in a similar way?" Michael didn't answer. "Come on Michele, I've heard you compliment and sing the praises of Black women hundreds of times. Now you've circled round to the dark side of your passion."

"You think so?"

"Yes, Lola's family and the Civil Rights movement have shaped you."

"Maybe that's true."

"Definitely; you're rebuilding yourself only this time with a male ideal, so, what's kind of guy do you want? Please don't tell me some JLS dude."

"They're pointless to me. I don't know. I'm not ordering a *male* bride." For some reason, they laughed at his ironic turn of phrase.

"So let's get out into the streets and find your dream boy." Countless Black youths, men, and women passed by.

"No 'boy', I couldn't. That would be like looking at my sons sexually."

They walked out of the Park and into the streets where the Carnival had started. There were masses of Caribbean's from all over the Islands. The women danced in the greatest Carnival spirit in costumes that defied Western decorum, and the men were dressed mostly in their light and dark brown skins, topless, wearing sashes and colorful trousers that fit tightly

57

around their bodies. Together the men and women's bodies harmoniously found the rhythm of the music in all the dances they did.

Tony shouted over the steel drums and percussion. "When you see so many Black people together, you'd think we were in Brazil."

"Oh wow! Can you spell that? Someone is cooking curry goat. I like it when it's cooked well. Lola loves it too but doesn't know how to cook it."

"Have you ever tried it at *The Old Country*? The food there is remarkable!"

"Yes, I have. Lola and I introduced you to the restaurant."

"Oh yes."

"Come, let's follow our nose and find some food." They kept moving through the crowds of fabulously dressed revelers and visitors. Many of the women in ragga gear of sequined hot pants and skimpy tops were a sight to see. They ranged from exotic to lascivious as they reached out to dance with strangers in joyous abandon. All around the two men, the language on the streets was a predominant mix of Patois, French, strangely accented English, Spanish, and Creole, which created a cacophony of vocal choruses. The hairstyles caught Tony's eye because they were far beyond anything he did at his *Salon Fabuloso*.

He took his smartphone out of his pocket and began snapping away so that he and the staff could discuss the hair at their monthly meeting. Michael spun his knapsack around and took out his iPad and switched it to video to capture the spontaneity around him. A lovely woman in her early forties grabbed Michael and simply began dancing with him and he followed without the slightest question. The Calypso dance was one he was familiar with so she loved the way he moved her around with complete ease and confidence. He stopped for just a few seconds to put his iPad away and then he gave her a great dance thrill. Tony watched Michael with empathy surging through his mind and body. When Michael caught sight of Tony's joyous face, he danced with even more gusto.

David saw Michael dancing with the woman through the ever-shifting crowd, and the laughter and joy in the woman made him stop and watch. He couldn't fully see Michael's face, but he was impressed at how well Michael danced with the woman. He said to his brother Solomon. "Solly I doubt that man is English, not with those moves." David and Solomon were dressed alike in khaki shorts and hoodie tops. David had his dreads tied into a samurai topknot that suited him.

"Maybe he's Brazilian," his brother replied as they moved on. Solly was a very attractive fellow with cropped stylized hair, a younger face than David, and he looked more African than Caribbean because he resembled his father. He was two years younger than David with an even greater virile energy.

When Michael passed the dancing lady into the hands of Tony, who also knew how to dance, David saw Michael for a few seconds, and he noted his intense topaz colored eyes but thought his beard and mustache obscured too much of his face.

A Black London 'Grime bwoy', clearly devoted to the subgenre of ten years past, dressed in homage street gear shouted. "David Bankole! Bloody hell, it's great you're here mate." His broad gestures were artful. "I'm Terry. Listen, man, when are you getting back on the radio? You and your banter were the business guy!" David could hear that his parents were from Trinidad, and the young man was from South London.

"I'm done and dusted with that, guy."

"Love you on *The Voice*!" Terry was a very cocky twenty-five-year-old with real street style. "How can you put up with that stupid bitch every week?"

"Tom Jones is so great, anything trivial, including her, just doesn't matter." They spoke for a few more minutes, and Terry flipped him a see-thru business card with his red contact details on it.

"Call me," he told David as he put his arm over his back. "You sent out a message last year about no more homophobic rants in our music; I respect that. We should talk."

"After the 7/7 attacks, I couldn't listen to anyone justify terrorist acts."

"What took you so long to say something?"

"Scared of the backlash. Over the last year I've learned, denying my reality is worse than being a liar. Promoting human rights is important. The level of global sectarian violence right now sickens me." David noted that Terry had the kind of London Black guy street beauty that is admired and copied by designers who always miss the point of self-made beauty born out of poverty, imagination, and improvisation that cocksure Black youth embody.

"Are you like – deeply political?"

"I'm British born with African and Caribbean bloodlines and strong Jamaican family ties to RAF service. I was born into a political consciousness from my first day at school. This Carnival marks my family's history of civil rights in Britain, so yes, I am political. Are you political about your rights?"

59

"Yeah, kinda." Terry tried to be serious even though he wasn't prepared for it. "On the radio, on TV and with your groups, I've never heard you talk this way," Terry replied unsure of how to stay on the same wavelength.

"If we can't speak the truth on this occasion then what the fuck are we playing at?" David eyed him, and Terry suddenly felt the erotic heat in David's seductive eyes.

Terry's friend came back with cans of drink, took a look at them and shouted. "Solomon Bankole! Fuck me, what are you doing here? Nice to see you mate." Solly gave him an appreciative smile and shook his hand. The tough London lad looked at his hand. Solomon Bankole; fuck. Oh look – and David! Did you guys come especially for Carnival?" They nodded. "Solomon fuckin' Bankole – the legend!" People turned in their direction, and they were pounced upon by fans of different racial backgrounds.

David took out his mobile, dialed, waited and then asked. "Where are you and where is she?"

"She's standing outside the bank with him, 300 meters from you, you're safe. The Barbadian float is blocking you from sight. I'll buzz you when to film." David smiled and hung up. Some fans bombarded Solomon with questions about football, Nigeria, the kidnapped schoolgirls, the World Cup and many other issues. Solomon was very good at handling people. As he dealt with them, David turned to Terry, who was eying him up. David winked, and Terry blushed. It was rather becoming, and he looked like a classic 'rude boy' who'd lived his life pushing other people's buttons.

David gestured to Solly that he was going to get drinks, and Solomon nodded in-between dealing with twenty questions.

David moved off and gave Terry a definite 'go signal'. They quickly kept weaving through the Carnival crowd as people were clearly affected by the good weather. The sudden smell of jerk chicken hit them hard and Terry though he must call his Mum before the end of the day. The swell of people had grown within the hour David had been there; and the mix of Black, Asian, White and people from the Far East was displayed everywhere they looked. Terry glanced up, and residents hung out the windows with flags of the Caribbean and South America flapping in the breeze.

David took Terry's wrist and pulled him away, down Cambridge Gardens, off Ladbroke Grove and led him to Solomon's XK Jaguar and they got in, and the black windows shielded them from view. Terry breathed heavily from nervous excitement. He eyed David once again, and David did likewise. "I'm going through something important right now, so this can't happen. But hear me; you got me, charged-up man."

"Let's see? Terry demanded, and David unzipped with full knowledge and gave him a look... "Fucking sweet." Terry said and made a move, but David stopped him.

"How did you know?"

"When you said enough of that batty boy pathology from homicidal motherfuckers who seed and breed without any thought except for their ego, I just loved you for that, and I kept thinking... are you gay? Even though you're married. And I thought what a great shag you'd be." Terry unfastened his baggy pants and pulled out. David looked, stared and gazed long and hard at him.

"Today I've got serious business to look after. But..." He looked back at Terry and stared into his eyes. "Everything in me wants to go... I haven't got down with a man in nine years."

"Nine years! What... so you're not gay but sometimes..."

"Oh fuck no – I'm the cocksucker every 'Brother' would kick the shit out of. I've forced myself to butch clown. And there isn't anything wrong with pussy galore except I don't want it anymore. I actually *really* love women. But more as a 'girlfriend' than a woman of mine."

"You're killing me, man; especially with that dick standing there like that!"

"We just met. If you can wait a few weeks, I'll rock the arse off you like shock therapy and sweeten your soul like a Pentecostal overload."

Terry loved the sound of that. He felt giddy and fell back slightly, so David kissed him, and they shook in their seats. David's mobile rang, and he had to stop and get it.

Five minutes later, he went back to Solly, guided by following his direction on the phone. When they were side by side, David told him. "Your fans still love you because u-da-man! And you're still so fucking cool about it."

"What happened with you and Terry?" he asked with ironic guile.

"Fucking gorgeous isn't he?"

"Don't go on."

"He showed me his stuff – sweeet!!!" David laughed happily.

"So unlike you; you use to like older men." David's mouth fell open at his brother's awareness, so he put his hands over his face. "But we know

Black men have 'it' so I'm not surprised. Maybe now *you're* a man, things are different."

"Gus will always be my man. Terry is a homie-sexual that raises the Black…" Solly eyed David candidly as only a brother can. "You gave him a taste."

"Are you mad? I'm here gathering divorce evidence on my wife. What kind of double-edged hypocrite would that make me if I fucked some bloke on the street?" Solly gave his big brother an even closer look.

"It's been nine years since I had flesh and bone sex with a guy."

"There ought to be a code red in the public sphere," Solly told him; "You're gonna teach that dude the real meaning of drum and bass 'Grime'.

"Shut the fuck up! That bitch and Horia are getting hot, move your arse guy!" They got a move on and fought their way through the crowd and David got on his mobile again. People were now kissing and cuddling as well as dancing.

David and Solly meet up with a solid bloke dressed in smart casuals, blending in, but his face and body showed that he'd been through government security training. He was, in fact, a London Transport police officer, earning some money on the side with this gig. In a pinch, he could outrun most people and take down just about anyone due to his ten year Terror Attack training by British Transport Police. Gareth was the kind of English bloke upwardly mobile young European and Black woman dated. David's father knew Gareth well, and he put him on the job to protect and support his sons. When Gareth learned that he'd meet Solly he needed no more convincing. He was a big fan of his when Solly played for the London club as a striker, and David was so well known on the London scene, he gladly took the job and the £400 a day which their father paid him to make sure his sons were always safe.

"She's getting frisky with him. I've got five men filming them all over the crowd."

He put his arms over David and Solly's shoulders. I know you want to do some filming of your own. We'll cover you as you planned but don't blow it. Gareth was only thirty years of age, but he had experience and instincts well above his rank.

Solly tugged David's arm and pointed his chin across the way, so David put his camcorder to his eye and focused until he had sight of Veronika and Horia, a gruff but happy looking Romanian, age forty. David zoomed in and caught sight of Veronika in a yellow summer dress as they swayed to the music and kissed easily. When they broke their kiss, she squeezed in tightly to him so she could feel his erection.

"Solly, record me filming them. Turn from me to them and turn back to me.

Solly did as David asked. He used the iPad to record David and then he quickly turned around to capture Veronika and her lover. Solomon switched points of view on the iPad to film himself. "Ok, this is the Notting Hill Carnival, and I'm out with my brother who is filming his wife with a man David suspects is her lover. David, what can you see through the camcorder?"

"Solomon, I've got a good point of view of my wife and her lover. I don't want there to be any misunderstanding of this footage being edited. You're filming me live."

"Yes, I am. Why don't you turn your camcorder on me and I'll turn this iPad on you." They did so and waved to each other and had a brief trivial conversation about the date, time of day and the exact location.

"You will be able to see in this footage that there is no sound break. This music you can hear is on my camcorder and the iPad." Solly continued to film David.

"I suspect my wife of adultery because I now have a fair about of recorded evidence of her and her lover Horia Tatarescu. I have the strongest suspicion that she and her lover will go to a hotel to fornicate later today. I'll capture the naked truth no matter what I have to do." The hatred in his words worried Solly. He and the family knew the kind of ferocious temper David has and the throbbing veins in his temple, and the manic look in his big brother's eyes under his thick eyebrows was as intense as men he'd knew in Nigeria who set their minds to vengeance and carried it out in bloody fury. Even though Solly was a man who enjoyed a fight, the steely angry look on David's face troubled him.

The Calypso steel drum percussion increased in volume as a float came by, and the phantasmagoria of dance and mime swished about in vibrant costumes in front of David and then came a cacophony of sounds overwhelmed the scene. The tonal shifts of light and dark brown skin kept blending into intermittent breaks of white and tanned Europeans lining the streets. The various expressions of joy in the crowd held the attention of the performers that floated by accompanied by every shade of pastel.

Veronika was spellbound by the procession as the Carnival passed by her. She received many admiring looks from men. "Horia, don't you love the display and drama of their music and dancing?" She kissed him, and he passionately returned the kiss because he wanted people to see she was his.

"You love these niggers, not me." His thick Romanian accent was coarse.

"Don't say that. They have struggled for dignity. I love how they celebrate their triumph of citizenship with this Carnival."

"Why don't we go to the hotel?"

"I don't see you just for that," she replied pouting.

"No? Aren't I better than that asshole husband of yours?"

"Don't talk about him."

"I'm twice the man he is!" He told her holding his head high and fixing his hair.

"If you say so."

"No, you've said so. Come on let's get away from this shit and go to the hotel."

She inspected him, and she was reminded of her home and everything she did to get away and find her freedom. She hated her life in Romania because it was so predictable. There was next to no freedom for her as one of two daughters who had to connive their way out of agrarian poverty. She left behind a life she could no longer stand, and she had no regrets. However, she did miss the smell and light of her country, some of the food and even though she never went to church in England, she did miss the ritual and family get-togethers on Sundays. Horia brought some of those things back to her because he had a newly rebuilt ex-pat family in London.

"Don't say anything horrible today about anyone or anything…"

"I will say what I fucking like as long as you are leaving me to go back to that nigger. Say it! Say I'm better than him at all things." She looked defiantly at him, and he grabbed her arm and twisted it until she finally gave in.

"Yes, you're better than him."

"Good – now let's get away from this monkey circus and go fuck." He pulled her by the arm slightly and she abruptly stopped; leading him away from the flow of people decorated with every fabric color imaginable moving west toward Ladbrooke Grove, where she knew she could get a taxi.

CHAPTER FIVE

Tony excused himself, leaving Michael standing on the street eating food surrounded by people in Portobello Road. Pleasure seekers came from all over the world to the carnival as a part of the vacation in London as well as coming to visit their extended families, and Michael liked being among them. Tony made a call and waited.

Lola was at home in Muswell Hill, when her mobile went off, and she stopped talking and checked the phone. She saw Tony's name on the visual display, left her daughter and boyfriend and went into the library to take the call passing her sons and their girlfriends on the way. All her kids were clearly mixed race. Lola closed the door to the empty library and answered the call.

"Tony, how are you?"

"Alright."

"Michael has told me pretty much the same thing. He's isn't seeing anyone. He wants me to date you, see you. He wants you to be happy with me."

Anxiously she said, "Tony, he must know."

"He knows you have feelings for me. But he hasn't hinted at anything."

"Michele is cerebral and very savvy. God, I feel so dirty…"

"There's no need. He speaks of you with love and kindness nothing to even imply he distrusts you. He's in limbo because he doesn't know what he wants he just has the belief he has to find something different. Some ideal guy… I tell you I couldn't even imagine this last year."

Lola lowered her voice, "And I kept telling you he was driving me mad, sleepwalking through his life not paying attention. The kids were impatient with him…"

"Listen to me. Will you marry me?" Lola's heartbeat jumped, and she looked all around as if everyone she knew could see her, but she was alone with empty book shelves in an incomplete room.

"I don't know. It's so strange to do this…"

Tony looked all around the streets, lowered his head and said, "Do you love me?" He anxiously bit his thumbnail waiting for her to reply.

She took ages to answer. "Yes, but I don't want to act like some heartless cheating…"

"We haven't done anything." Tony watched kissing couples and party people dancing and swaying, drinking, carrying on and flirting in the street. "You haven't betrayed your marriage vows."

"If we marry… I – I can't have Michael thinking I cheated on him when I haven't even kissed you."

"You leave that side of things to me. He has no negative thoughts about you."

"What are we going to do Tony?"

"Marry me; will you?"

She stared into space and took some time to freely think about her future.

"Darling talk to me."

"Yes, I will marry you."

"Good answer. Great – beautiful. We've got our entire fifties, sixties, and seventies to make a new life. I'm glad you haven't chosen to be a saint and slip into the past without any vision of what we're going to create for the future."

"We'll have to wait some time."

"No – no no. We'll marry as soon as we can."

"What about the children. They'll…"

"…deal with it! They have their life. Most of which you and Michael gave to them and made for them. They're not retarded dependents or idiots. They're all educated graduates, good looking, willful and sharp manipulators of social policies. Both of you have played gift bringer to them long enough. Let them go into the world and hunt and gather their food and shelter. They've never been tested like that."

"You can't ask me to abandon my responsibility to my children."

"No, I would never do that. I'm telling you to see the men and woman you've raised and let them show you *their* respect. They've run your life. With the exception of Roberto, their failure to honor their father is a bloody disgrace. He's given them everything you have and more. He's given them money to solve their problems."

"You're right…"

"Yes, I am because I've watched the two of you raise them."

"Do you like them? You sound so angry…"

"I grew up in the Favelas of Rio. That's with the army, pregnant girls and poverty everywhere under tin roofs. Over here families pamper kids and teenagers; afraid they'll be un-liked if they don't buy every piece of shit their kids demand. I love my mother and father for their heart and advice to me."

****

At a B&B reception two hours later, the six o'clock news headlines kicked off and Gareth and David shoved their faces right at the manager, and David told him. "Look at the picture." It was a wedding photo of David and Veronika. "My wife is up there shagging an Eastern European geezer who sends his fucking whores here. Do you want to find your business splashed all over the tabloids on Monday? I can arrange that."

Gareth said, "Give us the key or I'm going to arrest you for living off immoral earnings. Running a terrorist cell and facilitating human trafficking." The Romanian fella played tough but Gareth grabbed and twisted his nipple, and he yelped. "I've got a rat in that sack." He pointed to his colleague, a Rookie twenty-four-year-old Welsh guy. "I'm gonna dump that rat down your trousers and…"

"No!" The man begged. The Rookie noted how effectively that scared him.

Gareth put out his hand for the key; the man handed it over, and Garth said, "If he goes near that phone, smash his teeth in and punch him in the throat." Gareth looked at him as though he'd just seen the manager involuntarily defecate, now covered with shame.

Inside the bedroom, Veronika lay in Horia's arms. "You will always come back to me because deep down you know that fucking nigger is beneath you. He can never understand a woman like you. For God sake, what does he know about Romania? He's never even been there with you."

"I told him I never want to go back. You talk about him as a pure racist would. He never treats me like some white thing to amuse himself. He buys me everything. We're married. You'd never marry me, would you?" He didn't answer and wouldn't answer no matter how hard she stared at him and gave him dirty looks.

"You know the difference between you and him."

"His dick is under 18cm, and I am over 21cm. He's a fucking monkey, and I'm a man." She slapped him in his face, but he didn't dare hit her.

67

"You prick. He can give me a climax, but you struggle for it. He's a successful businessman, and you're a pimp! He plays music, makes stars, comes from a refined and intelligent family, and you didn't graduate school because you're lazy. He got me clean when you gave me drugs." Admitting that upset her, deeply.

"Veronika, sorry; sweetie, sorry: you were homesick, and you complained about everything you were living with the first time we met at the club."

"You don't understand women at all. I was depressed about my singing career. He did everything he could but every time I opened my mouth I fucked up a meeting or couldn't sing in the pop style." She flopped down despondently and might have cried if she was a weaker girl, but she wasn't raised that way and didn't indulge in self-pity.

"Do you think I'm still beautiful?" she asked desperately needing assurance.

"I love you." But his drunk thick accent didn't convince her.

"No, you don't."

"I prefer you to the other girls."

"Well they're hookers, and I've never been that; so big deal."

"What do you want now?"

"What would you do for me?" He stared at her, and he did like her above all the others, but he wouldn't let himself be 'played' by a woman. As far as he was concerned, she was cheating on her husband so he couldn't trust her. "I'll make you cum and go crazy the way you like."

She went to the bedside table and took some cocaine. She offered him and he inhaled more than most men could. She liked the sight of him and when the rush hit him the two of them interlaced their fingers and lost her senses for a time. She went down on him, and he moved into her, spat, and licked her private parts.

The door discreetly opened, David and Solly came in filming, as Gareth and his crew of four also came in filming David recording Veronika and Horia. They moved deliberately and quietly so that even after ten seconds of filming Veronika and Horia didn't look up immediately. David caught them in full oral consumption.

He shouted. "Good, you adulterous cock sucking bitch! You're busted!"

She turned, and Horia swirled around and saw the room full of strangers filming him. "You fucking nigger I'll kill you." He got up and made a dive for David who moved aside, and Horia fell badly. David tossed his camcorder to the Rookie; Solly recorded everything on the iPad, and David pulled a heavy belt from around his waist then proceeded to beat Horia as he rolled around on the floor.

David yelled with each lash. "You, have, no, business, fucking my wife! You're a nasty, filthy, pimp! Avoiding tax, trafficking girls in and out of Britain!" He gave him two lashes across his face. Horia screamed! "Yes, bawl – and beg." Veronika did not move to help him. Her hair was wrapped around her face as she struggled to see the man filming her. "Vermin like you must be driven out of the environment!" David caught Horia with a lash right across the stomach, but he didn't catch his penis: David spat on it, and Horia felt wounded.

"That bootleg DVD business you're running. I sent a letter to Time Warner and Fox about your rip-off." Horia tried to get up, but David dropped a lash down his back that made him ball up. David flogged his buttocks and made Horia cry and crawl away. "Don't, run, from, me!" People in the room watched enthralled because no one in there had ever witnessed anything like the terror on David's face.

"You're too damn rude, wicked and lie! Lie!! Bastard, I'm tired of your evil shit! I work for a living! You're a dirty thief! And I'm gonna put your arse in prison, where perverted criminals will fuck you over."

"Please, no – stop."

"Hell no." Lash! "You ever heard of the Carnivalesque? Of course not. I've had you investigated, and you're an ignorant peasant." Gareth, Solly, the Rookie and two others watched unsure of what would happen next. But Horia trembled on his knees as David stood above him.

"Today is the day when chaos usurps the status quo. Ever heard of Paul Bogle? Today's when the oppressed and repressed can override the normality people like you love. You've had it your own way, but on this day of Carnival, the enslaved can mock the master." David let out a cathartic scream that also sounded like the cry of a deeply wounded man and proceeded to bring his belt down on Horia with unrestrained fury.

"Turn your cameras off!" Solly ordered, and they did. He watched his big brother regain something that was taken from him at the age of seventeen. It was a day Solly never forgot because that was the day he cried watching his Dad beat David.

Lash! "That's for Stephen Lawrence." Lash! "That's for O'Neil Crooks." Lash! "That's for Patrick LuMumba. And this–" A heavy lash caught his hip and his scrotum. "Is for the disrespect you inflicted on me like I'm some 'black thing' you can fuck up."

David's consciousness of Black's destruction and victimization strengthened his arm and fed his psyche. The beating he laid on Horia forced Veronkia to scream out.

"Shut up you fucking slut!" Solly yelled, and she covered her head.

When David stopped, Solly turned his iPad back on. Horia was covered with welts.

"Now it's time to deal with you, Veronika." She screamed. "No, I'm not going to hit you. We're going to help you back to my house. You'll pack your bags and leave tonight. You can come back here or live in a bed and breakfast until we go to court. You're now free to shag everyone and take as much drugs as you like." She stood up and covered herself with the sheet.

"Car's downstairs." She walked out defeated because she had underestimated him. He was totally out of character, and she'd never have imagined him capable of physically beating Horia, even though she knew David could outwit him.

****

Tony eyed Michael listening to the Dominican guy he took a shine to earlier, and he was curious about how effortless it was for Michael to let the man talk about his preparation for the Carnival and his emotions throughout the day. The three of them were in a café bar on Portobello Road packed with people from across five Continents. The Dominican was a very expressive thirty-year-old with a smiling face and adoring eyes on Michael. Tony glanced around at the men and women who took no special interest in them. In the café's low-lit space, with sparklers sizzling over the patrons' faces, the heavy Soca rhythm of the Islands blended with the bossa nova playing in the café and Michael looked contented. The Dominican played with Michael's disheveled sunlit brown and gray hair. "On plantations, many of us willingly went to bed with the Masters because desire doesn't lie; we do."

"Michael, I'm gonna make tracks. Young man, nice meeting you – you guys have fun." Tony never imagined telling Michael he approved of him getting laid.

"No worries," Michael replied untroubled because he'd drunk nine rum coolers so he was mellow and bright. Tony got up and slipped him a condom. Michael secretly looked in his hand and then kissed Tony on the ear and said, "Call tomorrow." He let go and sat down closer to the Dominican and Tony rushed out, keen to go to Lola.

"I want to kiss you." That made Dominican really happy hearing that.

"I live twenty minutes away from here." Michael finished his drink and stood up, and the Dominican led the way. When they stepped outside the heat from all the bodies was thick with energy. They walked through the darken streets, squeezing through the crowd lit by shops and lanterns and Michael occasionally eyed his arse.

Twenty minutes later, Michael entered a darkened room lit with fireworks outside. He watched the sexy Dominican take off his parade custom, and he observed the way Michael eyed him with a specific glint of excitement. They were on the top floor of a social housing tower block, so they were totally unobserved as red, yellow, silver and blue light burst into the room. The Dominican loved everything about the day, particularly since he'd hooked an attractive man. Michael told him. "So much I want this." He moved in and they began kissing. Michael was instantly aroused.

"Fuck! your cock could get me pregnant." Michael laughed, took him to bed and showed him size has no skills if a man has knowledge and experience. Outside, the night of music, laughter, drink and love continued until the next morning.

CHAPTER SIX

David watched his father's reaction to the DVD recorded footage of Veronika carrying her bags with David following her and pointing at the front door. On the doorstep of the house, there were six Louis Vuitton suitcases. An overweight English cab driver took the bags to his taxi and came back for the others.

"David, where am I to go? What must I do?"

"If this was *Gone With The Wind*, I'd answer you." The cab driver darted looks at both of them. "Suit yourself; I have your sister's address, so I'll send the divorce papers there. If you take me for a nigger, try something, and I'll burn you and make the Nigella mess look tame compared to what I'll do to you. So, my adulterous wife, fuck off!" He slammed the door in her face.

When the DVD footage turned to snow and stopped, his father said, "Checkmate!" He turned to David and shook his hand. "Bradley, how does the case look to you?"

Bradley Weinberg was one of those Jewish men who lived by honor and devotion to his family. On first impression, he resembled Daniel Day-Lewis. He and Solomon met at a convention, and he liked Solomon, but he was greatly impressed by Cynthia. Like many men of his generation, born in London's East End, who'd moved up in the world through hard work and good social contacts he was unconsciously influenced by Black's cultural transformation of British post-colonial society. He respected the achievements of his race and used Black social confrontation to deal with the rising tide of anti-Semitic bigotry nationwide.

"You've got her dead to rights. Plus, you have that amazing footage of her going hell-for-leather with David. There's no way she can say you're not a passionate and willing husband that… satisfies her needs. Come our day in Court we're talking about her love of cocaine, sodomy, and adultery. In addition to her involvement with..."

"Rasputin!" His father said, and Bradley broke into laughter, and David connected to them quickly. "I mean I've been going through the files with

72

Bradley and that blood-sucking villain is a mess! How many illegal activities can one man have going on?"

"In his case, fourteen," Bradley stated. "Five of which he can do time for. The human trafficking is as bad as it could get, but I've got one of his girls to give evidence that he raped her and sold her Albanian arse to a Russian in France. Then there's the tax issue. Our biggest win is the DVD bootlegs. Time Warner and Fox want him nailed!"

"That's only half as good and the beating David gave him," Solomon replied.

"Well, I learned from the best." He looked at his father and a dreadful tremor shot through Bradley which he'd never felt before.

David's PA, a pretty ugly mixed race guy with a violent streak knocked on his glass door. Standing beside him was his girlfriend Sophia, David's PR and Marketing manager: a gorgeous Dutch woman who took her work seriously and handled his staff of seven with care and an iron fist. David glanced at them and switched off the monitors that faced away from the staff on the other side of the spacious Hi-Tech, multi-media steel, glass, and wood paneled office.

The staff sat on both sides of a long central desk, divided in the middle to feed wires to their iMac, PCs, and Apple laptops. From his office David could watch over them and in Sophia's glass office at the other end of the office, she could keep tabs on the reception area and the staff. "Talk among yourselves." David went out to see them.

The noise of overlapping speech in English, French, and Spanish was distinguishable as his staff sold and promoted his clients. On the walls behind the staff were projected images and streaming videos of his clients and their performances. The red, white and blue translucent lights gave the office an even greater technological feel. Outside, a giant crash stopped the staff talking as they rushed to the big windows and pushed it open. In Hoxton, the Techno center of London, two belligerent drivers were screaming at each other. The staff watched for 45 seconds, and David yelled, "Come on people, no deals no meals. We've got bookings and money to make."

"Slave driver," replied a fair-haired final year Welsh undergraduate.

"Why don't you repeat that and see if I'll fire you." The smile vanished from his face. "You haven't learned to respect the work have you, Ewan. If I don't see any online sales for Mr. Man, by the close of the month, you'll be going back to Uni' with a fail mark for this internship that is 60% of your final year mark. Candace has hit her target and exceeded your figures by £83K this quarter." David was impeccably dressed in a blue shirt and cream suit. Subsequently, Ewan felt shabby in his jeans, exposed pants, T-shirt and greasy hair, compared to the smell of hibiscus in David's hair.

"That's because she's £100K better than you," Sophia stated.

"Let's not say that," David replied; "but I know I'm offering her a full-time post before she graduates, and I certainly can't say the same for you. Of course, you could change that." Ewan was a blagger, built for media, but he didn't know how to sell in a consultative way. He always stated the obvious rather than analyze clients' needs.

"Get over there, book the clients and sell their work!" Sophia told him and he got a move on and hurried to his desk. "Fire him already," she told David.

"We're dealing with students' degree marks. We don't pay them much right now unless they sell, and I'll give them serious bonuses and commission for that; so we must treat them fairly and with care."

"You're too soft. Anyway, listen..."

Willy interjected. "Men's Word, the new giveaway magazine wants to feature you on style. Their launch mag is focused on London's Black style and meanings. They're doing post-Carnival happenings and sub-culture. There's a big show on Rude Boys, happening at Somerset House. You and your brother must go to it! That my advice for today." Willy handed him a folder of stills and text about the Rude Boy event. "I've worked two weeks on this so find time. Also, I figured you could take Mr. Man with you because he needs some good press. He can go with that Spanish girl. They make a right pair, his Jamaican temperament, and her Spanish temper."

"I hope that's not you stereotyping again, is it Willy?"

"No man," he said defensively with a nice blend of Cockney patois. "I was out with them at 1-2-1; they had a blazing row just for media spots: pure acting. They need to be out with some class, acting sweet. You can get that out of them."

"Print me up a copy of the riot act, on red letter paper with the red envelopes. I'll give it to him. Now I'm planning my divorce, so..."

"What?!" Sophia exclaimed. Willy looked dumbfounded because he knew almost all of David's plans, but this was a shock to him.

"Yes," David continued irreverently. "No bullshit 'un-coupling', thank you, Gwyneth. I'm getting rid of that bitch." Sophia and Willy swapped looks as David turned and left them standing. Sophia adjusted her tight red skirt and white blouse; Willy fixed his black tie, white shirt and gray suit. Willy cast his eyes over the staff stealing glances while doing business on the phones and computers. Sophia head back to her glass office and drew the men's attention to her behind because they all thought she was gorgeous. As she walked past all the technology, Willy was reminded why she was greater than everything in the place, so he adjusted his growing member and exit.

David said, "Give us the room please, gentlemen." They all stepped out. Solomon walked to the door and turned his back to face David. "Son... are you alright considering what's happened to your marriage." He felt deeply upset for his son, but he knew David wouldn't believe that so he felt compelled to convince him.

"She's an adulteress. I've *never* been with anyone since I married her. And don't think I haven't wanted to or haven't had the chance. But I know God is my judge. Each of us is tested in life, and I'll stand before God and he'll know I've never committed the crime of wickedness against anyone." He moved right into his father's face. "I learned that because of you."

"David please stop digging at me."

"I'm not. I just can't forget what you did." Solomon looked terribly weak suddenly not only because he was guilt ridden, but he couldn't feel any love emanate from his eldest son.

"I watched you beat that guy, and I swear it looked like you were flogging me."

David moved away with a smirk. "Not everything is about you."

"Do you want me to beg you?" Solomon asked pulling it his clothes.

"You almost killed me," David stated in a cool and accusing tone. Solomon attempted to speak. "Not here. This is my office – my place of business, my staff."

"You must talk to me because this mentality has broken out of you. The icy way you're planning to crush your wife and her lover. It's..."

"Business! They're... pointless. I've been victimized by forbearance and some twisted martyr ideal 'PC' society expects from me. The day I turned thirty-six I promised myself I'd be honest. So if you don't want to hear any more about it, you can go."

"I want to know what's in your heart."

David laughed and then stopped laughing. He fixed his shirt then sat behind his desk.

"Look at you sitting there, like Prince Fuck-U-all."

75

"Daddy, please don't upset me, because under your tutelage I've learned how to battle with anyone. The only thing I'm scared of now is my rage. But how I live with that is marked by *my* search for love. Love is our greatest salvation."

"And do you have any love in your soul for me?"

David took a minute, and his father went through hell before David spoke. "Yes."

Solomon's eyes blinked and refocused because he was hot and dehydrated. He licked his lips and desperately attempted to speak but couldn't.

"Daddy, are you alright?" David quickly got up and rushed to his aid. Solomon lost his footing and David helped him into his chair and went to the fridge and poured him sparkling mineral water then helped him swallow it. The Pellegrino refreshed him.

"You don't hate me?" David shook his head no, and his father began to cry, so David turned the chair around so no one could see and he kissed his father's hands.

CHAPTER SEVEN

Michael walked with masculine grace, through the Tate Britain Gallery with his Dominican boyfriend, Harry, and prospective new client, Jason, a thirty-eight-year-old English Dot.Com managing director who'd made his first million and wanted to splash out. Michael gave Jason an Art history lesson as he walked through the halls and galleries, but Jason was distracted by the attractive female tourists who passed him every other minute.

Harry was incorrectly dressed in a fashionable tracksuit and timberland boots, Jason was overdressed in a Hugo Boss navy-blue suit and red shirt, and Michael had on his tweed Inverness three-piece suit that was ten years out of date.

"Has any of what I've said given you an idea of what you'd like to buy Jason?"

"I appreciate the Art lesson, but I've always thought Art is whatever you can get away with." He laughed at his remark, but Michael didn't.

"Right now you have disposable income, but money is worthless unless it has a purpose, you have to put it to use."

"How should I do that?"

"This is why I've brought you here because you said you didn't like what you saw at Tate Modern and wanted something more stylish, more traditional."

"If *you* could afford anything in here, what would you buy?" Michael laughed and led them in another direction. "My tastes are very eclectic, but some works are timeless because they speak of and refer to myth, morality, and realism. Any work that encompasses all three usually fascinates me." He hurriedly kept walking with them quickening their pace to keep up until they stopped in front of Frederic Leighton's *An Athlete Wrestling with a Python*. Michael studied the bronze in reverent admiration.

"For me, this is the greatest modern sculpture that inscribes good and evil into our Christian perception of man and beast, temptation and disavowal." Michael addressed them for seven minutes on the subject of

Eden, the 'fall of man'; his industrious rebirth and his strength of self-preservation. "Whatever you buy, Jason, it shouldn't be fashionable, it should be fulfilling. And that's why I'd buy this."

"Well, you couldn't put that in a house. And it's a bit gay, isn't it?"

Michael grabbed Harry, kissed him and caressed his buttocks. People in the gallery actually bumped into each other gawking in disbelief. When Michael finally got his fill he opened his smiling eyes and said, "No, that is gay."

"You're totally outrageous!" Jason stated as his accent strained his voice.

"Well, I used to be a square…" Michael laughed out loud, and he suddenly stopped when he saw that his son, Roberto, was staring at him dumbfounded. Roberto's penetrating eyes switched to Harry and bore through him with pure hate. Roberto was twenty-two and looked like he was caught in a frame of *L'uomo Vogue* standing dead still. But he carried all the years of hatred in his look that his great-grandfathers would have if they saw what he witnessed. Michael approached him, and people in the gallery peeped and moved away sensing a dreadful confrontation. Roberto watched his father walk up to him, and he had no idea what to say.

"Who's that?" Jason asked Harry.

"That's Michael's youngest son."

"You're going out with a married man with kids," he said accusingly.

"No, I'm not." Jason looked confused and turned back to Michael.

Michael hesitantly said, "You're early. I was going to meet you in the café at five o'clock."

"Papa, is this why Mama said to see you and listen without judgment?"

"I suppose so."

"She said the separation is the first step in getting a divorce."

"Yes." Roberto looked back at Harry. "Did he do this to you?"

"No, I've changed." They stood in silence. "Come and meet him."

Roberto stepped back and threw his hand upward and yelled in Italian. "No! I will never talk to that… evil beast that has poisoned you. That she-devil, slut!"

Roberto threw Italian gestures at Harry that was both vulgar and damning. People in the gallery stopped talking and moving because Roberto was the most compelling sight contrasted beneath the statue of the *Athlete and the Python*. Although it towered above him, Roberto's clawed hand whilst spewing venom at Harry was a greater paradox.

Roberto worked himself up into such a state he ended up in tears, screaming at Harry and covering his face.

Through CCTV monitors, two security men watched Roberto and Michael. The cameras intercut between high angle shots and zoomed in close-ups. Michael took Roberto in his arms and comforted him as fathers do in moments of grief. The image of Roberto grabbing and clinging to his father compelled one of the guards to say. "Get down there and see if they need help. That guy looks like he's having fits." The distressing sight of them on the monitors contrasted sharply against the lifeless works of art.

Michael came into the bedroom carrying a bowl of soup and bread on a tray. Roberto sat up, and Michael placed the tray in front of him.

"Thank you, Papa." Tuck in, Roberto began eating, and Michael watched him.

"Remember the time you caught pleurisy from staying out in the cold at the rock festival."

"Oh yes. Mama was working so hard, and you stayed home to take care of me. I got better quickly didn't I?" Michael nodded. Roberto ate some more but then he stopped and hid his face in his hand. "That guy you kissed. I was so shocked. I never hated somebody all at once just like that. You won't see him; go out with him anymore, will you?"

"No, he's gone."

"I was so stunned. My God I was screaming in the Tate Britain!" He shook his head, and Michael took his hand and kissed it.

"It's alright. Maybe it's too much to ask you to accept of me starting another life or being someone different. You know me. I'm too romantic."

"You don't love Mama anymore?" he asked in Italian.

"Yes, I love her deeply."

"How can you divorce if that's true?"

"Remember in Luchino Visconti's films how he explores the question of love. And how contradictory the right and wrongs are. *Ossessione*, *Rocco and his Brothers*, and *Death in Venice*. I… I have come to understand I cannot deny my soul and my conscience. You remember in Woody Allen's *Crime and Misdemeanors* you and I kept going over the question of 'truth' and how it's become meaningless in politics today."

"Yeah, I think all political leaders are liars."

"I have been lying to myself. When I couldn't stand to treat myself like that any longer, I told your mother I had to leave to preserve our lives and yours."

"Is that why you've been so… isolated this past year? So vacant?"

"Good word – yes. It was like giving false evidence to condemn someone, but I was doing that to myself."

"You've been in that kind of pain, Papa?" Michael nodded. Roberto touched Michael's face, and his father's eyes hurt him deep in his heart.

"Those things I said to your… friend. They're not my feelings about you." Michael smiled, and Roberto moved the tray to the bedside table and said, "Come here." Michael nestled on top of the duvet, and his son rocked and cradled his father.

Two days later Roberto came into the sitting room, and Michael was on his laptop and mobile doing business. The expression on his face told Roberto his father was winding up a good business deal. "Ok hear me; I'll fly to Prague and acquire the painting for you. I'll come back here, do the paperwork, and bring the painting to you in Los Angeles. I'm going to email you the travel and expenses within the hour and, after that, we can settle up when you have the painting."

Roberto listened, and his face indicated he liked the way his dad handled the business, so he held up his hand for a high five. When Michael got the verbal confirmation he held his hand up, and they hit it when he put the mobile down. "Fifty grand, not bad for a day's deal and three months of aggravated back and forth. I'd been following the artist because I knew his work would appeal to my client, but the client was doing a number on me since he's hit it big with his movie. I even had to fly over to LA to talk him through the metaphysical aspects of his attraction to the work."

"What was his response to your explanation and questions?"

"Rubbish. I asked him why he paid bar tabs of $5,000 and spent in excess of $90,000 on recreational drugs in a month. He stated this in *Vanity Fair*."

"Who is he?" Michael told him. "He is a total pussy hound and coke fiend."

"I know… and he's a right wing zealot, fucking bastard; anyway, deal done."

Roberto half smiled and went and sat opposite Michael. Roberto looked distinctly mixed race as he settled his mind and pushed his hands through his auburn loosely curled hair. His full mouth and nose marked his mother's heritage in him.

"The other night I did something." Michael moved in closer. "I told you to get rid of what's his name. I used the worse kind of emotional blackmail. Considering we brag about our sexual conquests as a trait of our masculinity, I was really out of order to tell you to live without ever having sex." Michael sat back contemplating what Roberto said, but Roberto misread Michael body language.

"Believe me I don't want to put you down, make you despondent. Yesterday I was thinking how sanitized we've become. In your era, between radicals, sexual liberation, and the neo-realist artists – you guys changed the world. My 'PC' generation is so sanctimonious and judgmental. I don't have the right to lay down laws to you. I think we, me and my friends, get freaked out by our parents fucking. I could say having a love life, but to people I know at Uni, that equals parents and 'shock horror', grandparents actually fucking." Michael chuckled. "But grandpa and his sister had four marriages, and Aunt Daisy loves to say at sixty-one she has amazing orgasms."

Michael laughed loudly. "Life in Jamaica is very different from here. Aunt Daisy lives well in London because she is malleable. I love that about her. She reminds me what my parents might be like if they were still alive."

"Papa, after everything we've been through, I haven't earned the right to tell you how to live. You don't even do that to me." Roberto stood up and went over to the G-Plan sideboard and poured them whiskey and soda. He held out his hand, and Michael went to him and took the drink.

"Forgive me. Please..." Michael shook his finger at him.

"Stop, you've never disappointed me or insulted me. Especially the way I hear kids talk to their parent's today – unbelievable! No, the other day, 'you had a moment'." They toasted, and afterward Roberto scrutinized him with a half-smile that was reminiscent of his mother's spirit. Michael wanted to know more but refused to ask.

Roberto said, "Cesare, Fabio, and Maria are going to shit when they find out!" Michael laughed openly and then hugged Roberto briefly and stepped back.

"Your brothers and sister are really going to break my balls; I know it."

"They're not going to believe it because it doesn't show. Believe me. I know gays at University, and one of the lecturers is openly gay – he can't hide it. You don't have that..." Roberto gestured for the right word; "gay thing." They laughed once again.

"Well it's real, but I know what you're talking about. I've been to gay clubs and people ignore me. One horrible bitch said I was a fat old queen who shouldn't troll Old Compton Street. It's overflowing with its trendy young gays."

"He called you a 'fat old queen'? What a little prick! I'll tell you something, though. You could do a reboot." Michael was puzzled, so Roberto dashed and got his iPad and quickly returned. He gestured for his dad to sit beside him, so Michael did. Roberto opened his pictures, and there were over a hundred of his family, but the majority was of his parents; most of which were Michael and Lola in the early years of marriage.

"Look you and Mama are alive with the love you both inspired. Mama shines with beautiful love, and you are heroically virile playing games with Fabio and Maria. Look here, you at thirty with Aunt Daisy and Grandpa. This tough and beautiful man is who you have to reclaim." Michael looked at himself, and he had everything men wanted at that time: success, a wife and kids, virility and enough to live on.

"I cannot go back in time. My body and hair..."

"You've still got your hair. A personal trainer, a fitness program can work wonders."

"Yeah, but which one, and where?"

"This is London the greatest world city on the planet. The mix of people in every borough makes finding people a lot easier, and if you can't be bothered to do it that way..." He flicked out of the pictures and went online. "Write in whatever you want online and buy it. Everything is happening here. Traveling on the Tube used to do my head it until I read *Get Out of My Way* by David Bankole. He has survival tips."

"Isn't he the football player?"

"No that's his brother. David's the music producer manager to hip-hop artists. Wait..." He went online and looked up the Rude Boy show at Somerset House. "Yes, I thought so. He's going to be at this next Tuesday; you want to go? He is so cool."

"I'll be in Prague next Tuesday."

"I've got his book in my bag. They update it every two years. It's a bit of a Uni staple. International students studying here are always reading it." He got up and found his bag in the corner of the room. "Listen to this." He flicked through the pages to find what he wanted. "Ok, good here it is." He sat on the edge of the sofa. "He talks about dealing with idiots who don't cooperate and cause obstructions and shit on the Tube. This bit's about people who pack the door area and won't move into the Tube because they wanna get out faster, total fuckwits. Dave comes face to face with a cretin and says. '*Did you mother's pudenda collapse around your head during childbirth, so now you suffer from some neurological cunty-itis we have to put up with!*'" Michael laughed harder than he had all year and Roberto loved the sight of him.

"Here, take it. Read it on the plane. It's full of tips concerning how to deal with dumbass commuters on public transport and 'moments you know you're Black'. He talks about his awareness of being Black and reading White perceptions of Black culture. It's so dead on. It reminds me of times I hear shit from people about Blacks, and then I say my mother is Jamaican, and they turn deep red with embarrassment." He handed Michael the book.

"It's even worse when a client makes racist comments and jokes assuming I'll collude with them because I'm 'white'. I always add a surcharge: racist tax. Your mother loves that. I've made more than £400,000 on that alone." Roberto high-fived Michael's punishment against racist's and left the room.

Michael's mobile rang, and he took the call. It was Cleavon, Lola's brother. He told Michael that he had to see him immediately, urgently. "What is it? Is Lola alright, has something happened?" Michael's face and body became tight, and his voice was filled with anxiety.

"Just meet me now, name a place?" Michael moved to get his keys and wallet.

"Bar Italia in Soho." His brother-in-law ended the call and Michael headed out of the apartment and took the stairs because the lift was always slow.

Michael got out of the cab in Soho, and he saw Cleavon sitting outside the bar. He was a rich brown skinned man with an angry face. In his Def Jam T-shirt, gold chain, baggies and trainers he looked like a 1989 hip-hop throwback, but aged forty-two he really was outdated. Michael paid the cabbie, rushed over to him and sat down.

"What is it?" Hundreds of tourists from all over the world roamed the streets.

"My father told me you're a queer," he stated with a distinct East London accent. Michael felt his mouth and throat go dry at the insult and accusation of criminality.

"How long you been carrying on with this nasty shit?" Michael was going to speak, but Cleavon cut him off. "Stay away from my sister's kids. I'll talk to them. They should know you're an AIDS threat…" Cleavon looked at Michael with hatred. "You nasty white men can do anything and everything disgusting. I'm gonna ask you one time. Have you tried to fuck the boys?"

Michael punched him the mouth, and Cleavon instantly got to his feet, flung the table to one side, and pulled out an elaborate flick knife. Patrons and tourists backed away screaming as Michael yelled, "Call the police!" The people around them were afraid for Michael because Cleavon fit the image of a thug they feared would kill them.

Cleavon lunged at him at him. "All of you have fe dead with your abomination."

"You must have had your brain fucked out and you know what I mean by that!"

People were on their mobiles calling the police. A stocky Italian in his mid-forties who knew Michael told him to back away from 'the crazy black killer'.

"*Sto bene Gino, sono in grado di gestire questo pazzo bastardo,*" Michael replied.

"Did you just tell him that you fuck your sons?!" Hearing Cleavon yell those words, Gino made the sign of the cross. Michael saw a bottle of wine on a table, picked it up, dived at Cleavon, struck him on the right arm, and he dropped the flick knife.

"The cops are coming; I'll tell them about Mr. Murray to explain this attack." Cleavon was strangely panic stricken. Michael gestured for him to run. "Keep your mouth shut or your kids will never come near you again." Cleavon ran as the cops arrived.

CHAPTER EIGHT

Christmas 2014

David watched people move about with ease and joy at his firm's Christmas 'Do'. He'd hired a restaurant's upper floor overlooking Soho for the event and he invited some of his clients. They were under thirties, Black and mixed race. Dressed as a classic Rude Boy, David turned to Terry and said, "So here they are; my triple L.M clients from London, Leeds, Liverpool and Manchester." They shared the restaurant with another party. Terry was dressed in great street style, and he looked perfectly in place among David's employees and clients. David walked Terry over to a window, and no one noticed anything odd about them in the neon-lit Tapas restaurant serving a large variety of Christmas specials. In the low-lit brown and blue space, the smart multiracial Londoners were in half shadow and light looking young and chic.

Terry pointed at something and faked a smile. "If you don't fuck me in the next hour I'm going to the loo for a wank."

"Shut up," David replied laughing and gesturing to his friends and colleges. "My balls are so heavy they could fall off." Several people passed and David indirectly said to Terry, "I'm gonna get atomic on your arse; you'll think the world is coming to an end in five minutes." David turned away from the crowd and looked out into the neon night, and Terry turned and glanced at him.

"My dick is so hard right now."

"Save it because I've waited months for this day. My divorce has come through, and I promised to give myself a treat to celebrate. You *are* that treat." Terry liked that. "Nine years, nine dry arse years."

"Whenever you tell me that, I just freak at the thought of nine spunk free years." David laughed and pulled back to check him out.

"You are fucking succulent!" Terry was deeply aroused by David's compliment.

"Man you're always coming out with this language. What does *that* mean?"

"Stand right there, I'm gonna step behind you." David did so, and Terry felt David's throbbing pulse against his backside. David moved away and said, "Can you imagine what it's gonna be like later?" Sophia and Willy came over to them.

"Is it alright to bring your five apprentices to speak to you? They're very happy. I don't think they've ever got £10,000 a piece from a job before."

"Yes bring them."

"Also, the staff's very happy with their bonuses and the job offers."

"Great,"

"Jill was so happy she was crying in the ladies. And Barrington has a St Lucian holy vibe over there." Terry laughed, and Willy looked him over once again.

"Oh my God," Willy said. "Your wife is coming at you, 10 o'clock direction."

David inhaled and turned to face her. She was nicely turned out in a cream satin dress that complimented her figure, but she looked thinner. One of his employees took out her smartphone the second she saw Veronika enter the restaurant. Terry had never actually met her, but he disliked her because David wouldn't make love to him until he was divorced and rid of her.

"David I have to talk to you. Can you give me some minutes, please?"

"No." She had to relax because she hadn't expected him to say that. "It really is important." She cast looks toward the people around David.

In his best BBC voice, that was always tinted with an African cadence, he said, "From today when our divorce papers came, there is nothing of importance for us to discuss." Adrian rushed in and stopped when he watched the two of them faced off.

"What is this skank doing here, Dad?" Sophia and Willy became just a little anxious.

"Please David; let's not be horrible in front of these people." Her accent made her voice and her words distinctly vulnerable.

"You're out-of-order, to speak about 'horrible'," Adrian told her.

"Our son shouldn't see this."

"I'm not your child! You're nothing to me you stink, nasty, whore."

"Adrian, stop talking." He was going to answer back, and his father gave him a look that no African man ignores. The look always referred to the 'Law of your Father'. As a young man who loved the Jamaican psyche he'd inherited, Adrian sometimes wrestled with the choice of which aspect of his identity he wanted to be guided by.

David saw Grace coming over in beautiful Indian purple and green Sari, but Veronika sensed nothing because he quickly shifted his eyes back to her. "You should leave because I'm not interested in you, and I don't care about your feelings."

Grace walked up behind her. "David this whore better not be testing me." Veronika turned around startled and her temper rose all at once.

"Oh, right, you and the mother of your child. So now you can be together. Are you sure you weren't fucking her behind *my* back! I mean you've always wanted him." Terry looked at both women, and every instinct told him to stand back, which he did.

Grace slapped her in the face with the full force of her resentment for everything she believed Veronika had taken from her. "Take your dirty Transylvanian pussy out of here and keep your blood sucking mouth shut before I batter you!" Adrian whipped his fingers and laughed at Veronika. She looked at the mother and son and felt powerless to fight back. In Romania, she fought men, women, and livestock that resisted or gave her grief but she'd been sapped of strength throughout the months of the divorce. Additionally, she had been forced to give evidence against Horia and lie to save herself from prosecution, and now it had taken its toll.

David's new employee Jill, a hungry English girl from an upper-class background moved in closer, recording the altercation with her smartphone.

"Turn off the fucking camera, turn it off!!"

David told Jill. "If you stop filming this you can go and work for someone else because I've told you never miss an opportunity like this for any of my clients. Evidence is the key to good business, not rumor and gossip." Jill moved around nimbly because she was just twenty-one, slender, ambitious and loved to win at everything she did.

"You'll be sorry for this. I came here to be reasonable and talk…"

"Shut up. Go away." He eyeballed her. "Coming here like this was more stupid than I ever thought you could be." Feeling real contempt towards her, he walked away. Terry followed him, and Adrian gawked at her. Grace looked at her with disgust and pity and yelled, "Transylvanian disease."

An hour later David watched his staff enjoying their Christmas dinner and he suddenly flinched when his phone went off in his breast pocket. He saw who it was.

"Yes Mum?" He listened for two minutes as his mum fed back what Grace had told her. "I'm absolutely fine. Everything is good here." He listened. "No this is good. I'd never let you or your staff cook for my employees." He listened again. "No, I promise you nothing can upset me tonight or over the Christmas." He didn't eat very much because he was watching his staff and Terry, who sat among them. Sophia and Willy sat on David's left and right. David seldom missed the looks Terry threw his way and he allowed himself a minds-eye view of them in bed, later, having waited so long.

"Mum, my thoughts are all over the place. I'll call you tomorrow." He ate rather delicately because his father drilled them all on their table manners. The Italian DJ signaled to ask permission to come over to David, and he gave him the nod.

A couple of hours later his staff were in 'the fun spot' that the restaurant had made for dancing and the original mix of *Bootylicious* by Destiny's Child had everybody moving. Sophia took a great deal of pleasure grooving on the dance floor with each of the seven members of staff who she passed over to David. He had one Asian, three Afro-Caribbean's, and three British/Europeans all under thirty in his team now; with Sophia, Willy and himself bringing the full staff number to ten. David also had five apprentices on part-time employment rounding out to form a formidable firm.

Dancing with his staff, David remembered his father's advice to maintain their dignity in public. David never chanced getting too close with females in the firm because he wouldn't give anyone cause to accuse him of sexual harassment. However, he moved in a sexy manner with his female staff, and he stepped it up a notch when dancing to demonstrate his virility beside men in the firm. But no one could have expected what happened when Terry danced in front of him. Terry's break dancing moves were a sight to watch, and his only real competitor was Adrian. Adrian got on the floor and competed with Terry much to the delight of the staff and David, who stepped back to watch them both. Adrian's classic electric boogie and Terry's Urban Grime dance grooves inspired David and he showed his love for Michael Jackson and Usher when he took back the dance floor and his staff and clients cheered him on. The DJ dropped the beat of *Shut Up* by the Black Eye Peas and David called

Grace out on the floor. She moved with funky elegance in her Sari, and he took hold and she spun out of it and revealed her gold colored one piece swimsuit *a la* Beyoncé. Adrian cheered at the sight of his mum and dad because none of his friends' parents were fabulous. The cut *In the Closet* by Michael Jackson came on, and they danced so well together a rush went through Adrian because he revered them. "Show him, Mummy!" Adrian yelled, and she weaved her hips around David. "You Da Man Daddy." And David paid homage to Michael Jackson's original dance in the video while Terry ached for David in his heart and loins.

As David danced with Grace, he kept thinking why he asked the DJ to play the track and why he rehearsed with Grace the week before. He was determined to come out in 2015, and he wanted to drop hints. He reveled in the irony of the song and his dance. He was happy to be free of Veronika. He was also sure he and Terry had something. They've gone on thirty-two dates over several months getting to know Terry. Their clandestine meetings were a key factor in the thrill David derived from seeing him, and wanting him, so David danced freely to *In the Closet*.

****

Terry sat in the kitchen watching David make him a full Caribbean breakfast of cornmeal porridge, corn beef omelet and plantain, with banana fritters for afters. It was three days before Christmas and Terry was in a 'love sexy' state of mind. The two of them wore the same pair of oyster-colored silk pajamas: Terry dressed in the jacket, and David wore the pants. David watched him get the cutlery and plates for breakfast, and he studied the shape and form of Terry's imperfect natural body.

Unlike the rest of the house, the kitchen had everything the 21st Century demanded of health and safety, convenience, and style. It was kitted out in cream colors, with a high gloss red fridge and black stove dominating the space.

They began eating, and Terry turned to him. "How'd your wife start shagging someone else when you take care of business in the bedroom *and* kitchen?"

"I don't know, and I don't care if she wins the lottery or gets hit by a truck. She's gone, and I won." David laughed. "The state of her last night: man – Grace nearly tore her face off with that slap. Adrian was like... Goal!!!!" David concluded jumping to his feet.

"I don't get you and your wife at all."

"It doesn't matter anymore. Last night you gave me what I was craving." He kissed Terry.

"Have you thought about what I asked – us going steady."

"Yeah, that's nice: but you 'coming out', going public – Wow! Oops!"

"I did great business last year. No one's gonna drop me because I'm gay."

"And that's where your madness lies. You know what *we're* like. Every Black woman with a Bible and a brother with 'Street Cred' will condemn you nationwide." They ate in silence for a while, and David lost himself in thought. "This food's great," Terry said and kissed his forehead.

"Do you really think they'll be that kind of shit storm?"

"More! You're David Bankole, who's put ten Black British crews on the music map. You're the beloved brother of Solomon Bankole. You're on television! Mr. Man swears by you as his savior from a life of crime. Last year The *Evening Standard* featured you as a 'Leader of the Urban Community'. In 2011, you were a voice of reason in the Hackney Riots. They'll crucify you if you come out," Terry concluded a little out of breath.

"There are only so many lies I can live with. Last night in bed was the truth. I don't feel right with myself at times because I can't deny my soul and my conscience."

Terry slowly kissed his chest and held his nipples between his lips until David chuckled and pushed him off. "Eat your breakfast!" Terry's youthful smiling brown face was as charming as could be.

"Listen to me gorgeous, are you…"

"What did you called me?" Terry asked flabbergasted and enchanted. David repeated it and pulled him in closer beside him.

"After last night in bed, you proved to me why I couldn't go on as I was. The heat in you from your skin to your soul; and 2½ hours of Homie sexuality was great."

"Listen to you; this is why I loved you when you were on the radio! And I've never been with anyone who can fuck for that kind of time. Your dick made me talk patois man: plus the stop and go ice and tongue lashing!" David rocked with laughter.

"I knew you'd like that." Terry sat astride his lap to face him up close. "You did me, man! Maybe because you're a real man and know what you're doing but that is the first time anyone's made love to me instead of having sex with me. I came *inside*; which was amazing and then the blast at the end: fuck-yeah!"

"So," David took Terry's face in his hands; "since we connected perfectly in bed and we're good together, are you going to tell me *now* what you do for a living? After all, you took an HIV test, and we shared our status. What are you hiding?"

"It's just…" Terry looked away and took a deep sigh and breathed to calm himself. "You pioneered Nigerian High-Life and Drum & Bass. You've made over ten club classics! Twenty-something hits… Solomon **football God** is your brother."

"I already know who I am. What do you do? How do you make a living?" Terry stood up and walked to the other side of the kitchen to get a glass of water.

"Listen, as long as it has nothing to do with drugs or street gangs, it's fine." David studied his physique and waited because he was determined not to let it drop.

"I… work for Royal Mail," Terry said. "I'm a postman."

"Man, that's fine!" David said and went to comfort him, but Terry became very boy like in his naivety, inexperience, and insecurity.

"Dave…"

"David, always David never Dave or Davy…"

Terry withdrew and became noticeably introverted and insecure. "I didn't do very well in school, yeah. I – it… they were fucking horrible! Teachers pegged me as one of the black boys they couldn't bother with. And if I'm honest I did have a 'fuck-it' attitude."

"I wasn't that different at school myself."

"Excuse me; you went to private school and you have a MA in Business Studies. I've looked you up online. I don't have any 'A' Levels," he said defensively.

"You could go back and get them."

"No, I took them and failed. The point is… I'm a postman." He looked defiant but so inexperienced.

"What do you want to be, Terry? Obviously, you're not satisfied with being a postman, so what do you want to be?"

"What difference does it make?"

"Maybe I can help you."

"Excuse me, but people usually tell me 'sort yourself out I can't do it for you'."

"Is that your life? The way it's been?"

91

"Yeah, I'm not complaining, my job gives me money and freedom to do what I want. And I've never been on income support, living off the State. My mum goes mental about that, and my dad says only losers stay on it because they don't have any pride."

"That sounds like my dad."

Terry stood up straight and took his bowl to the sink. "I do want to do more, though, but I got no rhythm and flow rap skills. I'm not an artist."

"What's your best life skill, just something you've always been good at?"

Terry sat back down and continued his breakfast. "I can play church organ…"

"And the mouth organ…"

"No I… Oh! Fuck me you're nasty!" Terry laughed easily. "You got those skills?" David nodded. "I can play the saxophone too."

"Well, you'll have to play for me."

"You can't do anything for me like you've done for your crew. I'm just a postman who lives in a shit one room place in Shepherd's Bush." He started on the corn beef omelet. When the full flavor hit him he became animated. "Bloody hell, Dave…David, sorry! This omelet is better than my mum's."

"Do you want to move in?"

Terry stopped chewing and the thought ran through his mind very quickly. "No, I've got really bad habits; it drove my mum up the wall, cleaning up disorganization."

"Just ask yourself two things: what you want out of life and are you going to be a shag pile, humping around whenever you find the right bloke, then walk away… used."

"There's another side to that picture: if I'm not in a monogamous, I won't feel tired down or guilty if I meet someone else who I fancy. I've never been a one-man, serious boyfriend type," Terry proclaimed asserting his independence.

"Ok, it's early days. I should mention if you're going to do the rounds; I can't be with you. I just divorced a slut who put me through that."

"David, I'm not a slut. Traditional marriage demands fidelity. In this century, people have relationships based on freedom that may not include that."

"Ok, here's my offer. Me and my 'amazing sexual skills'. Sharing life with me: and my support *and* honor as a loyal friend." Terry pushed his food around and then quietly ate while thinking. Terry recalled the sensuality of the night before and their romantic and secret dates all around London.

"I don't know if I can do it? Not saying I want to be some slag. I don't know what it takes to live with a guy or be a couple living separately. I don't even know anyone who's happily married."

"Don't you want to see me anymore?" David asked in a sudden panic.

"Yes! No, I'm not saying that now I'm onto the next shag."

David tried to be neutral. "Please don't do that again. I have a fragile heart?"

"Attacks, strokes…Oh. Ok, I see."

"I can't shag around. I have a son. He wouldn't talk to me if he thought I was some… *fuck*ing queer. He will listen to me and understand when I explain my heart and mind. But cruising young blokes – no! He'd freak."

"Do you think he'd go off on me?"

"No, because when I tell him about myself, I'll tell him about the man I love and the man who loves me." David was instantly caught in reverie. Terry saw and felt the surge in him which compelled Terry to take his hand.

"When I tell Adrian what truly lies inside me." Tears that didn't fall filled David's eyes. "He'll still love me, even more… because he knows what I've suffered."

"What?" Terry asked knowing that meant something important.

David knew it would be stupid to speak about his father. "Long story."

"Suppose I did move in…"

The joy that flashed through David made him deeply appealing to Terry.

"I'll only do it if you don't come-out to anyone until I tell you if I can cope."

David reluctantly nodded to the agreement and Terry embraced him relieved he hadn't lost the only man to include him in his life rather than steal bits of *his* life.

Lola was furious. She stared at her sons and daughter and walked a circle around the living room with all of them watching her stalk them, dressed in her embroidered gold kaftan. "It's Christmas in two days. Your father told me he'd only come here if you treated him right," she stated while scrutinizing all of them.

"What does he mean 'treating him right'? He's divorcing you, isn't he?" Fabio stated. According to his girlfriends, he was gorgeous and athletic much like his twin sister, Maria, both of whom inherited Lola looks. Maria was uniquely attractive due to her Jamaican Italian parentage. Lola grabbed Fabio by the tie and pulled him out of the sofa. He stood above her, at 6ft 1inch to her 5ft 9inch. She stared at him and said, "How the hell did you get that 2.1 at University? Oh, wait! You're what my mother would call an educated fool!" She yanked him into the middle of room and Roberto told himself not to laugh, but he loved his mother's panache.

"Mum's gonna go Jamaican on him," Roberto told his eldest brother, Cesare, who was dark, rugged and serious. Cesare elbowed him to stop. They both bore their father's image more than the twins who didn't look alike but resembled their mother.

"Don't presume to know what's going on between Papa and me. You don't have to protect my honor, as if your father has wrong me, cheated on me or some other disgusting shit that your 'PC' generation do to serve your own ends."

"Mama, I don't know what you're talking about." She shoved him and he staged backward. She turned on Maria and pointed in her face.

"And you! What the hell is your excuse?"

"Mama, can you cut the dramatics and let's have a civil discussion." Lola walked up to Maria and looked at her with the full force of her Being. Maria started to crumble under the weight of her mother's gaze and she covered her eyes with her hand.

"What gives you the right to treat your father in this fashion?" Cesare looked away. "Shall I tell you the day Papa broke up with me?" Maria looked up at her mother. "On his birthday. You know the one; a few months back when you were too busy, too uncaring to attend." Maria bit her lip.

"Mama, stop bullying her." Lola turned speedily and marched over to Fabio and he backed toward the corner of the living room until he was flat against the wall.

"Bully her! You're lucky I don't batter you, but the night is young, and Lord knows what I'll do if you if you tell me any more shit!"

Cesare said, "Mama, I think we didn't go to see him because we didn't want to offend you."

"Darling, what's offensive to me is the way you've treated him. Papa loves you so much: each of you, all of you!"

"If he loves us so much, how did he abandon us?" Fabio said.

Lola swung around and said, "You twins can really talk some shit. I should have let you spend more time with our genius, Cesare." Fabio's friends envied his good looks and charm: his devotion to his sister and his solid work ethic which had got him two promotions at the software firm he worked for. But standing in front of his mother with his elder and younger brothers who were looking at him made him cry.

"I'm not really stupid you know Mama. And I do care about Papa," he concluded wiping away his tears with the back of his hand.

"Baby, Fabio… I'm sorry. I'm sorry." She went and comforted Fabio, and then she remembered a few weeks earlier when she was with Tony on her birthday.

****

Lola took his hand as they mingled with the theater crowd during the interval of *Book of Mormons*. The Prince of Wales bar was packed with people buzzing through spaces and the continual sound of laughter underlie the voices and clinking glasses. In his dinner suit Tony looked very dashing and Lola had on a lemon colored chiffon dress that complimented her size 14 figure. Tony had styled her hair into an eye-catching chignon earlier so she looked as lovely to everyone else as she did to him.

"I ought to be paying more attention to this. I know it must be good because the audience is laughing like crazy."

"It's your birthday, this is your treat. Enjoy yourself."

She took a sip of champagne and told him. "I can't believe I refused to share my fiftieth birthday with the kids. I thought it would be fitting to deny them the day with me because they denied Michael his day."

"It is apt, but this is one of the very few times you've ever stood up to them. You and Michael have always sacrificed your pleasures and wants for them. Believe me, in Brazil no parents would put up with the shit your kids run on you."

"I feel so guilty."

"I told Michael, giving them everything they want is not good parenting."

"That's easy for you to say, you don't have any children."

"But all my friends have kids, so I see and learn a lot. You must be strong now; because you're going to get through this. You have to tell them about us." She turned her back on the crowd, and he tried to comfort her, but she wouldn't turn to face him.

Michael arrived and looked at the two of them. Tony gestured, and Michael turned Lola around to face him. "Darling, what is it?" She forced herself to speak.

"Tony was talking about telling the kids about us. I don't know if I can do it." Lola forced a smile and looked into the crowd with the fake expression on her face.

"Hear me… both of you," Michael said. "For the first time in our lives we are not going to put the kids first. They have their lives. They have jobs, money, partners and their own flats. They are totally self-sufficient. They also have your blood and mine. That is more than they need for strength."

"Fabio and Maria…"

"Fabio is devoted to her. His strength lies in his psychological and spiritual bond with her as his twin. He's not so good at defending himself but that is where Maria looks after him. Cesare is a rock! He will listen to you. As for Roberto, he has all the courage and vision of you and me."

"Oh darling, you make it all seem easy when you explain."

"Today is your birthday. You have reached a pivotal moment in your life." Michael turned to Tony. "You're going to start anew."

"I have to admit," Tony began with anxiety. "I'm not looking forward to telling them about Lola and me. They might think we've been carrying on."

"I've thought about that. Lola, tell them you're divorcing me." Tony and Lola exchanged looks and then came to rest on Michael.

"And I thought this musical was weird," Lola stated.

"Oh, it is," Michael replied. "It's too bad it doesn't have a great score otherwise it would be a classic."

"Michael I see you're losing weight and too much if you ask me; but are you losing your mind? I was going to tell them we reached 'irreconcilable differences'."

"We've filed already. Tell them you're divorcing me for your own reason which is none of their business." Tony looked at him stunned.

"She can't tell them that. That forces all kinds of questions."

"Will you leave that part to me? I have a plan to help you two and myself."

"What plan?" She asked.

****

96

Maria went to Fabio and sat beside him. Cesare got up, poured a drink and handed it to Fabio.

"Understand this," Lola said. "I have decided to divorce your father."

"But he left you," Cesare said. "Doesn't he have a woman…"

"Do you just happily fill in the parts you don't know?" He made a typical Italian gesture to indicate 'what else could it be'. "Your father is not involved with another woman. He's living alone." She went over to the drinks stand and poured herself some Christmas punch and stated in a matter of fact tone of voice. "You'd know that Cesare if you'd gone to see him."

"I wasn't going to see him behind your back Mama."

She reached up. "God in heaven, please tell them: you're not paying honor and service to me by ignoring the only person who's made our lives happy and secure."

Maria tentatively said, "But when he left you were crying and upset, Mama."

"Yes! We've been married for thirty years. Maria, try to think beyond this judgmental era of self-righteous platitudes and proclamations. Not everything can be packaged as the media like us to think. Yes, I cried; the reason is not because I was wronged or shamed by your father. Michael has never been with any other woman. His virginity belongs to me."

"There is no other woman?" Cesare asked.

"None!" Roberto drew on his strength to resist speaking about what he knew.

"Then why are you getting a divorce?" Fabio asked, and Cesare keenly waited for her answer.

"That is none of your business."

"Mama that is ridiculous!"

Lola smiled, and Roberto loved her all the more. He didn't know what was happening, but he knew his father and her had agreed on something because what was happening bore the mark of Michael's personality.

"Maria, do you remember the times when you've had difficulties, and I've asked you what's the matter, and you've said again and again, *'Mama, I can't talk about it. It's too personal, stupid even. I'll get over it'*," Lola replied imitating Maria's voice. "All of you have told me things like this. Well, now I am having my own 'personal moment'."

Cesare said, "We have a right to know what's going on. He's our father."

"Oh, now you remember he's your father, Cesare. Where were you for him on his birthday? Fabio was managing your soap opera, Maria, with that boring, spineless boy you're dating."

"That's not fair Mama."

"It's a fair assessment of a privileged boy without character."

Fabio turned to Roberto. "You're very quiet."

"Don't put your mouth on me, because unlike Mama, I'll blast you." His brothers and sister eyed him stunned by his boldness.

"Children…"

Cesare said, "Mama tell him to shut up because he's just a baby. I'm the eldest, and I'll smack the crap out of him." Lola went for her mobile and dialed. "I can see you've forgotten who the head of his family is," she told them and walked out.

"What the fuck are you like?" Cesare asked Roberto. "Everything's going crazy, and Mama is so humiliated by Papa's… exodus with his books and God knows what else, now she's acting out."

Roberto said, "All of you. Try thinking about them and what this means to Mama and Papa. You guys are cross-examining Mama to deal with your shit."

"The baby has suddenly got wisdom," Fabio stated. "Where did you find enlightenment boy?"

"From my father." They cast looks between each other. Roberto got up and walked around the living room as if he'd just been struck by lightning, waving his hands in the air. "Yes, my father! I see the man who gave life to me every week."

After a few moments of silence, Cesare said, "What did he say?" Roberto suddenly stood dead still when he looked at the door, and Michael was there.

"Why don't you ask *me* what I've had to say to my son, Cesare?" Michael responded with a rich bass sound in his voice. They all stood and came to attention. Michael was a lot thinner, but he still had his beard.

"Papa!" Maria responded slightly short of breath.

"What is this bullshit I hear: that you *dare* to question your mother?"

Lola entered and went over and poured Michael a glass of Christmas punch and then brought it to him. He took it and kissed her on the lips. She sat down casually. His sons and daughter did not. He had on a new brown suit that fit him well. "Sit." They obeyed him.

"The last time I saw you all was… I forget. He circled the room talking to them. "It's almost Christmas, so I'll get to the point. Your mother is divorcing me; we have agreed on a settlement. In the New Year, she will re-marry."

"What the fuck are you telling me?" Cesare said.

"Maybe I'll take off my belt and explain things to you." None of them could have been more shocked that he said that.

"Since when the hell have you taken to corporal punishment Papa?"

"Cesare, I'm not taking questions!" Lola burst out laughing, and they turned to her and quickly back to Michael. "I'm here to make an announcement." He crossed the room to sit beside Lola and took her hand.

"I'm here to give your mother my blessing. She and Tony are to be married in spring when our divorce is final."

"You're joking," Fabio said. Michael took out his mobile and dialed as he walked over to his son. "How well do you think you know me?" Fabio failed to answer immediately. Michael spoke into the mobile. "Ok, now." He pocketed the phone.

"Answer me, Fabio."

"I know you, Papa. I honestly don't know what's happening to us right now."

"Have I ever given my word and failed to keep it." He shook his head. "Your mother and I have the right to be happy. Darling, can you please go and see to that." She got up and quickly left the room.

"Your mother and I do not owe you anything more. We have provided you with everything that's made you safe and secure. Now Mama and I have come to the end of this stage of our relationship, and we're going to start an even more... profound friendship based on our love and marriage and the life we've shared with all of you."

Lola came back into the room with Tony. "Alright, here they are." Their sons and daughter looked at Lola and Tony. "I give you my blessing, and I know we will all come to realize happiness is the most difficult thing to maintain so when it's there, use it to sustain your life."

"I'm not listening to any more of this," Cesare told them.

Michael said, "Do you suffer from *cunty-itis* that I'm going to have to make provisions for?" Fabio's mouth fell open, and Maria covered hers with shock.

"All of you owe your lives to your mother and me. Your 'PC' views on your rights don't interest me. I care about your rights and honor as my children who believe in the humanity of your elders. We've raised you with a true understanding of freedom."

CHAPTER NINE

Spring April 2015

At Arsenal stadium, David sat in his season ticket seat with Adrian beside him and four rows back Michael was there with his sons Fabio, Cesare, and Roberto. The four of them were shouting and cheering their team on. In the four rows below them Adrian was also cheering but David wasn't. He looked miserable and distracted staring into space. All around the Arsenal Emirates stadium, the crowd was getting more and more excited. The multitude of racially diverse faces created a unity among the Arsenal clan that exceeded their separate everyday lives. When Arsenal scored the goal, everyone erupted, and friends and strangers hugged one another.

David started hallucinating. He saw himself out on the pitch naked as the statue of David and then being kissed by Michelangelo and coming to life as his Afro-Caribbean self. In his arms, David felt magnificent, and the cheering fans added to his sense of renaissance. Suddenly two teams came charging at him One team was African, and the other European got him on the ground and started kick tackling him.

David's face was so drained Adrian stopped cheering and watched his father's depressed figure. He shouted and moved up close and repeatedly asked. "Dad, what's the matter?" Grief-stricken, David just stared out at the pitch but then eventually turned to face Adrian who shook his shoulder, but David couldn't speak. Adrian scrutinized him in their Arsenal official kit and felt a growing level of anxiety. David abruptly got up and pushed his way through the crowd with Adrian following him.

After fifteen minutes of struggling through the crowd, David ended up upside. "Please Dad, what's the matter?" Adrian asked concerned for his father.

"I want to be real with you. I don't want to lie to you about anything."

"Of course, yeah; what is it?"

"Would you still feel good about me no matter what?"

"Yeah, course."

"All I want is to be free. To… If you stopped loving me, I'd die."
David's thoughts drifted into the abyss. But the roar of the crowd came
crashing into their ears. "I'm gay," David said.

"What? I didn't hear you, Dad."

David's eyes darted about. "I thought I met someone who I love, but
it's not working."

"You met someone you love and it's working, but what about Mum?"
Adrian looked less than happy and a little disappointed.

"No, I *thought* I met someone, but I'm not in love." Adrian brightened
up a bit, but he wanted to appear happy, which he wasn't because he was
still troubled by David's level of stress which he could feel.

"Dad, why haven't you asked Mum if she wants to get married? She
loves you a lot. And no other bloke is gonna call himself my dad as long
as the two of you are alive."

"Your mother and I have something greater than marriage."

"What?"

"We're mates. I trust her more than any other woman beside my
mum."

"Yeah, but I'm talking about passion man. You know! Don't you
wanna get real after that nasty bitch you divorced?"

"Yes, I do."

"Then who's this new woman you thought you loved but don't."

'*I'm gay; I'm talking about a guy. His name is Terry*'.

"Dad?"

"Listen; don't pay any attention to me. I'm just disappointed. I'm not
in love." A gigantic cry of woe came out of the stadium and David heard
that finish his point. "See, even the fans are sorry for me." He forced a
smile, but Adrian wasn't taken in.

"Are you gonna tell me what's going on because you're *really* upset."

"I suppose I'm lopsided because it's my birthday, I'm thirty-seven and
wanted more in my life at this point. But it's not so bad: there are religious
conflicts, wars and chaos going on, so does it matter if I'm not in love –
not really." He tapped Adrian's shoulder. "But I do have a lot of love from
you and Mum, the whole family."

"Is there something wrong with you and Mum, because you two are as
close as I've seen, but you're not together when we should be."

"We are together. There's more to life than tradition. I want you to
study and learn that at York University. Do you like it there?"

"Yes I go to all my classes, and I am learning." Adrian eyed him knowing that his father was holding back the real issue.

"You're studying International Relations, and you're going to be greater than grandpa or me."

"My studies haven't got anything to do with your pain, shock or panic back at the stadium. I thought you were having a stroke or something."

David began to hurt all over again, and his taunt face convinced Adrian something was wrong. "Dad, I don't keep secrets from you. You're hiding something. There's something deep. Whatever it is, you can tell me."

"What do you think I'm hiding?"

"That's what's weird about this because there's no way it can be criminal. So what does that leave? You're not two-timing because you're single, and you're not in love. You can't have converted to Islam and support those issues. You're not going out to the Far East to shag lady-boys because Black men don't do that nasty shit. And considering how well your business is doing, you can't be going broke; so I don't know. Don't keep secrets from me; secrets are usually perverse or psycho."

"I'm not perverse or psycho. If I'm in serious trouble, I will come to you, OK?"

Adrian watched him dissatisfied with his excuses, aware of his dishonesty and David felt it. "You think I'm a child." He walked off, and David was distraught.

"Yes go ahead and leave me in the street on my birthday – thank you!"

Adrian realized what he was doing, so he turned around without walking back.

"I've had to beg my father for love. I'm not going to do that with you too!" David walked off. For ten seconds, Adrian watched him, and as David moved further from sight Adrian felt increasingly bad.

"Daddy!" He ran after him, and David lengthened his stride, so Adrian ran until he caught up. Neither one of them wanted to speak, so they walked together.

At that exact moment in time, Veronika entered Canonbury Pond Gardens. The lush trees hung draped in green leaves in what looked like an enchanted hideaway in New River Walk tucked away in plain sight. A twisting footpath led into and around the gardens, and a winding pond sat between the iron gates and benches occasionally placed within the gardens. Veronika walked for several minutes and then sat down and forced herself to breathe calmly. After two minutes, she was able to concentrate and cast her mind back to 2008 in that exact spot when David told her that he loved her.

David brought an iPlayer with him, and they sat and listened to hip-hop classics and told her. "My Dad says you're 'beneath us' but I think you're lovely. Do you have any concerns about me because I'm Black?" She said no. "Then will you marry me?" He took out an engagement ring, and she accepted his proposal. "Right now I'm on the radio building a reputation, making money, and I'm going to spoil you." She kissed him. Now she only had those memories, she thought for over an hour about how she lost him.

CHAPTER TEN

Edinburgh May 2015

Angus looked up when the grandfather clock struck three. Gustav Holst's *The Planets* played softly in the cozy cottage standing alone in the wondrous landscape.

Gazing at David, Angus felt younger than forty-seven, but a broken heart had taxed him. He was a dark, brooding Scotsman, of Greek heritage with stunning green eyes, shoulder length black and silver wavy hair that contrasted against his ivory complexion. His wide shapely lips scowled, holding David attention.

"When Adrian said secrets are usually perverse or psycho, I felt accused."

"Yeah, you and the rest of us: your Dad, Veronika, Grace and me."

"Were we perverse or psycho? I could be accused of that considering how I punished Horia and Veronika." David took off his jacket and loosened his black shirt because he felt hot, and he wondered why Angus didn't feel hot in his heavy kilt, knitted socks, boots and Shetland pullover.

"I wanted to kill your father." Angus crossed the room and sat beside him in the big sofa. "Grace wanted to spite you so she spoke to Solomon when she shouldn't have." His lyrical Scots brogue was entwined in a poetic meter. "Grace went diva because she was pregnant and your Dad rules by the 'Law of the Father' so he played her. But it's *you* who makes us all crazy." Angus could tell David didn't understand what he meant. He moved closer, still gazing at David, haunted by the memory of their past. The light of spring outside came into the room and created an ethereal environment.

"You're an *amazing* man. That's coz you were an incredible boy. As beautiful as anything God ever created. I came alive as never before the minute I saw you."

"No, your beauty and truth captured *my* soul Gus. You were everything I wanted and your kindness touched me."

Spellbound, Angus said, "I watched you play cricket, and my heart choked me." David asked why. "You were pure. And you survived brutality. But even now you're still striving to be heroic as a father and a man. You turn people into stars."

"For profit, I'm no philanthropist."

"Sneer all you want, but you're one of the reasons I can live in peace now."

"Why, we broke up; I left you to be a father."

"You left me for a higher purpose. But you loved *me* first and afterward you loved Adrian. I risked going to jail because I loved you." David buried his face in Angus' tummy and cried, so Angus stroked his head.

****

Michael sat in front of his iPad and fixed his hair. "So today I attended my Lola's wedding. It was beautiful. Tony paid for everything. He said I didn't put him in the shit with the kids, and so he was grateful for that. Lola was so beautiful. Anyway…I am now totally single now. I've kept my promise to Roberto, and I haven't seen Harry even though I think about that first time very often. The one-night stands have been a learning curve. I'm too old for the 'gay scene' but at the gym, or whenever I take off my clothes, people look at me, and they want it. I must change my appearance.

****

Venus, the Bringer of Peace played as David rest his head in Angus' lap and he gently stroked David's hair, cradled in his tartan kilt, and caressed his face. "Coz of you, I studied psychiatry and specialized in Black men's neurosis. I've helped hundreds of men now."

"Angus, help me. I don't know what to do anymore," David confessed. "If Adrian hates me… I'll kill mys-…" Angus pulled him up and kissed David to silence him. When he broke the kiss and looked at David, he caressed his face lovingly.

"Do you forgive me for leaving you? I honor everything you taught me."

Angus unbuttoned David's shirt and moved it aside to run his lips over his patterned skin. "These African signs; they hide your father's scars. I

105

remember when you were unblemished." Angus moved his lips over the patterns.

"I was fifteen, and you were a man. Born here but Greek: I idolized you. I told myself I could seduce you."

"Aye, but we waited, and that's why living together in Manchester..." David interrupted him because he felt distraught. *Mercury, the Winged Messenger,* began.

"I don't want to be a liar! I can't stay with Terry. I want to be free, help me Gus."

Angus gave into his instincts and eased David's clothes off. When Angus saw David's rich naked glistening brown skin, scented with oils, it excited him. However, what reached into his heart was David's face. Angus got lost in the cacophony of music and his internal combustion. He tore at his clothes and covered David in wet kisses and then lifted his kilt and moved into a state of complete bliss.

"You're bad for me, so – bad, God, oh darling. Oh!" Reunited with the love of his life, he laughed, cried, screamed and wept as he moved like a one-man full ensemble orchestra conducted by David's hands and baton fusing their passion together.

****

Staring into his iPad at precisely the same time, Michael said, "These Brits I've shagged aren't going to make me happy. They're obsessed with my dick, nothing about my intelligence or heart. To become that fixation would be ridiculous. When I started this self-analysis, I was sure my understanding of Jung and Foucault would help me overcome my fears. But that book by David Bankole on how to manage obstructive people in confrontational situations is excellent. I'm sure he's read Fanon. Fanon's work helped me cleanse myself of colonial sexual sublimation. This Bankole guy talks about 'Living in a Black Body' and dealing with life. I checked him online, and he's married to a Romanian woman. That mixed race relationship is one of the things that make his social commentary so interesting. I want a relationship with a man like that."

****

Spread out on a big sheepskin rug, David eyed the hair on Angus' body that looked like the shadow of a tree with its roots in his pubic, the

106

trunk up his stomach, and the leaves scattered across his chest covering his skin. "Don't look at me."

"Why not?" David asked.

"Age is a bastard… I'm getting soft."

"That fucking organ wasn't soft, nor is your arse."

"You still like 'em big, yeah?" Eyeing his imperfect naked body David nodded.

"Yes, especially after a nine-year absence. For me, sexy men are a vault of hidden power just waiting to spring to action: from their cock to their fists and brain."

Angus shook his head bewildered. "So you left me to shag and marry Veronika."

"I was obsessed with being straight so Dad would love me. Women mean something to me; so I blocked men out. But the only physical love that identifies me is us."

Uranus, the Magician, began. "Have I still got it?!!" Angus asked joyfully.

"Your psyche and amazing cock are just two of the great things about you."

"What are the others?" Angus probed with hopeful exuberance.

"You're instinctually kind. That's why I fell in love with you." David climbed onto Angus. "Would you give us another try Gus?"

"Sweetheart I can't. I've been offered a Professor post at the University of Amsterdam. I start in September." David felt utterly helpless.

"Whenever we Face Time or call I feel like we're still mates. We help each other cope. What will I do without you?"

Angus kissed him and said, "Be you own man." Naked, David got to his feet and exited.

****

Late that night, Angus looked in on David asleep in his bed. The moonlight was so bright Angus could see through the window, and so he turned and walked down the hallway quietly. He went back into the living room, picked up his mobile and dialed.

"Hello, it's Dr. Vassallo. I had to call." He listened. "You're my analyst, and that gives me the right to one late night panic call. David and I have been making love all day, and I'm caught in limbo. It's so fucking sweet, but you said I feed on the pain, so I have to talk now." He listened to his analyst caution him for twenty minutes.

"He needs me," Angus replied between his gritted teeth. He walked over to the window and looked out onto the hills shaped by the azure moonlight sky. Angus vividly recalled David breaking up with him in 1996 as they walked along the rainy winding bends of North London's Regents Canal, with its concrete footpaths, muddy waters, 19th-century locks, English laborers fishing, and colorful Narrowboats.

Crying inconsolably, David looked like a post-nuclear skinny urban teen dressed in denim gear and cropped hair. "Grace is expecting, and if Dad finds out about us he'll kill me. And he'll come after you. I don't want to put that on you."

"Aye, we can't go on clandestine. This is best," Angus agreed, walking tall and stiff in his Levis and leather jacket. "I'm a doctor, and you're a kid." His green eyes were bright with pain David could see as he grabbed Angus tightly.

"It isn't fair, I love you. But I have to be a man as the family expects. Dad gave me such a beating for getting Grace pregnant. Imagine what he'd do if he found out about us." Helpless to stop him, Angus watched David run off down the Canal until he was out of sight and then Angus bawled his eyes out screaming 'David' repeatedly.

The moonlit Highlands came back in sight as Angus told his doctor. "Suppose I don't want to be the wise man, loving and teaching my protégée to fulfill his hero's journey. What if I want him all for myself?" He listened without interrupting.

"Bollocks to that! Being a role model is overrated." Angus left the room and went outside the cottage and into the fragrant spring night. He took deep breaths and lifted his kilt so the night air could caress his buttocks. Listening and thinking, he fell once again into a trance as he remembered his brother in 1997.

Angus staggered out of a pub on Piccadilly in Manchester, nodding blatantly and shaking his shaggy hair in his brother's face. They didn't look alike because Angus was love crazy and Theo was morally offended. Theo watched Angus weave around on the crowded neon street at closing time, and he dared Angus to "Fuckin' say that again."

*"My **boyfriend** has transferred from Cambridge and come to study up here at Manchester Uni to be with me because he loves me," Angus defiantly repeated. "You have no idea how fucking beautiful he is. He's eighteen, tough as a Zulu warrior with an Adonis physique and face."*

*Angus clapped his hands and shook his hips as people passed them. "Dave's naked beauty would make Zeus so fucking hungry he'd spunk on the world! You can keep your girlfriend with her ripe fanny. I've got this amazing bloke with a perfect arse who takes everything I can give and blows me away!" Angus applauded his life. "Not just that... He's rich, he's posh, he's got a high IQ, and he fucking loves **me** more than the mother of his child." Angus laughed loudly, and Theo beat him in the streets in front of people who watched, but didn't stop them.*

Two years later, Angus was tidying up their flat in Salford, Manchester; but he stopped cleaning the kitchen as the music ended and David's voice came through the radio. "This goes out to the love of my life. Baby since you love me I sing; 'Sexy MF' by Prince. You're beautiful, and we've discovered how vile racism is. I love your Greek heart and soul, and my Black body is yours alone."

That night in the vast darkness of the gay club with its flashing lights, David danced madly in just football shorts as Angus danced beside him dressed in his kilt and boots. His bare chest dripped with sweat and David was all over him as George Michael's hit "Outside" played. Angus led him off the floor and up to the lounge room. "Beautiful Stranger" by Madonna blasted out as they sat down. People around them were high on ecstasy, and Angus told him how great he felt since the tribute on the radio.

****

The year 2000 was difficult for them. At their flat, David told Angus he was leaving to take care of Adrian and be a proper father. David looked terrible. Angus asked what was going to become of them, and David said he had to return to London.

"Aye! Just fucking stay there and forget me!!" Angus hit him in the face, and David barely flinched, so Angus kept hitting him until he ended up punching him.

"He's my son! Mum's begging me to come home." Angus stopped, defeated. Eventually, Angus gave him the nod in agreement that he had to return to his family and David clung to him. "Thanks, love." They sobbed in each other's arms.

****

"Dr. Sfakianakis, I recognized the logic and reasoning of your analysis, I do. I'll sleep on it. But nothing is in our way now..." He stopped and listened. "I know my Professorship is a personal best... I'll call you." Angus hung up and closed his eyes.

The next day Angus led David up and over the hills of Edinburgh. As they stopped to look at Edinburgh Castle in the near distance, alone, they walked in silence for a mile. This allowed Angus time to analyze David's symptoms and anxieties, and then Angus abruptly placed his hand on David's shoulder.

"Your symptoms are what I'd call a symbolic 'white knight complex' that manifests when you feel you're in peril. The mirage you envisaged on the football pitch could easily represent your frustration as a hero. You are lifeless until a *Guardian* gives you a rebirth: a kiss of life. That hallucination could symbolize you coming out. You're not kissing your knight on the pitch. But the significance is that you're kissing your 'Idol' in a space that attracts national media coverage. You were kissing him so that it could be broadcast. This is tied into your divorce strategy. You've gone both ways with men and women. You've lived 'double-consciousness' as Dubois explained."

"When I introduced Dubois and Fanon to Dad..."

Angus put his finger on David's lips. "Dave, focus; don't evade. You've gone nine years without touching a man. That's extraordinary. You divorced to be free and honest; now you're trapped by a guy who forbids you to come out if you want to keep him. It's a dreadful paradox, coz now your boyfriend, not your family is oppressing you." David contemplated deeply.

"I think that confrontation with Adrian is a manifestation of your rebellion and unconscious tendency to self-oppress."

"That can't be what's wrong with me..." David protested.

"Don't argue with me; I'm a psychiatrist. I specialize in Black male neurosis and institutional racism."

"Yes, but I'm living in this Black body, and so I know... Sorry, I'm listening." "Nobody loves a smart arse." Angus pulled him in by the waist unafraid of anyone's condemnation; "except me." He kissed David in the sunlight.

Memories of their life together filled Angus' head, and he held David closely. "O Sweetheart, if you think *you've* got it bad, spare a thought for me." David looked him in the eyes. "You changed my life, Dave."

"As much as I loved you, I couldn't leave my family."

"And I'd have thought less of you if you did. We had an amazing romance, and it's kept me going through the 'sex only' relationships I've had. Love isn't everything. I've researched and written seven books. Work has been fantastic for me. And coming back here was right too, coz we're standing in my place of life and death."

Angus looked out across Edinburgh, and the mist of May instilled the landscape with mystical tranquility. "Would you do something for me?" The mischievous thrill and passionate desire that played across Angus' face was unmistakable to David.

"What right here?" The smell of the land began to fill the air.

"This is the exact spot they gay bashed me when I was fifteen. They almost killed me. I was so ashamed of being gay I sobbed, right here. Mum and Dad called the police, they searched for ten hours before they found me; but I couldn't say I got a kick-in because some bloke tried to fuck me and I fought back, so his mates got me."

"Will it dispel your demons after what they did to you here?"

"Yes. I wanted to find where they lived, break in at night and slash their throats. Therapy helped me with that, and you changed me," he said valiantly. "When I took you to Paris and Athens it was so obvious you wanted to be existential, an alchemist, combining Classical and Cyberculture; I – adored you. The best of both worlds is what I loved about you, plus you were dead sexy, and you still are." David felt inspired listening to him.

"Get your pants off." David obeyed unquestioningly. Angus opened his sporran and took out the Trojans. David held onto a tree and looked over his shoulder. Angus said, "People across the world idolize Solly. Your parents are in the press, and you're on TV, and DJ's turntables. You've left me for women coz you can love both ways…"

"I can't do that anymore."

"Shut up! This is for your best-kept secret." Angus had him without restraint. He felt the change in David's body, and before long David heard the sound of his own erotic dementia in the atmosphere. Before long, Angus' thighs got hotter, and David felt the rumblings of his internal orgasm which they mastered in 1999, and soon the strumming galvanized David's body and made Angus scream while they were hyperactive.

****

Walking down Princess Street that night after the pubs had closed; the city looked like a Georgian village invaded by frisky predators drunk on cocktails and beer. In the lamp lit streets, lovers and friends sang and left Scots broth on the pavements of Edinburgh. Angus loved it all. "Dave, before; up in the hills, did I go too far?"

"No that was the fucking truth. My loquacious tendencies are a shield because I live in denial."

"Bollocks to that! Tell me the truth. Just talk to me."

David tried to speak and Angus put his arm around his shoulder. "It's me: *I* introduced you to the Classics to explain the legacy of your father and your fear of him. Even though it's twisted, I get! Of course, I'll never get why you married!"

David gathered his courage and took a breath. He said the words he wouldn't want any of his kin to hear. "Black men scare me," David confessed.

"Right, but Terry proves you've changed. Likewise, I'm fearful of white men because they've queer bashed me; even my own brother – *Mouní enós ándra!*" David liked it when Angus swore in Greek. "I'm obsessed with Black men because you guys are full of faith; even after everything we've done to you. My work exonerates me from institutional racism, and I'm glad!" David nodded. "I know a group for struggling Gay Dads, in London." Angus flagged a cab. "They're experts about our issues."

The cab took them back to the cottage and Angus rustled up a midnight feast for two while David watched him at work. Angus made salmon cooked in butter, herbs, and sherry; served with poached eggs, topped with chili seeds. They ate it with Greek olive bread, champagne, and malt whiskey. At one o'clock, they tucked into the food with smiles plastered on their faces, in the cozy, rustic, spacious kitchen.

"Food's great, but you always could cook," David said wiping his mouth with the back of his hand. Angus leaned in and kissed him.

"Up on the hill today… for the love of God; talk about fucking great! When I have you – there's no one to compare, and I feel like I've been struck by lightning."

Angus saw David blush and understood even more. "When we agreed to psychodrama; to discover the truth in ourselves, and society; we said no limits and swore we'd examine everything taboo."

"I remember; that's why we don't lie to each other."

"I was angry you dumped me for that Transylvanian muff. I've got eight fucking inches and brains. But you tossed me for her; to be a 'real man'. I use to fantasize about pushing the two of you onto the tracks at Euston station. But I'd mentally replay the time we spent in Crete when I taught you how ancient Greek men made love. Only you can give me an internal orgasm, and make me spunk my balls off! I'm telling you there's something supernatural in your soul. But you left me for that, *ómorfi kakó skýla*: I mean beautiful evil bitch."

His twisted face changed into a benign smile as he sat in David's lap. "You know what it is sweetheart?" David shook his head. "On your sweet sixteen, you came to me and gave me your virginity." His shining green eyes smiled.

"You changed me. The blood I spilled and the pain you suffered... I knew then; sex isn't a joke. It's the blood and dignity – the soul of a human being. When I see you on TV or dance to one of your 'club classics' I know I'll go to my grave loving you."

David got up, smiled at him slyly and then began humming, *The Heather on the Hill*, and Angus' face was transformed by adolescent joy.

"That's not fair of you, you bastard. I taught you that song because I love the absurdity of *Brigadoon*. Smiling, David shrugged, gestured and took off his T-shirt.

"Fucking beautiful – look at you! Take your jeans off."

"No." He took Angus' hand and danced him around, humming; knowing Angus loved the show. It was no surprise Angus joined him, humming and dancing with his kilt swirling as he imitated his hero Gene Kelly. When David was seventeen, he lied to the family about a sports training weekend and spent the time with Angus. Throughout the weekend, they made love, watched *Brigadoon*, and David played Chopin and Debussy, but Angus stopped him. With tears in his eyes, Angus confessed why he loved him.

Circling the kitchen, Angus was unexpectedly graceful as if he'd studied modern dance. It thrilled David to catch sight of Angus naked under his kilt. Angus astutely reversed the seduction because he was a truly great psychiatrist. Angus hummed and danced until he fell onto the soft and he allowed David see under his kilt. "Sweetheart, d'ya see my A-B-C?" David came closer, gazing under the cloth.

"Yes, your arse and balls are what a man should look like, especially with a cock like that." David rushed him and made love to him desperately.

David awoke with Angus holding him. He lay there listening to Angus mumbling inaudibly, and he could feel the pulse in his cock behind him. David's thoughts went back to 1993 in London when he walked off the field in his cricket whites and saw Angus in his black leather motorbike pants and red leather jacket standing beside his Suzuki VX 800, gazing at him.

Angus' stare made David tingle, and he was glad his school friends were gone, as they stood alone on the open green cricket ground in Islington.

"I could get arrested for what I'm thinking. How old are you? Do'ya have a boyfriend?"

"No, I don't have a boyfriend. I'm fifteen."

"You're beautiful. You play incredibly well. If this was 1993BC, I'd show you one of the things that made us Greeks amazing."

"But you're Scottish," David replied because there was no mistaking his accent.

"Born, yeah – but I'm Greek. Like you're West African but British yeah?"

"How do you know I'm West African? I could be Jamaican."

"Not with that pigmentation… and the posh voice on you. You've also got that cadence and tempo in your speech which is Nigerian, or possibly Ghanaian." David smiled and became luminous as people do when they're bashful and bewitched. "Don't look at me like that or I'll get the horn." David went right to him.

"You fancy yourself, don't you?" David told Angus.

"No clever clogs. I fancy you." David inhaled and smelled petrol, musk, and whiskey on him. His Greek face and bright green eyes had classic manliness distilled in his bone structure and DNA. His lips were pink and full, and David liked his large nose that was slightly crooked: it made him less ideal and more rambunctious.

"Angus – actually its Augustus Demetri Vassallo." He put his finger into David's shirt collar right next to his jugular notch and pulled him in close and kissed him. His tight fleshy lips made David stiff and yielding. David had seen hundreds of kisses on screen and instinctively knew theirs was better because it had no feminine touch. Angus pressed David's lips between his and quickly moved the tip of his tongue from right to left like a signature.

"Fucking gorgeous you are. Can I take you out?" Angus dipped into his pocket and took out a pen.

"Yes, anything," David replied. Angus wrote his name and telephone number in the palm of David's hand. "Gotta go, he's getting restless," Angus said pointing and at his groin with a devilish smile. When David looked at his protrusion, he bit his lower lips dazzled by the cover-up Angus couldn't hide. Angus got on his big motorbike and rode off, and David opened his hand. The name and number in red ink blazed in his palm and thrilled him.

David got out of bed, went to the bathroom and freshened up. He entered the kitchen and put the thick Cumberland sausages into the pan and then started making porridge. Forty minutes later the food was almost done, and so he went into the spare room and took a look at all Angus' degrees and awards, as well as his gallery of photos hanging on the wall tracing his life and his parents in Greece, London and then Edinburgh. Angus had the first photos they'd ever taken together in a Photo-Me-booth.

There were pictures of David at school as a teenager and lots of other photographs of David and Angus throughout his years at University as a student, an athlete, student protester, DJ; in California, New York, and Athens, and shots of them together at David's graduation. There was also an angry photo of his brother Theo at his son's Christening with his parents and a heartwarming picture of Angus' parents with David and Angus all hugging at the same Christening.

Angus came up behind him in his wooly green socks and black underpants. Angus remembered hugging him at the Scala Cinema Kings Cross, watching Jean Genet's *Un Chant d'amour* and *Querelle*. "I'll remember this when I'm in Amsterdam."

"What? But last night…"

"Was beautiful: but if it's real, if you're gonna be *my* man, call your Dad, no call Adrian and tell him you're gay, tell him you love me." Angus declared, exalted. "I'll fulfill my contract at the University for the year and do everything to make a home with you next year." He touched David's face. "Solly will help to smooth things out since he knows you've loved me all this time." Angus could see his fear creep into David's face. "You were mine before you married that beautiful evil, the *kalon kakon*." The thought of Veronika made Angus' mouth dry, and his eyes flash. "My analyst told me, if I started with you again I'd never recover." David gave him a long searching look, and Angus could see he was scared.

"Call him now," Angus gently coaxed. "Tell him you're gay."

Panic stricken David repeatedly said, "I'm not ready." Angus had to calm him down.

"It's alright... You just don't love me enough..." David placed his hand over Angus' mouth and went to get his mobile in the bedroom. Angus followed him.

He dialed and waited. "Daddy, it's been days, why haven't you called me."

"Hi, morning. I..." Angus hugged him comfortingly. "I'm... I'm. I came up to Edinburgh to see a friend. Actually, we're really... best mates."

All at once, David couldn't speak, and his hand began to shake.

"Daddy, are you still there?"

"Yes. Anyway..." David's heart started racing, he began to shake as fear ate at him. Angus saw how deeply it resonated and soothed him because he started trembling.

"You'll be seeing a real change in me soon. I... goodbye." David was angry at himself so he sat still and tears came down his face. "Dad's right, I am a disgrace." Angus couldn't do anything to console him because he was filled with dread. He stuffed his T-shirt into his mouth and then pulled it over his head.

BOOK TWO

Romance
Summer & Autumn 2015

CHAPTER ELEVEN

August 2015

Michael strut down Fifth Avenue proudly. He was lean, shaven and tanned. He moved like a man who had acquired power. This power in his mind and his body came from six months of self-regulation, diet, exercise, and self-analysis. His clean-shaven face and layered haircut totally changed his appearance. Dressed beautifully in a bespoke Italian suit in two-tone green and gold mohair, and tightly buttoned up in a orange silk shirt and red tie, he cut a path between people on the street. The man beside him had to quicken his pace to keep up. Clearly he was younger than Michael, but his thinning blonde hair, ruddy complexion, and heavy belly was due to the martinis, Italian cuisine and first-class lifestyle he enjoyed.

"I can't believe the change in you, Michael. You look fantastic!"

"Yes, it's my birthday, I'm fifty-one, and I can tell you a secret?"

His client, Westley, slowed down, and Michael stopped walking. Westley stared at Michael waiting to hear, and he looked like a predatory WASP.

"I'm gay. Last year I came to terms with it and now I'm free."

"That must have come as a real shock to Lola. She's so beautiful and devoted."

"Yes that is why we divorced, and now she's married to a wonderful man; her business manager. I like him enormously."

"How very… European and…wow! You're so cool about it too. Jeez, most of the guys I know would be in therapy for months if they left their wife and kids to come out as gay. In today's media culture, you hardly ever hear about this."

"Didn't Leonard Bernstein leave his wife and family for a man? Then later pursue a brazen gay life much to the shock of conservative America."

"I don't know. He was before my time."

"History is very important," Michael replied in a scolding tone.

"Are you with someone?" Westley keenly asked.

"No I'm looking, but I'm very particular."

Michael started walking again, and Westley began to think.

"Do you want to come to a party in the Hamptons? A friend of mine at Columbia, his parents have a house there. He's having a great summer party this weekend. You mentioned if I could get you some referrals, you'd get me a better deal on canvases. I would like something very special for my house in Vermont."

"Yes, I'll go to the party," Michael said, and they headed for the Plaza Hotel.

In the bright East Hampton sunlight, Michael walked out of the grand white beach house estate to join the couples by the pool. His casual walk and military physique was admired by the guests, particularly since his saffron-colored swimwear made him look glamourous. All of the guests looked like they were celebrities in 1950s Hollywood. However, they were America's wealthy elite rather than the American intelligentsia.

With Mozart's music piped into the gardens, Westley introduced Michael around to people. In a collage of colorful beachwear, the women took a particular shine to him. They were mostly single thirties or divorced in their forties, resigned to never meeting anyone new who qualified as potential marriage partners chiefly because they occupied the same circles and kept faith with the cliques of White America's Christian capitalists. Michael could smell how much money they had because they were washed in perfume. He could also see how much money they had because all the women wore their jewelry like medals and trophies. Michael remembered the scene in Visconti's *The Leopard* were the inter-bred aristocracy looked feeble.

A wealthy and prominent patron of the arts stood perfectly still scrutinizing Michael as Westley navigated him toward her. Michael saw her and knew she was a faded beauty, now a reigning dowager of the East Coast set. She was in fact so wealthy and powerful; when her son was involved in a scandal in Manhattan four years earlier, she was able to bring pressure on the DA and have the affair dropped so that no one knew her son was involved in a drugs homicide case.

As Michael was led toward her, he felt nervous; until he suddenly remembered a confrontation that David Bankole described in his book concerning survival on British Transport. *'Never tolerate unkindness. When I come face to face with a snob, a racist or a fool; I remember I am the son of a Nigerian QC, whose father was a high-ranking diplomat. I was first educated at a Private Boys School, and their philosophy of humane rights has kept me alive. When an obstructive or prejudiced person comes up against me, I am inclined to expose their vicious ignorance swiftly and directly'.*

Standing proudly in front of Mrs. Helen Madison-Langley, in his sandals and shorts, Michael was an imposing figure. No one there could know how hard he struggled to stick to his diet and exercise every day for six months. Helen dressed exquisitely, and her six-inch diamond and emerald brooch designed into a twisted caterpillar held her silk blouse together. Standing beside her was a dashing fellow in his early forties who was professionally groomed by the US Navy, and reminded people of Steve McQueen. He shared a glance with Westley and then spoke to his mother.

"Mother, this is Professor Michael De Farenzino, the Art Dealer I mentioned. I believe we have a lot to talk about."

"It's an unusual name, where are you from?" she asked cordially.

"Rome, madam, but I have lived in London for most of my life."

"Where in London?" she asked sharply. He told her. "Oh, charming. I know Muswell Hill. It's like a village up there."

"Now I live in the West End, near Regents Park."

"Oh, much nicer."

Michael smiled warmly. "No, madam, it doesn't compare to the home where I raised my children and lived happily with my wife."

"Westley mentioned that you're recently divorced. I'm Nathanial, Nate to friends." He offered his hand and met Michael's eyes with subtle allure. Nate had a smug look to him but as his friends at Yale would testify he was a good sport.

Helen said, "Westley swears that you're the right man for us."

Nate looked at his mother and then turned to Michael. "Whenever we want to buy a painting or find one, the minute dealers and galleries discover it's for Madison-Langley, the price goes sky high. We're tired of it."

"Damn right!" Helen interjected. "Nathanial talk to him; Professor, we've been looking for an honest man for years. If you and my son can come to an arrangement, then I look forward to the future." Westley helped her over to the other guests.

Nate told him. "People think they can take advantage of Mother because she's aging. Frankly, that makes me sick. Westley spoke very highly of you, and we're keen to do business with the right man." His New England cadence was rather poetic.

"My clients can testify to my professional practice. They're from Royal houses, banking, hoteliers, sports, and entertainment. Some are moguls, others have come into wealth, and they're generously endowed."

"Are you generously endowed?" Nate glanced at Michael walking beside him.

Michael stopped in his track and did a 360-degree surreptitious scan of the pool area, then the gardens, and he spotted some people looking at them but not suspiciously.

"You Americans are very direct. It is perhaps the nature of rugged American individualism and entrepreneur capitalism."

"I *was* trying to shock you. Excuse my manners. Westley mentioned that you divorced your wife when you realized you preferred men."

"What do you prefer?"

Nate glanced around and walked him in the direction of the beach because no one ventured down to the sea: guests stayed in the safety and catered environment of the estate. Approaching the beach, Michael waved at anyone passing them on the sands.

Nat told him. "Of course, I'm married, and my wife and I are intimate, and there were women before her. But I'm also 'familiar' with men: as one might say in England." Michael liked his turn of phrase and noted that irony was only lost on Americans of a certain class: particularly those that didn't know the difference between patronizing as a condescending attitude, and patronize as a discerning customer.

Michael laughed openly in a most becoming fashion as they made their way toward the sea and talked about art which interested Nate. As soon as they could hear the sound of the ocean, Michael was drawn toward the sea, and he looked out shielding his eyes with his hand above his eyebrows. Nate was able to take a really good look at him from behind and move up closer to study his muscular legs, upper body, and arms.

"How do you stay in shape? I'm only forty, and you looked twice as ripped as me. Westley mentioned that you're fifty-one is that right?"

"Yes, five days ago."

Nate moved in close. "What do you think it would be like to work for us?"

"I will consider it."

"Is there anything I can do to speed things up?" He fondled himself discreetly.

"You have to understand something. I take my work very seriously. As for the pleasures of life; I cannot get involved in something where I have to lie to my children. Are you the kind of man I can talk to about such things or are you mainly interested in what I do in bed?"

"Forgive me forcing things. We're a family who acts quickly, force of habit."

"I know I can travel and buy things for your estate. But I'm going to clear the air so we can work unencumbered by sublimated desires." Michael took his shorts off and stood before him. Nate was easily aroused. Michael tossed his shorts on the sand and walked toward the sea unashamed and Nate followed him.

"This is what God gave me, a body. I buy art and promote artists. I do not degrade myself for sex or money. My services are available to you. Sex and intrigue are not my business." Michael strode out and dived into the sea and Nate watched him longingly. Michael was proud of his conduct, and he knew the five sessions at the Gay Father's therapy group had helped him. He wanted to go back and learn more about life.

CHAPTER TWELVE

October 4th, 2015

Michael sat with the men in the Gay Father's therapy group. Each man went to personal sessions at a private clinic in Covent Garden; however, the group sessions were held in meeting rooms at hotels all around London so that no outsider knew where they'd convene. The men liked it that way because safety and privacy were paramount to them all.

There were thirty-three men in the conference room shielded by white blinds that blocked out sight from inside and outside the hotel. The men came from diverse backgrounds. All together they looked like international business delegates in their suits and traditional clothes. They were all over thirty except one Irishman aged twenty-nine. Half of the men in the room were from the Middle East. Nine men were of African and Caribbean heritage; the others were European and British. Herbert was the eldest man there, seventy-two, a great-grandfather and a vital member of the group because he was fearless in spirit which Michael discovered when Herbert recounted how his wife and her father had him arrested and imprisoned in 1961 for being gay. His life story fascinated Michael. Consequently Michael often sat next to Herbert and shared intimacies.

When the men convened as they did on that Sunday, the conference suites were filled with tension and hope, rooted in their need for solace and approval which manifest itself in the facets of dialogue shared between the men.

When David entered the room with Dr. Claude, he was acutely aware of the wealth and status of the men there. His instinct was correct because the combined wealth of the group amounted to approximately £5.5 billion. David was glad he'd dressed in his oyster colored Ozwald Boateng linen and silk suit, black vest, and African beads. His cropped hair and sideburns changed his appearance. Wearing expensive attire always gave him confidence, but David was reluctant to enter standing in the doorway with his analyst, Dr. Claude; even though he told Dr. Claude he needed to learn from the group.

Claude was Nigerian from an Igbo cultural background. He was dedicated to the welfare and sanity of men going through social agony. His landmark study on '*The Social Agony of Black Sexual Oppression through Ridged Family Practices*' was researched globally over ten years with one million men of African heritage taking part. His groundbreaking work brought him to prominence, attracting psychologists and psychiatrists from Asia, the Middle East; Africa and Aborigine backgrounds.

The doctors formed a partnership, meeting at conferences and members' forums to research and treat gay men who were fathers, whether they were married, divorced or single. Michael heard about the group when he took a canvas to Saudi Arabia for Omar, a wealthy client of his who laid on the finest hospitality imaginable.

Omar, who was forty-six but looked younger, introduced Michael to his doctor after Michael had confessed he'd been lonely since his divorce, and his 'awakening' to his true nature and identity caused him distress that even his sexual conquests couldn't pacify. Omar told him about his desires, his love for Ahmed and their growing peace of mind as a result of the doctors at the Gay Father's Therapy group.

Omar and Ahmed were on the other side of the room dressed in robes. Although they looked tranquil dressed in all white, their lives were a maelstrom. Michael saw it when they took him into their confidence. They consumed opium and made love in front of him even though he protested. But Omar offered him a million pounds to watch them. Ahmed told Michael: 'to bear witness to our passion is an affirmation I need'. Michael could not resist the money or the taboo.

Dr. Claude cast his eyes among the group who came to represent the discursive discourse within the Academy of Sexual Politics. Dr. Claude was a tall and bulky figure of a man who David identified as a father figure quickly because Claude was fifty-six, gay, a father of two, and he understood the Nigerian 'Law of the Father' rules and contradictions extremely well. Angus begged Claude to help David. At the door, David told Claude something in Yoruba and Claude patted his shoulder comfortingly.

Michael was talking to a friend so he didn't see David at first but the second he did he could no longer hear anyone. He heard his heartbeat in his ears. He was fixed on David. Across the room, David saw Michael and his mind started to pull the past into the present. David kept thinking, but he wasn't sure if they had met. As he contemplated he heard *If Its Magic* from *Songs In The Key of Life* by Stevie Wonder.

Dr. Claude went to the front and spoke to them all. "Gentlemen, it is good to see you all. My fellow colleagues and I continued to gather research and facts to help you. I will remind everyone of the private environment we occupy when we meet. Any violations of this meeting space and discussions will be taken very seriously as documented in the confidentiality agreement that you have all signed. I'm happy to say that in the three years of this group's meetings we have only had to prosecute two people for breach of confidentiality and violation of personal safety."

Ahmed stood up and pointed heavenward. "I can promise you, the dog that violates our lives will be punished." His doctor, Nasir, a North African Muslim with an exceptional gift for exegesis, explaining religious practice the psychological neurosis in African and Middle Eastern culture, stood up and Ahmed sat down. Dr. Nasir commanded Ahmed's respect principally because of his avuncular disposition and deep-rooted love of Islamic peace and the Koran. Ahmed adjusted his headdress and sat calmly as Omar took his hand.

"We all understand the damage that social media leaks causes so please respect each other. Recording of these meetings is prohibited." Claude moved from the front over to a refreshment area. "Please help yourself to anything." Michael quickly went over to David. He gazed at him for a moment and then offered his hand.

"Michael De Farenzino and you are David Bankole, yes."

"Yes, good afternoon."

"Have we met? I get the feeling we've met."

"No. I have been following your advice for the last six months." David didn't understand. "I re-read your book, every week. It's been very important for me. I must speak with you after this meeting. Are you free?" David felt the intensity of his expression and the eager light in his topaz colored eyes.

"I had an engagement later, but I'll re-schedule. Please come and sit beside me." Michael flushed a bit, and his smile sent a frisson through David.

"Gladly." David got a glass of sparkling water and pointed to the range of food and drink. Michael declined, therefore, David led him over to his seat. There weren't empty double spaces, so David turned to the man next to him.

"I need to speak to this man urgently. Is it alright if he sits next to me?" The middle-aged Ugandan nodded and moved to the front. David felt light headed, and Michael liked David's aroma of bay rum and hibiscus.

Half an hour later, the first speaker, an MD from a finance firm hesitantly came to a conclusion by stating. "Considering the world we live in, if you're an Olympic diver like Tom Daley, you can come out online and get on the *Jonathan Ross Show* and the country may be on your side because you're a twenty-something 21st century boy. But I'm fifty-three and my four kids treat me like an old pervert. The things they say make me feel dirty." He stood still and silent for almost a minute. He was a middle-class everyman, but within the minute he slumped over, and his words pulled his face into deep reflection that left him feeling dejected.

The men wrote affirmations concerning their dignity and human rights: recalling key moments of social agony trying to cope with abusive behavior and their personal fears. Dr. Claude stood up and asked the men. "Do you have any words of comfort or survival strategies?" Each one of the men got up and went and gave him letters they'd written days before the meeting.

Etienne, the French concert conductor who was a strapping frame of a man with a face rather like Jean Dujardin said, "My wife is kind. Since the divorce, we have enjoyed life. But my children, they sometimes threaten to tell the media I am gay and destroy my career. I have reached the point now where I hate them. My own children and I detest them!"

The Ugandan got to his feet. "This is what the regime in my country is doing, brainwashing kids' minds and the population with repulsive stories about our lives. If I tell my sons I am homosexual, they would run to officials like Nazi kids and turn me in. I know men who have been abducted and then found dead."

"But the Uganda anti-gay bill was declared null and void last August," David said, even though he only planned to listen on his first visit.

"My brother I tell you; I wouldn't place any faith in that. I have been granted asylum here in England, thank God and I would never go back, for fear of death. I am documented as a homosexual, and I know people would kill me."

David was clearly distressed to hear that and it showed. The men in the group saw the transition of worry and fear write itself across his face. Michael took his hand as if it was totally normal and David squeezed it and closed his eyes for a few moments to steady his mind and body.

Omar was moved by his anxiety and asked David. "Young man, tell us what you hope to get from the group because we all confront this question in the beginning." David opened his eyes and took a deep breath.

"I want to tell my son the truth and receive his blessing afterward."

"What age is your son?" Etienne asked.

"Twenty, we're good mates. His mother and I are very close; but my father…" He stopped and couldn't speak even though he tried to.

"Is he a motherfucker?" asked Preston, the African America. He was almost age fifty, with a dark and bitter face as a result of his family having him committed to a mental institution during the AIDS era, as a young man of twenty.

"No, my father's background… Anything that isn't law abiding is seen by him as weak or worthless. He believes this because he's highly successful."

"What does he do?" asked a young father from Kuwait, who was still married and leading a double life because of the laws in that country which oppressed gay men.

"He's a QC," David replied, and all of the men noted his pride for his father.

A smartly dressed Jamaican guy who had a dark brown, Trench Town presence that scared most English people outside of London asked. "So, he's a big lawman. What do you do, David?"

"I'm a music producer and Events manager, promoting Black British…"

"Fuck! Yes, you're the producer, fused Nigerian 'High Life' with drum & bass, manage Black Youth musicians," the Jamaican said as he whipped his fingers. "You manage Mr. Man! You was on the television. But I didn't recognize you because you cut off your dreads."

"My sister died and I cut off my hair and buried it with her."

Liam, a handsome ginger haired Irishman said: "Sorry for your loss mate." David nodded and sat down.

David lowered his head and prayed silently, and then he became increasingly upset. Michael put his hand on top of David's and he looked up. A faint light of gratitude and relief emanate from David. Simply sitting there trying to calm himself was difficult. Michael looked up at one of the doctors and indicated he was going to usher him out so David could regain his balance. Dr. Claude nodded at Michael, and he helped David to his feet and led him out of the room without people looking at them strangely. In several sessions, some men had to take a moment alone or receive support from staff and mentors.

They left the Savoy Hotel and walked for five minutes toward the Embankment at the River Thames. A lot of tourists and Londoners crisscrossed the streets heading toward the Houses of Parliament and across the bridge to Royal Festival Hall. David stopped and took several deep breaths. He looked directly at Michael and a smile broke out of him. Michael saw David's trust in him and it gave Michael the feeling that he'd just completed his National Service and once again arrived in London now he was free.

David said, "I seem to be a mess today. I'm not usually like this, far from it really, but it's my first time, and I haven't seen Dr. Claude for long."

"How long have you been a part of the group?"

"For two months," David replied, and Michael rubbed David's back.

"Give yourself time. I've only been seeing my analyst for three months."

"How's it going?"

"I still can't tell my daughter, but I have come out to one of my sons. I also tell my clients now." David didn't understand what he meant by clients. "When I say, clients I'm referring to my work, I'm an art dealer. I buy paintings and *object d'art* for clients. Sometimes they're looking for new art, other times they want a celebrated work. I also have five artists whose work I sell to promote them and extend my business."

"That sounds fantastic. I have some fine *object d'art* at home, art nouveau; I totally love the movement and style."

"You're very young to have such an appreciation. I commend you." Even though Michael was a stranger, David didn't feel as though he was, he felt comforted.

"People think I'm showing off or trying to be 'different' because I like it."

"I think it's important to be different. Uniformity and convention bore me." Michael pointed at the thirty-seven strings of African beads sitting on his chest. "These are beads of mourning. These are Ghanaian, these are from Cameroon, this one is from Sera Leon; the rest are Nigerian, these of the Igbo culture and this one's Yoruba."

"How do you know this so precisely?"

"I was a Professor of Art History and Diaspora Culture before I left that to start my own business. I love Black Arts and Culture, from Africa

128

to the Pacific Islands. There are fascinating things to learn about mysticism and magic in these places." David settled down and breathed easily because all at once he liked Michael even more.

"I know a nice place to have Japanese tea and cakes. It's a not far away."

"I'm all yours," he replied with a wonderful smile that made David flush. They strolled toward Blackfriars as the sunlight kissed London. They displayed sartorial elegance, and sightseers noticed them because David's suit had treated silk thread in the material that glinted like mother-of-pearl in the warm October light and Michael's cashmere tailored suit was the exact shade of bluebells, contrasted with his open collar flamingo pink shirt. They walked in step moving as easily as holidaymakers discovering a foreign city. In fact, people who spotted them thought they were foreigners because they were too dressy and groomed for Londoners on a Sunday stroll in the city.

Michael was so flabbergasted at meeting David, he started fifteen sentences in his mind before he spoke. He sensed David was gaining his equilibrium because the fresh air did fortify David. Consequently, he glanced at Michael periodically, but he didn't speak; however he felt ebullient, and Michael sensed it.

"My son gave me your book last year. I read it all the time; I've found it inspiring. Your confidence in handling situations…"

"Yeah, look at me today. I wrote it when I was at University and based it on my years of traveling on public transport. Strangers think I'm some African cleaner who doesn't have the right to say anything, therefore, when I've confronted them with logic or intelligence, lots of them are flummoxed; it's too funny."

"Also, I saw you on television and instead of being bitchy about so-so singers; you offered them advice about further study, voice practice. That woman with the dreadful voice who was ridiculed in the press, I loved what you said: 'wanting to sing and lacking the gift must be a deeply frustrating experience'. With you, always compassion instead of cruelty; it's a most becoming virtue."

"My Mother firmly believes acts of kindness give us true strength. I love her for that. She's an amazing lady."

"You have that love in your heart for people; this is why you are so charismatic on television."

"Stop," David replied dismissively.

"No, I'm speaking the truth. I watched you and looked you up online. When I read that you were married, I thought…" Michael bit his lip and turned away.

David looked at his strong masculine profile with his tight jaw line and full lips, and he found Michael, even more, desirable. "You must finish that sentence Michael or I'll think you're a wicked cock tease."

Michael turned to face him and sputtered out words in Italian. "Excuse me," he laughed and concluded in English. "I'm not as you say. I admire your humanist attitude. When I discovered, you are married with a son you became a prototype to me. I wanted to meet someone gay who possessed your qualities. Never in my mind did I think this would happen. Me, meeting you at the group today: when I saw you standing in the doorway… *Bellisima!*"

David reached up to Michael and pulled a hair out of place. Looking into his eyes, David focused on its topaz color and in a flash he remembered. "You were at Carnival last year. You were dancing with a very happy lady." He kept thinking. "But wait – you had a beard, and you looked different."

Michael recalled it, so he took out his mobile and showed David a picture of himself in 2013 with his family at a wedding. "This is me: lightweight Pavarotti. And this is me." He was on the beach wearing a white sarong showing off his six pack abs.

"I started an intense weight reduction program. I've lost 25 kilos. It took me almost a year. I totally changed my diet and exercise like a prisoner; it was incredibly difficult, but I wanted to look better because fat men don't stand a chance on the gay scene. And I wanted to feel and look younger."

"You're no old man."

"I'm fifty-one."

"Exactly, you're in the prime of your life. Granted now you do look better, but when I saw you at Carnival, I was impressed with how well you danced. But…" David gave him a seductive glance: "you do look quasi Adonis now." David laughed and his smile, which Michael saw as exclusively for him, played its way around his body. Michael laughed because the convivial nature of the man he'd yearned for clearly seemed attainable. He touched the back of David's neck, and energy made them both jump from the shock between them.

David suddenly dashed across the street, and Michael chased him. When they caught up, they made their way to the south side of the

Thames so they could walk beside the Millennium Bridge, Shakespeare's Globe Theatre and the restaurants nearby. The footpath was crowded with tourists, but the smell of food, the sound of music and the scenery of London's City landmarks elevated their spirits.

"Can I ask a personal question, David?" David looked a little anxious, but he nodded. "Are you free or are you involved with someone?"

"I'm free without any entanglements." Michael was delighted. He walked a bit faster, and David quickened his step and pointed him toward the Japanese cake house.

The Japanese tea house gave a perfect view of the City of London. The Thames River cityscape was iconic in the sunlight. "Don't you love London?" David asked. "I do, especially at this time of year. The light is so evocative of Turner's art."

"You appreciate art – wonderful! And your voice has a lot of harmonic tones."

"I'll put that down to my family, and school days. But mostly, Dad insisted we study our diction. Slang was strictly prohibited. I use to think he was ridiculous, but he's taught me so much."

David ate his cake and drank his tea without saying a word for eight minutes. Michael's feelings rushed back and forth. His entire body was racing with energy and impulses. He told himself to go and see his analyst soon, but then he went back to thinking about David's cultured voice, brown skin, and his physique.

"You're so handsome, David." Michael grunted. "I sound like Dante Alighieri, but you are no Beatrice. You're bellezza dell'Africa in eleganza Britannica." David didn't understand. "True Black beauty," Michael translated.

"Dark skin, Black guys usually make people nervous."

"I don't believe in demons…"

"Don't joke. My brother and I have studied how to avoid police profiling, and how to repudiate sexual harassment. Grandpa was a West Indian volunteer in the RAF. He was eventually decorated. He spent ages teaching me about race relations. Living in a Black body, I see every nasty thought played out through people's attitude and perception." David took Michael's hand. "But I'm not preaching today," he concluded facetiously.

"You *are* amazing!"

"No! Anyway, please Michael, tell me about you."

Michael sat back as if the wind had been knocked out of him.

"You know you're the first man to ask me that?"

"What do you mean?"

"My dates aren't interested in my family." David was puzzled.

"Lola is Jamaican…" David leaned in with a respectful smile that many Black men reserve only for people they are truly impressed by. "I've always loved Black women and Caribbean life. It's not so different from Italian life. My kids are very… self-conscious of their background. Lola is fiery; I love that …" Michael took an hour to explain the personalities of his family and David listened with intense fascination.

David told him. "I love how you went home before your divorce and laid down the law, concerning 'who runs things'."

"I got that from you! In your book, you provide countless examples of self-determination. I adopted that mentality with the kids. I planned everything with Lola and Tony, and I refused to allow the kids to call the shots. Your refusal to be victimized was inspiring for me." David's reticence about compliments was very endearing.

"Dad knows some of the most important Black folks in the country; I've learned from them." David became briefly plaintive. "I've read all President Obama's books; *Dreams From My Father* is my favorite. Obama believes people can transform their lives – I admire his perspicacity and faith. Something about us meeting today is working me. Don't you think circumstance is a part of transformation?"

Michael replied facetiously. "Two formally married fathers undergoing therapy for help and happiness: yes, that's a circumstance of profound kinship. We have a common enemy."

"Patriarchy?"

"Heterosexism: a lot of gay men have patriarchal power because lots of us are still living undercover. Heterosexism, on the other hand, is pernicious because it employs sexual dominance as the worse kind of oppression against women and men."

Their scrutinizing gaze was intrusive yet benign; and every instinct they had, told them, in different ways, this was one of the most important moments of their lives. Michael had dated enough men to know, David, unlike the others, was interested in his life. Likewise, David was certain Michael had a heart of passion and an intellectual mind.

Michael lifted David's hand and kissed it, and somehow it reminded David that he had kissed his father's hand similarly. An East End thirty-year-old taxi driver sitting nearby with his girlfriend who witnessed Michael kissing David's hand said, "Oy, you queers wanna get out of here with that gay shit?"

David's eyes flashed with fury. He got out of his seat and went up to him and said, "Shut your mouth and mind your own business or I'll knock your teeth out!" The fifteen Japanese and European patrons were confused. The Cockney taxi driver looked unsure of himself for a moment, but he figured, 'queers' are weak, so he'd push back.

The cabby said, "Don't fuckin' tell…" David stepped back and kicked him in the face, and he fell off the chair. Michael got a hard-on staring at David's kickboxing stance and dominance over the cabby. The Japanese and European tourists couldn't take their eyes off David either. Michael stood up, adjusted his big throbbing erection and moved toward the door, as he indicated with his eyes to David to get out of there.

Pointing at the cabby, David told his girlfriend. "Take your pussy, home!"

David took out a £20 note and slapped it down on the table behind them.

Outside, David caught up to Michael, who gave him an admiring look and held up his hand for a high five. David hit his palm just right, and the slap sounded like a beat. Michael put his arm around his shoulder, and they went off into the crowd.

Life has a strange way of resuscitating the soul, and that happened to both of them in different ways right at the same moment in time. David took off his jacket, and Michael saw how the fitted sports vest hugged the contours of his upper body and led down to his arched back and pronounced buttocks that confirmed his solid athlete's build. The sight of David ignited a great deal of heat in Michael's flesh.

CHAPTER THIRTEEN

David and Michael were on the London River Thames boat trip sailing down the Thames past the Houses of Parliament. "David, you shouldn't have splashed out like this on the tickets; they're overpriced. You must let me take you to dinner. I know the greatest Caribbean restaurant in London. In fact, it's less than ten minutes away from my flat. It called *The Old Country* on…"

"Great Portland Street. I know it. It's my mother's restaurant."

"Shut up!"

"Really, that's my mum's restaurant."

"I've met your mother. She was very nice to me on my birthday. The kids were too busy to come, so Lola and I went there, and your Mum fit us in, gave us the VIP table, and champagne to help me enjoy our evening. She understood some Italian; I remember now. She was rushing out to a birthday party…" Michael's mouth slowly opened into an expanding aperture. "That's when I told Lola we should part. Do you have someone in your family with a birthday on July 1st?"

Shaken by the coincidence David quietly replied, "My son: Adrian's birthday is on July 1st." Michael and David searched each other's faces.

'If this isn't a sign then I don't believe in anything' David thought. *'I've hoped and waited for the right man; he must be the one'.*

'God hear me, please' Michael thought. *'This has to be your blessing to me: a man with truth and spirit. All these overlaps between us have meaning'.*

David's mind was suddenly flooded with music; he heard every word of Stevie Wonder's *For Once In My Life*. At the same time, Michael couldn't get Tony Bennett's song *Just in Time* (*I Found You Just in Time*) out of his mind. By the time the boat arrived at Battersea Bridge neither one of them had spoken for fifteen minutes.

"Where's your mind been, David?"

"Thinking about you, finishing your national service and then marrying Lola, moving to London, your kids and your career; you've been so focused and sure. When I was married, I was focused, unsure and determined to be straight."

"Why determined to be straight?"

"Back home and in Black Britain there's a plague of disgusting words inflicted on us. I had enough of that homophobic language. So I've written a clause in my contracts with artists stating I'll drop them if they use sexist, racist or homophobic slurs."

"I know these issues well, my brother-in-law is totally homophobic, the Jamaican brand." David pulled a face indicating the severity of what Michael was saying. "The Group is deeply important to me because of the doctors' knowledge of 'honor killings' and the social agony of Black sexual oppression. Lola's brother accused me of fucking my sons." Michael took a breath. "I need help, and I think we can do that together."

Some Spanish and Australian tourists moved between them, so David went to the other side of the boat. Michael came after him. "Finish what you were saying."

"Only once before have I felt something like this... the spark between us. It was with my first and only true love, Angus. I met him when I was fifteen. He protected me and taught me a lot about life."

"What age was he?"

"Twenty-five. That first year he didn't try to seduce me, he took me out and spoiled me. I loved it and on my sixteenth birthday..." David looked around to make sure it was safe to speak. He pulled Michael in by the hem of his jacket and whispered. "I gave him my virginity on my birthday." David stepped back and looked into Michael's eyes for any sign of moral judgment, but there was no sign of it."

"I lost my virginity when I was seventeen with another boy."

"My God; what else do we have in common? What was that like for you?"

"I tell you more when I take you out next time."

"You want there to be a next time?"

"Talk sense David. I want you." They went under Putney Bridge, and when the darkness covered them, Michael embraced him.

"Michael, there are so many things I could say one mustn't speak of on a first meeting..." David gestured for him to speak. "I want to take your clothes off and kiss you all over." The sunlight fell over everyone as they journeyed toward Kew Gardens.

Tourists moved to the front of the covered 30ft long Perspex and garish red and green interior and exterior. David and Michael moved to the back of the boat, but there wasn't anywhere to share a kiss, so David felt, even more, amorous. In that emotional state, he turned away to adjust himself. Fortunately, Kew Gardens was only a few minutes away, so they prepared to get off the boat along with the tourists. Michael stood behind him, and in the crowded space, he pulled David in around the waist and pressed himself next to David, who turned around startled by what he felt next to him. "Is that you or bottle of juice?" Michael pressed harder against him.

Kew Gardens offered one of the great pleasures of living in London. The gigantic botanical gardens were filled with exotic plants from around the world. Walking around gave the impression it could be the 18th or 21st century. On any given day, tourists could hear experts and amateurs pontificate on the subject of horticulture. Michael and David walked around the colorful gardens looking for a spot to share a kiss but everywhere they went they encountered families, couples, and grannies. On that Sunday afternoon, it looked like half the city had taken sanctuary in Kew Gardens.

Unsettled by their carnal instincts, and loiterers; Michael and David became agitated. They noticed how sloppy most people looked. Both men were raised by families that wore their 'Sunday best' and they didn't intend to break the tradition.

David said, "We've just met, we're talking, and I can wait… until we kiss."

"No, today demands visceral contact." Michael saw a roped off area and jerked his head for David to follow him. They walked under the trees, among the people and headed for the roped off area across the green landscape which resembled a University quadrant and palatial gardens. Finally, they got to the manicured green clearing and clear blue skies. They walked on the grass and headed toward the far wall. As they made their way there the sound of people slowly died away.

"Finally!" Michael was so fervent he looked like he'd escaped from hell.

"Yes, Michael." He kissed David's eyebrows, bright eyes and brown plum lips.

"Incredible…" Their kiss filled them with testosterone and adrenaline. In what felt like frenzy, their hands grabbed for each other and David pulled Michael closer until he could feel it throbbing next to him. Michael nodded, and David ran his hand over his long hard muscle beating under his suit. "Careful, I have a month's fuel in there." With a look of gleeful disobedience, David unfastened him, took out his hefty flesh and gazed at it. If David met an alien, he couldn't have looked more fascinated.

"Do you have a license for this cock?" The blaze that shot through Michael's anatomy showed David that no other man ever felt better about himself. Undoing David, Michael whispered. *"Mio dio tuo cazzo e le palle è fottutamente perfetta*. I've dreamt this, but now that I see it… *you* are even more beautiful." David loved what he understood of the compliment, and his face couldn't hide it. Michael touched him and then pulled his hand away. "Fuck – he's hot."

David couldn't resist touching him, so he put his hand inside Michael's pants. "You're not just cocky, you've got balls too. Man, I'm gonna get high on this!" They quickly fastened their trousers before they got arrested for indecency.

****

The packed streets of Covent Garden were alive with people, lively shops, pubs and street actors performing to tourists and travelers. David carried a bottle of rum in his fist and passed it to Michael who took a swig and cleared his throat. "So Michael, we have all these things in common but answer this: What are five things you hate the most?" Michael thought about it and laughed to himself.

"Ok! Cruelty to people. Rap music, screaming hate at me. Celebrity gossip. Guys who take me for a prick because my cock's big. Oh yes, and The Turner Prize."

"That is specific. And the five things you like."

"Lola. My son Roberto; he is my favorite even though you shouldn't do that, and, of course, the other kids. Lord Leighton's *An Athlete Wrestling with a Python*. Italian, Arsenal, All the work of Puccini and Federico Fellini's films. Barolo wines. Caribbean cuisine – *absolutamente*. Naked Black bodies. Meeting you today."

"There are things on your list that coincide with my favorite things."

Michael moved ahead of him and played virtual football; dribbling the ball across the street intricately. He looked so good doing it, David just watched him. Onlookers also liked what they saw. His footwork was fast and agile. After he kicked and scored, he shouted. "And De Farenzino scores a hat trick and all of you hear this!" Michael sang *Volare* with such panache and seductive Italian butch charm he even added a swagger in his hips as he sang to David. This thrilled David immensely. Michael took off his jacket and tossed it to him to hold. People gathered to watch, and Michael liked it because he was half cut on rum and reeling from the knowledge that he met a man he could take seriously. Michael told everyone in Italian. "I want to sing this for a great love that entered my life." He sang *Grande Grande Grande*, the original Italian version of *Never Never Never* made famous by Shirley Bassey.

He sang it, and people were entranced by his impassioned face and Italian. David was stunned to hear the song in Italian. Angus loved the song very much, and David took it as a sign that he was passing from one stage to the next. The light in Michael's eyes was heartwarming, so when he finished, David whistled loudly.

He bowed and walked David away from people toward the main street the Strand, and David followed him to Trafalgar Square, which was lit up and glowing in the autumn evening warm night. They sat next to the lions and had a bit more to drink.

"I'm going to get into a taxi soon and go home. It's been a big beautiful long day. You're a beautiful guy, and I must see you again." David was thrilled.

"I'm not going to play it cool, like some arrogant bastard! I'm taking you to dinner on Tuesday evening." Michael eyed him up again. "When I think of you naked, I can see God smiling and the devil in agony. What do you want to do with me?" David blushed, turned full circle looking up at the sky and then looked at him joyfully.

"I want to take you to bed and do *everything* you like." Michael adjusted his cock and shook his head which tousled his hair.

David got up and stood between Michael's parted legs. Standing there, Michael pulled him towards his lips. "I love the taste of you: your smell, everything." The taste of rum on his tongue delighted David all the more.

"Michael, do you truly believe in God?"

"Yes, I couldn't live without my faith in Jesus and the power of God's spirit."

"That's good because I couldn't go out with a man that had no religious faith."

"Why not?"

"When I introduce you to Adrian I want him to understand we have God on our side." In the luminous evening light of London's most famous square, and the flashing car lights coming and going in red and white, Michael eyed him and his desire and heart mixed well with the rum in his blood.

"I must go now. I need to lie down and dream of you, my beautiful friend."

David didn't care who saw him, and he knew in such a public space he could have been snapped on a mobile. But he found Michael irresistibly sexy sitting on the wall of the fountain with his face upturned and his legs apart; so David kissed him, and the heat in their kiss made Michael quiver all over because it was romantic rather than explicit. When Michael pulled back, David's eyes were still closed, but he was smiling broadly.

Michael said, "Amazing erotic energy in you." David opened his eyes and Michael seemed transcendental. David had never seen that kind of aura or power radiate from anyone except his father when he imparted African philosophical psychology to Solly, his sister and himself.

The difference with Michael was that David had no sense of fear with him and he could feel Michael's capacity to love. Michael got to his feet, walked to the curb and flagged a taxi coming toward him from the Mall. The taxi pulled over, but David didn't want Michael to leave him. He wanted Michael to stay and banter, flirt and look at him with his topaz colored heartwarming eyes.

"Until Tuesday my friend." Michael got in and the cab drove away. David started walking with a dance pending in his step and the greatest smile on his face.

CHAPTER FOURTEEN

Michael was rushing back and forth and Roberto was following him from room to room. "I must get the fuck out of here because I can't bring David to this place. This flat is like a place for some retired foreigner who thinks this chintz is elegant. When I take David to the new house, he'll love it. If you knew how smart and sophisticated David is, you'd like him."

"David who? Papa you've been rambling since I arrived." Michael put down the glass of wine and the white shirt. He took hold of Roberto by the shoulders.

"This is top secret; I kick your arse if you say a word." Roberto smiled at the suggestion of Michael beating him because he'd never hit him.

"I met the most beautiful man. Not since the day, I first saw your mother have I felt love so strong! Like me, he's divorced, and he has a son. By a miracle or chance his son and I have the same birthday. This man who's come into my life and my spirit is lovely. He's Black, of course, from a very high-class family." Roberto was fascinated and happy to see him in that state of mind. "Last year you said to me, not to go out with a guy…"

"Papa, I also said I don't have the right to tell you how to live."

"I'm glad you remember because…" Michael punched the air. "I want him. And he and I are…our lives and interests are deeply interconnected. I want to tell you who he is, but you mustn't leak it." Roberto shook his head. "David Bankole." Roberto started thinking, and his entire face lit up, and then he opened his mouth.

"He's married; he's a media celebrity on television! Wait – he's a father."

Michael knocked him on the head with his index finger. "Hello… son!" Roberto inhaled and shook his head.

"Tell me more, tell me everything!"

Michael dragged him to the sofa and held his wrists and recounted his day with David.

****

David sat with Dr. Claude, and he could barely keep still. Claude studied David and his white leather bomber jacket, black T-shirt, cream chinos and desert boots. They were in Dr. Claude's well-appointed examination room with hundreds of medical books and journals in interior lit glass cabinets. The chrome and glass furniture and the replica swan chairs in four primary colors gave the office a characterless ambiance. David swung from left to right in the red chair, and Dr. Claude sat still in the white chair. "I mean being with him was like something out of a French film. Have you seen *Diva*?"

Dr. Claude shook his head, observed him closely and continued to take notes.

David abruptly stood up and began pacing back and forth. "We walked and talked. He was incredibly understanding because when I left the group, I was so… fucked up and grief-stricken or scared. I don't know but this guy: no this *man* soothed me. He wasn't insincere or working me in any way."

"What do you mean when you say – 'working me'?"

"In my business, I get a lot of bullshit and sometimes I have to put some out there to promote and handle my client's best interest. Michael had read my book, and he's used it as a self-empowering text!" Dr. Claude didn't understand, so David explained most of the events from Sunday.

****

Michael told Roberto "I sense he's afraid of his father. There is something there, some bad blood. Anyway! I am sure I can help him. He was so relaxed with me."

"You can't be his counselor or father."

"No, no I want to be his inspiration, his love, his happiness."

"You're racing ahead of yourself Papa. Can you be sure he feels…"

"We kissed!" Michael rushed into Italian; which made his eyes dreamy and his voice poetic. Roberto embraced him, and Michael cupped his face. "David's heart and his misery clashed in his face," Michael said flashing his fingers. "His hard-on beat next to me. Sometimes his hand shook and other times he was a powerhouse."

"I'll bet no other son is having this conversation with his father."

141

"Excuse me... I forget it must be difficult for you to hear this type of..."

"Papa no! Yes – but if you started lying to me or avoiding me because you couldn't speak; that would upset me. We don't go to priests. I know your thoughts on the Catholic church, only now I realize it's because of their views on gay people."

"No one in robes is going to tell me their shit."

"Whoa slow down."

"No, I must have him." Michael got to his feet. "I must get him and keep him."

"You're convinced he feels the same?"

"*Absolutamente!*" We kissed, and it was like... nothing that has been written. It was real." Michael just smiled gloriously. "Now I have to find something to wear for our date." Roberto led the way to the other room, and Michael followed.

****

Dr. Claude said, "Bearing in mind your own words about Angus, namely: 'even though he was everything you wanted from love, you were determined to be straight, so you left him'. Then with Terry: 'as Black gay men who understood the law and the rules of being men, you left him because he lacked courage. What do you want from this?"

"Michael has qualities I admire in a man. I want to go to him unafraid."

"What if it develops into what you want? What will you do then?"

"Tell my family."

"Can you cope with your father's judgment?" David looked unsure, and he became uneasy. "David you are not a boy..."

"But why can't Dad just love me? He's grief-stricken by my sister's death. Do you think he'd give me a chance now, rather than damn me for being gay?"

"You must show and tell your father what your rights are." David fidgeted and searched as though he wanted a cigarette. He sat down and folded his hands in his lap.

"If Veronika and I had those kids, Dad would have been different to both of us, my God he hated her."

"You're doing it again David."

"What?"

"Avoidance: how would your father react to Michael? He's older, white, a parent, married and divorced?"

"He'd be hostile and unaccepting."

"So… will you strive to become what your father expects?"

David thought about it for 15 seconds. "No, I can't masquerade as a man who's into women any longer. I want Michael." Facing the truth, David knew the consequences that affected any Afro-Caribbean man from a bourgeois and religious background proclaiming his sexual freedom and identity. There is a small percentage of Black folks that will support and protect their sons and daughters and then there's a moral majority who are punishing. "I have to think of a way to get through to my father, but I wouldn't be surprised if he killed me."

"I will not allow that to happen."

"My father is one of the most cunning and powerful men in London; he's defended some top notch people. The CPS dread coming up against him. He'd find a way to justify his … temporary insanity… or dissociative psychotic break."

"If you introduced me to him and I could lay a foundation…"

"I want to tell him to his face. If you reached out to him – Oh fuck! You know what! I can't think about this today. I've met a man whose spirit and potential love can help me overcome everything I've been afraid of." Dr. Claude felt good for him. "His kiss was… love."

"What about your son?"

"Well he *does* love me, but if he turns on me; calls me a 'queer'." David began shaking. "I trust Adrian. He'll understand I'm not a bad person. Positive thinking… Positive thinking! 'Yes, We Can' 'Keep Hope Alive'."

"Calm yourself David and come back next Monday same time and we'll continue. Go and buy something nice to wear…"

"Dr. Claude have you met a man and known right away 'he's the one'?"

"No." Dr. Claude considered it best to stick to the truth. "I could envy you."

"Dr. Claude, are these the symptoms and meaning of the Social Agony of Black Sexual Oppression Through Ridged Family Practices?"

"Yes, it is, but David; I've researched and treated this condition for years."

"How many people are living happier lives after your treatment?"

"All but nine, out of the one thousand I've personally worked with."

143

"What happened to the nine?"

"I'm not going to discuss the bad news when the good news is so much greater."

David found his spirit again and got up and offered his hand. Claude shook it. "Don't expect everything at once. Both of you have to find your ground and build on it."

"Did those nine people end up dead?"

"For heaven's sake no: our lives aren't a wretched gay story where the stupid, ignorant writer kills off all the Black men or gay characters."

"I fucking hate that kind of hetero-terrorist pathology."

"Me more than you." Claude smiled at him reassuringly, and David felt better.

****

After lunch, David was in a meeting with Sophia, his office manager, and Willy his PA. She cultivated the persona of a siren love goddess in the mold of Uma Thurman.

They were watching a video of Mr. Man doing a fantastic dance routine with digital special effects. He was a master of breakdancing and 1960s funky strut. All three of them were watching on a large wall monitor when a grungy looking cycle messenger came toward his glass office. He held up a red box and pointed it at David. He gestured for the messenger to enter and tugged the lapels of his bespoke gray suit.

"Urgent delivery for Mr. Bankole Esq." David signed for it and looked over the elegant red ribbon box. The messenger left, and David placed the ruby red box on his desk. Sophia and Willy went back to watching the video, but they periodically glanced at the box. At the end of the video, he told them. "I like it a lot. Would you liaise with the web director because I want this on YouTube and Tweeted by Thursday. Willy, set up a meeting for Mr. Man with me for Wednesday?" he nodded. Fine, then we're done." They left, and Sophia looked at the box once more before leaving.

David kept looking at it while he took a nicotine patch and put it on his arm. He picked it up knowing it was from Michael and opened it. A card read:

For our first date, you are cordially invited to dinner at
The Connaught Hotel Mayfair at 8 pm. Formal evening wear is required.
I'm keen and eager to see you.
Dr. Michael De Farenzino MA

There was a wrapped gift in the box which David opened. It was a white silk scarf. David put it to his face and inhaled. He began thinking of what to wear and sat down for ten minutes and searched his mind. He could see his staff through the glass wall watching him, and he pulled his laptop closer and sent them all email that read:

'Watching me won't earn us any money. The first person to close a deal today will get £100 cash in hand. You have four hours left'.

When the email message got around, they went to work, focused on winning. David re-focused and went online, typed in 'men's second-hand dinner suits'. Within ten minutes, he found what he wanted and took his mobile to call and get information. The seller had his size, so he left to go and buy the dinner suit.

On his way out Willy stopped him to ask a question. "I pay you to think, William, work it out and talk to me afterward." Five years earlier David called him over to his family home, and William sat in front of David, Solly, his father, mother, and Grace. David told him. "My family now considers you close to us. We're Nigerians. If you come to work for me, you must change. The 'street image' has to go! I am never stopped by the police nor is anyone else in this family. Dress and speech are vital social skills you must cultivate. If you agree to that, you can work for me."

William studied David's masculine chic as left the Hackney entrepreneur Co-Op building, one of the big success stories in the borough. All the start-ups in the building were making a profit and 'boomerang funding' the scheme with a return of investment. David exit the gray steel doors and into the autumn sunlight.

CHAPTER FIFTEEN

The next evening Michael waited for David in the deluxe Hotel Coburg Bar. He looked very elegant in his tuxedo, evening shirt, and bowtie. Sitting with his feet casually crossed drew attention to his handmade side lace shoes coupled with scarlet red socks. He had checked in at four o'clock that afternoon, napped, bathed, dressed and now his mind raced waiting for David. Other guests caught sight of him and they appreciated the red socks as a sign of his audacious personality.

At 8 p.m., David entered the noir lit, elegant Coburg Bar. He'd dressed in a black velvet and satin lapel tuxedo, a black silk shirt, which his father gave him for Christmas and Michael's white silk scarf which he tied into a Regency gentleman's cravat. The white silk against his smooth mahogany skin made a rich contrast. At just under six foot, he walked taller in his burgundy suede boots. Michael noticed that his cropped hair glistened because David had put silver glitter in his hair. Michael stood up, and David approached him, as his father had taught him to meet dignitaries.

"Professor, it gives me enormous pleasure." David's façade worked to pump blood into Michael's vital organ and kept a smile on his face.

"You look wonderful; I love how you wear the scarf."

"And you – with all your 'Bond' Italia. I'm sure you have a hidden weapon on you." They sat, and David called the waiter. "Good evening: I'll have your figs and dates covered in Grand Marnier, a bottle of Pellegrino, and a black and white Russian." David gestured for the waiter to leave. Michael was mesmerized by him.

"I love this manner you have tonight. It's so splendid."

"When I knew I was gay, I learned homo-erotic supremacy," David stated and then gazed at him quietly. Michael burst out laughing!

"What a statement. How do you do that?"

"I combine women's instincts and men's impulses." David's three-minute silence charged the atmosphere with more explicit heat than Amsterdam's red light district because profane and sacred thoughts rushed through their minds and lingered.

The waiter brought the figs, dates, and refreshment. David gestured, indicating he wanted to serve. He fanned his fingers into a fist and Michael leaned in toward him. He offered Michael a fig, so he parted his lips and David popped it into his mouth. Michael sat back, and David had a date. They eyed each other and chewed.

"Your style is a mystery in itself."

"Style is *very* important to my Dad. I'm what we call a Nigerian 'great' Briton. Dad is the quintessential Nigerian Great British gentleman. So... tonight I'll be on my best behavior," David eyed him up, "particularly since I want to kiss you. What's for dinner?" he concluded casually.

"Me." David looked at him with enticing approval, so they surveyed the menu, ordered, and their evening steamed ahead.

Over dinner, Michael noted how well David handled everything going on. After he had finished his second course, Michael asked how it was. "My mother's menu is better, and she puts food on the plate rather than just decorating it."

"Your mother's place is my favorite restaurant in London. I love Caribbean food, even more than Italian. What about the wine?"

"Fantastic! I'm not a wine connoisseur, my specialism is cocktails." Because he didn't mean that as a salacious comment, he heard it that way, which made him laugh so much Michael joined in. Michael's heart was warmed by the mischievous glee in David's face as he tried to stop the phallic implications from flooding his mind.

"Feel free to slap me if you must." David started laughing again. "Sometimes I'm just like a child. Even my son notices it."

"Sex was always a joke in my house. Lola can laugh her tits off from a good joke maybe you share that trait. The kids especially loved to share smut between themselves. If I asked what they were giggling at, they'd pretend it's nothing, except for Roberto. I remember when he was eleven he said... 'Papa listen. *There was an old man from Guyana, he wanted to play the piana; the foot peddle slipped and down fell his zip and out pop his hairy banana'.* Lola nearly fell on the floor laughing, but I was already there rolling around."

"Lovely. Mum is very shy about sexual connotations even though she was Miss Teen Jamaica and rather a smoky love goddess in her own way. Dad adores her. That's his major redeeming feature. He loves Mum more than anything or anyone else. I *do* understand that. I love my son for his dignity and heart. He's very bright too."

"Have you and your son always been close?"

David waved it away. "Another time, I promised myself when I was getting dressed I wouldn't get into complicated stories about my Ex, my big love with Angus, or stuff."

"It's who we are, though, no?" David nodded and finished his dinner quietly.

Michael told him. "I was so up in the air about this date; I called my son eight and a half times." David didn't understand. "Eight calls and one text. Also, *8½* is a film…"

"Fellini, yes I know. *Amarcord* and *La Strada* are epic."

Grinning, Michael said, "And you admire Fellini – wonderful! I've never taken a man to dinner like this." David looked up at him.

"No, after Lola and I separated, it took me a while to get my bearings on what I wanted out of life and then eventually we met at the… Father's group."

"This is serious for you too?"

"Yes, that's why I'm staying in the Carlos Suite upstairs because I can't think properly in my current apartment. I hate it. So I booked a three-night stay here."

"What's it like up there?"

"That depends on you. If you come up with me, it's the greatest place on earth, if you go home soon; the room is just a hotel." David gave it a lot of thought and called a waiter who came over.

"Bring me the bill please, my treat. And send up a bottle of Moet 1966 and a bottle of Calvados to this gentleman's suite." As the waiter moved to leave, Michael tried to stop him. "Young man, I don't condone disobedience, do as I asked, and bring me the bill." The waiter left. "I'd love to go upstairs with you. Are you going to give me a *hard time*?" The smile on David's face was glorious. Michael watched him; trying to figure out why he wouldn't let him pay, and soon he came to the conclusion it was a statement to advise him that David wouldn't let anyone buy him.

"Carnal hedonist abandonment," David said in a slow, hushed tone of voice. "I want to see you naked and bow down to your alter ego: the full triad. Manhandle you when you think it's all over. Since you've been stockpiling, let me kiss you where it hurts." Michael felt sticky listening to him. The waiter came back with the bill, and David didn't even look at it. He just gave him his platinum card and the waiter took it.

Twenty minutes later Michael opened the door to the suite and let David go in first. The suite was as grand as David expected. Michael put down the champagne and David sat himself down. "So Professor... I'd like to see you undress just for me."

With savoir-faire, Michael took off his clothes piece by piece knowing the game because he was no longer an amateur. "My wife is the only person who knows all about me, but now I going to show you because you're as beautiful as she is." Michael undressed and he saw the excitement in David's eyes as he stripped away his silk and cashmere evening attire. David opened the Calvados and poured two glasses for them. He took a gulp and sat up to see the pattern of hair that lightly dusted Michael's Mediterranean colored skin. The muscles in his chest, torso and thighs were filled with power after months in the gym, starving himself, and taking fat burners. When Michael was barefoot in nothing but his black silk boxers, he walked right up to David.

"Give me a hand?" Michael's voice unlocked all David's fascinations with ancient African sexuality, Greco-Roman eroticism, and Cybersex; he pulled Michael's silk boxers off, and the reality stared him in the face.

"Thank God." David gazed at Michael's body; then he got to his feet and stripped off as though his clothes were scorching him. Naked, David stood high and mighty with anticipation.

Michael said, "You see, reality is better than porn." David caressed him and it fueled Michael's outstanding erection.

Michael's strong hands worked everything out of David and before long Michael slipped into a psychological kaleidoscope of incandescent sensuality. Making love, Michael saw David's sweat and tears, so he stopped and started as David adjusted. By midnight, David was so far gone he felt as if he were walking through clouds and the only tie to earth that held fast was Michael's flesh but once he withdrew he rained over him like hail and they screamed out loud.

****

Five minutes passed as their interlocking bodies were caught in the jouissance of erotic pleasure. Neither one of them could move, so they closed their eyes and drifted. And then, an hour slipped away. David turned around to Michael in bed and told him. "Michael, Michele... I still can't move."

"No really darling, did I hurt you, are you Ok?"

"Can I have a cigarette? I was so nervous before I got here I had one. They're in my jacket pocket." Michael got out of bed, got him the cigarette, lit it and got back into bed. David took a hit, and it helped. Michael took it from his lips, and they smoked it together for a post-coital decadent moment, but all of a sudden Michael pulled it out of David's mouth and rushed into the bathroom. David thought he was a comic sight dashing about naked with his hefty flesh dancing around the center of his body and his hands and arms propelling him forward. A minute later, Michael returned and stood by the entrance to the bedroom. "Smoke alarm and hotel managers threatening to kick us out." David laughed and tried to get up, but he couldn't. "Help me to the bathroom."

Michael rushed to help him out of bed and into the bathroom.

Michael kept watching the doorway into the suite's lounge, waiting for David and after a time, he returned calm and collected with a bottle of Moet 1966 and champagne flutes. David walked towards him in the nude with the glasses and bubbly, and Michael was entranced by the reality of David in his birthday suit.

"Look at you, my God I thought I'd die making love to you."

"I thought you'd kill me," David replied.

"Why, I was too crazy, too rough?" David put the glasses down, opened the bottle and poured them champagne.

"Now I understand the meaning of – 'be careful what you wish for'. You were rocking me like Mount Vesuvius!"

"I saw the pain and then the frenzy in your face. It burned me: *palle e il culo*... on my balls and my arse." Michael was elated. "You're amazing."

"And if you're not the best of Italy, they can rewrite history."

"But you; like an Olympian..." Michael moved his hands as though he were carving a body out of thin air. "All over, how do you do it?"

"Diet, gym, acupuncture and Judo."

"I watched the video of you at the music awards when you hip-hop danced onstage and dropped to the floor and break danced. And the day you and your brother ran the London Marathon. Everyone looked a mess but you and Solly looked strong. My kids adore Solly. He's very handsome – butch; but you, you are beautiful."

David climbed onto Michael, touched, kissed and caressed him over and over and over again and again. "Please, please don't play me. I like you; I couldn't wait to see you tonight. I dressed for you, and when I saw you downstairs in all your Bond Italia chic and beauty, wow! And later watching you strip off that cashmere suit and black silk, all for me."

150

Michael pulled him in tight and spoke to him first in Italian and then English. "*Caro*, never in my life could I hope for a nicer man."

"What gets me about all this is how easily you ruled my body without forcing me to do anything. With a cock like this, you could be so obvious. Instead, you're like Venus and Mars," Michael protested. "Yes! I could have said porn star and poet because your voice does one thing to me but the sight of you... fucking sexy."

"At fifty-one, you make me feel twenty-five: what heart you have." Michael kissed him tenderly.

****

David stayed with Michael all the next day. They went to the hotel spa, exercised, had lunch and walked around Mayfair. They went back to the Connaught, and Michael explained how they could make love without the strain that briefly disabled David. Michael showed him a crossed leg nook position that Lola adopted to cope with him. Making love between the skin but not in the flesh, was comfortable for her, especially since Michael's cunnilingus abilities were exactly to her liking. Subsequently, David discovered they could make love with unexpected satisfaction and unimagined power.

****

In the bathroom, the following morning Michael begged him to stay another day. "I can't Michael; I run my own business." The soap flew out of Michael's hands onto the floor. They looked at it, and David said, "I'm saying nothing!" Michael laughed, stooped down and kissed his balls. David watched the water beat down on his head, and broad shoulders and he became woozy, particularly as Michael's big hands ran up between his thighs.

He fondled David. "Can you spend the day with me?"

David hesitated but finally said, "No darling, I can't; if I fail to show up for work today it sends a bad message to my staff not to come in when they don't want to."

"You're the boss." The water splashed over David's face, and Michael looked disappointed that he wouldn't stay. David didn't want to leave with any misgivings between them. All at once Michael saw David's eyes flash as he got down on his knees and took hold of his hefty cock and sang

151

the chorus of *The Best* al la Tina Turner. David handled him like a solid microphone with his balls in the palm of his other hand. Michael laughed until he was finally able to get his words out.

"My God you're so loveable." David got up and looked him over, but he couldn't speak. "David if we had ten, twenty dates I know then what I know now."

"How can you be so sure? My Dad's known me for thirty-seven years, and he isn't sure." David pulled back, turning his face away. Michael took his face between his hands and him around.

"You're a beautiful person. You're going to meet my son because I know what's good for us. Go to work and then come back. Roberto will be here." Michael pulled him closer and kissed his eyes and David smiled pensively.

CHAPTER SIXTEEN

David rushed into his office in his jeans and T-shirt at ten o'clock. The staff was busy on their phones and Mac-Pro laptops. It was also the day that his five apprentices were in the breakout room brainstorming the info they had gathered from clubs, gigs, and events across London. Sophia walked up to him in her tight gray suit and high heels looking gorgeous and pissed off. "For fuck sake man, you're late, where the hell have you been."

"This is *my* firm! I do not clock in and report to you!! Do not ever talk to me like that again if you want to work here!!!" Sophia bit her lip and struggled to stop herself from crying. She ran out of breath so fast she became light headed. All the staff stopped working, stunned by his outburst. They knew he could fly off the handle with punishing effect, but he and Sophia had a great mental bond, so they were shocked.

David's trusted PA. Willy came up to him in his butch casual way and said, "Dave, you're out of order."

"Open your mouth and say something else and see what will happen." The furious look on David's face reminded Willy of Solomon, who genuinely scared him.

"The two of you, go to my office." They did so, and David looked at his staff and they snapped out of it and went back to work. He went to the loo and locked the door, staggered over to the sink his hands were shaking. He looked in the mirror and asked himself through gritted teeth: "What the fuck are you doing? How dare you talk to her like that? Get in there and apologize." He took the time to calm himself.

When he walked into his office Willy was holding Sophia's hand and she was breathing evenly to settle herself. She'd obviously been crying. "Sophia, please excuse my appalling and fucking outrageous rant in front of the team. Wait…come with me."

He went back outside and held up his hand and waved at them. "A minute please!!"

They put their phones on hold or stopped. "When I came in I had some kind of Gangster rant like say me-no-have-no-manners!" He told them in patois and continued in the same dialect. "That fuckeries was a disgrace! You nar go see it again because I love this woman and I respect all-a-you." Sophia looked at them and then turned to David. "I beg your pardon, Sophia," he concluded in his best English.

She nodded and he told her. "Words are needed, Miss Lovely!"

"Yes you crazy bastard, I forgive you." He embraced and hugged her for half a minute in which time Willy became slightly jealous. David moved to him and whispered. "Go to Ruby Café and take Sophia I'll meet you there in 20." He nodded. "Thank you people, ramp up, and continue to make money." David went back to his office and went online, found what he was looking for, then called to make a booking.

David entered the café and the staff gave him the nod because he was a regular. The brick walls and unpolished wood tables were all too casual trendy/'cas-tre' as the Tech-city staff of Shoreditch called it. He took off his red pullover and Sophia said, "Ok who is she, this woman you're seeing."

"I'm not seeing any woman."

She forced a fake hollow laugh and tossed her hair over her shoulders. "You look like you've been on a marathon fuck; you're bulked and psyched with the craziest look on your face." She poked his biceps. "You don't do drugs so what about this pumped up mind, body, whatever you want to call it?" She said unable to hide her Dutch accent.

"Listen to me. I've booked you a full day of lady's spa treatment all in at the Angel Therapy Rooms. You can go on a day that suits you. I'll give you a fully paid day off when you want it. Take it in the next two weeks. I hope this will make up for my conduct." Willy looked at her.

"Thank you that's great... wow. What made you so crazy when you got in?"

"I only discuss my private life with my mother or my brother." He thought about it and added, "Sometimes my son and his mother, depending on the need-to-know."

"Please don't tell me, Veronika..."

"Have you ever noticed I never ask about the two of you?"

Willy said, "Ask whatever you want David." Willy dressed and looked like so many sports stars that were 'in' therefore he was happy to answer any question in praise of Sophia and his Caribbean mixed-race machismo.

"It's none of my business." An undistinguished waiter came to them.

David ordered. "Lime in hot water and a fruit cup: pineapple, melon, and grapes."

"Hot chocolate and a bran muffin," Sophia told him.

"Sausage and bacon roll with chutney, and a black coffee," Willy said.

A half hour later they had got through the review of the previous day. "Ok, today I have a VIP coming in. Michael De Farenzino…"

"From where?" Sophia asked.

"He isn't media or music. He's a Professor and Art Dealer. I want him to see the running of the place."

"Is he from somewhere?" Willy asked implying a financial connection.

David thought about the best way to answer. Waiting for his answer Willy and Sophia watched him while exchanging looks. "He's… someone I know. A friend and I want him to see how my business has grown."

"Are we being taken over, or merged?" Willy asked.

"No, we made a million last year. We've never made a mil profit and yet we've hit that already, and it's only October." He held his hand up and they Hi-Fived him.

"Thank you, Mr. Man," Willy added.

"Fuck yeah!" David pointed at them. "We need another one like him."

"Any ideas David?" Willy asked.

"I dreamt about a major event for Rome."

"Is this Michael guy here for that?" Sophia asked.

'Get on it David'. "Yes, I have plans; he's… into me and my ideas." *'Yeah, he wore and tore me last night. No kind of Obeah in the world of black magic could do me like that. I'm still loaded. Especially after the spunk he washed over me. Shut up before it shows. Oh fuck, I'm getting hard. Think of something vile… Naomi Campbell… Her assaults – 10.9.8.7.6.5… and blood diamond day in court – 4.3.2.1. Good – turned off'.*

"So please give him the full treatment."

"If the deal goes through will he co-produce or sponsor?" Willy asked.

"We shall see."

'Stop lying, just tell them the truth. Say he's my boyfriend. Daar! He's fifty-one, he can't be my boyfriend. Say he's my lover. Fuck-in-hell! That's so Carrie Bradshaw… I'm having a Carrie Bradshaw day. I can't be Carrie, I need to be more Charlotte, I've already had a Miranda bitch fit. If I were gonna be Samantha, I'd tell them about Michael's amazing

fucking cock and what kind of sex-planation he gave me last night. David!
You're a Black guy from Hackney, raised by a strict Nigerian QC and
devout Mother from one of the county's elite families: Man-up! You run
your own business. You've got an MA, a big cock, and own your own
home. You're not some white girl from a television series'.

"Actually, I want to tell you more but I can't. We live in a world of
gossip and betrayal, and if I said anything more about Michael and you
repeated one word of it I would fire you. I'm not joking."

"Is he some kind of Italian extremist…"

"You see Sophia; the work has created an occupational hazard in you.
If you hear a bit of 'something' your mind rushes to the worst
conclusion." She pulled a face.

"David it was one of the key things we learned on the MBA, withheld
facts always have stories behind them. Follow your instincts and the key
players."

"He isn't a key player, he's a friend of mine," he replied irritated.

Sophia said, "Ok, kid gloves when he comes in and…"

"No, listen, I'll handle it myself."

Willy told him. "David, no leave it to me; I'll take care of him."

"Fine," David got the bill and asked them to get back and oversee the
staff. Sophia and Willy left and he got his mobile and called Michael.

David went to the far corner of the café and sat by the window, alone
and comfortable he called Michael. "Hello darling." Michael then told
him where he wanted to kiss him and David lit up and turned away from
people. "If you kissed me in my armpit I'd be bouncing off the bed." He
listened again. "I don't speak Italian. Say it in English." He looked out at
the city full of people and traffic intersecting from all directions. "That
sounds great. Listen I'll see you at one o'clock. I was talking to my staff
and they're determined to know more about you. I said I might be
considering an event in Rome to throw my assistant off the scent as to
why you're coming in; she's primal." He listened and Michael concluded
by saying he loved him. "I don't believe you. See you later."

Michael came into David's office at one o'clock sharp, dressed in a
gray suit and primrose-colored shirt. David was in the closing minutes of
his meeting with Winston, better known as Mr. Man, his star client.
Winston was born and raised in Layton. He started as a DJ and then
turned to hip-hop preaching 'nuff-respect for the beauty of Black women'.
He gained a massive following on the subject of dealing with 'Black
Woman Blues'; which was the new album due out for Christmas. David

started socializing with him in 2011 and when he listened to everything Winston said about his love for women based on the dreadful and violent treatment he witnessed his mother go through at the hands of her abusive boyfriends he vowed he never become one of them.

David immediately spotted the USP and got two lesbians to write for him, but Winston didn't know that. Black women immediately responded to him not only because of his regard for them but also he was thirty-four and single which made him a real catch. A little controversy arose because he appeared to only go out with white women, but once he started seeing a Black woman, he became even more popular nationwide. It helped that Winston was really articulate and told the press he would not be put on trial for who he went out with. David had personally organized and scripted that interview for him.

Within three months of David putting his debut single on YouTube, he went viral. Over the last year, Mr. Man moved from strength to strength with David's careful management. The year before, his five tracks placed him on the media map. Now David was planning every aspect of his tour, events, and back-to-album format. Fortunately, Winston was old enough to know when he was treated with respect, so he took David's advice.

Michael saw that David was in a meeting as Willy took him to the Apprentice Breakout room on the other side of the techno office. Michael was impressed by the 80ft space with it glass fittings, hi-tech lighting, videos and images of Black hip-hop Artists everywhere and a fantastic blow up of David, Sophia and Willy with his father, mother and son in the newly finished office not long after they opened for business. A billboard poster captured David's pride standing beside Solly with Grace and Adrian.

"How long have you worked here Willy?"

"2010, a year after he started."

"What do you do mainly?" Michael asked him genuinely interested.

"Logistics; manage the research and develop new business. I also handle the events on site staff, wherever we go. Do you have somewhere in mind for Rome?"

"Not yet. There are all kinds of outdoor spaces for concerts and other events." He stood in the corner and watched the five teenagers on their iPads projecting text and images on the Apple TVs, talking about what they'd captured in public with the performers. One English guy who looked like the teens that skateboarded under London's Southbank showed his video of a man performing on didgeridoo in one of the

London Overground stations. When the musician finished a funky rhythm, the Apprentice interviewed him and asked one of the five set questions they all asked.

"What impact are you hoping to achieve with your performance and playing?"

"Most people think these sounds are ancient and sacred. For me, it's about composing new material for the didgeridoo and expanding world music as popular but not processed pop which I fuckin' hate. I'm really onto new age jazz, and I want to bring that to the world."

"Fuck yeah!" a mixed raced Malaysian African girl shouted. "You gotta show David that. He could book him for the Dalston Arts and Music Fair. This year they're doing the Tri-Borough, Hackney, Islington Tower Hamlets hook up."

"Right," the skinny English guy said, "let's put this together and show Dave."

Willy told Michael, "David sends them out to gather info based on their interest. David believes in people. It's an inspiration to us because I have trust issues."

"Me too; the world is full of dirty, violent bigots and tyrants." Sophia came in and offered her hand. "I'm David's confidential assistant, and office manager, Sophia Van Dyck. He's free now, come this way, please." She liked the look of him so she put a touch more sass into her stride. Michael watched her arse and Willy noticed.

As they walked through the office with its desks end to end and facing each other, Michael heard them speak several languages, rushing the conversation along. All the staff were nicely dressed, and he noted that they were racially diverse, and all under thirty years of age. "What part of Italy are you from?" Sophia asked.

"Rome, but I live in London. You are from Maastricht." She stopped walking.

"I can hear your dialect; I have a good client from Maastricht." Through his glass-fronted office, David saw them coming so he opened the door.

"Michael, good of you to come."

"David, it's my pleasure."

In perfect Italian, Sophia asked Michael. "Would you like a biscotti and espresso, perhaps something with wine?" She tried to be casual, but she was so full of herself. Michael liked the look on her face so he went and embraced her, laughing nicely.

"Surprise me. You look like a woman who can do that." Michael told her in Italian. She moved closer to him, and she could feel him on her thigh. Sophia gave him a look and a playful smile.

"I'll get you some cold meat, a Valpolicella, and genzano."

Michael patted his stomach and said, "*Bellissima*, small portion." She left them. "She's very sharp. She even offered me bread that's very popular in Rome, where did you find her?"

"We did our MBA together. She was at another firm, and I poached her."

He nodded and took a look at David's multimedia office. "Nice. How's business?"

"Good, I've made over a million in profit this year."

"Fuck me," Michael replied looking at him sincerely impressed.

"I'd love to." Michael laughed loudly, and the staff outside looked at them, wondering what kind of business they agreed since Sophia's email indicated a great business prospect was coming. Therefore they must be on their best behavior for his visit.

CHAPTER SEVENTEEN

That evening back at the Connaught Hotel, Michael relaxed with Roberto in the suite's Reception room. In his new autumn clothes from Benetton, Roberto looked young, healthy and very upper middle class in tan corduroy pants, white T-shirt, brown and red plaid shirt. Michael dressed in Austin Reed casual clothes and loafers.

"David's office is totally dynamic hi-tech. Videos on screen, his staff on Macs, and researchers projecting iPad content in funky casual media breakout playrooms, where people draw on glass boards and use paste up composite ID flow charts, storyboards to post and script ideas." David got up and poured them sparkling mineral water.

"Was David like... all over the staff barking orders or cool..."

"He let them get on with it. And when he introduced me to all of them, they didn't act like it was a prison inspection and they had to mind what they said. They were easy. He has a 'Confidential Assistant'," Michael muttered in Italian about Sophia. "She made a move on me when I hugged her to check me out. I could feel it."

"You can't always hide it, like now." Michael looked down.

"You know what that's like, you got yours from me. But it's like nothing if you're 60 seconds instead of 60-minute man or if she doesn't scream and love you."

"True... and poor Fabio didn't take after you; only me and Cesare."

"Ah, but Fabio is so Adonis, girls flock to him, and Cesare is more like me than you. Women really want him," Michael said proudly.

"Hey, but girls love *me*. In Italy, Paris, Jamaica or London, everywhere I go."

"You should see this Sophia. High maintenance? She'd give a paraplegic a fucking hard-on. Have you seen Almodovar's *Talk to Her*?" He shook his head, no. "I've got the DVD in storage. I'll lend it to you when I move out of that old folks flat and into my new house. I can't wait to have my own place. Get my books back. You must come and stay after I've got it fixed up. Have you been home and seen your mother; how is she?"

"Papa you're rambling."

"I don't feel nervous. I feel great. David's so beautiful! So heart... Oy!" He poured another glass of water and pointed at the drink on the bar, but Roberto declined. Michael drank and considered the truth for a minute. "We made love last night." Roberto's face shifted between shock and curiosity.

"Can I tell you?"

Roberto never imagined he'd ever have such a conversation with his father, but this was a time for him to test all the things he believed about himself as an egalitarian Artist. He fancied himself as a novo realist filmmaker with something different to say about life and Italian experiences. He wanted to be like his father who never said dreadful things about people's identity when it came to race, class, or sexual identity; and providing Michael knew about someone's spiritual belief he kept his hatred for the Catholic Church in check.

"Alright tell me," he said sitting forward. Michael quickly moved to the sofa in front of him. He took a quick breath and quietly spoke.

"It was magic," and then he sat back in the sofa pleased with himself.

"Is that it?"

"Pardon me... child. I cannot sit here and tell what went in where etc." Roberto laughed. "You're my baby. I can't talk about those things with you."

"Do you think they're wrong? Against God's teaching, un-natural, dis..."

"*Basta!*"

In a distinctive patois that Roberto learned from his mum's brother, Cleavon, Roberto said, "You know people say batty man have fe dead." Michael's spirit came crashing down at the sound of those words. The statement drained his life within a minute.

"Papa, I didn't mean to say that. I was joking..." He took Michael's hand.

"I hate that Jamaican bacca-yard shit. Oh my, God, I tell you."

"I won't talk like that again. Papa sorry."

"We know when to speak patois; your mother always goes to it exactly when it's necessary. It's a part of your life. But those words are so fucked-up and hateful." Michael went and poured himself rum on the rocks and swallowed in one go. I shouldn't do this; it's bad for my figure."

"You look great, spoil yourself a bit."

161

The phone rang. "He's here!" Michael rushed for it and told reception to send him up.

"When he arrives let him in. I need a cold cloth and a minute." Michael rushed to the bathroom. Roberto went to the bedroom mirror to check how he looked and once he fixed his loose curly hair with his fingers the door rang and he went to let him in.

David stood there in a steel gray EA7 tracksuit with a fitted red Arsenal vest and black designer trainers. The Arsenal vest stood out against the gray.

"David, hello. Wow! You're so Arsenal," he said delightedly.

"Yeah, I mean Man U it's never gonna be."

"They're cunts I hate them," Roberto replied with revulsion on his face.

David stuck his hand out and Roberto patted him on the shoulder. "We've got seats at Emirates in Box X section Y," David stated.

"Bloody hell, Papa and I are three rows up from you in Section Z."

"I've been taking my son, Adrian for years…" David stopped to think about it. "It's so weird with your dad and me."

"Yeah right gay dads!" Roberto struck a pose like a sissy boy.

Watching his mime, David said, "I know – what the fuck?! But I also meant the threads that link us. This is another one. I knew he liked Arsenal, but I didn't know we were sitting in shouting distance from each other."

Roberto cringed inside as he thought how badly his gay mime could have gone.

Michael came in and David turned to him and then fell silent, gazing at him.

Michael approached him. "You always look different – formal or informal. Hello, darling." David wanted to reach out to him and Roberto could see it, but David couldn't. David glanced at Roberto and quickly back at Michael.

"He knows I'm crazy about you," Michael remarked casually. "It's alright."

"What do you want to drink, David?" Roberto asked.

"I'd like a Guinness."

"Anything," Michael told Roberto. He gestured toward and sofa and they sat together. Michael took his hand, rubbed it and finally kissed it. Roberto saw and he was oddly moved. He picked up the phone and ordered room service.

Roberto started a conversation about Arsenal and their performance, and all three of them stayed on the same subject for nearly seventy minutes. Roberto's passionate and physically dynamic body language said a lot on the subject. Their clanship mentality for Arsenal removed any difficulty they had talking to each other. When the phone rang again, reception told Michael, Omar and Ahmed had arrived, and Michael told them to send them up.

"By nine o'clock Michael, David, Roberto, Omar and Ahmed were all together talking easily and interrupting each other with points they thought were important. Ahmed and Omar were in casual western clothes: Omar in a cashmere V-neck pullover and Japanese slacks, Ahmed in black silk trousers and a crisp white cotton shirt. The two men looked very cozy leaning on each other and snuggling together. They seemed like youngsters rather than men in their mid to late forties.

"But listen," Roberto said to Omar. "Papa and David have divorced and are getting started because they feel great forces have drawn them together, they have so much in common trying to escape the depression of lying and deceiving their families and themselves. I get that. But if you two love each other…"

"Roberto…" Michael interjected, and Omar gestured to let him finish.

Roberto lowered his voiced and continued. "Doesn't it get complicated for you two being married, with kids and sneaking away, flying to London to share your lives?"

Omar said, "I understand it might appear hypocritical, full of paradox and intrigue. But if Ahmed said anything about me in Kuwait or I said anything about my feelings in Saudi Arabia, we'd be locked up, whipped, attacked on the street. The scandal would bring down our families; even my kids would be a pariah."

"What do you mean whipped?" Roberto asked.

Ahmed moved up closer to Omar and took his arm. "I know a man who decided his wealth and Western education put him above everyday laws that affect people's lives. He was dragged from his bed through the streets. People threw rotten food at him and then he was stoned by a mob." Ahmed kissed Omar's arm, and he caressed Ahmed.

"The kids at school taunted his two sons and daughter with vulgar expressions. His eldest son tried to fight for the honor of the family. The local boys grabbed him at school…" Omar had to take a moment. "They took him to a remote place. Collected packets… They excreted into paper earlier in the day and threw it at him."

Roberto was horribly upset by that, which they could see from the way he covered his mouth as the fear and indignity at the child assault rocked him.

David said, "It's the main reasons why I took up boxing and martial arts. I know the level of violence people are capable of. I know people who've been gay bashed. When I knew I was gay, I armed myself with Judo, karate, boxing, and martial arts because I wasn't going to let anybody else beat me up."

"Anybody else – what do you mean?" Roberto asked.

David nervously tried to cover up and cover over his past. "I mean anyone." Everyone in the room sensed he lied and was hiding.

"Somebody used to beat you, didn't they?" Ahmed said.

David quickly tried to answer and Omar jumped in and said, "It was your father."

"Listen, we're in Mayfair at the Connaught Hotel. This conversation is too heavy." He went and got some rum from the bar on the other side of the suite. Michael followed him over and they spoke in whispers.

Roberto asked. "So Omar, what are your kids like? How old are they?" Omar took out his mobile. Here are my three. "These are my two sons, and this is my daughter." He showed Roberto about forty pictures. Ahmed got his mobile out and moved over Roberto. "These are my three. My two daughters, Fatima, twenty-one, she got married earlier this year."

"Amazing wedding," Omar said. "Things were flown in from all over the world." They looked at each other and chuckled. "This is Shiya, nineteen, she's at University in Paris studying Chemistry. And this is my son! Nadim, he's a wonderful person." Omar agreed. "He graduated from LSE and London Business School. Works for the family really does us proud. Married two years ago, one son!"

"And we think he has a boyfriend."

"We don't know that it's just your mind working overtime."

Michael took his mobile over to them, and Roberto put his arm around his dad. "Here is my eldest son, Cesare, he's twenty-six. He's a literary agent. This is Fabio, he's a journalist…"

"Wow! So handsome," Omar said.

"Maria, his twin, they're twenty-four. She's a copy editor at a big magazine."

"They don't look alike at all."

164

Roberto said, "What's missing in their physical similarity is made up for in their temperament. They're a couple of drama divas on the same wavelength – they're *so* alike!" he stated. "Nothing like me: I'm more…"

"Like me," Michael declared.

Roberto laughed. "Yes!"

"In a way, Fabio and Maria are like my wife, but Lola has so much fire and power, my God I have still never met a more beautiful woman. Cesare is like me, but the serious side of me. Which is why I was surprised he didn't recognize my depression as a 'life stage' because he's introspective with a gift for reading people."

"But he doesn't have a worldview; he only thinks about his immediate surroundings."

Michael said to David: "They're all so competitive."

"He likes to play big brother with me and it pisses me off. Papa is head of the family." The acknowledgment clearly meant a lot to Michael.

"Darling, show them your son," Michael told David.

David became spiritually alert when he took his mobile and showed pictures of Adrian. "He's such a compassionate person. He's at York studying History and Politics."

"He doesn't know?" Roberto asked, and David shook his head. "When you tell him? How do you think he'll react?"

David asked Michael. "You will help me with Adrian?" David thought about Adrian turning on him. "I pray and I beg God to have mercy on me and let him still love me. If he stopped loving me because I've changed, because I've stopped lying to myself and others I'd be destroyed."

"Have you told your family you're gay now?" Roberto asked.

Omar and Ahmed moved in closer. "My brother, yes, and my mum kind of. My friends and father don't know."

Roberto asked. "David, do you want me to be with you when you talk to Adrian?"

"What do you mean?"

"To explain how I feel knowing Papa's gay and why he needs me as he never imagined he would." All four men looked at Roberto astounded by his support.

"Why would you do that?"

"There so much heartless violence and persecution going on: I won't add to it." David placed his hand on the side of Roberto's face and all the kindness and love he knew from his mother's gentle care settled in his heart and Michael felt deep love toward him and enormous pride in his son.

****

An hour later Dr. Claude was there with his partner, Dr. Nasir, the North African. Michael also invited four ladies over who were clients of his. The ladies were buyers who ran a club for women with breast cancer. They all mingled in the suite. A little later Michael opened the door and Lola came in with Tony. She threw her arms around him and gave him a great kiss. She had on a gold colored silk fitted dress with a decorative belt and a green satin evening coat and Louboutin evening shoes. Roberto excused himself from the ladies he was talking to and went to his mother. Lola gave a little shout for joy at the sight of him, and Tony vigorously shook Roberto's hand.

"Everybody! This is my former wife, Lola!" The group gave a collective 'Hi'.

"Darling I almost ran here when I got your call. Hi, people!" She said throwing her head back. "We were at a thing, Yuk! Then I got Michael's call," she told guests.

Michael turned her around and whispered in her ear and then took her around and introduced David.

David bowed his head slightly and then looked her in the eyes with a confident smile and said, "I've heard only great things about you."

"They're all true," Lola replied in a generous convivial manner.

"Mum, David was a key guest judge on the television new singer's show, and he manages Mr. Man!"

She took a breath. "I love that guy. His confessions and praise on Black women are a monumental step forward in hip-hop."

Michael told her. "David's mother is the owner of *The Old Country* restaurant."

"Shut up! That's my favorite restaurant in London! The food is excellent."

"That's because my mum's amazing."

"And you must be one hell of a guy to be here. Michael doesn't suffer fools and bores. He loves visceral artists and visionaries."

166

"I'm those things but never on the same day. At my best I'm bold and at my worse, I'm perilous because I don't know who I'll have to deal with."

"Him sometimes, he's got some dreadful habits." She caressed Michael's face. "But none of them are disgusting."

"You're very beautiful… you remind me of Shirley Bassey in a way."

She stood back and pointed at Michael. "Did he tell you to say that?"

"No, you have that sparkle and freedom of movement; your smile and hair."

"We do bear a similarity."

David led her away from the crowd over to the bar. "This is difficult for me. There's a chance for Michael and I but if I see him, is that going to be difficult for you?"

"This isn't the place for that conversation. But I'm very happy in my life and if you ducked out of the scene because you think I'm some kind of Mrs. DeWinter who haunts Michael you'd be wrong. You're not my replacement, and I don't think you can be some 'boy'. Michael called me on Sunday and said he found love. Michael told me your son is a major factor in your life?" David nodded.

"The kids mean a lot to Michael because he's a great father. If he left me for another woman, I'd have ripped him to shreds. The fact we parted because he wants what no woman can provide. It's left me without remorse. I'm his only love, and he was my only love. Now… we've both discovered more about our lives."

Tony took David's arm. "Michael's happy at last. You made that possible."

"People are going to condemn me and maybe even inflict that special brand of homophobic Black hatred that's instilled in Jamaican and Nigerian culture. The only way I'm going to handle it is if we're on good terms, and you don't turn on me."

"That's not who I am. Also, I know our 'laws' subject can be hysterical."

Tony said, "On our honeymoon we went to Jamaica, and you should have seen this lady deal with the old country." Lola looked at him as if he'd revealed a confidence, but he stared back at her challengingly. "Come on, you struck a blow for women's freedom."

Lola paused for a few seconds and then hooked her arm through David's and walked him away from everyone.

167

"We went to Jamaica so I could introduce Tony to my father. He's a respected Professor of Caribbean History at the University of the West Indies."

Tony said, "Your father commands respect because he's rich. That's what speaks to the majority of people in Kingston." He turned to David. "She's an heiress." Lola saw innocence in David when he smiled, and she was certain Michael saw it too.

"My story, excuse me. So – I didn't want to discuss the reason for our divorce, so I trotted out the 'irreconcilable difference' and my father cuss a long strike of bad words and finally I told him the truth. He didn't listen he just heard *gay* and went into a homophobic rant calling Michael all kinds of things and I slapped my father's face."

Picturing it again, Tony said, "The slap was like thunder; a strike for women's freedom against a father's power. Lola pointed in her father's face and said 'Shut your mouth. You're only half the man Michael is'." Tony was still stunned by her action.

"My father has power," Lola continued, "and he's very smart, but he lacks compassion. My brother's the same. Michael is the opposite, and so is Tony." She looked into Tony's eyes, and David saw that they were definitely in love.

Tony said, "The best part of all this is the strength it creates in us. If we had an adulterous affair, I couldn't have been a friend to Michael when he needed that. I couldn't expect Roberto and the other kids to accept me in the family."

"Adulterers are just fucking greedy," Lola added. "I could never look my children in the face after coming back from a lover's bed. All that lying and disgrace, no thank you. I'm happy now because I didn't dishonor myself or my family."

David leaned in and told them. "When I was thirteen I knew I had 'tendencies'. Eventually, I tore them out to be a father and a man. I never committed adultery during our nine-year marriage. It's great to know we're all like-minded." Lola and Tony escorted him back to Michael.

An hour later, Lola was engrossed in a conversation with Omar and Ahmad. Tony was talking to Dr. Claude, and Michael and David were speaking to the four ladies. Roberto stood back and watched them all, thinking about things. Lola quickly excused herself and went to him. "What it is darling?"

"Papa's all lit up, he's really in love. I know it. When I was a boy, the way he looked at you assured me you'd never divorce because my friend's parents didn't look like you. Does this hurt you? Are you here to check out if...."

"Stop fretting. Dad's going to be alright. David is no lightweight or gay tramp.

"I hear you. Besides," he whispered in her ear. "He and Solomon Bankole are brothers." Lola covered her mouth because she was stunned. Roberto nodded at her. "I promised Papa I wouldn't tell, but you're my mother for God's sake." Tony came over.

"What is it? What, the look on your face; what is it?" Roberto walked them onto the terrace, and Mayfair's streets and rooftops were aglow in the night light.

"Ok, since you love Papa and never shagged my mother." Lola hit him. Roberto looked into the suite and back at Tony. "David's brother is Solly Bankole."

Tony spun around and whipped his fingers mouthing a muted, "Fuck the planet! Can there be a more famous Black Brit alive? He must be worth fuck-you millions!"

"Calm down," Lola said.

"Fuck no. Solly is the greatest Black player England ever lost. And my country signed him." He laughed like the cartoon character Muttley in the *Wacky Races*.

"Listen, people!" Michael announced. "When I've moved into my new place you're all invited to my housewarming."

"Where is it?" asked one of the ladies. Lola pulled Roberto and Tony back in.

"In Canonbury." Lola tried to behave casually and Tony was ready to burst.

"Where is Michele getting his kind of money?" she asked Roberto.

"Not sure, but he's been doing great business with those Arabs." He ushered her away from people. "They're worth billions."

"Money isn't everything. I have you kids, Tony, and Michael. That's plenty."

"Cesare, Maria and Fabio may have a totally different take on this party."

"I know. Cesare has adopted too much from my arsehole brother."

Michael walked David past his doctor, Nasir, and he winked at him happily. Nasir was amused and easy about the two of them mainly because Michael had taken steps to keep his lifelines to Lola and Roberto, who Nasir was delighted to see at the gathering. He knew very little about David.

Michael told David. "From now on, we are going to keep company with people like this. Granted some of them are my clients and that's not the same as my lifelong friends, but Tony is here and he's like a brother to me. Are you OK with the people?"

"I think Roberto is one in a million. I thought he might be of *your* making mostly, but Lola obviously has a lot of say, because look at him with her now." They looked over and back to each other.

"Are you happy?"

"Yes, very... I feel really lucky we've met."

"This isn't luck; we are destined to be together. I feel almost ready to face my kids. I've been telling my clients I'm gay: if I can tell strangers why not my kids."

"Because you can ignore strangers but family is a different story?"

"When am I going to meet Adrian?"

"Soon, he started his second year at University, but if I invite him down, he'll come for a weekend." David looked at Dr. Claude.

"Darling, look at me." David turned back to Michael. "If it wasn't for you I couldn't do this."

"Michael, I want to kiss you so badly my head's spinning." Michael was thrilled.

Tony came over to Michael. "This is a very smart move, Michael."

"What is?"

"Holding court at The Connaught Hotel."

Michael turned to David. "He's very clever, knows me like no one else."

"David I like how you roll. You've cultivated some great British talent.
I'm not a hip-hop guy, I love *bachacata*. But you've made stars; should be good for you!"

"Thanks. I have nothing against samba, if you know musicians, call me."

"Give us a minute." Tony did a Favela cool move that was street 'smart'. Michael took David outside. In the empty corridor, Michael pushed David against the wall and gazed at him. David saw the kiss coming but ducked under his arms.

"CCTV." Michael looked up and around the empty hallway. "Let's go outside.

170

They walked out the entrance and onto Mount Street where they strolled for a minute without saying a word. The streets of Mayfair were almost deserted, but the streetlamps lit the posh area as if it were enchanted. They walked past the redbrick 19th century buildings and ducked into a doorway and David kissed him without restraint.

"Michael, tonight, your son, Lola, everything – it's lovely: and you!" David kissed him, and Michael felt him up.

"David I want you to feel good about us. This could be an infatuation since it's been less than a week, but I know it isn't. I know when God's blessed me. Give me a chance to prove myself. Before Lola and I parted, I was impotent and let things slide. In the last stage when I knew I wanted to live again I regained my lust for life. Since I read your book and we met on Sunday I have fire and guts again." They heard the sound of people coming, so they stepped out of the doorway and walked on.

"Michael, come to my house in Camden for the weekend. Can you spend the weekend with me? I'll get everything in. I'll cook." Michael nodded. "My brother is coming to London. You must meet him."

Michael looked over his shoulder for an all clear, he saw it, so he manhandled David and kissed him. David grabbed him as they staggered around the pavement. "Tonight... oh, my balls feel like grenades... we'll make love so great..."

"No, I have to cool down – rest, and get up early." Michael was so disappointed. "I need to recover. You're fucking large, you know."

"Oh, bloody hell, have I hurt you?"

"Kind of agony and ecstasy." Michael looked concerned. "As much as I loved it, that won't be why I love you."

"What will it be?"

"The day I stand up to my father and tell him about us; that will be a turning point for me. I'll get to be what I think I am." He kissed Michael again and then ran off up the street shouting "call me." Michael didn't chase him; he watched and thought about why he was falling all the more in love with him.

****

Two days later in David's living room he and Michael were alone surround by many album covers on the floor. They were totally at ease and barely half a minute went by without them smiling at each other as they played music and talked about growing up.

"This room is lovely. Can I see upstairs?"

"Not tonight."

"Too bad." David gazed at him, and he liked him all the more because Michael had dressed so well for their date, bought ten bottles of Barolo and the simple fact that he didn't lose his cool about sex. Michael was on the verge of speaking, but he wanted to make his point without sounding aggressive or condescending, so he contemplated; basking in the joy of David watching him.

"Back to the discussion; *you* know music from the 1960s and 70s retrospectively. I was a teenager buying American music in Italy as a teenager during my National service. Motown, The Temptations, James Brown. Aretha, *Rock Steady* I love it!" David went to his record collection and played Aretha. Michael got up and grooved to *Rock Steady* as though he graduated from the Tom Jones School Dance. His sinuous 'fucking' Boogie made David hard: he could barely sit still watching Michael.

"To hell with ballet and belly dancers, you my man bring the juice!" David said in distinct patois. "Are you sure you haven't got any Afro-Caribbean genes in you?"

"Not yet!" Effervescent laughter poured out of David until he simmered down and took another look at Michael; knowing they were in tune and certain he wanted to seal a friendship between them.

David told him. "Don't make a fool of me. I like you even more than you know…"

"Why do you get so upset out of the blue like this?"

David took his hand. "There's so much horror and wickedness out there. Some psycho crashes a plane into a mountain killing 150 people, beheadings, and terrorism: and out of you comes nothing but kindness; which makes me so happy."

"You saved me remember." Moved by Michael's honesty, David embraced him.

"Alright, another groove: what's your favorite song?"

"My God what a question: I love opera, jazz, classical. Let me think." He saw how important it was for David to hear the answer and Michael wanted to please him, but he also wanted to make a point. "Ok, I know but it's one single out of millions: *Bridge Over Trouble Water*." David took a moment to think about it and then he got a CD and put it on. They lay on the floor, looked up and the ceiling and then Michael took David's hand and they lie still and listened closely to Simon and Garfunkel.

When the song ended, Michael turned to him. "There is more to us than musical tastes. What choice have you made that's shaped your life, David?"

"Being a father, trying to be straight, running my own business." David thought hard and initially he took his time because he enjoyed Michael's flirtatious eyes. But after a minute, he searched himself and then he knew the answer, but he considered the cost before he spoke.

"Since we met I've asked myself are we going to change each other's life."

Michael went and sat on the sofa and he gestured for David to join him which he did. "I'm going to head back very soon. When we next meet, maybe some action?"

"Yes I will, and you're going to love it."

"Are we playing by the millennium rules of dating practices?"

David was slightly taken aback and he had to mentally re-group. "No," he said quietly. "You broke my arse the other night, and I just need time."

Michael grimaced. "Oh...please forgive me if I was rough." He walked toward the corner of the room. He clearly needed a minute to contemplate before he spoke.

"It's a paradox you know. Everyman wants to be big, to overpower women with their gross fantasies of sexual mastery. It's pure phallic egotism. Women must bow down to it, and men worship it to the heights. But when a man... like me... is just a fucking pain to his wife or lover, what joy is there in that?" David stared at Michael's back and although he couldn't see his face he felt his turmoil.

"Were there difficulties in your marriage, concerning that?"

"Yes: but I learned to be sensitive, tender you know." Michael turned around, and his eyes pleaded for understanding, even his face looked darker to David, because Michael was embarrassed to speak.

"I've always had a love-hate relationship with my body. After I married, Lola talked to me about a woman's body, sex, pregnancy, birth and sexual pleasure. I learned how to be loving and not just a prick. Gay men are utterly different to have sex with. I've heard: 'you've got ten fucking inches'. One guy told me to 'megafuck him'." Michael was gravely upset to recount the way he'd been treated. "I hate the whole cock and bullshit about machismo." Michael's entire expression displayed distress, and David had never imagined a man could feel like that.

173

"At dinner the other night, I love your expression, 'carnal knowledge': to learn how to sexually please a loved one. Will you teach me? I want to give of myself."

David went and embraced him. "The family jewels are only a *part* of you. I totally get it because lots of people think I'm carrying the fucking jungle in my pants. I don't need Darwinian ape to man notions to make me feel like a superman. This body is God's blessing, so is yours." Michael caressed his face. "you're a man not a prick."

"I hear you. I know you see *il mio cazzo e le palle*. In English Michele! You see him resting in my pants, big and bold, and I know you like it. But when I asked Lola to teach me, we became real lovers. I want you to teach me, so I become your man, a lover and not some..." He searched for the right words in English. "Nothing pornographic." Michael was revolted and horrified at the idea of it. "That's not love." Michael stared at him until all he could see was David's face and he got lost in the joy of a man who understood his cry for help.

CHAPTER EIGHTEEN

David and Mr. Man walked through the city of York with Adrian and people on the streets gawked, pointed and tried not to look but couldn't resist. Even though it was a major University City with lots of International students' four Black men walking together caught people's attention, especially when two of them were media and celebrity people. Willy made a remark that David agreed with. Mr. Man was fitted out in designer sportswear and fantastic reflector sunglasses. At 6 foot 1inch, he was an impressive figure of a man, but Adrian topped him because he had a kinder face, and looked totally natural in a crisp white shirt, new Levi 501 and polished leather boots.

They were standing outside the magnificent York Cathedral in its gothic splendor when Adrian spotted people who took out their mobiles to point at them. David said, "So everything is good?"

"Yes, Dad. I'm really glad you took time out to come up yourself and bring him. The Student Union Director would be dead chuffed to get Mr. Man booked for the Christmas party. And it will make me look good for setting this up."

"No worries. If I can get Mr. Man booked for this and the May Ball with a media hook up that would be fantastic. I really came up because I wanted to see you. I've met an amazing bloke, Michael De Farenzino, former Professor and Art Dealer; we've started doing things together. He's keen to back me up in new areas."

"Are you branching out?"

"Yes, I don't know what's best as yet but I want to build a relationship with Michael. His kids are Jamaican Italian. His ex-wife is one hell of a flame."

A fourteen-year-old English kid came up to them. "You're David Bankole from television, does the hip-hop kids online audition."

"Yes, hello."

"I don't know how to get the Audition program to work on my laptop."

"Have you called the 0800 number?"

"No."

David took out his mobile and turned on the camera and pressed record. "OK tell us what your name, phone number and log-in problems are." The kid spoke into the mobile and Adrian looked heavenward and smiled.

"Will somebody really call?" the bright-eyed kid asked.

"Yes, I'll see to it."

"Thanks mate," and then he rushed off. Mr. Man came back displeased.

"This town is so white; it gives me the creeps, like, say the police are coming to arrest us and fit us up for whatever unsolved crimes are on the books up here."

"Pure paranoia," David said. "This is York; they don't do things like that here."

"How do you know? When I come back for this gig, I want security."

"You're too well known for anyone to pull that shit."

"You forget that everyone from Ashley Cole to Idris Elba can be accused of everything in the media. Last year Idris was just working, and the media went nuts about his exposed dick. The man just had a phone in his pocket, but he got tagged."

David told him in patois. "Easy, me no tell you say, nobody a-go-do you fuckeries."

Mr. Man turned to Adrian. "Your Dad's a master of deception – Nigerian, Jamaican, businessman, scholar or media politician, he's a style master me-tell-you-sa."

They continued walking. David pulled Adrian closer, and Mr. Man caught sight of women on the street, so he strut his stuff in the best 'badass' style.

David told Adrian. "He's pleased with himself." David intentionally changed the subject. "Would you be vex with me or denounce me if I said I was going to date somebody else white, or…"

"Dad date who you like. I couldn't get vex because she's white. That prejudice is what I've been reading about this year. Black people don't have the power to be racist but lots of us have prejudices that are as nasty as institutional racism and other kinds of bigotry." David nodded to him. "Are you seeing somebody else that's white?" David nodded, yes. "Cool, just make sure before you get serious that real love is flowing back and forth between the two of you."

"Yes, Obe Wan," David affectionately replied.

"Shut up," Adrian replied secretly delighted that his father considered him to be wise. "Wait, you're not getting back with that bitch are you?"

"Fuck no!"

"Thank God. Mum would rip your balls off, and I wouldn't talk to you. She defined disgusting to me. Doing drugs and miscarrying two kids because she couldn't live without the cocaine up her hole: nose or where ever she put it."

"I had no idea you felt that strongly about her."

"I could have had two brothers and that degenerate took their lives. You really fucked up there, but oops there goes my mouth." David yanked him to one side away from people on the street and Willy and Mr. Man stayed back.

"Dad don't give me a lecture in the street about your marriage because if you killed someone, shagged half of London including blokes or stole money to the tune of millions I'd still love you but that woman offended my mother, the family and me."

Mr. Man came forward and pointed in Adrian's face. "Don't chat your business in the street or talk to your father like that." Adrian smacked him in the face, to the astonishment of David and Willy.

"Don't put your mouth in my business," Adrian told him. "Go over there and wait and don't move until I'm done talking." Mr. Man made a move as though he was going to hit Adrian, so David shoved him back.

"Have you gone fucking crazy or something? Don't lift your hand against my child." People across the street twisted their necks to see more.

Willy rushed in. "We're on camera."

"I don't give a shit," David said.

"Dad, they love him, and this is business. Play nice: it's show business. I mean I think he's a fucking joke, but that's just me. You admire him. And count yourself lucky my Dad does. Now move I'm sick of talking about you." No one, anywhere, had ever told Mr. Man anything like that before. He backed off and walked away.

"What's with you and him?" David asked.

"He's such a loud mouth media hog; he gets on my fuc...flipping nerves."

As they began walking, David looked back and saw Willy was consoling Mr. Man.

"Are we ok?" David asked Adrian.

177

"Yeah, I mean yes Dad, but don't test my limits because if you intend to mess up your life with some degenerate conduct, expect to hear from me."

"And what constitutes degenerate conduct..." David asked him agitated.

"Dad please don't do that. I'm talking about you doing things you're ashamed of, and you were ashamed of her. That's why you apologized to me a million times when I was growing up about her bullshit. Now can we just go to the Uni and get that Ragga dude back there, booked, because my only interest in him is gaining marks. If he wasn't a fake, I'd still think he's dick, who actually doesn't love any woman."

"Why'd you say that?"

"He shags any girl he can get his hands on. If you think of girls as a cum bucket that is not love. He gives me the creeps."

"Well, I'm on the verge of real love and I'm happy," David said petulantly and wondered why Adrian was in such a bad mood but refused to blame himself for it.

CHAPTER NINETEEN

Michael entered David's bedroom dressed in a sports vest and jeans, and he kept looking at everything. "My God this house is fantastic and I love this room especially; the bed, and those Egyptian veils – incredible!"

David was mentally and physically excited just seeing Michael's toned biceps and pectorals bulging in the white vest. Michael started a crash diet mid-week, and now he had the fat and water reduced in his body he looked even younger.

"I'm glad you like the whole house," David said.

"I love it! Your house is better than a Fellini set!" David laughed easily, so Michael gladly held him and inhaled David from his neck to his armpit.

David turned him around. "What do you think of that?" Michael saw the *Athlete* replica statue and quickly moved around the larger than life model.

"You have this in your bedroom!" He reached for David, who came to him. "I invited you to The Connaught to impress you, but this! It is my favorite work of art. We *were* destined to meet; don't you think?" David nodded, and Michael turned back to the sculpture and ran his hand over the snake arm, buttocks, and the inner thigh.

"I'm still a virgin you know. I want you to change me."

David quickly realized what he meant. "You and your friend Alexander…"

"We were boys; some things we didn't do." Michael's face confessed.

David crossed the room and put on Mahler's *Symphony #9*. He didn't know what Michael liked, but he was sure he'd appreciate Mahler symphonies which had the perfect dramatic narrative. Michael smiled knowingly.

"Let me tell you a secret. I'm an expert at hiding my true feelings. I've fooled everyone I've ever met. I refined those skills better than Jekyll and Hyde. I know the true meaning of Black male mystique, my father, Solly and my brother-in-law Erwin are compendiums I've studied. Only one man knows me, my ex-lover and guardian. What you told me about the way men have fetishized you as a big prick, I won't do that. A man's heart and his philosophy inspire me. I admit it turns me on if a man is loaded. But, I love romance more than sex." David was all the things Michael hadn't imagined, so he willing went to bed with him.

Most men don't make love, they have sex. David made love to Michael and discovered his erogenous zones and spots above and below the skin. They were clean inside out therefore David's lips and fingers found the secrets and the pride that amounted to Michael's body and soul.

It was strange how well *Mahler's Ninth* spoke for them. They were inside the canopy of David's bed with the lights glowing in, sealed in the white encampment of the luxurious bed with the hieroglyphics on the veils.

The prelude led to their intimacy and Michael couldn't believe what was happing to his skin and his nervous system as David's abrupt and subtle movements took him into the sphere of the uncanny. He knew what was happening because David turned him around as though they were circling the compass. Mahler's opening passage torn at Michael's heart and at the same time David's erection forced his eyes open. In the realm of Michael's sexual anatomy David made a meal of his fecundity which strengthened and mellowed his flesh. Unable to control himself, Michael burst out laughing because he felt marvelous.

After a time, their sexually fused bodies led them into a kinetic ebb and flow. David bit the soles of his feet and Michael felt an undulating reverberation shake him internally, and before long he was involuntarily going through his first arid orgasm. Michael went out of his mind and found heaven. He lost all sense of time and place, but David kept at him until they were conscious of their ferocious ejaculations. A sense of nirvana overtook Michael, and David collapsed on top of him.

Neither one of them could speak for a time. They lie still and in their separate ways they reached out to God to ask for salvation. David knew all his loving moments with Veronika didn't bring him the peace he felt now, and every element of love he shared with Angus didn't overshadow what he felt for Michael. In Michael's mind and body he knew he'd never experienced sensations of the kind that darted through his Being.

David stood, lifted Michael like a war buddy and carried him over his shoulder into the bathroom that was warm and lit in orange. They quickly got into the sunken tub and David filled it with bath salts and crystals, along with other oils and bath herbs. When the tub was full and hot, David moved toward Michael, and he held onto him.

"David," he whispered. "Now I'm yours darling, all yours." They washed each other, caressed one another; and stayed in the fragrant herbs and crystal water, topping up the tub with more oils, minerals and hot water which heightened all of their senses.

"You said carnal knowledge Michael. I think that was a good start."

Michael laughed rapturously. "I have a great friend in Rome, Luca. He used to be my priest, now he's a painter and my client. He told me he was re-born when he lost his virginity to the man who became his husband so to speak. He said when his flesh was willing, and his soul was in a state of grace he felt no fear. Now I understand."

"Excuse me if I feel great about getting you to that level."

"This is why I believe in God and not the Bible. In the flesh, something amazing happened to me, and I spoke to God, because everyday happiness, in a world of want, is for me like an ordinary miracle. Making love, you gave me affirmation of my rights, to renounce sin. Your flesh in me is not sin, it's sacred."

"The things you say, your mind, it's incredible."

"I studied 'greatness' in religion, art, philosophy, literature: also by bringing life into this world and protecting my children." With humility, he looked away from David. "I've never considered myself great. My life is measured by acts of courage and 'decency': but naked with you in the flesh, seriously; I feel like I'm God's creation; free of original sin," he declared looking directly at David, full of life.

"I'm speechless," David said and didn't know where to look.

"Every guy who wants to be the alpha male has yet to discover what it is to be a fearless man. You had me and I feel no fear, no feminization, no... weakness." David could barely cope with what he was hearing so he lowered his head.

"Darling what is it... what, what?"

Michael moved closer to him. "If this doesn't work I'll die. Something in my soul will die. Or I'll walk around..." David felt humble and strange; "but I'll be dead."

"I felt it when we met: when you were inside me; when I was in you!"

181

David's face was momentarily illuminated with mental and physical euphoria, and Michael fell in love with him differently and knowingly once again.

They grabbed each other tightly as though the world would end any minute. Michael comforted him and when they got out of the tub, they went to bed together and slept soundly.

****

David woke up at six o'clock, turned and saw Michael fast asleep beside him. Just watching him forced many thoughts into his mind. In repose, Michael looked totally at peace. David remembered the night before which easily brought a smile to his face. He got out of bed, went to the closet and took out a present in a large Selfridges gift box. He looked at the card again…. *'Welcome to my home. Luv – David'*.

In the kitchen forty minutes later, David was half way through cutting up pineapple and papaya. The aroma of ginger tea filled the kitchen with warmth. He set the table and poured the blended smoothie. When Michael entered in his silk black dressing gown with red piping around the collar and the edges he looked very suave.

"Good morning darling." The sight of him made David tingle. "Thanks so much for this robe." He turned with his arms spread wide. David hurried to him and held Michael in a fond embrace.

"You look beautiful." Michael was touched to hear it. "Are you alright?"

"Yes… I'm just dealing with my brainwashing." David didn't understand. "There is so much hysteria about protecting your arse."

"I think what's more terrifying for most blokes is not the thought getting fucked, it's liking it." Michael bumped his fist against David's.

"That will be my thought of the day."

"Do something for me?"

"Anything," Michael replied.

David went over to the stove and turned off the porridge. "Will you pray with me?"

Michael was taken aback because he'd never been asked to do that. "Yes."

David took his hand, and they stood in the middle of the kitchen as he closed his eyes and said, "Dear God Almighty, I want to thank you for bringing us together. This beautiful man is what I deserve because you

182

know I've had to protect myself. The world is so full of hatred based on religion and egotism, and that is why I always pray to you for guidance. Thank you for my life today and the strength to tell my family the truth with the support of this loving man." He concluded with the Lord's Prayer.

When he opened his eyes, he saw that Michael looked worried "What?"

"Between last night and this now, it's a lot."

"Oh I'm sorry; I didn't mean to make you feel trapped like I'm a needy, obsessive freak..." Michael put his hand over David's mouth.

"No darling it's nothing like that," Michael confessed. "Your heart and spirit reaches me." David was relieved. "I have such an incredible feeling about us. Last night was so amazing for me."

"And thanks for coming with me today because I couldn't go home and do this. I need to be on my turf to face my mum. Some men back in Nigeria would move against me and kill me to restore the honor I'm going to violate in my family. But my honor is not living by rules that crush me. It's living with my own dignity."

"The idea of an honor killing is so medieval it shakes me. But we're going to protect each other. You don't have to justify yourself to me. I understand." David could see that Michael truly understood what they were facing.

"Alright, let's eat." David showed him the full Afro-Caribbean breakfast which pleased Michael.

They didn't speak during breakfast; they simply made sounds depending on what was tasty and how they felt looking at each other. Afterward, Michael insisted on doing the washing up while David went into the garden to exercise.

CHAPTER TWENTY

Fear and anxiety rushed through David as he sat nervously in his office with Michael. The two of them were smartly dressed, but David couldn't sit still. "Listen, I have to go outside for a cigarette because I can't meet them like this."

"Do what you have to darling." David tried to shake the pins and needles out of his body, but he couldn't make it. He went to a cabinet in his office and took out a packet of cigarettes ad excused himself to go outside and smoke it.

In the Hoxton area, it was fairly quiet at ten to eleven in the morning but David hopped around as though he were freezing, smoking in the cold but it was a hazy sunny, mild autumn morning. "You can do this David. You're a tough bloke born and raised in Hackney. You're not afraid of anyone. Dear God, have mercy, please have mercy." He finished the cigarette and darted back inside and entered his office suite. He went into the kitchen and found mouthwash and aspirin. Making his way into the loo he stopped to look at the office which looked lifeless on Saturday. He turned on the lights and Michael looked out of the glass office into the staff area. David headed for the men's room.

Twenty minutes later David got a text. "They are parking and heading in." He got up and bounced around and began shadow boxing so Michael went and kissed him to calm him down. His breathing slowed down and his heart rate returned to normal. "I'm gonna be fine, I'm gonna be fine, I'm gonna be fine." He sat in his executive chair behind his desk and Michael sat facing him in the comfy side chair.

His mother came into the office escorted by his brother Solomon. She was dressed well but by no means dolled up in designer clothes. She wore a simple peach and black polka dot dress that complimented her complexion and figure, and Solly wore the best casuals money could buy in Nigeria. She waved at David as she walked the twenty-something feet toward his office. Because Michael had his back to her, she couldn't make him out. David got up to let her into his office.

"Hello honey, Solly's been so mysterious about everything. First, he flies in early and… Oh." Michael stood up. "Mum, this is Michael De Farenzino, he's an art dealer and former art professor."

"Mrs. Bankole, glad to meet you again, I came to your restaurant on my birthday; you took care of my wife and I, even though we didn't have a reservation."

Cynthia tried to remember. "You were rushing to your grandson's birthday before he had to go off to University."

She thought about it and his eyes came back to her. "Yes, it was over a year ago."

"Correct."

"Small world." David and Solly simply snapped their fingers at each other. David said, "Still scoring goals and recruiting talent into the Motherland?"

"Shut up and earn some more money." David was happy to hear Solly rib him. David pointed at a chair, and Michael moved onto the sofa so that Cynthia was at the desk in front of David.

"Mum, I have something important to say. I'm glad Solly flew in early. I asked him to bring you here because I couldn't enter your home where you might throw me out."

"How could I do that?" She looked at her youngest son and then at her eldest.

"The fact is I'm gay." She was stunned as she looked at each one of them.

"Mum, I swear before God, I haven't done anything that shames me in the eyes or spirit of God." David got up and sat next to Michael. "I've been so unhappy and empty. God sent *this* man to save me from lies and misery."

"Mrs. Bankole, I was married for over twenty-five years. I have four children and my depression was so severe I tried to take my own life. The day I met David I knew I was really saved from a life of nothing since my divorce."

"You knew about them, didn't you Solly?"

"I've never seen David carry on with any homosexual business."

"So why haven't you jumped over there to beat him?"

"How am I supposed to beat up my big brother?"

"You think you're funny, but I know your father won't find this funny." She turned to Michael. "What do your wife and kids have to say to this?"

185

"My wife loves me…still. I'm working things out with my children."

"Have you told Adrian?"

"No, but I'm going to. I can't live with Dad's hate and Adrian's."

"Your father doesn't hate you."

"Yes he does; nothing I've done makes him…" He stopped because he couldn't say it in front of Michael.

"David, I need time to… think through this." She got up, and Michael was about to speak. He offered his hand, but she held her hands to block everyone from touching her. Michael immediately backed away, and she moved to leave, but when she got to the door, she said to David. "You should have come to me privately."

"I couldn't Mum, I need Michael. He might do a runner now he knows how serious I am, but this isn't some kind of infatuation. Michael if you want to bail because this isn't as sexy as you might have thought than dump me now."

"No David; you have to help me with my children."

"How did the two of you raise a family knowing your preference?"

"My wife and children are my preference. And David was destroying himself to be everything your family prefers: now David and I want to be who *we* are."

She took hold of herself and said to Solly. "Come, drive me home." She left David's office and kept walking.

"This is the easy part, Dave." Solly hugged him and suddenly pulled back and looked him in the face and grew angry. He slapped him so hard David could taste blood. "You've been smoking! If you smoke, I won't have you near my kids. I've fucking told you, kick the habit! I'm watching you." He pointed at Michael. "We got things to talk about Michael. I hear you're an amazing bloke. Later." He flexed his shoulders, and his leather jacket rode up on his back.

****

When Solly closed the car door for Cynthia, he quickly got into the Mercedes. His mother covered her face and wept and couldn't stop. Her entire body shook. It distressed him so much he could barely hold himself together.

"When did he tell you?" He didn't answer. "Do not lie to me!"

"I've… suspected him since he was fifteen. Mum, he's tried to fight it. He married, and he never went with anyone."

186

"Was he running after other boys?"

"No, he just kept fighting it. He's never actually been with a guy. He'd get freaked out by what would happen if you and Dad found out. Dave's a tough guy to fight it all these years. I know sportsmen who are all mouth about women but get their jollies with blokes. Dave's turned away from that to be a faithful husband and father."

"So really he's not actually gay."

"A mixed race person can pass for white but if your DNA is Black…"

"Yes… whatever he hasn't done can't dispel what he is."

"Mum, David's a very loving person, and you know that."

"Your father could kill for the honor of his family and this scares me."

"I just lost my sister, I'm not about to accept an honor killing because David offends Dad's sense of Nigerian dignity. I hear this anti-man, homo rant all over the place in Nigeria. How *they* have a right to kill because 'homos are an abomination' and all kind of shit! No one is gonna kill my brother. No one is gonna touch him!!"

She caressed his face. "Baby, shhh, baby. I'm here, and I'm alright."

"Mum, I'm not a child! I'm married with kids and make my own living. Anyone raises their hand against my brother…" He thought through the most dreadful consequences. "I'll fucking kill them. I don't care if I go from famous to infamous."

"Who'll take care of your family?"

"All of you until I get out! You're my mother, but Dave's been more loving to me which is amazing because you're great and I wouldn't be alive without you! But Dave's kept me alive at school, on the streets, in the press."

"He does rate you above any man alive."

"Except Adrian." She half smiled. "So… I can't listen to any shit about killing and Obeah again."

"Hush, don't talk about it. You were so cool back there."

"He told me he's reached a changing point in his life; I didn't know this was it."

"If only he'd have married Grace."

"She should have kept her mouth shut, and he might have."

"Your father isn't a monster you know. Back then he just… freaked."

"Dad's always been great to me and wonderful to you… but he's obsessive about David." She agreed. "But David's moved past all that. Back at the office, he handed Michael an invitation to leave him, and he didn't. Have you ever heard of two guys backing each other up like that to deal with their kids?"

"I don't know any gays."

"Mum, bi and gay blokes are all over the place. In Nigeria on drunken late nights you'd be surprised what people ask for." She looked stunned and he nodded and started the car. "David isn't some gay slut or sneaky married man, out on the prowl for victims. David's repressed what he is. But I think Michael's changed that."

"If this is serious, and it must be for him to confess to me."

"Mum don't worry, I'm back now. I had to get Amy and the kids out before the Ebola turned into an epidemic."

"This is why I told you to have the kid's here for their security."

"Well, I'm back and thank God I've still got my sponsorships and the rest."

CHAPTER TWENTY-ONE

David and Michael sat in Canonbury Pond Gardens, and it appeared that they had escaped the hustle of the busy city on Saturday afternoon. The lush magnolia trees hung draped in leaves surrounded by well-kept green gardens. The gardens were like a hideaway in plain sight. It had a twisting footpath that led into and around the leafy gardens and pond, where benches were periodically placed within the pond gardens.

David took Michael's hand in his and told him. "I had to bring you here because I've always come here as a sanctuary when I've had to think or realize what's happening to my life. I came here with my first love, Angus. I'll tell you about him when I'm ready. But I told him that I loved him right here on this bench. I brought Veronika here and told her when I loved her. And I did, we did, in the beginning before she went druggy on me." David looked up and saw that they were alone. "Now I've brought you here to tell you that I love you." The moment he said it he smiled from his heart. "It's young, and it's so mysterious, but there's no doubt about it." Michael stared at him speechless for a good while.

Veronika came into the Gardens, and she was heading for their old spot, but she stopped and ducked out of the way when she saw David was there with Michael. She watched them, and there was an intimacy between them that she felt even though she was thirty feet away. She went into her handbag and took out her phone and searched for the camera App.

"I'm happy you tell me this David because everything between us is like we were destined to meet. I feel great empathy with you, as new friends: also passion that makes my philandering, before you seem stupid. I've had you and you've had me. Our lovemaking is fucking primordial! The virgin and beast in me are touched by your soul. And now today with your mother: you have incredible strength, and I beg you to help me tell my kids, I'm afraid they'll run from me." David couldn't see anyone in the Gardens, so he kissed Michael.

Veronika watched them through the moving image on her phone. As she did so, she cursed under her breath and walked under trees to get closer. She held her breath, stealthily moving closer, taking clearer and better photos of them. Her heart raced as she watched the intimate exchange between them; and then ran away before she was spotted. Michael said, "Your son should know."

David took Michael back to his house, and Michael kept walking around the large 30x32 foot living room. They went from the front to the back of the house. "I must say, David, you have a really good eye and taste. "This furniture is…"

"All replicas of the 1900s classic art nouveau furniture: I didn't have the money to buy the originals. But the great thing about what's in here is that it'll last, and the condition is sound."

"What made you choose cream and black furniture?"

"The room needed light and contrast."

"These shelves for your records are good: the curve and swirl of all the shelves, the elegant chairs, sofas, the tables, and lamps; everything including the wall coverings and the curtains." David appreciated his compliments.

"Shall I tell you my inspiration for the house?" Michael nodded. "The movie The *Picture of Dorian Gray*, from the 1940s: I love the book, it's one of my five favorite books of all time. *Autobiography of Malcolm X* is my favorite by a long shot." He went and prepared them a Crème de Cassis. "There is one room here that I hate. It's a pink pussy cat palace. I haven't even been able to bring myself to go in there, it's locked. Veronika hated this house, and she insisted on having a room for herself. I gave her one of the bedrooms, and she turned it into a pink girly playpen. It's the kind of glam palace that typical teens and gays love. All that Kyle, Lady Gaga… Rihanna. That's pure shit to me."

"Aretha Franklin, Ella Fitzgerald, Diana Ross, Madonna and Joni Mitchell are women I like and admire…"

"I love Joni. And where do you stand on the Streisand question?"

"I have never been interested in her." David brought him the drink; Michael took a sip and liked it.

"You can lose your gay license for saying that." Michael laughed loudly, and David liked the sound of his laughter and the fact that he could make him laugh.

"She means nothing to me. My daughter, Maria, likes her a lot. Anyway… what's more interesting to me is how many albums and CD you have here. I've seen them before but in the daylight, wow!"

"There's 7,209. I collected them from everywhere I've traveled and during my years on the radio. There's just about everyone in my collection except Elvis because he makes me sick and Lady Gaga because she makes me yawn."

"So now *you* tell me, who do you like above all the others?"

"Michael Jackson or maybe Stevie Wonder, but I love Michael. The racist media just worked their worthless arses off to criminalize and pathologize him. At times he didn't help himself or protect himself; tell the press to go and shit on their mothers. Back in 2009 when he died, I just cried." He went to the CDs, found *Thriller* and put it on.

The bass line for *Billie Jean* came on and David performed the famous routine perfectly, prolonging the moonwalk on his lacquered floor, and Michael watched him stunned at how well he danced and moved.

"So many surprises spring out of you like a force of nature. I can imagine when da Vinci, Michelangelo, Caravaggio or Botticelli were inspired, it manifests itself when someone possessed your fire and heart. I must photograph you, for all kinds of reasons."

"I could listen to you sweet talk me all day, but the food will not cook itself so come to the kitchen and keep me company." Michael stopped him leaving with an embrace, and he felt him up and down. "I want to see you in your birthday suit again."

Michael eyed him in sexual desperation and pulled him onto the floor, and they had each other without restraint.

In the early evening, David and Michael rested in the media recreation lounge which looked like an installation in a gallery. The room had hidden lights of pink and violet contrasted with a frosty green so that it looked like a nightclub in the evening and an exhibition room by day. There was a giant plasma screen on the wall and five huge pastel leather sofas around the room where anyone could see the hundreds of DVD films and box set TV series in glass cases. He also X-Box games as well as the top of the line TV stereo sound system. The walls were crowded with framed album covers of his favorite artists and magazine covers of people he represented. There were headlines on the Grime music scene, stories about his mother's restaurant, his brothers' victories at the two London football clubs and Solly's new role as a headhunter scouting Black young talent in the UK and introducing them to football clubs in Africa. There were also stories about his father's famous cases in the Black press. Additionally, David's five awards for producing newcomers, his radio show, and his television appearances sat proudly with everything else in the room.

Around nine o'clock they watched Todd Haynes 2002 film *Far From Heaven* about a white woman in 1957 who discovers her husband is gay and the only her African American gardener is able to help her. Because the characters have the sensitivity and intelligence to comfort each other, they fall in love. "This is my favorite film of all time."

"How wonderful you share it with me." It's tricky watching your favorite film with someone because if they don't like it, it feels like a personal attack. But they snuggled together on the leather sofa with a bowl of cherries; intensely consumed by the love between the socially divided couple whose racial difference was contrasted with sexual repression and guilt. An hour into the film they stopped flirting because they were deeply affected by the drama which they understood by implication and association. At the end, David was in a flood of tears.

"Darling, easy, take it easy. Why do you cry like this?"

"This story is so real. I know this situation." Michael asked him to explain. "Don't pay any attention to me. David left the room with crockery and went to the kitchen. He tried to calm down, but he stuffed the tea towel in his mouth and sobbed, heading out into the garden to cool down.

****

At Kings Cross railway ticket counter, Veronika was well dressed in a trouser suit as she went up to the window. "A day return to York now please." He sorted it out, and she took cash out of her purse and paid. He handed over the ticket, and she moved through the station to get on the train.

On the train heading to York, she played cards and recalled the conversation she had with her sister on the phone and the voices echoed in her head.

'You have some dirt on him, give it to the media and they will ridicule him. Make him a liar,' Veronika told her sister. 'His father threatened me and I think that man would personally kill me. David isn't violent with women, but his rage is terrible. He has the videos of Horia and me. He'd use them because I signed over the rights to him. I don't want to see my ass on websites he has access to from his company. He has a dreadful temper. One time a guy called me a stupid white cunt, and David Kung Fu him, out in the parking lot; knocked him out, drag him between parked cars and shit on him. That night in bed he fucked me. It was like the

192

greatest guitars riffs rocking through me. I'd be stupid if I underestimate him. When he beat Horia... who's still fucked up and has to see a prison shrink because he can't believe a black could best him. Horia said David's just a black savage, and I have a bigger dick and his wife. Why do I find idiots like Horia and fuck up?'

'You're insecure that's why,' her sister replied mercilessly.

'But why am I dissatisfied with what I've got?' The ticket inspector came into the carriage, and he loved the look of her so he stood there giving her the eye as she went through her purse to get her ticket. She liked his attention. He was an able-bodied sex maniac but a simpleton with no money in the bank. Except for David, Veronika had always attracted men like that. She found the ticket and handed it over. He told her to enjoy her trip and call on him for anything.

Ten minutes later she settled back into her game of solitaire, and the voices swam around her head again. 'What the hell is he doing kissing some guy in public? I never saw any gay signs with him, and I checked his online laptop history when he was out. I watched him at clubs, and there were no women he left me at the table or bar to go for a quickie with. I had that shit with Max once; what a bastard.'

Her sister said, 'After you, he went queer because he can't handle women anymore.'

'Don't be a bitch. I have this hot item, and I want your advice what to do.'

'You hate his son, rub it in his face.' Veronika was going to York because she really did hate Adrian. She convinced herself he hated her because she was white. When she miscarried the second time, Adrian said to her. 'You killed the baby with drugs.'

She yelled, "Fuck off you little bastard." But she wasn't sure if he ever told David what she said. The fraught voices in her head continued. 'Why don't you trash David on Facebook and put the pictures there?' her sister goaded.

'I think he'd kill me. He comes across like sensitive man, but I remember once, a reporter told David; Blacks are drawn to crime, and violent music and David pushed past all the journalist right up to this guy's face and said: "You cocksucking bitch!" Veronika's nipples tingled, and she came out in a flush.

'The studio went tense; red hot with danger. David's Black musicians were ready to tear the white guy apart. The media don't dare examine Black British political rage because Blacks will annihilate the class masters who keep Blacks powerless. I've been to hundreds of clubs and met enough Blacks to know these guys, and their women are dangerous. So I can't go too far, but I want him to hurt as he hurt me.'

'You are too afraid of him to do anything. You should just delete the fucking pictures,' her sister yelled down the phone.

'You turnip! You didn't have the ambition to leave home, and you put your mouth on me. I will show you how afraid I am!!'

Veronika smiled, convinced that she could push Adrian over the edge.

CHAPTER TWENTY-TWO

After the movie, Michael looked around the rather messy kitchen and asked. "How do you know these healthy macrobiotic low-fat diets? You also cook the food so Mediterranean and Caribbean." The P2J Project Grime classic *Hands In The Air* was playing. "The photo of you two years ago when you were heavier and the body you're showcasing now. It must have taken a lot of work. I'm trying to help you with that."

"Would you help me?" David nodded. "Please take this horrible music off." Michael's eyes pleaded with him. David looked for the remote and turned it off.

"Oh thank you: so horrible."

David pulled a face. "I'm sorry."

"It's alright now: just talk to me, I like the sound of your voice so much."

David wanted to cover over that gaffe, so he returned to the subject and spoke quickly."

"Veronika was very food conscious, and we both went to the gym three, four times a week to keep everything tight and clean. So many people are full of shit because of the junk they eat. I detox to get rid of all that shit."

David took their plates and began to sort out everything around him in the kitchen. He knew exactly what he was doing and exactly what to do with everything.

"I'm aware of your hygiene. Some men are so dirty," Michael replied sickened.

"I've been with two women and two men and now you: that's my history."

"Only one woman for twenty-eight years."

"And the men?"

Michael was reluctant to answer, but he told the truth. "You're the twelfth man."

David put the plates and pots in the two dishwashers. "I thought you were going to say thirty or…"

"My God no, that would make me a promiscuous prick!"

195

"When I confirmed Veronika was an adulteress," his jaw tightened, and his eyes flared like a panther's. "I planned exactly how I'd get rid of her." He had a butcher's knife and a frying pan in each hand. "I'll tell you the truth about something. I left a man who loved me…so I'd be straight. I went back to the family, and Grace was happy because we had Adrian, friendship, and intimacy and I wanted to be a man and a loving father. Everybody was pleased with me. I won them all back. That's when I began my life as a fake." Michael felt David turn malevolent. His physical stance changed and his body language altered.

"Dad invited us to formal dinners and Embassy parties. Solly and I were in the public eye as heroic sons of Solomon the QC. I devoted myself to Solly, Adrian, Grace and building a career. But dad and Grace wanted me to have more children. She told him about our intimate life." He stopped talking and put the frying pan and knife into the dishwasher. "One night dad introduced me to a diplomat's son from Ghana, and he said: 'Safe sex hasn't prevented him from having four children'. I knew Grace told him I used condoms. I was so angry I cut off the family and moved to Jamaica for six months. The radio station I worked for wanted a hook-up with Kingston, so I took it, but my heart ached to see Adrian. I use to Skype my Mum and she'd bring Adrian to the PC…" David was overwhelmed by sorrow. "Solly flew out and brought me back home."

"When I saw that the children didn't need me any longer, that is when I became suicidal. Lola tried to kick start me back to life, but I needed them, to feel alive."

David reached out to him. "You understand?"

"Your father and Grace were not allowing you to determine your life as a man."

"Yes! But after I left I felt guilty. I sent money to take care of her and Adrian, but I felt like more of a fake; especially being absent and not participating as a father should." Michael placed his hand on the side of David's face, and that heartened him.

"To repay Solly I started promoting him in the media, I found this house and I started to see Gus again, spent the best part of my time with Adrian. And then I met Veronika. We were determined to reject racist stereotypes." Hesitantly David added, "Also, we had quasi-homicidal impulses against people who thought we were just bloodsuckers and cocksuckers."

"You are far more interesting than your work. You share a lot with the modernist artists battling convention, from Vincent van Gogh to Oscar Wilde."

"Remember what I said about *Dorian Gray*. Anyway, Veronika adored me because I wasn't like anyone else she knew. She made me feel like such a man, I really enjoyed sex and everything with her."

"What did Angus say when you started with her?"

David turned away, "He was upset." He walked to the far end of the kitchen, opened a cupboard, took out a packet of cigarettes and lit one. Michael got up from the table and walked over to him, removed the cigarette out of his mouth and took a hit.

"What did Angus say about it?" Michael looked at him as only fathers do.

David tried to decide how to say it until he just said it. "He gave me a beating." Michael looked horrified.

"Wait, no – don't think he's some kind of a bastard. He's my best friend, I deserved it. Three times I seriously fucked him over and hurt him. After the beating, he felt so bad he couldn't bring himself to face me for years. I kept writing to him, and we resolved things. If it weren't for him, I'd have never got into the Father's Group. We'd never have met." David went and poured them two glasses of ice cold vodka from the freezer. He gave a glass to Michael, took a mouthful, went to the kitchen door, opened it and spat it out. "I must stop smoking."

"You only seem to smoke when you're nervous."

David nodded and replied, "You don't smoke, but you take a hit now and then."

"I smoked for twenty years. But you started to tell me about your wife's adultery."

David pointed at him and nodded. "Yes!" He continued tidying the kitchen. He grabbed utensils, crockery, and plates. "My first clue was her smell. I detected Old Spice aftershave. Why does a woman have that smell? She started speaking in her own language when taking and making calls. That was odd because when I first met her, she said teach me English, I'm turning away from the old world. Then there was the night I caught her… She was bruised anally." Michael laughed even though he didn't mean to. "I know!! What a paradox." David grabbed serving bowls and a carving knife and headed from the dishwasher. "I stopped anal to go straight, and my wife is out there with some prick up her arse. I was determined to find that prick and break him!" David said clutching the knife. I told my father about her adultery, and he put someone on her to track her every move. I knew Dad would help me because he hated her."

"How long did it take to get the evidence?"

"Two months or so: the more I knew about Horia, the more I intended to whip the skin off him. Cut him to the bone!!" David said slamming the knife into the chopping board. The vengeful blues and self-awareness that David revealed made Michael realize he preferred it to the ethereal persona that initially shrouded David.

"I had no intention to kill him. I was going to use my belt as a whip." Michael loved the sight of David laughing because twenty-five years of research convinced him life was a battle between wicked impulses and righteous instincts.

David sat down and looked up to Michael, pointing heavenward. "I gave that fucking bastard, Horia, a beating that would make his mother hold her womb."

"That sounds like something."

"I'm not joking. I'll show you." David led him into the media lounge and asked him to wait. Michael looked at the headlines about David and his family. With each headline and image, Michael was sure David fought to get ahead because he knew the discrimination his mixed race kids had put up with, never mind color prejudice.

David came back with his laptop and clicked through the Apps and icons to get the videos playing. Michael watched David burst in on Veronika and Horia. The beating David gave Horia excited Michael because it was real. Michael didn't believe in brute force but watching the beating was a lesson he was determined to learn because he was sick of people taking advantage of him.

"My father kept telling me: make her regret her deceit. He said to take away her hope of marrying the lover. He began a full criminal investigation of Horia and discovered he was involved in human trafficking and the drug dealing."

"What about Veronika?" Michael asked at the end of the recording.

"I'd never hit a woman. I fucked her for evidence to show in the divorce I was a sexually active husband responding to her desires and fancies. You wanna see it?" Michael said yes and David played him the edited footage of Veronika and himself. As Michael watched, he became aroused as he never did when he watched porn. Before the footage was over, Michael climbed into David's lap with overwhelming hunger.

"You're a 'badass' as the Americans would say."

"If anybody tries to make a fool of me I'm not the forgiving type."

"There's a lot more to you than most people think." David read his remark in many different ways, and Michael could see him pondering over it. "I bet most people who've seen you on television think you're funny or 'cool' by today's definition.

"Most people don't see me. They see their version of me."

"What's that?"

"A nigger."

"No, no darling no."

"Yes. There are small variations to 'the nigger', depending on the level of people's malignant racism. The police force in America – very high, the Liberal in the UK, rather low; providing we don't get in the way of what they believe they're entitled to."

"I think your intelligence and wit, unsettle people but what really scares stupid people is that in their brainwashed head, you are so far removed from the myth of the inferior and servile African; you threaten their ego. I don't know if you're fluent in sciences, but your knowledge of the humanities subjects is most impressive," Michael declared.

"I had great teachers." David could not mention Angus or his father.

"For the average idiots, you conjure up fucking chaos, first because the discursive conversation will leave idiots floundering: and second your face, that amazing arse and wicked cock is everything a rich man can't buy and a poor boy dreams of." David burst out laughing. Michael just loved his brown face and shiny eyes when he laughed. "Do you want a cocktail?"

"Yes," David replied trying to calm down.

Michael got up from his lap, opened the fly on his trousers and took it out for him. David's belly laugh reverberated throughout his whole body and Michael delighted in the sight of him.

****

Veronika unpacked her bag in the bed and breakfast room. It was modest, and she clearly didn't like it from the way she looked at everything. She went to the bathroom and showered and then came back and looked at herself in the mirror. She struck a pose and point out. "You think I'm immoral and cheap, but it is your father who's a queer, a cocksucker!" She took a moment and repeated, but she wasn't pleased with its full effect. "I've come here to tell you your father is a liar. He's

199

queer. How do you say in your language? A batty man?" She shuddered after saying that.

"I better not say that. They go mental and get violent if you say that."

She went over to her bag and took out a silver case that had a joint in it. She lit up, and three minutes later she started to feel mellow. She went back into her bag and took out a vibrator and lay back. She turned it on and let herself go.

CHAPTER TWENTY-THREE

Michael returned to the garden followed by his brother Solomon. Solly was very sporty looking in every way. Michael got up to greet him, and Solly took a look at him in his jeans and sports vest and turned to David and said, "You always like them butch and buff." Michael punched Solly in the arm.

"Shut the fuck up, shit stirrer." He turned to Michael. "He's referring to Gus." Michael looked a bit worried.

"Are you still friends?"

"He doesn't live in the UK anymore. Solly was ribbing me, but he knows that I don't keep something on the side, right?"

"True, he doesn't do that. Sorry if that sounded like I was shit stirring. David has never before done what he did yesterday. Mum's adjusting to what you said. She's gonna come round. She knows you're a decent man. Not some bastard who lives a secret life bed-hopping."

"Is she alright?"

"She's ok. She wanted to come to this, but she couldn't. How did you forget she's afraid of heights?"

"Oh, bloody hell! Oh yeah. Blast! Let me call her." David rushed inside, and Solly and Michael sat down. They looked at the spider web staircase climbing from the garden up the back wall.

"I love this house; I've never seen anything like it."

"It's great isn't it? Lots of our school friends and design people worked on it following David's exact instructions, God help the fool that doesn't do as he says when David's fired up. Have you found that out yet?"

"Are you against us?"

"No man, no. But if you're one of those thrill seekers, you're messing with the wrong guy. David is everything I want from a brother. He's kicked guy's arses for me when I was a kid at school. Helped my wife and advised me when I left the London clubs. Plus he's had it tough: our family live by a strict code."

"Can you tell me about that?"

"David will explain. But you tell me. Do you love him?"

"Yes."

"In what way?"

"On a human level, sexually, spiritually; with the truth that God gives us."

"That's serious. You put me in mind of Adrian with the words you use. But of course, you and Adrian share the same birthday. When you meet him, you'll see just how right David is because he gives the best of himself to his son. If he shares that with you too, you've struck goal my friend. Dave will be your friend for life."

"My son likes David very much too, so I understand your concern."

David came back. "Mum said we should wrap up."

"What have you got planned now? This weekend is already incredible David."

"Come with me." Solly clapped his hands and told Michael to look up.

****

Michael looked up and then caught his breath. When he took in the sight of London's cityscape, he turned back to David, who was beaming with joy. "Happy?"

"What made you hire a hot air balloon, this is so wonderful." The aerial view of London's landmarks was unmistakable on that bright shiny morning with its warm autumn air which invigorated them. *Feeling Good (Birds Flying High)* was playing on a portable CD player.

"I've wanted to do this for the longest time," David told Michael. "But I knew I could only go under certain conditions." The Thames River sparkled as they flew across the city. Michael's face was luminous with joy. Solly and his wife, Alice, a Tanzanian beauty who gave up her career as a foreign correspondent journalist in London after Solly asked her to marry; was equally thrilled to be there. Solly and Alice had only known each other two months when he proposed. She was assigned to do a feature on Diaspora Africans who had achieved great success and Solly dazzled her with football social and club life. Now she could see that Michael was moved by his happiness and she saw in David a sense of peace she had never seen in him before. Together the men looked enchanted rising up in the air, free from anxiety of any kind; which profoundly moved her because after her eleven years of marriage she still felt deeply loved, so she reached out to Solly and he took her hand. Sitting next to Alice were two of their four kids, aged nine and ten. The other two were with Cynthia's sister in North London because Solomon had left Nigeria after the Ebola disease became more widespread and he wanted to protect his family.

"I'm never going to forget today," David said and he snuggled beside Michael.

"All my life I wanted to tell my family I'm just me, no ideal; no role model. When I was married I never once gave in to temptation. It took willpower not to go with a man. There's no happiness in sacrifice. I want to be happy with you."

"This has been one of the greatest weeks of my life. For you to have the imagination and spirit to do this for me; only Lola has ever been this kind to me. In the group, we hear about honor killings and disgusting violence against us. I know about the Black hatred against us and what we'll have to deal with, but your spirit and courage touches my heart." He sat still, silent and took David's hand and tried to regulate his breathing. Alice, Solly, and David saw that he was out-of-sorts.

"Michael is everything Ok?" Solly asked. Michael nodded and kept breathing to steady himself.

"Darling," Michael whispered, "I want to kiss you so much my stomach's cramping."

Michael kissed him tenderly as if the world had no judgments against them. Solly watched and as much as he loved his big brother he found it a little unsettling to see him kiss a man. However, David and Michael were caught up in their own exaltation; consequently, the longer Solly looked, the less strange it appeared. David pulled Michael in close as the flight operator glanced over and then turned back to his work unfazed. In their intimate embrace, David and Michael weren't crushed by the edict of patriarchal bigotry. Like all rebels conscious of their internal and external torments, they refused to acquiesce to fear of violence. Therefore, they spoke to each other in the unbroken kiss that professed their love.

David pulled back, and he had to try and regain his equilibrium. Solly had never seen his brother that openly honest. Solly thought of his family and friends and felt deeply protective toward David. Eventually, David said to his niece and nephew.

"Come and say hello to the city and to Michael, I love them both." Solly moved them around so David could hold them safely as they looked out. "You know how Daddy loves Mum?" They looked at Solly and Alice, then back to him. "Well, I love Michael like that."

203

"But he's a man Uncle David," his nephew replied.

"I know, he's my man, aren't you Michael?"

"Yes, I am. My kids are grown-up, but they'll be happy to meet him as much as I'm happy to meet you." He offered his hand, and both kids shook it. David moved toward Solly and Alice. "I know its shameless emotional blackmail, but I need this,"

Alice said, "When you called and asked for our help I said it *wasn't* going to be an issue. We don't bring the kids up to hate. "What's we've learned will help them. Today the beheadings and terrorism disgusted me, scared me – especially in the name of righteousness." Alice confessed.

"It's weird isn't it," David asked her. "To think we're up here feeling free and below us, people are fighting and doing dreadful things to each other – madness."

"What are his kids like?" Alice asked.

"I've met one; he's great. I haven't met the others as yet so my heart is in my mouth. But I suppose they couldn't hate me any more than dad will." He leaned in and Solly and Alice drew closer. "After I got off the phone with you, I threw up anxious about Dad's reaction. You've helped me with Mum; but Dad – yikes."

"Dad might surprise you because he loves you more than he lets on," Solly told him. "He wants you to love him, Dave, he's told me; full of all kinds of pain." Michael touched his shoulder, and he jumped. Michael caressed his face, and that calmed David.

Veronika knocked on the front door of Adrian's student digs and waited. It was a chilly empty morning with no traffic driving up or down the residential street. She was a bit overdressed in her Burberry pants suit and their iconic tan tartan scarf, but her barley blonde hair styled into wavy curls made her look so sexy. He came to the door in jeans and baggy T-shirt, and after a few moments, he switched from his early morning daze into sharp focus when he saw her. "What are you doing here?"

"I'm here because I'm very worried about your father. Something dreadful has happened to him." He dismissively waved her away as someone totally unimportant.

"I have to come in and speak privately. I can't risk anyone hearing me."

Adrian doubled his fists but then put his hands in his pockets. "Unlike Dad who was raised under the strictest Nigerian high-minded discipline, I'm more basic so wha' you want?" he said pointing in her face.

"I have to come in to speak privately."

"If you come in and chat shit, I'd have to fling you out, and I'm not going to jail for touching you. So talk or piss off."

"You've become so hard and horrible. Don't be proud of it." She came closer and said quietly, "You father has turned into a homosexual." Adrian heard her, but he didn't register it. "He's queer; he has a boyfriend, well, a man he's involved with."

"Get your lying arse away from here. Chat shit. What the hell you…" Veronika held up her mobile and showed him the picture of David and Michael kissing. He looked and kept trying to focus. "You bring your cheap whoring arse up here to tell me some shit about Dad with photoshop queer pictures. Listen, bitch, fuck off!"

He went in and slammed the door in her face. Unperturbed, she went into her bag and took out an envelope of pictures that showed David with Michael in Canonbury Gardens and pushed it through the letterbox and then she casually left.

After a few minutes, Adrian came out of the living room into the hallway, saw the envelope and picked it up and opened it. He looked at them and with each one somewhere in his soul he knew they were not fakes they were candid images. The hallway felt as if they were closing in and the untidy house shrank as he made his way back upstairs bumping into one of his housemates on the stairs. He was a final year, exceptionally gifted IT designer who was unfortunately saddled with a dismal face.

Adrian went into his room and locked the door. He had one poster of Nelson Mandela, one of a gorgeous Black woman, the poster of his family of the day he David open his business, and a lovely picture of his father during his radio days on air with headphones with friends around him. Adrian picked up his mobile and went down the list of contacts and came to Mum and dad and his finger twitched between the two.

He sat down and stared into space trying to make sense of what the photographs told him and what he knew. Adrian never thought that his dad could be gay. He rushed and got his laptop and Googled: '*What to do if your dad is gay*'. There were many entries and blogs along with advice information so Adrian began reading them over a three hour period of time and discovered Robert De Niro's father, who was an artist, was also gay. When he looked up famous gay men, he was flabbergasted by the number of well know people throughout history who were gay. He found the London Lesbian and Gay Switchboard and called.

"I just found out my Dad's gay. I'm twenty; my Dad's thirty-seven. We're close, like real friends. Dad loves football, and he's great with my mum and he's been married but recently divorced. Should I tell my mum or ask her if she knows?" The staff provided him with excellent advice and continually asked how he felt and if he needed to be referred to see someone but he told them no he didn't.

After he had hung up, he went to the bathroom, drew a cool bath and got in and kept the hot water running until the tub was exceptionally hot. He lay there and searched back in his mind for links and clues that would tell him or show him where he should have spotted the difference between straight and not. He suddenly remembered the radio show where David announced we should put a stop to homophobic rants in rap, ragga, and hip-hop music because it degraded people's life and struggles and denigrated their humanity and human rights. As the water cooled down, he became more heated because now he asked himself why David didn't tell him. He got out of the tub ready for a fight and left the bathroom in just a towel.

Liz, one of the girls in the house, saw him walking up the corridor and stopped. Liz was one of the 'darlings' of York. She was a popular and well-loved girl because she was pretty and stylish. She was Sanja's girl. He was mixed race and a nice friend who Adrian liked because he was a good scholar of politics and social theory and he supported Arsenal. Adrian didn't like Liz because she frequently asked impertinent questions about what Blacks are really like. Whereas Sanja was from London, keenly aware of Black and White social history and he understood multicultural politics. Liz was a County girl from Plymouth, who was racially naïve. Adrian didn't understand why she didn't learn more, considering the guy she was going out with; so he mentally filed her as irrelevant, but he tolerated her.

"Finally, you're up and out of your room. What have you been doing? Have you got a girl stashed away in there?" Her facetious tone of voice really needled him.

"Don't make my life your business."

"Oh fuck you then."

Staring at her scornfully, he said, "You're pretty but really ugly." When he walked away, she couldn't get the scornful look on his face out of her mind. Back in his room, he sat down despondent and depressed and after a time he called his mother.

CHAPTER TWENTY-FOUR

By late afternoon Adrian arrived back home in London, he opened the front door and let himself in. Grace came out of the kitchen, and he pulled back from the hug she wanted to give him, and she saw it. "What's up? You sounded so serious on the phone. You've dashed back home, what is it?"

"Is it true about dad?"

"What? Is what true? What's..." and she ran out of words.

"Veronika came up to my digs this morning and told me..." He walked into the living room and sat down and then stood up again. He pressed his lips together, and he seemed to be on the verge of an outburst, but he clenched his fists and spoke. "She said..." He closed his eyes. "She said dad has turned into a homosexual."

Grace threw her hands up and shouted. "That filthy cunt! You're not going to pay any attention to that blood sucking whore."

"She had pictures." He went into his jacket pocket and handed them to her. She looked at them, and her anger and anxiety wrote itself across her face.

Adrian knew her so well he said, "They don't shock you! They don't horrify you!!! You're not disgusted by what you see?" She slapped him to calm him down, and he grabbed her wrist. "You know about this, don't you?"

"Do you think your father is a pervert?"

He took a moment, and he was clearly angry at her words. "Dad is not a pervert; don't you dare talk about him like that."

"I have loved your father ever since I saw him heading off to private school. I was fourteen. He was nice to me. We became friends and instead of us going out together we became confidants who'd tell each other everything. He was so well mannered, had that African intonation in his voice; spoke correct English." She went to the telephone and dialed. "He always looked impeccable in his uniform. I wished my family were rich like his. At my school boys smelt stink and looked worse, but David talked to me on the way to school and came here when he got back. He had knowledge beyond his years, so he knew I loved him and we eventually started going out. Our families were so happy, especially your Uncle Erwin." David answered the phone. "David I have to see you immediately. That vampire you married went up to your son's student house and told him you're a homo and gave him pictures to prove it: you and a white guy kissing in a park." He listened. "Adrian came home, he's right here." Grace listened and then ended the call. "We're going to your father right now."

****

David and Michael got out of bed and rushed about the room. "Let me call Roberto, he can speak to your son... they're sort of peers. He'll understand Adrian's mindset since they are dealing with us turning away from heterosexuality."

"Yes! Oh darling thanks, call him. I was going to speak to Adrian this week, but Veronika went up there with destruction on her mind. I'm going to make her sorry."

"She took pictures of us, because of what you have on her." Michael got his mobile and called Roberto as David dashed into the bathroom.

David looked at himself in jeans, African shirt with an African necklace and a crucifix. "This is the wrong way to go. I should be formal, so he knows as his father I have the authority..."

"No really stop it. You are his father. Wear anything." He kissed David.

"Who'll get here first, Roberto's coming from Bar Italia in Soho..."

The doorbell rang and David rushed to it. Michael followed him. Roberto was at the door. Michael rushed to him and spoke rapidly in Italian. Roberto nodded and listened to his father closely as they headed into the living room briefing each other for two minutes.

As Michael continued to speak and listen, the bell rang again. Roberto touched Michael's neck with the flat of his hand and nodded at him. David took a breath, left the room and went to the front door. Grace came in first followed my Adrian.

"Before we say anything, there are people here I want you to meet Adrian. I'm sorry Veronika came to your place like that. Michael and Roberto are here." He led them into the living room, and Roberto came forward at once.

"You guys, take a minute before you get all defensive and parental. Hi Adrian, that's my dad, Michael, I'm his youngest son Roberto." He walked Adrian out of the living room. David was a bit confused but introduced Grace to Michael. "This is Michael. Show me the pictures Veronika took."

"Adrian has them,"

Michael said, "Your ex, saw what she saw. That's part of the truth, but pictures don't always tell the true story. Grace, we should have met differently, but it's good to meet you." Michael offered his hand, and she took it unhesitatingly.

In the media lounge, Roberto said to Adrian. "Papa and your father, they aren't shagging, they're in love. Papa was almost suicidal before the divorce. When I first found out, I saw him kissing a guy at the National Gallery in public, bold as brass. I had a bitch fit like some hysterical girl who keeps texting you after you've broken up. I cried – I mean Gwyneth Paltrow blubber, it was ugly. Don't break his balls if you love him, do you and your dad get on?"

"Yeah, I got in a twist after that slag came to my digs this morning. Imagine that. The bitch comes all the way up to York to tell me Dad's gay."

"Fuck her, let David tell you. I want this to be good for all of us. We're going to be family from the way Papa's talking, so it's best we get it right from the beginning. You might need to help me with my elder brothers and sister because whatever your dad has to say when we go back in there, it's a preview of the hysteria I'll have to deal with when my brothers and sister do their... 'Oh my God this can't be happening to us' opera. I'm talking Italian meets Jamaican indignation, plus the homophobic shit," Roberto switched to patois. "You understand wha'-me-a-say?" Adrian was gobsmacked.

"Italian and Jamaican, what's that like?" Adrian asked bemused.

"Pure drama and totally hilarious at times. My Mum is the business. She met your dad and thinks he's nice." Adrian was clearly surprised. "I know; you came in late so you've missed half the match. I'll tell you the rest after Papa and your dad turn their guts inside out trying to explain how much they 'love each other'," he said dramatically. "I'm actually instrumental in introducing Papa to your dad."

"What do you mean?"

"I'll tell you later. Let's get in there. Your dad must be bursting by now." He pushed Adrian ahead of him and they left the cool room.

They entered the living room, and David braced himself and shot a look over to Michael. He took Grace's hand as if he'd known her for years. Ordinarily, she'd never tolerate that level of familiarity so soon, but Michael was shaking and she couldn't stop her concern for him. She placed her hand over his as Adrian and Roberto sat down.

David said, "We're gathered here like it's some kind of who-done-it where the murderer will be exposed when I've displayed my ingenuity and powers of deduction. Let me save you that long winded mess. Adrian, Michael and I met very recently; we're right for each other. I psyched myself into being married, but it wasn't difficult because I loved Veronika. I rejected everything gay and remained faithful."

"Dad…"

"No, wait. I'm in love with Michael. My marriage showed me I can't live a lie. I've seen analysts and fought with my demons in the face of praying to God for salvation and truth. Your mother knows I've struggled since I was fourteen. She was my lifeline as a kid; that's why I love her, and we started going out and then had you."

"A lot of Dad's secrecy was necessary because we know Nigerian and Jamaican laws about manhood…"

"Grace, do you mind, he's my son…"

"Yeah, but you're not telling him what you ought to say. Your father dragged you to Nigeria and put you through some Voodoo Obeah shit to make you normal."

"Grace shut your mouth!!" She pulled back, and Michael and Roberto shared a look. David steadied himself as tears came to his eyes. He took a breath and went over to Adrian. "Your grandfather thought I was possessed with something evil. I don't want to talk about that. I did my best to live as our community expects. The whole Black man, pussy posse, tough righteous, Empire Windrush, Black British pride t'ing. In the beginning, Veronika understood this more than you'd think. I loved her disavowal of racism because she isn't a racist. She also gave me unconditional love in the beginning. She was looking for meaning in her life too. She was tired of the vampire, communist, peasant shit that people labeled her with. We shared a lot."

"But she still managed to kill your two kids, though, don't forget that part."

"Kill your kids?" Roberto asked stunned.

210

"That drug fiend," Grace angrily replied, "put all kind of shit into her body and miscarried! Twice mind you! Me, Cynthia and everyone that we knew comforted her after the miscarriage." Grace stood up and pointed at David. "He defended her on the grounds she was depressed. If that bitch had been a decent, honorable woman and loving mother, he'd have two other sons. But no…she wanted to be a star. One time she told me how much talent she has, but the bitch couldn't sing."

"That's what depressed her Grace," David said pleading for compassion.

"Did I get depressed when you married her and not me, yes! Did I take drugs – No! You know why? Because I'm not a deluded nasty slut!"

Roberto told her. "Grace, you're gonna love my Mum when you meet her. The two of you will chat forever. But we're getting off course. Your ex-wife isn't the issue, David. Clearly, she's fucked because if she thinks she can bash a Black man and get away with it; she must be back on drugs because that shit is a beating waiting to happen." Michael's look of pride in his son was unmistakable. "The point here is Adrian didn't know you were gay and it doesn't matter why you're gay now, the point is you love Papa, and the two of you want to be together, right?"

"Yes, but I can't be happy if you cut me off. Or condemn me to that damnation that belligerent Black righteousness demands. I can't lose you, boy; you've always been the happiest part of my life." Tears fell out of him.

"Daddy, please don't… I could never do you like that. No matter how much love you got for me, you're ten times that in my heart man." Adrian got up and pulled his father close to him. He led David out of the room and Grace watched them profoundly affected by the bond between them.

"I'm not some shrill bitch, but that wretch took a lot from me. She was supposed to look after my man. Instead, she turned nasty, and then this morning she takes her arse up to York to hurt my son; degrading his dad as a queer." Grace silently cursed a stream of profanities under her breath, but Michael could see her mouth moving.

Michael told her. "Don't reproach yourself, Grace. If she was dealing with my ex, we'd be in the police station now…" Roberto laughed knowingly because their family knew not to provoke Lola. "Lola would have torn her face open because no one fucks with her! She has that Jamaican rage that will strip any crazy bastard."

Grace told Michael. "That is a Sista of my Clan. You married a Jamaican?"

"I have a passionate admiration for Black women. I courted and married Lola because she is the most fantastic woman I've ever met."

As only a Black British woman of Caribbean heritage can command, Grace said, "As you know, David is nothing like a woman."

"True, but he has amazing Afro-sexual power and intelligence. When I set eyes on him, I was totally captivated all at once."

Grace turned to Roberto. "You don't have a problem with your dad being gay?"

"I'd have a problem with him shagging blokes and lying to me. But Papa falling in love, and coming back to life is something I'm grateful to David for."

Upstairs in David's office surrounded by photographs of his family Adrian spoke in hushed tones. "Less than two weeks and you're sure about Michael, living a gay life and dealing with the shit to come?"

"Yes; he's a Professor of Black Culture, he never chats shit about 'blacks' because his wife has taught him a lot. For some amazing reason, I don't feel afraid anymore. He's kind to me. The man is solid me-tell-you-say!"

"Are you getting it on?"

"Yes," David replied without flinching, looking away or any embarrassment.

"You've been fighting this since you were fourteen?" David nodded. "How did you do that?"

"Prayer, analysis, counseling, more prayer: but what really kept me straight is knowing I am your father. As a teenager, I wanted to die. Every dirty utterance that Africans or Caribbean's said about gays terrified and haunted me. Even now it makes me crazy to hear that kind of homophobic shit! It's a kind of psychological terrorism. I've escaped gay bashing, but I know what it's like."

"What did Grandad do to you?" David started trembling, and he couldn't speak. "Tell me." David shook his head. "Tell me, or I'll go over there and get in his face…"

"No, leave it. He hates me enough as it is."

"How can he hate you when you're a credit to our name? What did he do?"

David looked off and spoke. "When he discovered I had gay tendencies he wanted to cleanse them out of me," David told him everything and Adrian broke down in tears. David took his hankie and wiped his son's face and told him to blow his nose.

"After all that, I regained my sanity by defying dad." Adrian was fascinated. "Gus, the first love of my life, he helped to cleanse me of the brainwashing and crap they did to me. He's a brilliant psychiatrist, he worked on me for years, and I gave him what he needed. He loves Black life, not like some of the fucking horrible Wiggers I've had to talk to in the media and industry, Angus is a man of learning and taught me a lot. He got me into the Men's Group where I met Michael."

"Did your wife know about any of this?"

"No, I couldn't tell anyone except your mother. It was only today that I told your Aunt Alice, and her kids, Uncle Solly knew about me as a boy, and he kept his mouth shut. I told grandma yesterday. I was mentally all over the place, gathering strength so I could come and tell you. I didn't want to fall apart."

"And all of this is because you met Michael?"

"Yes, I love him no doubt about it. The two of you have the same birthday. He and his sons sit three rows behind us at Emirates; his favorite restaurant in London is Mum's place. He read my book and was inspired by me before we even met."

"His son Roberto was telling me something about that. Talk about six degrees of separation."

"That's not all. The night I first said to you 'I'm gay' was on my birthday. But I got drowned out when Arsenal scored a goal." David could see Adrian recalling the day. "Well, Michael and his sons were sitting behind us. On top of that Lola, Michael's ex-wife and Mum are from the same Parish in Jamaican but never met.

"You told me you are gay?" He thought about it and remembered the football match when David suddenly became overwrought. "That's the night you were nuts. I knew there was something weird. So you did try to tell me. In fact, you told me before everyone else."

"Yes."

"What does it feel like to disown women and sex with them?"

"Sex means nothing to me without love. I like women because I'm not threatened by them. I struggled through all kinds of mess thinking – If I tell you I'm gay and you become like Dad; cold hearted toward me…" Adrian oscillated between emotionally reaching out or holding back, but he ran his hand through David's hair. "Anyway, the years of agony is over; if Michael can put up with me and not flee because I'm too much. You need more than sex to maintain a happy, lasting relationship. But I think we stand a good chance because I totally like his son."

213

"He's so 'take charge' and in your face, I only just met him, but I like him."

"Well, I have his others sons and daughter to meet. That could be tricky. But I say that knowing Michael is going to have to deal with Dad."

"What about Veronika. Since she came to shit on me what else is she plotting?"

"If she's planning to 'out me' I have to beat her to the punch. I mean her heroine is Catherine Tramell." Adrian was puzzled. "*Basic Instinct*."

"Dad, don't go public. In social media, there are evil psychopaths. They'll say you've been living a lie. Some people will feel it's their right to assault you."

"Another guy said the same thing. I'll confound the homophobic diatribe by showing I fucked her." A wicked smile crept onto his face. "I have some of the hottest footage of Veronkia and me. I'm shagging her deluxe and doing anal."

"Are you serious?" Adrian asked, shocked.

"If I put that online she can show her pictures and talk whatever shit she wants. I've had her and also kicked her boyfriend's arse." Adrian was confused, so David explained filming her at home and then filming her and Horia in the hotel room.

"To fuck her and whip his arse! That is so miniMum wage vengeance!"

"No one is going to humiliate me and I just take it."

"You're no pussy. You're balls out tough." He grabbed David and hugged him longingly without a trace of fear, shame or discomfort. "You must be the 'man'?"

It took a short time for David to really hear his question but when he did, he stepped back and said, "Michael and I don't do that." Adrian didn't dare ask his father anything else.

When Michael came into the room, there was an awkward moment, but Adrian kept looking at him suspiciously. "You better be for real because if you're playing with my dad," he smiled beguilingly. "I'm going to be violently happy to kick your arse from here to hell." The smile vanished, and they locked eyes. Adrian felt sweat break out on his chest and down his back.

"Papa, get Adrian down here!!" his son shouted from downstairs.

"Roberto is waiting for you. He wants to take you to a club or something. For sure there will be wall-to-wall pussy so get going. He has the key for my flat in town. Park the car and take a cab from my place to where you're going in town and take a cab back. He has a credit card of mine, use it. Do not let him drive after you get to the flat."

Adrian paid attention to what Michael said and nodded that he'd look out for Roberto. "Can we have lunch tomorrow, Dad?"

"Yes, come to my office. Solly and Aunt Alice are here so I'll hook us all up." Adrian kissed his father and offered his hand to Michael, who kissed him on the head. He looked at David and Michael. "Gay Dads, that's no joke." He left, and David reached out for Michael rather unsettled.

CHAPTER TWENTY-FIVE

Roberto drove Adrian through London's city of night, and it was clear Adrian had a lot on his mind. "This is weird for you, right? Knowing about your dad? Did you suspect?" Roberto asked him.

"No, nothing, he's not gay in the way I see gays at University. Dad's not interested in hair, make-up, pop girls and boy bands. He can build things; he loves Arsenal, football in general. He won the Duke of Edinburgh Award for sports. He has a ferocious kickboxing martial arts temper if he's pushed too far. You won't see him run from a fight and gays that I've seen don't go violent if someone is out of order. Dad doesn't make creepy dick jokes the way Graham Norton acts... girlie."

"Nor does Papa: he is every inch a man." Roberto let out a loud laugh and couldn't stop.

"What?"

"The whole family was on holiday in Jamaica once when some babe was drowning, and Papa swam out to save her. After he carried her back to shore, he then gave her mouth to mouth he got a boner. My brothers were shocked, and my sister was freaked. When Maria told my mum, she said: 'a real man always shows himself in life and death situations and Papa is the best'. Maria said it was nasty and Mama told her to pay more attention in biology and watch more nature programs."

"Was Michael embarrassed that you guys saw him like that?"

"No. Sex isn't taboo in our family. We sometimes heard them in the middle of the night, and it wasn't even like a dirty joke to my brothers or me. There are nude photographs of them in their 20s and 30s in the house, really beautiful; it speaks of their European and African equality, their heritage and culture. The PC philosophy of don't let the kids know parents fuck is totally sick! We grew up always knowing they loved each other mentally and physically. I'm glad because moral guardians and uptight religious freaks make me sick."

"Growing up was very different in my house. Mum is really involved with the Black Pentecostal Church were Christian emotional outpouring is Ok. But sex isn't something that's flaunted. Mum lives by those standards, my grandpa loves her for it. I've only seen Mum… sexually blatant maybe three times, ever! Dad has always had an alpha sexual mystique that women love. I looked it up a few years back when he was swamped with fan mail after his appearance on TV."

"Yeah, I saw that."

"He danced up the aisle and onstage, gave his acceptance speech and danced away with a babe presenting him with the award. All the girls thought he was hot and the boys thought he was cool. I was such a star at St Alfred's after that. Do you know it; it's a great school that builds creative intellectuals." Roberto nodded. "Dad never comes on strong sexually with women, they gravitate towards him, and I've seen him back off. But maybe that's because he was more interested in blokes, I don't know. What do you think they're like in bed?"

"The ins and outs don't matter, it's Papa's psychological transformation and the rebels they've become." They drove up Euston Road and turned off into Great Portland Street. Four minutes later Roberto parked, and he told Adrian to come up.

Inside the lift up to the flat Adrian asked. "What do you do?"

"Filmmaker, I'm in the final year of my MA at the European Film School."

"Have you made lots of films?"

"About twenty documentaries. Papa paid for me to study here and in Italy."

"Dad paid for me too."

Roberto smiled at that, led him out of the lift and into the flat. Adrian didn't think it was as grand as the address and location might suggest.

"I know, it's shit, but the new house in Canonbury is fantastic."

"I didn't say anything." Roberto closed the apartment door and threw his coat off.

"You didn't have to. I have to change for the party I want to take you too. Beautiful girls will be there. I met them at Bar Italia earlier today. Have you got a girlfriend? Do you want to come?"

"Yes, we're dating. These girls, are they Italian, Black, Asian babes, what?"

"Latinas from South America and Italy; they told me to come over."

"I'm not exactly dressed for a party."

"We're about the same size; take a look in the wardrobe."

"No, I can't wear your clothes, no I'll be fine."

217

"Adrian, something amazing has happened to bring us together; our fathers have fallen in love and want to be something special. How many guys are in our situation? For the bigots and idiots, they can fixate on the moral taboo but us we have to ask, 'what is a real man?' This could change what kind of men we grow up to be. I don't want to be a media bloke who thinks like other naïve drones. I want to be a great thinker and important filmmaker."

"This whole day, from that bitch coming to my place, then traveling down from York, the family drama and this is doing my head in."

"Don't bail, there's more to you than panic and denial. You've got your mum's fight and your dad's courage; this is the time to grow those balls."

Adrian was about to speak, but he couldn't get his thoughts and words to come out of his mouth. The events of the day sped through his mind and he was suddenly consumed with anger and distress but before he could stop himself he dropped his head and arms onto his knees and began crying terribly. Roberto watched him and then he sat next to him and put his arm around his back. Adrian sobbed, and Roberto pulled him in close.

"I do love him still, I do. Why did he have to turn queer and…" He couldn't say anything else he just cried and Roberto held onto him tightly.

****

David strutted about his living room enraged. "Tell your sister to call me!" He listened. "Don't fucking tell me you don't know where Veronkia is because you maybe in Romania but I'll have cops over at your house!" Michael and Grace flinched. "Your drug loving cunt of a sister distressed my son this morning. She tried to make me disgusting in my son's eyes." His stalking came to a dead halt, and Grace smiled because she knew him and she'd seen him like that before. Michael, on the other hand, was seeing another side of him.

"I will burn down the flat she lives in. So tell that blood sucker this cocksucker isn't afraid of anyone on this planet! She calls me in under ten minutes or she'll be homeless and prostitute, I mean destitute." He switched off his mobile. "Get me a sweet-lash!" Grace didn't move, and he gave her a look that threatened to erupt if she defied him. She got up and went to the bar and he got on the landline phone. Michael watched them stalk and move around with power and rage. The room felt alive.

"Bankole here. Use the DVD film and move to phase three. I told you she'd never be able to behave. She's a vile junky, I want her to feel the first lash on Tuesday morning. I'll contact my lawyers, but I have full rights and clearance on the video. If it isn't online Tuesday morning, you're fired!" He hung up.

"What are you gonna do?" Grace asked handing him his glass of white rum.

He gave her a sinister look and his mouth twisted into a smile. He sat beside Michael.

"You'll love it. It's made of Jamaican rage and Nigerian punishment." He took a sip of the drink and gave it to Michael. "63% alcohol overproof."

Michael drank some. "Fuck me! What's the aftertaste?" he asked whipping his fingers.

"Vanilla," he and Grace replied and laughed together. His mobile rang, and his entire body stiffened up as his face tightened. He answered the call.

"Yes." He stalked the room listening to her. "The last bastard who fucked with me is now living in poverty in Africa." He listened. "Most people in the world think that Blacks are depraved and inferior. I didn't need to go to University to learn how evil white supremacists are. I am going to take a leaf from that book and deal with your degenerate existence." Michael felt his accusation and threat head on. "You're like one of those lying white women who got Black men lynched and castrated. Not this time!" Grace watched him excited by his rage and Michael studied her.

"Do you remember when we discovered you have no talent and you fell into a depression? Then you took to drugs. And even when you tried to kill yourself, I helped you recover from that. Then today you took yourself up to York to demean me and yes, you did injure my son." He listened to her.

"Yes, I have turned queer. That's true I do suck cock." He sneered and bit his lip and yelled through clenched teeth. "You don't know if I take it up the arse. I know *you* do!" Grace covered her mouth.

"Since you're a Godless unclean witch! I've arranged a bit of Yoruba retribution for you…" She was cursing him, and he switched the mobile to speaker so Michael and Grace could hear her.

'A dirty pervert like you who lied to me… did you fuck a lot of men and hide behind me? In the divorce did you slander me and hide the fact you're a queer cum slut?'

"You're so boring. Remember when you called me and cried poverty I said if you were desperate I would help you because poverty is no joke."

"You offered to help her!" Grace cried.

"Oh, that mother is there," Veronika said. *"I had the best of him!! He rejected you for some reason… whatever! Maybe it's because you're a nasty bitch!"*

Grace got off the sofa, shoved her face at the mobile and yelled, "I'm the mother of his son, and your pussy is a drug cesspool. But as my son reminded me, if *you* gave birth, what kind of Godless evil Xenomorph would we have in the family." Michael was shocked by her statement.

"What does that mean? Answer me you fucking cunt!"

"If I see you I'll drag your arse to a church and drop you in Holy water and then you'll die as all satanic creatures should." Grace said with her fingers arched.

"Veronika, you had your say this morning when you went to my son. I will have a response to that soon. You can say whatever you want about me to anyone you like. There was only one person walking this earth that use to scare me, and I'm about to deal with him: a word of warning. Add one lie to anything you say about me, and I'll eviscerate you." He cut her off.

"What are you going to do to her?" Michael asked.

"Get my money's worth. I'm putting our sexual exploits online. I have the film ready to go with voice-over commentary and text. I have her letter of confession to adultery with that convicted human trafficker and all kinds of shit. She can tell the world I'm 'queer', but the fact is we're not. I reject those terms as much as I reject being classified a nigger."

"What did you mean, get your money's worth?" Grace asked him.

"When I première the sexual truth of our marriage it will be free for 12 hours in Europe and 12 hours in the US. After that, it will be on a paid site. And I've had people working on a pay-per-click which will bring in 'fuck you' money."

"Are you willing to risk your reputation?" Michael asked.

"Don't play with your enemies, destroy them."

"Not even Lola has this level of confrontation. And she hit her father."

"Great… hold that thought." He got his mobile and dialed again. David walked over and gave him a kiss. That was the first time Grace had ever seen him kiss a man, so her Christian philosophy with its moral worldview, her life as his best friend, and knowing she shouldn't have told his father anything about David's tendencies played mayhem with her emotions.

"I love this room," David said to himself. "Gus would be so proud of me right now."

Michael told Grace. "This morning we were sky high, and now we're in orbit."

"Hello, this is your son. I was going to come to you and plead and beg for your understanding, but I changed my mind. I have a newsflash: I'm homosexual, meaning, I have a man who I have luxurious sex with. So – the treatment and voodoo shit didn't take." He listened. "Yes, I know what time it is." He pulled faces to show Grace and Michael his father's response. "No, I'm not joking. I am in love with a... marvelous... gentle man. He got a big cock, loads of money and a high I.Q!" He listened. "Since you're screaming at me I know you're awake so goodnight." He hung up.

"I can't believe you just did that," Grace told him.

"I can't believe I did *that*." David had a bewildered expression of fear and fascination on his face. "Instead of pleading and humbling myself, I just told my father I'm in love with a man and he can smoke it." He laughed very nervously.

"Darling sit down," Michael told him, and David complied.

Self-mockingly he said: "Oh Dad – please I beg you, with all my heart try to understand I'm not a pervert." He changed his expression into that of a willful teenager without a conscious and sullenly stated. "No! I'm in love with a man; Fuck you if you don't like it." He laughed and fell silent. Michael decided he was burnt out.

"Grace. I don't have my car. If I pay a minicab for you will you be Ok? He has to stop now. He's had too much for one day. He has to stop, and I can't leave him."

"You're going to take care of him?"

Michael looked her in the eyes because he heard her questions in two ways. "Yes." She got the answer she knew and at the same time didn't want to hear because she also knew she'd lost him. Michael saw her ambivalence and took out his mobile to call a cab. He left her with David and stepped out of the room.

****

At 07:25 a.m. the next day David was at the gym dressed in his brown belt Judo Gi suit with his Keyi his Judo trainer. Michael had his eyes on David filled with tension and anxiety because David looked ready to commit grievous body harm. His trainer, the thirty-year-old Japanese black belt went for David, and David blocked him and threw him all over the place. Even though Keyi got up quickly, Michael thought it looked dangerously painful, and his tense face revealed everything he felt.

David and Keyi spent twenty-two minutes in violent training but David bounced back with every throw and after he pinned Kayi down and got him to smack the mat three times in surrender they got up and laughed together. It was a sight that pierced Michael's tension. David brought Keyi over to Michael. Sweating, but smiling he said, "Keyi, this is Michael. He's my boyfriend, but he's really a man."

"No more wife?"

"No," and he turned to Michael, took him in his arms and kissed him.

Keyi clapped his hands together once, and it loudly echoed in the gym. He said in Japanese. "Congratulations, it takes balls to be a man's man," and then he repeated it in English. He bowed to Michael and smiled at David.

"Will you teach him the art of Kung Fu, Keyi?"

"Please you run ten times," Keyi pointed around the gym, and they both ran.

They jogged, and Michael said, "Listen; say I'm typical white guy watching your video. What will hit me is your dominance over Veronika. I could hate you because she's a white woman and you're a Black man and that history is as violent as it is nasty."

"That's why I going to expose her. If you think I didn't learn from the Michael Jackson media trials and other Black men accused by vicious bitches you're wrong. Living in this Black body, most people think I'm depraved and inferior."

"Let me help you with this. I have a brand new house. You can present a media show. People like you, Veronika is a nobody. I know very powerful men and women around the world I've bought Art for. They'll back me. Lola and my kids will too." Michael increased his jogging pace.

"You'd do this for me?"

"Give me 24 hours to turn you from a scandal monger into a man reclaiming his life from a Siren. Expose her adultery, the death of your sons and most of all her journey to York to destroy you in Adrian's mind. Her actions are unjust and if I know anything about life since 9/11…"

"Bloody hell, we're on the same wavelength." They both said it together. "The public will find her guilty."

"The weird thing is how stupid she's acting," Michael said. "We've just met but I know messing with your son would be my biggest mistake."

"I won't be her victim. People will see her as a white goddess, so I'll use evidence to prove she's a dishonorable lying bitch. Can *you* face coming out in public?"

"Love untested is just *fucking* talk: all ego and no spiritual heart and truth." Michael took off, alone, and he kept running around the gym gaining strength. David watched him and the grit and heart that filled Michael brought a smile to David's face. Keyi watched David and looked at Michael running and studied the two of them.

"This is the first time I see love in you," he said, happy for his friend.

"Maybe: he's so beautiful." Running around the gym in his trainers, shorts, and vest, Keyi saw the energy and weakness in Michael's aging body and David saw the grace and power of him.

BOOK THREE

Love and Hate

Winter 2015

CHAPTER TWENTY-SIX

Willy and Sophia watched David beam at them happily in his Monday meeting. Dressed in his purple mohair and silk three-piece-suit, brilliant white shirt with a short collar and narrow black tie and standing in his blue suede shoes, Sophia eyed him up. She couldn't explain what it was, but he seemed haughty. Willy was perplexed and strangely threatened by David's demeanor. At the start of the meeting, Willy thought it was their clothes, but he was also well dressed in a gray suit, and black shirt, which he filled out nicely. However, he felt outclassed and vulnerable throughout the meeting.

David moved away from his desk toward the glass wall and observed his staff. They were all hard at work. He got a great rush as he recalled Michael making love to him earlier with the pounding beat of the album *Controversy* by Prince playing in the living room. When they returned from the Judo class, they were of one mind. Consequently, David was now conscious of the fact he was truly loved, and in love, and that's what Sophia and Willy couldn't deduce.

David turned around to face Sophia and Willy. "There is a sex tape that's going to be aired online tomorrow, and I want you to help me manage the media campaign."

"Sounds nice, whose tape is it?" Willy asked smiling.

"Mine – me and Veronika." His voice was neutral, but his face was gleeful.

"Motherfucker yes!" Sophia turned to Willy disapprovingly. "Sorry just listening. Mess her up! The number of times that bitch sent me for her shopping."

Acerbically, Sophia asked. "Why are you doing this David?"

"Because I want to," he replied laconically, with a smile.

She crossed her legs and began fidgeting, so Willy tried to conceal his amusement.

Willy said, "Woman, you're giving off a negative vibe, and you sound judgmental. If Veronika was running her mouth on David, he'd just be a mug getting slapped, by some bitch with issues." He went off on a

Jamaican rant, and she eye-balled him with scolding eyes. "Look at me however you want, but you'll never know what it's like to be the black villain with the dirty cops looking to frame you, and people slander you because being Black makes you the blank space to write nasty shit…"

"You're referring to a *tabula-rasa*," David said.

"Look there, the man knows language and issues. You gal dem have you business, and you-no-know how the man-dem…" He saw clearly that she was getting angrier. "Look don't put yourself in Black man business; you don't know the history."

"And don't come up on me like this, or you won't get no pussy tonight," she replied in mock patois. David laughed and clapped his hands together.

"We're getting off point. And Sophia, I have to say living here for eight years can't cover the life expectancy of any Black man dealing with institutionalized racism so Willy is entitled to speak even if it rubs you up the wrong way."

"I know, but sometimes he works this black and white experienced history…"

"Epistemology…"

"Yes, whatever," she replied, even more, annoyed.

Willy said, "Don't do that… 'whatever' shit. We're talking about men's lives getting trashed and bashed in Britain, that isn't a *whatever*. That brutality is nasty. I didn't go to University like you two but I've had the Met and the racist executives in suits spit on me and that, Lady, ain't no joke!"

"Hey Willy, easy. As a mixed race man in a bi-racial relationship…"

Sophia said, "You were in a mixed relationship, David, what did you learn? You divorced her because she was a two-timer who went back to one of her own. I mean, what does that say about your marriage?"

"As accusing and vicious as your comment is Sophia, I'm not dealing with that right now."

Willy said, "She does that all the time, instead of listening, she slams you with personal troubles and pains we've lived with."

Sophia said, "You're not even Black so shut up!"

He looked at her. "When I get stopped by the Met you think it's because I'm white?"

"Enough already!" David told the two of them.

Sophia said, "We were just having a discussion; I wasn't condoning police misconduct."

Smiling, David said, "A little more love is what you both need." They looked at each other and silently agreed they were both hot headed and naïve.

"My tape is a documentary now. Tomorrow is the launch and the after-party."

"Where? What's booked? Who's coming?" Sophia asked.

"Michael De Farenzino is handling most of the event."

"That hot Italian guy?"

David couldn't stop smiling and then trying to suppress his smile. "Yes, that hot guy."

"What's with you, man?" Willy asked. So David sat on the end of his desk.

"You should both know I've reached a point in my life where I've come to terms with the truth. I'm gay, I'm in love, and I'm very happy."

The smile slipped off Willy's face as though a man felt him up.

"What do you mean gay?"

"Just that; I could say I'm Bi, but that wouldn't be the truth."

Willy backed into the chair, and Sophia was genuinely dumbfounded. Confused, Willy asked David. "Grace, beautiful Grace is the mother of your son and Adrian is proof of your manhood; how is that... gay?"

"I'm telling you, I'm in love?"

"With who?" Willy demanded to know getting to his feet.

David watched both of them and in all the years he'd known Sophia he'd never seen her lost for words or puzzled as she clearly was. He moved away from them and when and sat in his seat behind his desk.

"Michael De Farenzino," he replied with a straight dead on look.

"What!!" They both exclaimed. Sophia stood up, and David swung from side to side in his executive chair as if he sealed a million-pound deal.

Michael was at his gym lifting weights with a gym buddy spotting him. His friend was a forty-year-old bouncer from one of London's nightclubs. He was the kind of Jamaican you shouldn't mess with because he grew up in Trench Town and even though he'd been in England for over twenty years the Caribbean toughness was instilled in him. At 20 stone, not many people befriended him because he was dark brown with a face like a bronze sculpture. Six months earlier he hit it off with Michael immediately because Michael understood the way prejudice work in people's minds and so when he offered Barry friendship without judgment they bonded quickly.

Michael finished the reps and Barry put the free weights back on the stand as he sat up. Michael's personal trainer Enzo was coming straight towards him. He was a typical fit gym character. He was a third generation Italian, but he'd never been to Italy nor did he speak Italian; he had a light West London Cockney accent which everyone heard when he yelled at Michael. "Can I talk to you?" Michael gave Barry the nod, and he stepped away. Enzo got in close and said to Michael. "Where the fuck have you been? I called you like thirty times all week, and you ignored my calls and text. I…"

"Shut up. We're finished. I met the love of my life last Sunday, and I've spent the week with him. It's been fantastic."

"Don't fucking tell me to piss off. Who is he?"

"That's none of your business. All you need to know is we're finished."

"I'm bound to find out who he is." Michael made no attempt to mask his boredom. He looked over at Barry in the near distance and chuckled for a second. Enzo looked over and saw their connection. "You can't just throw me aside."

"Go home and shag our wife. I'm sure she misses you."

In a cajoling tone of voice with pleading eyes, Enzo said: "Mikey, don't be horrible."

"Shut your mouth you big woman! I don't want to fuck you!!" Enzo heard a barbell drop in the gym. He looked around, and men were staring at him.

"What are you talking about you fucking narcissist." Michael punched him, and he staggered backward. He grabbed Enzo by the shirt, but he didn't see Barry come up behind him to eavesdrop.

"If Angelina knew it takes ten fucking inches to really get you off do you think she would divorce you or ask her brothers to beat you into a disabled mess?" Michael knuckle punched him in the mouth with the back of his fist and Enzo fell on the floor. As Michael walked away, he realized Barry had overheard him. Enzo was deeply ashamed when he saw the men in the gym look at him with contempt.

When Michael came out of the shower, he stopped abruptly. Barry was sitting on the bench in the changing room. Carrying 20 stone and a lot of anger he looked threatening. Michael went off in Italian and switched into English and said, "Yes, I'm in love with a man! So shove your Black righteous condemnation, or I will kick your arse here and now!"

'God give me strength; he's a heavyweight, but I'm gonna drop this bastard!' Michael took a fighting stance ready to attack. His whole body tapped into his military training and the vision of David fighting. He was fueled with Italian bravura.

"Rest yourself, man. I know how it is," Barry said as he got to his feet.

"I've got a great man who loves me. What have you got besides your hatred?"

"Not much. It's hard out here for a DJ, Bouncer. Especially when the man I fancy just told me he's got a man who loves him."

Surprised and stunned Michael said, "You're gay?"

"Yes. Enzo Dis' me one time, said he was no dinge queen; said you were his."

"What's a dinge queen?"

"A scummy white boy who only like likes 'Thugs' to fuck him."

Barry could see that Michael was physically horrified. "That is so disgusting."

"So you don't look down your nose on Black men."

"My ex-wife is Jamaican our kids are… my bloke is a Black man!".

Barry fondled himself which made Michael flinch and blush. "No way, no, no, no! I love David! This, nothing is gonna happen. *Basta*!!"

"Ok."

"God would smite me if I touched another man. Get your clothes on." Michael got dressed as quickly as he could. Barry asked him to wait.

"I have to arrange an Event party. I've only got a day – wait! You're a DJ." Barry nodded. "If you want to make some money for a DJ gig, meet me outside." Michael grabbed his things and headed out.

Barry came out the door onto Baker Street, and Michael waved at him. "Great! Time is important so let me ask." People rushed about the busy street in all directions. "Have you got everything to gig tomorrow night? Transport, help, lights and so on? I called a guy I know who does gallery DJ shows. I've used him before, but he isn't picking up so he could be overseas. The music has to fill a house."

"What kind of a house?" A Black woman caught sight of Barry and eyed him.

"No furniture, newly decorated, it's in Canonbury, North London; three floors. I want it to look like it's a house where Santa Claus hides out and watches sublime porn. The lights and props must be on a theme of Christmas in sexual paradise."

"I know a few guys. One decorates sets in a theater; another does events for a corporate firm. I have all kinds of speakers and sounds, a ton of tunes from every era – Black, Brazilian, Techno, House…" Michael cut in.

"Do you have any samples or scenes from your past gigs? My DJ has scenes on his iPad." A young executive banged into Michael and walked off. He stood still for a second and then went after the guy and grabbed him by the arm and stopped him.

"Hello, you can't just walk through me."

The French exec pulled his arm away and told him to "Piss off." Michael spat on his suit and told him in French to go and fuck himself.

Barry pulled Michael away. "You're in luck because my last two gigs are online." They started walking, and Michael rambled on in Italian until he calmed down.

"Do you live far away Barry, should I get my car, take the tube, can I park?"

"I'm in Paddington. You can park if we take your car." Michael led the way.

****

David kept looking at Sophia as she walked around his office and eyed the staff and then settled her accusing eyes on him. "That's one hell of a bomb to drop. When the Italian guy came in, I didn't get a gay vibe off him."

"You didn't get one off me, but here we are."

"How can you really be gay? I mean I've known you for years and no signs. No eyes on the staff or anyone at the Events… and no comments; no anything."

"I don't have to justify myself to anyone."

"You can't just spring this on us."

Willy came back into the office and handed him a letter. "That's my resignation." David's eyes narrowed. "I don't work for queers." Michael inhaled and sat upright. "All this time David, pretending to be my friend…"

"I haven't pretended to be your friend; I am your friend."

"Fuck you! I don't have no business with batty man!" David lost focus and tried to swallow but his heart rate jumped up and he began to shake.

"Not half an hour ago you ran your mouth on the subject of bigots," Willy said. "Now you sit there talking shit. Revealing yourself as a hypocrite and…"

"Shut up before I batter you," David said softly with the most violent intent.

Sophia spread her arms to keep them apart. "Hey, you guys. Cool it, the staff is out there."

"Your resignation is accepted so fuck off out of my firm!"

"Your firm; I'm going to take Mr. Man from you because when he hears how your arse is full, he'll kick the shit out of you. I would do it, but I don't hit women."

"Alright you little prick, outside in ten minutes: I'm not about to lose money while my staff are distracted by what going to happen."

"In the Rec garden? See you there in ten." Willy turned and left the office.

"You've got to be kidding me. What is this, High School?" Sophia yelled in a hoarse whisper.

"This is happening. Do you still work for me?" She nodded. "Watch the staff. Keep things busy."

"When I'm doing that, and my best friend and my boyfriend are having their Black macho battles downstairs how am I to stay cool?"

"Figure it out." She was more upset than she knew and it wasn't until she faked a smile for the staff that she cracked inside.

****

David came into the Workspace Recreation Garden in jeans and T-shirt, which he kept in his office. He snuck out to the toilet to change before coming down. He saw Willy sitting there with a troubled look on his face. David figured Willy let his mouth get him in trouble once again. It was his biggest weakness. However in the past that hadn't mattered because David considered him a family friend. They had gone to church, matches, and parties together. Willy was a person that David's mother had come to consider family because he was devoted to her since his mother went back to Jamaica to look after his grandmother. He and David shared jokes about women, sex and what every Black man needs to know about handling himself in London.

231

David looked at him, and he could see the pugnacious pride in William's face. David reached for two sparks of inspiration: his brother Solly and Erwin, Grace's brother, who was almost like a brother to him. He walked up to Willy in a lackluster manner, and Willy looked at him deeply conflicted, yet still with deep contempt. David punched him in the face and the neck, hit him with a left hook under the chin and literally jumped back and struck him with kickboxing body blows that really hurt. Willy took a wide swipe at David but he overreached, and David kicked him in the stomach and Willy puked.

David bounced around the place. "You're a loudmouth Jamaican clown! That is *no* match for the Nigerian!" David stomped right up to his face. "You must be bloody crazy to come up against me when I was trained by my father. That means no pussy whipped pussy loving tough guy who *believes* he has to right to beat down 'bitches' can tear me up!" David yanked his T-shirt down. "These scars are the mark of strength."

"You fucking bastard Dave. You fucking liar. You were supposed to watch my back. Instead, you stab me in the back telling me how you love some bloke."

"It's my life, my truth! My choice; *my choice* – my arse!"

"You've shamed your son and your family with this white sickness."

"Oh fuck off!" David told him saddened by his ignorance. "Get this; Mr. Man is under contract to me. You try and run a sideline or take him off me, and I'll take you to court and take every penny you've earned under my employment." David headed inside and didn't look back even though Willy wanted him to come and help him up. He had little to believe in now that he was beaten by a self-confessed homosexual.

David made his ninth call waiting for Isaac to a pickup. He adjusted his suit and his call connected. "Isaac, it's Bankole, I have a situation with my ex-wife, she's trying to hurt my son and me, fuck with my business and my career. I need your help."

"What do you need? It's done."

"I want to invite you to an Event. There's a sex tape of Veronika and me. I've made a documentary. It features the tape, my life, my clients and people I work with. The Event is food, booze, music and people like us."

"No worries there, man."

"Plus there's a newsflash about me and my work."

"What's that about?"

"It's an exclusive. You can watch the sex tape from noon tomorrow online. I'll send you the link. At the Event, I'll come out, and explain my reason for the documentary because there's no way Veronika is going to 'slam' me. The documentary isn't made by a snake like Bashir." Isaac asked a few questions.

"Yes, I am shagging her in the film." He listened. "Shut up, you're too nasty!" They both laughed out loud. "Yeah fine rate me if you want. I'll see you at the Event?" Yeah, my Mum is fine, I've spoken to her. Dad hates Veronika even more." He stood up and looked at Mr. Man's video playing on the company website. "I'll text and email you the link and the address for the Event in Highbury, thanks for backing me."

He hung up and took a breath. He scrolled down his mobile and speed dialed another friend. "Yeah Kwame, it's Bankole, I have a situation with my ex-wife, she's trying to hurt my son and me, fuck with my business and wreck my career. I need your help."

CHAPTER TWENTY-SEVEN

That afternoon Michael was in his unfurnished new house with Barry and the freelance technician David used for many of his clients' shows. Michael guided them into the rooms and around the house. There was some tension between the technicians. The lighting designer was an Englishman in his forties who'd showcased musicians in studios and outdoor venues worldwide. Barry didn't have a degree, but he could design sound and music in a family home or the best club venues globally. Therefore, he felt 'the lighting guy' was borderline arrogant, which was compounded by the fact he imposed himself on Barry as an expert with academic qualifications to prove it.

Michael proudly showed them each room that had decorative mosaic tiles covering the walls. One room had gold colored titles; another room had titles in various shades of red, emerald green tiles covered the walls in the third room, and sapphire blue colored tiles gleamed in the fourth room. The kitchen had sheets of steel around workspaces and marble throughout the rest of the kitchen.

The 'lighting guy' as Barry thought of him was clearly impressed as they figured out where things should go. "How much did this set you back?" Barry asked.

"Three million." Barry was shocked. "It's half the price of Hampstead because Canonbury is so close to 'unfashionable' Hackney as far as snobs are concerned."

Barry hired four unemployed Black teenagers to lug the sound equipment into the house, and he warned them, three times, not the bang into any walls or doors, so they carefully brought things inside in a to-and-fro rotation.

Later on, Barry ambled through the house and found Michael in the attic. "The patterns made by these tiles in all the rooms are very elegant."

"The floors and wall coverings set me back a million, but it's gorgeous, no?"

"It's a little palace. What kind of security do you have?"

"None as yet."

"Ok, listen now." Barry looked anxious but determined. "I can provide security for tonight and nights to come." Barry began to stutter. "You're always traveling; you can't leave your house unprotected. If you rent me a room, I'll protect your house. You can do a criminal background check on me..." For a tough guy, he began truly fragile.

"Considering our mishap in the locker room I don't think so. I don't play games. David and my family mean everything to me and they'll reside here."

"Now I know you're a family man, that won't happen again. I will protect your home and your family. When you're away on business or here; let me prove it?"

"After the Event, we'll talk. I'd want total protection for David and my kids."

Barry nodded. "Let me call the decorators." Barry took out his mobile and called them, got an update and feedback. Michael went to double check something and bumped into Roberto on the way up with Adrian following behind him looking at the house.

"Hey, guys you Ok?" Roberto nodded, and Adrian concurred as he looked into the rooms. "Roberto show him around. I'm about to call your brothers and Maria. I spoke to Mama earlier. She is coming. Adrian, have you called your father?"

"Yes, I'll see him later. He's with some of his friends at London Live TV."

"Did he tell you about the theme of the Event?"

"He told me about the...tape. And the documentary he's made concerning it."

"What do you think?" Adrian leaned in and Roberto pulled them into a huddle so that the 'lighting guy' and the movers couldn't hear them.

"I get it. Telling the world, you're gay when dad puts out a film showing he's into pussy complicates things. It's a form of Disinformation."

"Corporations, governments, and the Church use it a lot. I want to protect your father." Adrian was attentive. "Confusion can be very useful. Your father and I are 'coming out'. Since we have sons and a daughter people can't say we're not 'real men' because, by their own definition, we've proved ourselves. Not only with you guys but we both built our own successful business, and our clients trust us."

"I totally get it," Adrian replied.

"Your father must protect himself against Veronika. An Indian guy I taught was stalked and sexually abused by an English student. He was a great scholar, and she was lazy; forcing him to write her work. No one believed him until he killed himself and the staff read his suicide letter. When we first spoke to her, she played the upper-class girl who wouldn't dirty herself with an Indian 'boy'. History documents the virtue of the blonde Venus and 'evil' black beast. Despite 'PC', millions of people still think in black and white. We must help David discredit any lies," Michael stated pointing at them, and they nodded.

"Tomorrow you'll meet the rest of my family. I have to call them now. You give me half – hour?" Adrian nodded. "Listen to me son; I love your father as much as I loved my wife. I know some very powerful people and I'm trying to make sure homophobic rage, especially the Black kind doesn't touch him."

"Ok," Adrian said hoping David wasn't walking into a trap of his own making.

"Papa, Adrian is very worried that homophobic backlash will destroy David. Last night we didn't go out, we talked. So take care of this." Michael spoke to Roberto in Italian for half a minute, and then he reassuringly placed his hand on Adrian's neck. "I'm Italian: love and vengeance are my specialty." With indefatigable spirit, Michael took his mobile and left them to make more calls.

"That was scary," Adrian said.

Roberto flicked his eyebrows. "Racial discrimination really makes him furious."

"It's odd, but after sobbing and waffling all night, I feel like we've been friends forever." Roberto felt wonderful because he didn't have many friends. Casual people found him domineering. He tickled Adrian, and he jittered and flapped about.

"Come I'll show you everything." Roberto pushed him forward affectionately. They went upstairs and entered a room with Barry working on his sound equipment.

Roberto looked at him for a good few seconds and asked. "Hi, who are you?"

"DJ. Getting this place ready for business." The sound of footsteps came up the stairs, and three gay guys appeared in a fluster. They were conspicuously gay. Adrian eyed them, and they felt it and calmed themselves. They typified Adrian and Roberto's image of 'sissy boys', especially since they were all pretty and chic.

"Hi, we're the decorators!" All three of them looked around. "Nice place."

Barry pointed at the door, and they were about to leave, but Michael entered.

Barry came forward. "These are…"

"The decorators – *ciao!*" Michael said joyfully. "Listen, guys, the event's for a fabulous man, I love him, do me a favor; we're 'coming out' so make it wonderful for us." The three guys rushed toward Michael and promised to surpass themselves.

"Tomorrow evening, you are invited. You're my guests. I want you to oversee everything. I'll give you £1,000 bonus if everything is fantastic!"

The set designer Bruno, who was sexpert with more admirers than everyone in the house put together, waved at his partners to get moving. "Signore De Farenzino…"

Michael interrupted him. "Italiano?"

"Yes," he replied and continued in Italian. "The minute I heard your voice on the phone I knew you were a sophisticated connoisseur and gentlemen from Rome..." Michael walked him away with his arm over his shoulder and Bruno felt very special.

"There he goes. Papa has a way of acting like he's known you forever."

"You get that from him." Roberto's eyes were searching. "You're the same."

Barry watched them leave the room and he wished he'd spoken to Michael six months earlier even though it wouldn't have changed things.

David was in the kitchen in his vest and jeans with a Bluetooth earpiece connection, gesturing to Adrian to hand him things. Sonny Rollins' *Saxophone Colossus* was playing as he moved about rather jolly but irritated by call waiting.

"Yes, I'm holding!" He put wheat germ, dry fruit, and yogurt into the blender. "It's totally low fat everything this week. Last week, between drinks and gorging on the finest, I've totally blown my regime. I cannot get fat. Michael is really fit."

"Are you being ironic again?" Adrian asked sarcastically.

"How was it last night with Roberto, did he take you to the party?"

"No, I was exhausted." Adrian stopped to consider. "Roberto's nice. And he's not after anything, like people conning me to get to Uncle Solly or you. He told me his brothers and sister are pissed off with Michael because he hasn't stayed in contact with them," he said probingly.

"Excuse me!" David ended the call and removed the earpiece. "They snubbed him on his birthday, his fiftieth. They've placed him as 'in case of emergency' then call Dad. He's their father. According to Lola, he gave them everything!"

"Rob said Michael was deeply depressed for about a year before the divorce." Adrian felt ready to tackle his father. "Before, were your blokes mates or lovers?"

"Mates." David stopped the blender. The lie paralyzed him for some time, and he thought of all the other lies he had to tell throughout his life. His eyes lit up, and Adrian watched him suspiciously which David felt. As he twisted his vest, he looked strange to his son, but Adrian didn't reach out to him because he wanted to know his father's secrets. Guilt rattled David. He went over to a cupboard and stood still and then opened it. Watching his father, Adrian felt he was seeing someone else because David physically took on a different stance. He took rum out of the cupboard and drank from the bottle and then he eyed Adrian intent on refuting his judgment.

Defiantly he said, "Last year I was seeing a guy. Like me, he knows there are few things more dangerous than being a Black gay man. Unlike me, he's afraid of people. My first true love: Angus. I loved him because he's fearless and he adores me."

"How do you control wanting a man and needing a woman?" Adrian asked as he walked straight up to his father. Adrian took the bottle from him and swallowed a mouthful of booze and as if to test his father he took out a cigarette and lit up. "No spin, just tell me the truth." David pulled the cigarette from his lips and stamped it out. Adrian had never looked more like a man than right then and there.

"Getting into a ring and beating the shit out of someone is a breeze compared to twisting myself into a facsimile of what 'certified men' expect of me." His voice was distorted by a lifetime of resentment towards every heterosexist tyrant he'd ever met.

Adrian spitefully said, "You have all the answers for this don't you."

In a gesture that not even Al Pacino could have made any larger, David said, "That's because I've been dealing with the questions my whole life!!" David's body expanded, reached its height and then slowly retracted. Adrian had never seen him like that and so he became anxious, and for the first time, it felt as if they were from two generations.

"I'm not disrespecting you, Dad."

"I've already kicked one guy's arse today so I can deal with this."

"Last night my head was filled with you and Michael. In bed, in love, gay dads; your wives, your sons, and daughter." Adrian searched for a way to contain his feelings. "It was a sexual puzzle like a Rubik's Cube: and if that wasn't enough, you're going online. Everyone will see you shagging Veronika... naked."

"You've heard me say; 'Living in a Black body'. Do you understand what I mean when I say that?"

"The philosophical psychology of liberation that rejects the colonial doctrine."

Snapping at him, David said, "Deconstruct that?"

"Regardless of Eurocentric superiority in their use of Christianity and capital to aggrandize themselves and demonize their enemies you won't be enslaved because you believe in equality," Adrian replied having discussed the subject with his Uncle Erwin.

"8/10. It also means I renounce racists' perception of me. I can stand naked because I have no shame. God knows I use to – I was guilty of everything until Gus loved me and now Michael's perception has freed me. You and the family, my friends, and enemies, can see the true me naked."

"But the world-wide-wankers and populous will see your dick; doesn't that bother you," Adrian asked troubled.

"Son, do you think they've never imagined it? We exist as sexual phantoms in the minds of malignant racists." Adrian took a moment to consider that. David snatched the bottle from him. "Men and women have found their heart and soul in bed with me." It was David's most sacred confession, and once he'd uttered the words he wished he had said it to his brother rather than his son. Nevertheless, he did not regret saying it because had it not come out of his mouth spontaneously, he'd never have realized it.

The self-realization drew his son closer to him. Studying his father in an unbroken stare, forced Adrian to see how little he really thought of David as a sexual practitioner. He saw him as a romantic, a symbol, not unlike Usher; but a man who was politically correct in his behavior towards virtually everyone.

"What do you think Mum and Gran'ma will say when they see you naked?"

"I'm not afraid of anyone. Solly loves me without question. That's... important! I've lived in fear for years. The psychological terrorism of heterosexuality turned me into a Jungian 'Shadow'. A phantom of evil." He stated unapologetically.

"What does that mean Dad?"

"I forced myself to be what society expects. A reproductive, money earning, aggressive bloke who thinks he's normal."

"But that's not you?" David shook his head. "This psychological and political stuff, how do you know these things?" Adrian asked confused.

"Gus is a psychiatrist. He taught me about the world. We'd be a couple now, but I left him to become your dad and not simply your biological father. The only reason he forgave me is because he loves me. I was never brave enough to be gay. Instead, I masqueraded as straight, but now I don't care who hates me, as long as it isn't you. The family, Gus, and Michael are all I have." David felt a jolt in his chest.

In Yoruba, Adrian said, "Daddy I can feel the weight of this life-change in you. I just don't want you to be out there naked where people will be vicious. What do you think Grandad will say when she sees you *fucking* naked?"

"I'm not worried," David replied in English.

"I can't imagine any other Black guy as cool about their gayness as you are."

"Homosexuality isn't a tragedy; there are countless well-adjusted Black gay men."

"How do you know?"

"They've asked to go to bed with me." Adrian walked away because he had to think again about his father. "There's beauty in me inherited from our ancestors that no one can erase. I intend to disrupt the perception of Black masculinity in sexual politics."

Adrian took the bottle back from his father. "How?" He took another swig.

"By defeating Veronika and changing my father. I'm fighting for the love that's tested me: my father's, Gus' and yours. If I win; Michael and I will last forever."

"I don't understand all this, but at least you're not conning me and lying."

"As I said to you before; Michael is the first man that I've felt truthful with."

"I want to meet the rest of Michael's kids and his wife. Roberto said she's Jamaican, kind of a diva."

"She is, and I think your mother is going to like her."

Adrian was about to leave. He started walking, but he stopped to confront his father.

"If you were born gay, how did you come to have me?"

"I love your mother."

"And all gay men are turned on by women?"

"No; but we do love women better than most of their lovers do."

Adrian started out of the kitchen. "I have no clothes to wear tomorrow. I came back without anything. Another day in these clothes and I'm going to stink."

"Take my Platinum card on my chest of drawers. Go to Selfridges tomorrow and buy anything you like. The pin number is your birthday, 1.7.9.5."

Adrian nodded and went through the door but stuck his head in. "What's for dinner?"

"Go to the fridge and sort yourself out. I'm on a skinny day. Oy! If you don't want to watch the DVD on my... tape and interview..."

Pointing at him, Adrian said, "I'll watch it now." An elusive smile crept onto Adrian's face, and David came at him in haste and grabbed Adrian's shirt.

He looked into his son's eyes. "With the amount of porn that your generation watches, and posting yourselves online, is this only bizarre because I'm your father?"

"I'll tell you tomorrow."

"Sons and daughters often *speculate* about their parents. You'll be able to tick the box now." In a challenging gaze, David asked. "How are things with Ivy?"

Adrian made a happy face. "Have you thrilled her?"

Resentment twisted Adrian's face, when he said, "Yes."

"She's beautiful and highly intelligent. Don't get into a macho funk to keep her. Women respond to mental and physical beauty. Being erotic is vastly different than being a prick."

"Is there anyone else out there who can say he's seen his father in the groove?"

"I'm sure there is, but I appreciate that is difficult."

Adrian flung his arms out and mimed a face that stated, 'Ok, now you see things from my point of view so gimme a break'. Adrian left him standing and went to watch the DVD. David took tentative steps back into the kitchen preoccupied with the substance of his conversation with his son.

CHAPTER TWENTY-EIGHT

Michael laid flat on the examining table as his Chinese doctor, a distinguished man with more medical qualifications than most GPs, continued to work on his legs. Michael's stomach, chest, and arms were spotted with acupuncture needles. His doctor moved to the top of his head to insert the last five needles. Michael flinched and fluttered, and after the second needle, Dr. Zhang said, "Michael, relax ok."

"I'm trying to but I have a big day ahead, and I want everything to come together for my partner's big day."

"It's a surprise for her?" Michael shook his head.

'There's no her, it's him. I have to look incredible today. I have to do this for David. If he sees nothing is too much for me to manage he'll know we're a perfect match. I couldn't tell Dr. Zhang, today is for my boyfriend, though. David just did that yesterday. He so brave. Michael fell into a light sleep as the sounds and smell of the aromatherapy acupuncture treatment along with music and jasmine overtook him.

David opened the door, and Angus came in and hugged him tightly. "Fuck me, look at you, all bright eyes fuckin' sexy! No need to ask how you're doing." He put his suitcase down and looked all around the house. "My God this is beautiful. You've shown it to me on your iPad but actually seeing it! He walked through the hall and poked his head into the living room. "O aye, this is fabulous! He went in, and David looked at him affectionately and followed behind him. "It's splendid is what it is."

"You really like it."

Angus took him by the shoulders and shook him. "Yes, you silly sod. What's the rest like?" David took him upstairs, and he noticed how nice Angus looked in a pilot's flying suit. David showed him into his bedroom. "O man this is the fucking sweet spot!"

"Obviously, you're alright!"

"Aye, if you take the ferry over from Amsterdam you have your own cabin for a good night's rest. I feel great. And coming over for this! Aye man, you've found it!"

"What?" Angus unzipped the RAF flight suit and pulled it down to his waist.

"Courage, your steel!" Adrian came into the room. "Fuck no! Is this him? Bloody hell he's so tall, and good looking too: takes after you then. Hi! I'm Angus, a good mate of your dad. I've known you since you were born Adrian." He shuffled in clearly waking up at the sight of the gregarious Scotsman. Adrian knew he was gregarious because Angus moved haphazardly about with his suit rustling and flapping around, his bangles and gay rainbow necklace sounding off and his voice impassioned as he shook Adrian's hand. His wavy graying hair fell over his eye, and Adrian noticed the muscles in his neck jitter when his spoke. Standing there in his black vest, the tattoo on his inner forearm with a heart and the initials AV&DB caught Adrian's eye.

"Do you shag all your patients or just my dad?"

Unfazed, Angus said, "I'd expect that the kind of talk from a lout with a low I.Q." His violent green eyes and enchanting smile unsettled Adrian. "How do you expect to work for the United Nations with this kind of prejudice?"

"How do you know that?"

"Like most handsome, smart, straight men; stupidity runs high among you. I'm Dave's jilted lover and a psychiatrist. I know everything…" he said with triumphant power. Adrian backed away, but Angus went for him. "You're experiencing a mental readjustment to F.E.A.R. I'm talking about False Evidence Appearing Real." Pointing in Adrian's face, Angus told him. "Your mind is leaking with residual anger and love for Dave." David tried to stop Angus. "Shut up! Dave hasn't changed. He's just stopped acting. You get it. There is no 007, there's just Sean Connery playing Bond and all the other wannabes."

"You're saying being gay doesn't change who he is?"

"I'll tell you who he is. He's your devoted father who was terrified your family would expunge him if he declared his true self. When he takes that mask off he's the Prince of Passion. Angus moved toward David. "The love of my life." Angus reached out to touch David's face but stopped and pulled his hand back. Adrian saw that David was captivated by him.

"I didn't mean what I said before," he told Angus.

"I know; you just want Dave to be normal and real. Good news – he is!"

"People think…"

"Most people are stupid! Your Dad is going to face all the cunts that expect him to bow before them because they're the gods and goddess of normality."

He pointed at Adrian. "Your Dad's going to tell the world there's more to life than their values. He's got the balls to say, in spite of what you see I'm a Black gay man." Angus kissed David's forehead. "We've seen Obama as President, and Oprah as the 'earth's mother'. Online today this Black Brit, your Dad, is going to change things."

Adrian moved toward David. "It's fucking brilliant, isn't it?" Adrian replied. David and Angus turned to him. "Dad, for you to come out as gay with that documentary showing of 'Black men rule' is great."

Angus let out a great laugh. "Dave was worried you'd be 'damaged' if you knew and I said you're more than a trophy kid made of money and image."

"Right, I'm a Bankole, so my family's guts and money have made a man of me." He turned to David. "In the documentary, I thought I was watching someone else, but that *machismo* is the real you." David felt accused and proud. "I've been asking questions because I needed to be sure you and Michael aren't getting off on Dad." Adrian punched the air out of his way. "You've exposed your privacy, so I'll let you into my secret." Angus looked at David. "I'm not sweet. I always have to check myself because I have Mum's rage and your vengeance. That is blood and fire!" His eyes and teeth flashed. "Anyone tries to take you down they have to come pass me."

"Fucking love it! Dave worries about you, but it turns out you've got that Ni-Jam force..." Adrian and David looked totally confused: "Nigerian egotism and Jamaican rebellion that marks ferocious Leaders."

"Dad's given me everything, what else could I be? Tonight *will* change things."

"Shouldn't we get going to your firm Dave? I've called a few of our friends, and they're coming so we need an update from your bloke, Michael."

David said, "He's got some of his best people working this. We're going to swing by his place after I check the office."

"What are you doing?" Angus asked Adrian.

"Going to buy some clothes; I dashed down when Veronika ambushed me..."

"Yeah I heard what she did... You were very smart to stay cool when she spat that venom in your face. But you know Dave, considering the stupidity of her behavior; in my professional opinion, I think that bitch could be bipolar."

"Or suffering from cunty-itist! I don't give a shit. She messed with my son!" Angus looked at him and the broadest smile spread across his face.

"I love it when I'm right." He clapped his hands. "Pure Ni-Jam force."

The air cooled down and David settled after a time. "It takes an Athenian to know."

"Too fuckin' right, so get a fuckin' move on Dave. I've crossed water for this: can't wait to meet your Mr. Wonderful."

"You're going to like him."

"Why? You chose him over me didn't you?"

"Don't hate me, not today. I have to face my father. I need all of you."

"Do you want me to come with you?" David shook his head. "Do you want a slingshot?" Each of them knew Solomon in different ways so when they thought about it, tension grew out of them and filled the air. "Remember what I've taught you." David began breathing heavily and his skin tightened on his face.

"Daddy let me come with you, Gramps..."

"I have to confront him alone. Go and buy some clothes." Adrian sensed a growing level of fear in his father.

****

David sat in his father outer office and his Nigerian Clerk, Akoni, was torn between watching him and doing on his work. Solomon's office was in a third-floor space in Cavendish Square. It was an 1889 building that was once a residence that had been converted into a shared three-floor office building. It had typical feature outside and retained some woodwork with a slam-door brass and wood lift, and a curved, ornate ceiling in the 20^{ft} high rooms. The handmade files, desks, and fittings along with the ambiance and environment transported David back in time. "Pardon me I have to say I love you on the talent show. You're so professional," Akoni confessed.

Solomon came out, and David stood up immediately and put his hands behind his back. "Good afternoon Father. I'm glad..." Solomon pointed at his door and David went inside like a boy entering the Headmaster's office. Solomon threw a glance at Akoni who made himself look busy. Solomon went into his office and closed the door. He took one step forward and looked at David harshly.

"Come here." David didn't move and his father pointed at the spot for him to come to; and stand still. Solomon's force of will and power was so strong David couldn't resist. He moved and stood in front of his father. Solomon unbuckled his belt and pulled it from out of his trouser loops. David watch and he started shaking, losing control of his ability to stand his ground. He saw the belt lengthen and dip toward the floor. All the saliva in his mouth began to dry up.

"No listen to me Daddy, I was drinking that night and I know I shouldn't have called and woke you up, or spoke to you like that, it was very disrespectful. See I just got nervous because I knew you'd hate what I had to tell…"

The brutal look on Solomon's face made David shout. "Don't! I'm thirty-seven, not seven you can't, you mustn't hit me." Solomon boxed his face and lashed him with the belt.

Neither one of them moved for an entire minute. Outside the door, Akoni had his ear at the door. He was positive Solomon struck David. He covered his mouth and listened as closely as he could.

"You cannot tell *me* what to do. You're my child." David moved back and then he rushed for the door, and Solomon grabbed his jacket and spun him around.

"If you lay that belt or your hand on me, again I'll leave. Go to the police and have you arrested for assault. I'll go public. Get a restraining order to keep you away from my son. I'll have you disbarred. I'm not sure on what grounds but I have my own lawyer, and you know what a triumph it would be to hand him your head."

"You wouldn't do that."

"Try me. I've come to see you, and you think you have the right to beat me. You're a man of the law and officer of the court."

Solomon whispered, "You're a homo: my son, a degenerate; a disease."

"No… cancer is a disease; it killed my sister. I don't have any kind of a disease; I've never even had an STD so you can shut up about that."

"You shut your mouth. You ever wondered how you might die? A crash, heart attack, brain tumor. I'll tell you how you're going to die. Today, right now – Your disease mustn't touch my grandsons or dirty our name." Stunned by his father's condemnation David searched his dark angry face all at once!

'Jesus Christ. He's going to kill me! Holy Father forgive my sins, accept my soul'.

A shot of urine came out of him, and he felt as if he'd hit his head. Solomon grabbed him by the neck and David saw Solly standing in front of the family gloriously happy on the day he became a national football star, and the family toasted him. Michael flashed through his mind, singing *Volare* and so did Angus watching him tenderly on the day he gave his virginity to him. The sight of Grace and himself on the day they Baptized Adrian. He felt his blood chill too cold as it descended and he screamed; horrified by death.

"Adrian!" David cried, but he blacked out with his father's face loomed in front of him, and his hands strangled him.

****

Michael was with Fabio and Maria, Cesare and Roberto in their Muswell Hill home at that exact moment. "You must come and hear what David has to say."

"Why do I have to listen to it?" Maria replied.

Lola told her. "Because you're not a heartless bitch without any human feeling, you're my daughter. You're a loving person, and this is important for us all. Let me ask all of you. Isn't your father entitled to some happiness?"

Michael shuddered with fear. "It felt like someone just walked over my grave. Listen, if anyone should be giving me a hard time, it's your mother. I'm blessed to find David and his son; otherwise, I could be running after young guys and disgracing myself. I've organized a wonderful show so come. You might surprise yourself and not hate him."

Roberto said, "Only thing to hate is the bigotry we have." The family eyed him.

****

Akoni pulled David from Solomon's hands as his father fell back, consumed with bile and rage surging through his body. His mind was lost in a demented state of fury. Akoni was utterly panic stricken as he tried to revive David without any effect. Solomon saw Akoni trying to bring David back to consciousness, and he realized he was shaking uncontrollably. Akoni rushed for the first aid box and Solomon looked at David as the dreadful reality shocked him into action. "Tunji, baby…" Solomon moved swiftly as David lie there. Solomon felt the pulse in his neck and quickly gave David CPR. He was consumed with fear and his heart raced horrified at what he'd done. He continued the cardiopulmonary resuscitation, giving him mouth to mouth pinching his nose and pressing his heart.

"How did this happen?" Akoni asked. "He's your son; how did you do this?" Solomon pinched David's nose again and breathed into his mouth, and then massaged his chest. A few seconds later David coughed and gulped to breathe. Solomon gasped, and tears ran down his face. He lifted David into his lap. "Yes, baby, breath and keep breathing son. Come on, Tunji..." He could barely hold himself together uttering David's Nigerian name. "Breathe." David opened his eyes, and his father kissed him on the eyes and on the mouth. "That's right my baby. You're going to be all..." and Solomon's whole body shook as he sobbed. "I'm so crazy. Why do I get crazy with you? Why do I get so mad at you?" Akoni watched the two of them, and he was drawn to Solomon weeping uncontrollably.

Solomon was so shocked by his own homicidal compulsions he confessed to his son in Yoruba. "Something must be wrong with you and me. I always want you to be me." Shame ripped at Solomon's mind and his soul.

"I let Solly be himself, but I want you to be me, only perfect. British Nigerian, honorable and respected; brilliant... loved. Why have I wanted you to be the perfect *me*? Your brother and sister did right: I didn't punish them when they went wrong or did bad things. Why have I been so obsessed with you?" He found himself crying out of bewilderment and the faintest suspicion that he might be mentally unbalanced.

"Daddy... you nearly killed me – again," David replied in Yoruba while pulling himself up. Akoni was shocked, and then David couldn't speak for a minute.

Solomon told him. "Go and get me a cold, wet cloth please, hurry." Akoni went immediately. "Your defiance provokes something primal in me, and I know what it is, Tunji... I know what it is."

David's pleading eyes looked into his father for an answer and Solomon could see it. "My father crushed me. I wanted to defy him, and I tried to defy him, sometimes. I was severely punished if I did. I know we cannot brutalize children. Your mother taught me how wrong, how crazy it is to beat our children, so I've been *mentally* punishing. Solly and Roslyn didn't question as you do. With you, it was also something else. And it rejects me as a man and your father." David wanted to speak, but he also wanted to hear his father.

248

Akoni came back with cloth and Solomon wrapped it around David's neck and held him in the fold of his thigh and calf. Watching David look up at him, Solomon asked himself what kind of madness drove him to try and kill his own son, and it shook him once more. He was overcome by fresh tears. "You think your success means nothing to me? Friends of mine congratulate me for you and speak of your achievements. Your eloquence on television, when so many talk shit: it reveals your nobility. This chastises me, because even though my VIP colleagues and diplomat friends respect me, you and Solly are the true nobility of our family."

He touched David's face, and the tenderness of his gesture was as deliberate as a faith healer's touch. Solomon wiped his eyes with the back of his hand. "Adrian worships you – I wish I had that with you. When you cut off your hair at the grave and buried it with your sister, I felt cut inside by your spirit. Like your mother, you have so much love. In a way, it's feminine, and I haven't been able to embrace that delicacy in my Being. The men in my family could not allow that fragility to be a part of who we were, or we'd have been doomed." David struggled to breathe evenly.

"It's one of the reasons I made you read Chinua Achebe's *Things Fall Apart*. We had to protect ourselves against the pernicious effects of the British Empire in Nigeria. I came here to prove my equality."

The loving need in David's eyes moved Solomon even more deeply. "What a paradox... to achieve professional superiority and sink to the savage primitivism of murder, goaded by jealousy of your tenderness. You've inherited so much from your mother, instinctively, and still, I have not learned despite all her guidance with me." Solomon tried to calm himself. Akoni took his hand and held David's hand as well. They exchanged looks and David understood the balance of life and death would never come back. He was in the moment with his father and the stranger. He closed his eyes and prayed. He asked forgiveness for provoking his father. He didn't feel hatred or even disdain. He was glad he wasn't dead.

Akoni hummed and began to sing an old Igbo song. Solomon looked him in the eyes with an intense kindred spirit even though he was Yoruba. The song of male kinship and unity resonated through all three of them and Solomon touched Akoni's shoulder, and David sat up. Leaving his father's arms and pulling away from his body felt like a separation to David. Solomon helped him to sit up and then Akoni aided Solomon in getting David up on his feet.

When he was standing David pulled himself together as the men continued to sing and there was no doubt in David's mind that he would always be more African than Caribbean. He pulled Akoni to him and told him in Yoruba. "Thank you, my brother. Let me speak the truth," he said deeply hoarse. "I honor and love gracious women: but I'm a man who needs the love of another man. I found him."

Akoni said, "That is good for you, Tunji. Love is the true meaning of our survival."

"Why've you beaten and tried to kill me, Dad? I'm not an ideal. I'm simply a man with a brother, a son; someone you've raised not to be threatened by Britain. Why isn't that good enough for you?"

"It is good, Tunji…"

"How can a man of your stature condemn his own son based on bigotry: unless you're like that fucking savage in Uganda!" David staggered to him and pointed in his face. "Are you?"

"No."

"If you're lying, I curse you with misery and renounce you as my father."

"I don't agree with human rights violations."

Gaining his voice, he said, "You're wise to repudiate that mess." David coughed and stood tall eying his father and watching Akoni. "How can you be my dad? You attempted to murder me, so what father kills his son?"

That question struck Solomon like a solar plexus punch. He was recovering from what he'd done and David forced him back to his raison d'être to rationalize his history of mistreatment.

"You know what Nigerian's honor of masculinity means," Solomon replied. "Weakness and femininity are abhorrent to any man who values his identity."

"I denounce that justification under human rights laws. I see a psychiatrist; he is Igbo and knows us; I want *you* to see him."

"I am not going to a psychiatrist; there's nothing wrong…"

"After the attempted murder of your own son you say that." David accused him with the judgment of a prosecutor's acumen. "The psychiatrist will help you. I've been seeing him so he can help me love you, even though you don't love me."

"I do love you."

"You can't. You dragged me out of school and put me into the hand of those…"

250

"David!" Solomon looked over at Akoni, and David stopped because he knew the depth of his father's shame. David placed his hand on his father's heart.

"Daddy, OK, alright. Tonight you have to come with me to a very important event. I am going to publicly expose Veronika. Even though she isn't a Susan Smith I have to stop her from casting me as a pathological Black man."

"What is she doing?" David told him about her visit to Adrian.

Four minutes later he asked. "How is he?"

"He's alright. I wanted to go to Adrian and explain things myself but he ran home to Grace, and she brought him to me."

"And you thought that 'wife' was nice: a drug taking, adulteress whose 'habit' killed my two grandsons! Back home she would have killed herself for shame."

"She wasn't always like that."

"She's a Jezebel, but you were naïve and rambunctious, so you married her to punish me. Grace could have cured you of everything; *she* is beautiful."

"I was happy with Veronika for years because I alleviated her paranoia about her Romanian identity and the myth of her infectious and depraved femininity."

"She's filthy!"

"She has her demons. But married to her I felt ten times more a man than I did with Grace and you watching me."

"Tunji, you care about a woman's dignity and feelings, have loving sex with women so how can you tell me you're homosexual?" Solomon asked him in Yoruba.

"Sir, contradictions are in all of us. We see it in every case," Akoni said. "One year a man loves his wife the next year he kills her. We believe in the sacred oaths of Bible, Law, and Family and the next thing we hear is someone justifying their murder of members of their family for money, sex or the honor of their name. I love my wife, but I've had sex with two other women. This doesn't make me less of a man – it makes me human."

"Thank you," David said sincerely. "I'm not after boys. The man who's in love with me is also divorced with three sons and a daughter. He's a professor and art dealer. His son likes me, and he's helped me with Adrian."

Solomon asked. "He doesn't think you've seduced his father away from his family."

"No. I didn't know Michael when he was married. But his wife, Lola told me she's glad I've saved him. He tried to hang himself before he met me: now we're in love." David concluded revitalized by just the thought of Michael.

Akoni asked. "David, this man, what is he really like?" David was relieved to hear a reasonable question come from a fellow Nigerian.

"He's beautiful. Come and meet him tonight." He nodded. "Dad, I expect to see tonight." Solomon contemplated for a time.

"Imagine what will happen when I tell Solly, Mum and Adrian what you did. I know Mum; she will leave you; and my son and my brother will cut you out of their lives. They will do it even if I have to play the victim…"

"How can you be so ruthless?" The vein in Solomon's temple pulsated and his complexion deepened to an earthy brown tone.

"You were strangling your son," Akoni told Solomon. "You can't say *he's* ruthless."

"You'll see a psychiatrist. I've paid for five sessions. It will be strictly between you and Dr. Claude. You're terribly ill, and it will help you, father." Solomon felt something inside his body crack having his son dictate terms to him.

****

Adrian was in the guest bedroom trying on several things he had bought earlier. The room was decorated with coffee and cocoa brown colored Art Deco reproduction furniture. The hidden lighting and the warm glow from the lamps in the room took its design from a Manhattan hotel room David shared with Angus in 1998.

Angry voices invaded the room, and it stopped him dressing. He had on his new jeans, but he was bare-chested and barefoot. Adrian stretched his neck, cocked his ear and froze in that position. He couldn't hear clearly, but he heard all three men's voices muffled by the walls. Drawn by a force he couldn't explain, he left the room and walked with stealth apprehension down the hall. His trim diver's body moved sinuously as the carpet under his feet silenced his approach. He heard Angus' anguished Scot's voice asked. "David, how can you say that? He could have killed you."

Inside the stripped wall bedroom with no furniture but a perfectly made bed, David, Michael and Angus stood facing one another with palpable hostility. David only had on his jeans so the tribal bare chest was exposed. "Granted I didn't expect Dad to do that, but I had to confront him and show him how irrational his thinking is."

Michael said, "You risk your life without speaking to me. Don't do that again."

"Listen to me both of you." Adrian looked into the room hidden away behind the door. "Both of you have got me here. I came to you Gus when all I had was fear and the hope of being loved. I learned what love is. You can't stand there and tell me you want to kill my father."

"He's should be... neutralized," Angus said through clenched teeth.

"Don't let your pride and vengeance consume you," David cautioned.

"I'm Greek, and there comes a time when 'PC' and analysis can't excuse evil. You've got to overthrow tyrants," he rebuked with animalistic angry green eyes.

David pulled Angus toward him by his green shirt. "*Oedipus Rex, Medea, The Oresteia;* you read them to me and we read Shakespeare together. Gus, vengeance is tempered by justice. If I raised my hand against my father or let you do it, it would ruin us."

"Angus let me say something." Michael gently interjected. "My children abandoned me, not my youngest, Roberto. Discovering they didn't need me made me so angry. I told myself I'd punish them for their neglect. I accused them in my letter and put the rope around my neck. I knew the misery would punish them forever but couldn't do that to them."

"How did you overcome that anger?" Angus asked genuinely interested.

"Roberto kept me alive; he's our Angel, that's his second name. To help me out of my anger and weakness, he gave me David's book, and after I had read it, it inspired me not to let life victimize me. If my mindset didn't change, I'd be out there as just a big fucking prick, and I'd be lonely." He took Angus' hand. "I didn't know you were Greek, but now I understand how your psyche and David's fear grew into love." Michael took Angus' other hand and asked him in Greek. "You had David's first blood, did you give him yours?"

"He's the only man who's ever had me," he replied in Greek. Angus turned to David. "You always think you can cope, and then you get beaten or fail. Besides Adrian, your brother, Grace and your Mum, you love the wrong people."

"Was I wrong to love you? Am I wrong to love Michael? Something's changed! Since my first day with Michael, I now feel strength instead of fear. Willy, passed his vile judgment on me yesterday, and I beat him up – I liked it!" Through the crack in the door's hinge Adrian wanted to see his father up close but he watched them all closely.

Michael said, "David told me he loved you and I was jealous. Now I see how a Greek man of your profession loves and protects David I could be even more jealous, but I'm not."

"Why aren't you jealous of me?" Angus asked.

"Because you are a man and not an ignorant gutless fucking prick." Michael pointed in his face. "You have honor. Both of us have first blood with David. We understand love and equality. Let that be the bond of our friendship."

"You're a smooth talker alright but why shouldn't I stick around and try to take him back from you. I'm willing to break the rules to keep him safe."

"If you touch him, I'll kill the two of you; and then myself." Michael struck fear in Angus right to his soul. Behind the door, Adrian was enthralled because he liked *Goodfellas* and *The Godfather* but what was happening before his eyes was real.

David stood between them, touched their faces and then buried his face between them. Turning from left to right they fell silent and very slowly placed their arms around him. "Swear by the first blood you've both shared with me; you won't harm my father." David stepped back and opened his palms, and they kissed him in his right and left hand. "Besides my family, you're all I've got. I'm not sure who my friends are, but I'll find out tonight. I have to teach my father what my rights are, and I will change him."

"Can you really defy your father?" Angus asked challenging him.

"Good point," Michael said to Angus. "Solomon's set himself up as lawmaker and life giver. It explains how he tried to kill his own son and still make demands."

Adrian was horrified to hear that Solomon tried to kill his father.

"I thought I was going to shit a brick when Dad tried to kill me, but I won, and I'm going to have to fight men like him. Can I count on both of you?" They gestured to signal their loyalty. Adrian was stunned by the power David had over both men.

"They'll attack thinking we're diseased weaklings. I learned Judo knowing it would come to this." He grabbed them. "I've got your blood and spunk in me – ready?"

"Fuckin'… look at you!" Angus said through gritted teeth and a warrior grimace. "I'll take on any straight bloke and rip his balls apart… I hate them."

"Why?" Michael asked.

"You guys are telling the world you're real men because you've had wives and kids. The only cunts I've ever fucked are the pricks that cheat on their women. I'm 'Out' and I command respect. If any fucking breeder tries to queer bash me again, I'll sink my teeth in and rip his throat open," Angus replied snarling.

"Michael?"

"You're dealing with Cleavon, so you can count on me for anything."

"Who's that?" Angus asked.

"Michael's brother-in-law: he's a villain that's threatened Michael and his kids." David lifted his arm and brought it down like a sword cutting the atmosphere in half. "I'm going to mind fuck him!" David's violent reaction pushed them back.

"Shush, Adrian's here," Angus said and Adrian jerked back from the door.

"I don't care; I swear on my son's life and the spunk you put in me, I'm going to break him. Nobody fucks with my people!" David began speaking in Yoruba and then he switched to Greek and told Angus. "You gave me the love, and then the will, but I didn't have the courage before. I'll protect Michael as I want you to protect me. I loved you first and that's why I love Michael now."

Stunned, Michael said, "You speak Greek."

"I taught him everything a Greek should: from the *Iliad* to Philosophy and Eros. And he taught me Greek's tragedy: to love and to suffer. Now before I stuff my big fat Greek cock up both of you, get out." They shared awkward looks and Michael turned to him and kissed him on the neck. Adrian tiptoed back into his room. Inside, he sat down and thought how little he understood about his father's life, his mind and true nature.

CHAPTER TWENTY-NINE

Michael and David pulled their warm dark overcoats tightly up to their necks standing in one of the smart cul-de-sac roads in Canonbury. Michael pointed out some of the features of his new detached house to David, such as the lit black and white marble garden path leading to a white marble front wall with a shiny steel door. Out of the cold dark night, Mr. Man approached and aggressively called out David's name. Michael turned around abruptly and saw his angry face. Even though Mr. Man was very nicely dressed, he looked rough. This was due to the poverty he grew up in back in Jamaica and his jaunty body movements. His lean, tough physique and brown eyes were charged with malice as anyone in their right mind could tell. Just before he came to a stop, he flexed his shoulders and stood threateningly close to David's face. Michael stepped back and got on his mobile to call the bouncers he hired for the night.

"Willy come to me yesterday, tell me you beat him after you declare you're homosexual. What kind of shit you carrying on with? Is true; you turned to batty?" David was about to reply but Mr. Man told him. "I can't associate with those things."

"Then piss off." People came up the path, and Michael greeted them, gestured to the entrance and the comforts inside. Michael's hired ushers were inside the doorway to take coats and guide people.

Winston Manley began cursing David in patois and then switched to English. He berated him, and David watched his lips move but stopped listening because his heart and blood were racing. David scanned the two narrow alleys on the east and west side of the cul-de-sac road and moved toward it. Mr. Man's eyes were filled with rage and David watched the spit build in the corners of his mouth as he sprayed his homophobic condemnation in David's face as if it were vitriol. There was no end to his rage so he went on unaware David was leading him into the darkness. Winston's face loomed larger and got bigger and bigger until David couldn't see anything else.

Michael saw David's maneuver. Therefore, he told the bouncers to watch the door. Michael remembered everything he had learned in the army during his younger years and went to protect David.

"After I tell the others what you've turned into, you won't manage nothing but unemployment benefit." His indignation blazed across his face.

Michael jumped in and punched Winston in the lower spinal cord, and Winston doubled over. Michael got a grip on his cock and balls which Winston couldn't shake off and inflicted excruciating pain on him. "Move you gutter fuck, or I break your balls." Michael pulled him into the cul-de-sac and punched him in the heart. "Darling, leave us." David gave him the eye and went back toward the house. Winston crumbled as he tried to focus, but he saw David vanish into a blur.

"If I give the order, I know guys who can disfigure you." He punched Winston in the eye with his knuckles. "After they pour acid in your mouth we won't have to listen to your shit." This was the first and only time in Winston Manley's life that he was ever truly terrified. When he took on the persona of 'Mr. Man' he feared nothing but now Winston felt he was staring death in the face. Michael punched him in the gut and he thought he was going to vomit. "If you open your mouth I'll burn your tongue out with acid and chop your hands off." Spiraling into fear, Winston wet himself.

"You got a contract with David Bankole. If you don't fulfill your contract, I'm going to take out *another* contract on you." Michael's Italian voice left him in no doubt.

"I will dead before I work for a batty man and his roughneck Mob man," Winston defiantly exclaimed, bleeding.

"Alright: rest in peace." Michael let him go started to walk away.

Winston wheezed. "Wait..."

"You're not as stupid as you look. Go and clean yourself up, you'll hear from us. But if you're really stupid; mention David's name to anyone and I will tie you down, take a pig's foot and fuck you in the arse with it." The threat made Winston throw up.

Michael hurried back to David, who was in the foyer greeting people as they entered. Michael smiled at the guests and under his breath told David. "He's a mess. Follow me upstairs." The house was decorated with sheets of tissue paper shaped into angels. The uncarpeted stairs were noisy so Dr. Claude, Omar, Armed, and all the decorators saw them and Bruno followed Michael. "This is David. Bruno and his colleagues dressed the house. I'll be back soon." Bruno asked him something in Italian and Michael replied, "*Sì, aspettami, le mie cazzo di palle mi stanno uccidendo.*" He rushed David up the stairs. The gay boys asked what he said, and Bruno replied.

"His fucking balls are killing him but in Italian, it sounds better." The decorators were amused.

****

Michael locked the bathroom door. The luxury of the place in marble was a total contrast to the dark alley. Alone in the Greek style enclosure, he took David's face in his hands. "Are you ok darling?"

"Yes. He reminded me of African extremists, killing and persecuting gays and I just wanted to take a bull whip and beat him to death."

"No illiterate Godless gutter swine without honor is going to hurt us."

His words gave David a frisson. He ran his hand over Michael's bulging arms and chest. "I feel like I'm having a Jack Bauer day. Or our own kind of *24* episode. It's like we've been through a Leopold and Lobe or Bonnie and Clyde initiation."

Michael searched his pockets, pulled out a condom and gave it to David. "Give me a boost to go out there." Michael's reverberating Italian voice got under David's skin, and blood lifted his erection. The sight of Michael's face in the mirrored marble sanctuary and his deep voice begging crashed into David's central nervous system.

"Do it," Michael begged. "Take me," his voice echoed in the bathroom. Michael's topaz bright eyes sparkled against his Mediterranean skin. He kissed Michael wildly, and they struggled to take each other's coats off. "Nothing and no one has your beauty or fucking power." David dropped his clothes on the floor and Michael stripped. Looking at each other on the brink of ecstasy their passion filled the air like lightning at twilight. "Is it me or do you feel something mystical when we kiss?" David kissed him in agreement.

Over at David's house, Adrian paused before knocking on the bedroom door because he could hear Angus crying and talking and even the Greek music he was playing couldn't mute his voice. Adrian turned the handle and entered the room. Angus was sitting on the bed speaking in Greek on his mobile choking with emotion. He had the mobile on speaker, and two Greek voices were coming through. His anguish filled every word, and Adrian was immediately affected by it. Angus looked up, and his green and

258

raw eyes were streaming with tears. "…Mama, *bampás*, I'll call you back… I'll be alright." He listened to them speaking quickly and reassuring him. "Yes I love you too Mama, thanks *bampás*, love you," he concluded in Greek.

"I know about it, I heard the three of you earlier." The level of distress crashed against Angus once again, and he couldn't control himself. He turned around and cried loudly. He covered his face and his mouth but his shaking body hid nothing.

Adrian went over to him and patted his back. "Has something else happened?"

"I've lost him forever! I'm always second choice. I lost him to your Mum but I understood that. It hurt so much that I called your Mum and she was very nice to me."

"My Mum knows you?" Angus stared at him.

"Yes, when I was…upset I called her, and she met me. She's nice, I like her rage. When David married that cunt, your Mum called me and we meet again. We tore Veronika apart with Pagan curses. I took your Mum on a holiday to Athens. My parents looked after the both of us."

"Why didn't Dad tell me about that?"

"He doesn't know about my friendship with your Mum. He can't have all of me," he said resentfully. "I've tried to find someone else, but it's no good."

"But you're smart and fit; you've got a good heart. Gays want that…"

"Other men fall for me, but I can't get your Dad out of my blood."

"How can I know so little about my father's nature and character?"

"He covered it up and hid it so you wouldn't hate him. As much as he loves you, if you turned on him, he'd kill himself or go mental. I think it's the core between him and Michael. That's why Michael's loved-up now. Dave's soul is true at last." Angus wiped his face. "Physician heal thyself!!" Angus yelled in Greek.

"What?"

Angus translated for him. "Your Mum and I are under the same spell, only she sees no one but I fuck around."

"Why's everything we're all feeling about Dad never talked about online, on television, in social chat? Most people think gays are failed men, but Dad must be one hell of a man to get you all this crazy. Do you see leadership in him? I mean we've spent hours talking about Equality, or is it some kind of bond and phallic power…"

"You're Dave's son alright, brains and instincts," Angus interjected studying him. "I told you about *false evidence appearing real*/F.E.A.R. Look into it, especially considering the career you've got in mind." Angus crossed the room, opened his suitcase and took out a gold suit. "Cost me a fortune this. Dolce & Gabbana; got the shoes and everything. Dave loves style and brains. Looking this good I thought I'd win him back, but Michael's the one. Dave's discovered the hero within himself. I couldn't get him to do that." Adrian understood and recognized what Angus meant.

"After the girls were kidnapped in Nigeria I decided to work for the UN in some way. Now Michael's shown Dad his Human Rights, it's made him sexually political and fearless, hasn't it?" Angus nodded in agreement with Adrian's analysis.

CHAPTER THIRTY

Michael walked David past his friends and colleagues in an imperial manner. Dressed in a tuxedo but without a shirt; a gold crucifix lay against Michael's bare board chest. David's black leather sci-fi suit displayed his strong African body. His neck was wrapped with African, Aborigine and new age men's jewelry that hung down his chest in a multitude of colors and shiny silver. The two of them were the center of attention as they moved among the guests.

Throughout Michael's house, all the rooms had red and white balloon figures in various states of embrace, juxtaposed next to wire-frame human figures. The thin silver, black and white steel figures were clearly men and women with large breasts and protuberant members. The male and female figures were arranged into gay-bi-hetero sexual post-coital positions. The balloon couples were sprayed with fake snow and in the midst of the balloons, there were Santa's. The Santa in every room had one hand on his binoculars and the other hand in his pants watching the loving couples.

A camera and photo crew followed David and Michael into the room as flashlights lit in their faces. Cesare, Maria, and Fabio watched their father approach them, and Maria was stunned by Michael's appearance because he looked so virile. The three siblings were casually smart in their trendy clothes, but all three of them weren't expecting David to look like a sex symbol. His smile was as enchanting as a great star in World Cinema, rather than a media personality. Fabio said, "For fuck sake, that's Bankole from the TV talent show and London Live TV media program."

Michael's sons and daughter felt disconcerting levels of shock when they watched their father and realized he was involved with David Bankole.

Maria added, "Yeah, he's in that amazing clothes Ad where he's dancing, getting dressed to go out." Figuring out the implications of her father and David distilled an ambiguity of distaste and admiration in her face and body language because the erotic and romantic energy between them questioned her perception of her father.

"Fucking hell!" Fabio stated with glee. "His brother is Solomon Bankole,"

Maria said, "Wow! That is one Black man I *would* go out with in a heartbeat."

"Why didn't Papa say it was him, and not just some guy?" Cesare asked.

David stopped in front of Michael's sons and daughter, and he embodied nobility and radiated great erotic magnetism as though he was a renowned star. The fact that his father knew 99 of the top 100 African artists and introduced them to his sons and daughter helped David's confidence and self-esteem.

"Michael, these must be your sons and daughter," he said in a distinguished tone, filled with character. He offered his hand. "David Bankole; please, your names?" David looked straight into the faces of each one of them.

"Cesare," he responded and offered his hand. He didn't smile, but he didn't look hostile. David noted his auburn hair was curlier than Roberto's and he looked more Afro-European than his brothers because he favored his mother, Lola.

"I am Maria," she told him curtly made no attempt to offer a hand.

"Fabio." Just then, Roberto arrived with Lola, who was dressed in a classic Chanel ladies suit. Fabio continued. "This is very unusual, this event gathering..."

"I know," Michael interrupted. "I planned it that way."

The DJ switched tracks to Grace Jones' album, *Nightclubbing*. The one hundred guests throughout the house suddenly gave him a shout-out for his selection.

"Oh for heaven's sake!" Lola said. "David, please introduce me to your mother, I don't have time for this mini-drama; I must talk to her about her restaurant." She hooked David's arm and led him away.

Impatiently Michael told them. "Don't start something you can't finish because after the day I've had, I'm not in the mood."

Tersely, Maria said, "We're here, aren't we?" Her soft face was hardened with cynicism.

Michael glared at her. "When you made that dreadful mistake with the English boy who told you about being Black do you remember how Lola and I helped you and dealt with him?" Maria was definitely uncomfortable with the subject. "I see you remember; all of us felt that insult based on his bigotry. Don't repeat his stupidity, it will discredit you." It was only her parent's love and strength that got her through that misery.

She moved closer to Michael and pulled his arm close to her. "Sorry Papa."

He kissed her forehead and walked her into the crowd. The three brothers watched until Michael and Maria were gone. Fabio turned to Roberto. "Bankole is very exotic."

Cesare shook his head. "He looks like a rockstar affiliated with Lenny Kravitz's clique."

"Not really," Roberto replied. "He's wearing that gear more as a statement. He's conflating sci-fi with tribal Cyber chic. He's very Luc Besson meets Almodóvar." Roberto's brothers didn't know World Cinema. Adrian arrived and came into their huddle, full of smiles. On the other side of the room, Maria saw him, and she liked his style and pride that couldn't be concealed especially as he was sporting a happy face, dressed in a silver-gray skinny-suit, thin red tie, narrow collar white shirt and wearing red suede Chelsea boots.

"Adrian, these are my brothers; this is David's son." Adrian happily reached out to them and his affability and youthful zeal connected with Cesare and Fabio.

Adrian told them. "You look as wound up as I felt on Sunday, it's cool, though. I met your dad; such a great bloke. They aren't weird or nasty. Dad's ex-wife came up to York to 'Out' him and hurt me. But you should see them together. Black and white dudes you've seen in buddy movies, *Pulp Fiction*, that's shit; with our fathers, it's real!" Despite themselves, the brothers laughed.

"Yeah, and when Michael talks about my Dad, he gets serious, really sincere like Fabio Capello talking about the England team." Adrian put on a stern face and tried imitating an Italian dialect when he said, "We play without fear, and experience the spirit of the game." Adrian's impersonation wasn't too far off the mark.

The brothers liked that. Adrian snapped out of it and told them. "Don't get me wrong. Dad's loyalty is as tight as his love for my Mum and Arsenal."

Cesare asked him. "How the hell are they gay with those butch credentials, and us?"

"Wow!" Fabio said. "The three actors over there are the biggest Black stars in British film." Adrian watched the brothers' fascinated faces search out stars in the room and exchange gossip between each other. "And

263

there's Solomon Bankole..." Fabio said excited by the sight of him walking into the room beside to his father.

Adrian shouted. "Uncle Solly come here!" He came over to Adrian. "Uncle Solly, these are Michael's sons." He stood there in all his football glory as tough and casual as his heroes Pele, John Barnes and Ian Wright.

Roberto shook his hand first, and Fabio pushed him aside slightly, but Cesare waited for Solly to offer his hand, which he did after he'd greeted his brothers.

Starstruck, Fabio declared. "Great to meet you mate! serious: amazing work in building that team of Black footballers, and your work when you were in London!"

"Incredible!" Cesare added happily agreeing with his brother.

"Much appreciated," Solly replied. Across the room Maria fancied the pants off Solly, so she kept her distance. Nevertheless, her vulva played havoc with her body.

"This is my father, QC Bankole." Cesare was really impressed, particularly by Solomon's sartorial elegance, but Adrian kept tight control of himself otherwise he would have lashed out, knowing that his grandfather assaulted David earlier.

Michael's friends socialized with the guests. They were art historians from his former University, as well as clients in London who Michael bought for. The difference in dress and class between his academic friends and his wealthy friends was telling. His wealthy friends were fashion conscious, and his academic friends weren't. His wealthy clients weren't that old whereas his academic friends were all in their fifties. Three of the four artists that Michael represented were also there: two European women and one Haitian Black Parisian guy who moved to London three years earlier. Every face in the room had its own life history of struggle, egotism, courage, and beauty.

David's friends were well-known musicians, actors from television, film and theater. Some of his other friends were DJs and some of Solly's football friends arrived along with members of the Black Professionals Association, and The Urban Nigerian Entrepreneurs who ran their own business. Some staff from the Black LGBT and friends who came to him after his statement on anti-violence in Grime and Raga music also circulated within the crowd forming an alternative London Fashion Week.

People came to David from all over the house as they arrived and found him mixing with guests. Each person asked if he was ok and commented on the 'sex tape', the tweets, online blogs, and the online reaction. Sophia made her way toward him and took David's arm. Her style was distinctly 1980s Versace. "There's so much online chat about you and Veronika! The company comments page is jammed with messages of support to you and remarks about you punishing Horia!"

"Are the blogs positive or negative?"

"Mixed, but some people really have obscene things to say about you."

"Good!" Grace and her crew of girlfriends, including Amy, her neighbor came to David and offered their support. Amy's loyalty and strength were truly palpable.

Cynthia felt beautiful accompanied by Solly and Grace. Dressed in vintage 70s Halston fashion, Cynthia called David over, and Solly signaled to Adrian to create a huddle and Cynthia said, "Adrian, your parents deal with things very openly. David, I'm still proud of you. Now explain to Adrian that his mother has the right to a life too. Child, don't distress your mother. I'm tired of her depression, trying to live for you and David. Let her live, you understand me, boy?" Contrite, Adrian nodded.

"Grace, find a man who'll love you." David and Adrian searched each other's faces, and Grace was thankful. "This past week everything's been so strange; particularly since I like your man's wife, Lola." Cynthia lifted her head and caught her breath. "I never imagine I could say that. I tell you, today, God help people who live in the past."

"Mum, I know I'm asking a lot from you."

"I can manage. And from the conversation I had with your father today, even he is prepared to accept you've changed." They all took a moment to consider that.

Angus entered the room dressed in his gold shoes, gold suit, and gold shirt. He drew more eyes to him than anyone else chiefly because he was full of sublimated rage and sexual frustration. He gave off a powerful energy that no one could ignore.

Adrian approached him through the thirty people in the room and Angus said, "Back off, I'm giving it the red carpet star appearance bollocks. I can't be fluffy. Love you." Adrian winked and backed away. Angus headed toward Dr. Claude and Dr. Nasir, and they were about to greet him when he turned off and stopped in front of Grace. Because he was one of the few white men in the room, he really stood out.

Grace said, "Hello dear, you look grand." Angus casually led her to one side.

People in the room wondered who he was, and Barry eyed every detail of Angus' £5,000 gold colored evening wear. His black and silver wavy hair shaped his strong Greek face and Barry wanted to get the measure of him.

"Are you alright?" Angus asked and studied Grace closely when she nodded. "You've done a great job with Adrian, I've been talking to him and he's handling everything really well. Don't worry about him."

"Incoming – David's on this way over." Angus stood tall like no other man.

David eyed Angus, baffled by the familiarity between him and Grace.

"Don't ask me how I'm friends with Grace…"

Grace felt their tension. "When you married that creature we became friends." David thought about it and told himself, 'why not'. The realization was nonetheless awkward face to face, particularly since David sensed Angus had trumped him.

Cynthia approached Lola and her brother Cleavon. Both women had taken an instant liking to each other because they had a lot in common back in Jamaica and professionally, therefore when Lola introduced her brother to Cynthia, she was gregarious. Cleavon's hip-hop casuals somewhat aged him.

David came straight over to them and Cleavon said, "Your video is one hell of a bump and grind your drop on that white gal. Me like the part when you bust-up the dirty white bwoy fe thief your wife punanny." David knew how much Cleavon un-nerved Michael so he was casual and cool because he intended to smash him and walk away unperturbed. David felt instant loathing and violent hatred towards him.

"Cleavon give me a minute, will you?" David asked with a genial smile. They moved and David quickly led the way to the top of the house as *Got To Give It Up* by Marvin Gaye came through the sound system. The array of casual and formal dress among the guests displayed a historical line of couture and street fashion worldwide.

David and Cleavon entered the empty white bedroom, and David closed the door. It was lit with ultraviolet. Therefore, their faces appeared deep purple with ghostly eyes and teeth. David yanked Cleavon's arm and flipped him onto the floor. Cleavon landed badly, and David placed his boot on his groin so Cleavon kicked and bucked his lower body but the pressure David pushed down forced him to stop. Cleavon looked up at him and David's eyes and teeth seemed to loom out of the ceiling as everything threatened to come down on him.

"Tonight, I'm going to announce to the media that Michael and I are a couple." At first, Cleavon didn't understand, but when he worked it out, he was stunned. He tried to get up but David stepped on his knee and he yelped. "Lola didn't tell you that Michael and I are lovers because she knows you're homophobic."

"But I watch you wax that pussy in the film. What distortion you-a-go-on-wid? You and Michael, you have sons and daughter."

"Of course; sorry… you're stupid." David's posh voice needled Cleavon. "You've never really been the same since your teacher molested you at school," David casually stated. He took his foot off Cleavon and hauled him up by his arm.

Cleavon took a swing at him, and David's three Judo moves landed him back on the floor. Cleavon doubled his fists straining at the jaw as fear spread through him. "Who tell you that shit?"

"Michael of course." David rolled his eyes. "Don't worry; I'll get the facts right when I talk to the media about it." Cleavon's ears blocked as if he'd climbed 100 feet in seconds. "You were raped, so obviously you *are* homophobic."

"Shut your dirty mouth!" he replied. Rolling about due to the pain in his knees he said, "I'm gonna fix Michael. All of you un-natural bastards deserve hanging…" Cleavon cursed him in patois and as he did David heard a huge chorus of voices rather like a choir coming out of his mouth condemning all gays. Cleavon got on his feet.

During the sexual abuse, Cleavon suffered physical paralysis and trauma, and the shame of it made him extremely violent as a teenager. He tried to regain a sense of his manly authority through violence against men who threatened him and dominance over women he got involved with, but the shame he felt now knowing Michael told David everything, paralyzed him. He wanted to fight, but David had everything he lacked.

"Leave Michael alone, or I'll tell how your teacher fucked you for… a year was it? If someone tried to shove his cock in my mouth I'd bite it off." Cleavon felt worse.

"If I was sodomized, the way you've been, I'd knife the man who degraded me and to hell with the police and my day in Court. But *you* let him back in…" Cleavon looked around the room as it began to tilt and spin as if he were drunk.

"I love Michael so much I'll do anything to hurt you." David took out a sheet of paper from his jacket pocket, unfolded it and showed Cleavon. "This is a mock up. I took pictures from your Facebook and photo-shopped them into a gay porn scene with you and S&M guys fucking you. I put the Priest in the scene just to make it less boring." Cleavon was horrified at the sight of himself, and David measured his shock reaction.

"I could break you. You're over forty, weak, and stupid. I might even help you to deal with the awful pain, and the debilitating impact that man's rape has had on you because that *must* have been vile and frightening for you as a boy."

Distraught, he asked. "So how come you treat me like shit!"

"Because I don't care about you and I'm not interested in your life."

The hatred in Cleavon's eyes would have forced a weaker man to fear retaliation, but David didn't fear him because he understood psychological violence and fear.

"I'll tell the media I'm happy to be gay because, unlike you, I wasn't raped by my teacher for two years. I'll get my father to track down your teacher and charge him. There's no statute of limitations on raping kids, since the Jimmy Savile case. My father's a QC, and he'll do what I tell him. When we get to Court, the whole story will be public." Cleavon was panic stricken and David's face never looked more sinister.

"A year ago I would have pleaded with you for our happiness, but you're nothing but a psychopath no woman wants. Michael is *my* man! If you raise your hand to him," David's bright eyes flashed with fury. "I'll use my father to get you in the witness box and detail how you used a tampon to hide your shame." The memory of it brought tears to Cleavon's eyes. "Now get out of this house." Cleavon had no strength so he slowly left the room humiliated.

Seeing Cleavon defeated David breathed to regain his equilibrium. He got down on his knees and said, "Dear God. How do they do it? Most straight men can humiliate and degrade people as if their lives depended on it. I've learned from people who hate us, and say the most dreadful things. I've learned even more from gays who have suffered the brutality of their family. These twisted men who act like terrorists because they believed in their sexism; I won't cower to them. I prayed and you sent me my guardian. Michael is kind and beautiful. In the name of Jesus and God Almighty …Lead me not into temptation and deliver me from evil," he kept repeating.

CHAPTER THIRTY-ONE

David stood tall. "Good evening to Michael's guests and all my friends, family, employees. May I ask, have you all seen the tape online today?" Everyone had seen it. Subsequently, there were catcalls, barking, and cries of 'Yowser'. A single voice declared, "Mash-up Man!" A guy from the Men's Group turned to Omar and Ahmed.

"Alright, here's a documentary interview that will be included with the tape as of tomorrow. A Q&A will follow this screening."

Grace called out. "Don't say you're retiring; we won't believe it."

"That ladies and gents, that's the missus, my son's mum, Grace. Babe you should know me, I'll never step out of the spotlight." His friends and family's applause and good will filled him with confidence. "Can you please prepare questions and I'll answer them shortly. I'll get out of the way for the next 45 minutes."

The monitors switched images from David addressing his friends in the house to a black & white introduction of him walking through the streets of London with Eugene Martins, the Black cultural theorist. David was dressed in an Ozwald Boateng gray suit and he presented himself as an aristocrat would. Every aspect of his private school background and his father's social training in etiquette supported him.

On all three floors of the house, people watched the monitors as Dr. Martins began the interview. "I was surprised to get your call David, but I'm very pleased to have this conversation with you." They were walking through the City of London's financial district. In the summer evening light, London looked fantastic with a bright ethereal sky and landmark silhouettes.

"You said you wanted to talk through key points of Black men's rites of passage and how white supremacists demonize Black male identity."

"Yes, my Romanian wife and I shared two passions; political and erotic enlightenment." In vivid color, a shot of David and Veronika, post-coital in an embrace came onto the screen. The intimacy between them was deeply warm and personal. They were both smiling and caressing each other's faces. The scene dissolved back to black & white with Dr. Martins and David sitting on the steps of St. Paul's. "When you called you said, out of the break-up of your marriage you've discovered things about yourself and Black male identity. What have you personally learned?"

"My wife's adultery was very upsetting, and it compelled me to ask what I didn't give her and why she threw away the values we shared."

Dr. Martins tactfully asked. "Did she tell you or did you discover why she became involved with another man?"

"I discovered her adultery as a result of her drug dependency. She became more careless in her social life. We have the same mobiles and one day she took mine, and I had hers. I was stunned by the text and photos of her assignations."

"Were you angry?"

"I was more shocked, considering I gave her love, money, independence and freedom to live her life without controlling her."

"Did you feel betrayed or did you have an open relationship where *you* were free to see other women?"

"An open relationship isn't a marriage. I've never had sex with anyone since I got married. I come from a very traditional background; so did she." He took a moment to contemplate. "Things weren't easy for her. She's been in rehab four times. She was never the same after she miscarried both of our sons due to her drug addiction."

Stunned, Eugene Martins said, "I don't imagine she'll thank you for discussing her business in public."

"She's going to discuss my personal business. Recently she's done something that's compelled me to release 'the sex tape' and make this documentary."

"What has she done?"

"She's forging a racist attack on me to present herself as the white goddess and me as the 'black' beast; based on the media's myth of Black men's pathology."

"What do you mean by that?" Dr. Martins asked him critically.

"Racists prefer to imagine a pathological Black male. In *White Racism: A Psychohistory* by Joel Kovel, his studies detail the neurosis and pathology of racist thought extremely well. My father gave me the book to prepare me for life. I've learned despite my education, achievements or work; some people still twist me into their racist fantasy. I constantly have to deal with *their* frame of reference. Namely, the niggas they love to hate."

270

Dr. Martins pulled back and replied, rather alarmed. "That's one hell of an assertion."

"No, it's based on my everyday lived experience. The fact that I'm on TV; manage urban crews in music and have a BSc and MA is immaterial in the minds of pathologically disturbed people. I know people like this are everywhere in modern society; I just didn't figure there was one in my bed."

Their discussion ended as the scene switched to Veronika on the bed saying: "Take me from behind, go on, do it, thrill me." The words out of her mouth changed from a whisper to a compelling plea. David moved behind her and fulfilled her desire.

The documentary focus changed to black & white as David and Dr. Martins walked through Canary Wharf past numerous people, but they were the only two Black men in sight. "Veronika is not a racist she's an unconscionable woman with a rapacious pathology. She's prepared to make people think I'm a sexually immoral 'black' beast. Historically the media has forged this maladjusted thug."

"I've investigated this subject for my book *Othellophobia*."

"That's why I contacted you, Eugene. Most Black men don't know how to cope when they are falsely accused by white society, and particularly when the accusing voice is that of a white woman. Historically, the media has taken the side of the perceived white goddess over their demonized 'black' beast."

The location switched to David's office, where a montage of images depicting Black men throughout modern history played on flat screen monitors. From the jazz age to the hip-hop era there were all kinds of men. The wall behind David featured heroes, and on the wall behind Dr. Martins, there were the media's demonized villains.

"Yesterday you were talking about the media demonizing Black men, and the way they are victimized. When did you become conscious of this?"

"Through my father's work and his struggles: he's triumphed over all racist myth of Africans inferiority." Angus looked away from the screen and over at Solomon sitting among David's and Michael's friends. Solomon was stunned by David's statement. Cynthia took his hand, and he looked around the room until he found David sitting next to Solly and Adrian. Solomon spotted Michael sitting beside his son and daughter, and he wondered if David had told him what happened earlier. Barry's lustful eyes were all over Angus, but he wanted to watch the documentary, so he was truly distracted. Angus knew Barry was eying him and he intended to have him later.

On screen David said, "Once a white woman accuses a Black man, he's socially criminalized. Dr. Angus Vassallo is one of the leading specialists in Britain on Black male psychology. His work carries on from where Frantz Fanon's left off. His case studies examined the socially criminalized Black and how the pathological racist psyche imagines an evil 'black' hypersexual who threatens the white imago."

Eugene Martins pointed to the Black heroes. "David it's most interesting that you've included scientists, political leaders, philosophers and artists from all over the Diaspora in the montage running above your head."

"We have to look beyond hip-hop media history. Some women consider Black men as socially inferior with specific sexual traits. This is why we're so often accused of rape. Initially, Veronika was puzzled by me because I didn't fit anything she learned about 'blacks'. Consequently, our courtship was full of endless delights. But drugs distorted her mind. I'm talking about cocaine, heroin, and crystal."

"Did you do anything to help her?"

"I spent almost £200,000 on rehab. I took care of her. My mother looked after her. My sister helped her recovery in every way she could."

A montage of home video movies of David with his mother and family played. The scenes showed David growing up from an eight-year-old boy playing football, learning to swim and going off to school. He was in the school play, studying computers, taking the hard-drive apart and putting it back together. In front of the class, he solved a complicated equation with a reward from his teacher at the City of London School for Boys.

The scene changed as Dr. Martin interviewed David's former teacher. "What was David like as a boy?" the bespectacled middle-aged man in a neat tweed jacket said.

"He was one of a kind. We never knew what road he'd take because he was good at several things. I thought he was going to be a musician; he plays the piano very well. My colleague thought he'd go into computer sciences because his understanding of hardware and software was clearly evident. But our Headmaster was right when he said David could have become a local MP; he was interested in people and how they lived."

The scene cut to a montage of his clients and employees. They were all from diverse racial backgrounds. Mr. Man stood in a video recording studio and said, "If it wasn't for David I wouldn't have this career." He told a well know DJ from a London Urban Radio station, and then one by one David's clients praised him for the integrity he'd shown in managing their careers.

Dr. Martins asked him, "How does that make you feel, hearing your clients speak about you like that?"

David was bashful yet clearly very proud. "My mother told me if you can do someone a kindness and help them it will make you feel great. She said it would lighten your spirit and remind you how dreadfully wicked people are."

"Do you share her values in life?"

"My family is my inspiration, and Grace has given me the greatest happiness of my life because our son is amazing." The footage cut to the past Christmas when David and Grace danced together. He watched it, and he was clearly delighted.

Dr. Martins sat in a lecture theater and waited for students to file out the door. Angus past students and stood beside Eugene Martins. Above the lectern, the lecture title read. 'Crime and Passion: criminalizing Black Identities in media society'.

"Dr. Vassallo your new book has come out and I wanted to take this opportunity to clarify terms. You've researched social media pathology. David Bankole cites your work as vital to his ability to cope with bigotry. What's the core of your research?"

"The 'pathological psyche'. By that I mean unconscionable people who discard equality and inclusion which strives to achieve democracy. People with these traits fixate on *their* concept of entitlement. They believe life owes them everything."

"How does David's life experience exemplify your research?"

"As a psychiatrist, I won't discuss David's sessions, but he won't mind me saying I've helped him recover from the death of his two sons. My studies have shown me that David has built what I call 'the champion trait' to sustain his masculinity. Certain Black men have a victim mentality because they lack the power to overturn the supremacy which the State gives to a majority of white men and some women. Men who construct a champion identity do so because they're advocates of liberty and equality."

"Why have you spent your professional life studying Black men?"

"Like millions of white blokes, Black men fascinate me. We've done dreadful things to you guys throughout history, and I won't perpetuate that." Angus got up and collected his book from the lectern and handed Eugene a copy of *Crime and Passion: Criminalizing Black Identities*. "I love you guys; that's why I do this." The smile on Angus' face was frozen into the film frame and it faded out.

David's face faded in. In a montage, home movies showed great moments between David playing kids games with Adrian from birth. As a seventeen-year-old with Grace, they looked young and happy and Cynthia and Solomon looked proud. In the final minutes, David and Solly were together with Adrian all around London, at football matches, with Solly's wife Alice at their wedding, and then David and Adrian's faces watching Solly play football on TV and the two of them kissing him the screen.

Back in David's office, Dr. Martins said, "You do have your detractors."

"That's reality. Some people hate me," David replied casually. Five minutes of footage showed people from all walks of life in a Vox-pop giving their opinion of David. They didn't like him for one of many reasons: he was too popular; people said he was too opinionated, too visible or too willing to sell his African heritage for a marriage to a white woman. A West London gang of six boys said he was soft on gays.

The blurry image of Veronika naked with a camcorder in her hand faded into a pixel distortion of David's erection and then traveled up his body to his smiling face.

Veronika sang Madonna's *Like a Prayer*, but she really could not sing. Her rendition had no substance. "David tell me about this?" Dr. Martins asked.

"As you can hear it's a cover recording. It's my ex-wife. As sexy as she is, she didn't have the stuff that stars are made of, a voice. I spent a fortune on producing and promoting her, but no one anywhere would buy. This reality destroyed her. She couldn't cope and turned to drugs to live with her pain. There are girls and girl groups that have even less talent than Veronika, but they're stars because they're Brits. Veronika has a heavy Romanian accent, and people couldn't understand her. They just made the usual vampire jokes, and that cut her up. She hated those comments as much as I hated the nigger slurs and pathological myths about 'blacks'."

"How far did that go as a bond between you?"

"It's one of the reasons we got married. I can prove I'm not a maladjusted nigger, but Veronika's idol is Catherine Tramell, the character in *Basic Instinct*, a predatory vamp. You can't disclaim the myth of a savage or a vamp if you idolize it."

Footage of Solly being interviewed on Nigerian TV came onto the screens above their heads and David looked up to his brother over Dr. Martins' head.

A Nigerian journalist who was clearly a fan looked pleased with the scoop. "In summing up, what do you think has made you the man you are?"

"My brother, David, he's a fighter; he's wise because he reads all kinds of things and meets people who he listens to. He's great with women; they love him! David taught me the true meaning of discipline: study, practice, and win. At eighteen until I was thirty I was too busy playing for my clubs and England to learn intellectual stuff. But my Dad and David taught me true Black pride. With my Dad, it's history and law. With David, it's human rights, romantic love, and Judo. Because of Dad and David, I have a successful marriage, loving times with my kids and all this. People don't like bullies; a loving heart will draw people to you." The footage cut to Solly's fans cheering.

Footage of David and Adrian playing football faded in over Solly's face. David and Adrian were clearly enjoying tackling each other, and then Solomon came onto the pitch and he joined them. It was a rare sight. On the sidelines, Grace and Cynthia were cheering their men on. The camera was handed to Grace, and Solly ran onto the pitch and joined his family and the laughter went on and on as the film ended.

"You told me you've learned about yourself and asked for this meeting?"

"I've reached the end of my patience with heterosexism. It's self-destructive. I'm a man's man and I will fight for my right to love who I want. After that marriage, I know the truth." David got to his feet and looked into the camera. "I prefer men." Without the need for another word David stared at the world. Dr. Martins' reaction changed from detached inquiry. Anyone watching could see that Eugene Martins was a bit shaken. What no one knew was the fact that he dare not make the same declaration. A smile sprang from the deepest level of Eugene's depression.

275

"How… I mean where do you get the nerve to go public on this?" Eugene had hidden away everything that he truly felt about life from everyone; therefore, his eyes searched David to understand his state of mind.

"Eugene, most of my life I've been afraid. I'm not anymore. I'm looking for real, honest love with the right guy." Dr. Martins got up and stuck his hand out and David shook it. Dr. Martins was clearly surprised David was calm and confident.

The lights came up on all three floors, and people's faces registered their shock. Angus looked at David and clenched his fist. The crew from Five Live TV turned on their cameras, and he waited for David's signal. "Love is an overworked word when it's dishonest. But this is the truth. I've found my heart's desire, Michael, darling, please stand up." Michael did but he was breathing heavily and looked somewhat anxious.

"You've changed my life and I'll love you forever because of it."

Cesare could see his father's anxiety, so he went to him. Michael took Cesare's hand and squeezed it tightly. Silently, Cesare spoke to him, and Michael tried to stop shaking. Roberto also went to his father and Lola got up and said.

"My husband, ex-husband; has everything to live for, now he's found the courage to live in the face of condemnation. If I won't condemn him, why should anyone else?"

David approached Michael and Lola took him by the shoulders and planted a kiss on his forehead. Cynthia stood up, went over to Lola and embraced her. People in the room felt the intense level of truth and angst. It was unusual for a media event because they're often characterized by insincerity and aggrandizement.

Maria also felt her father's anxiety. Their estrangement bothered her, but she couldn't bring herself to discuss his sexual identity due to her religious beliefs and the fact that as his daughter she couldn't cross-examine him because as an Italian Caribbean she'd never have that right. Michael looked at her desperately and she couldn't resist her father because he'd never been unkind to her. And although they hadn't talked in ages, she knew she was still his princess. When she came to him, he almost cried. He turned away from cameras and people and rocked her gently from side to side telling her thank you.

The Five Live TV crew filmed people's reactions and eventually Michael turned to the crowd, held up his hand and kept it aloft until people quiet down and his face appeared on monitors in rooms on all three floors of the house.

"Good evening. I am Michele Giancarlo De Farenzino. Tonight in my new home I have my former wife, my three sons, beautiful daughter and members of my partner's family here. For David and me, as fathers and formally married men, changing one's life is not easy, especially when you're over fifty. Finding this extraordinary man who loves me has been my salvation." The media crews captured people's disbelieving faces, and as they sequentially appeared on the monitors, Michael continued. Ahmed and Omar looked towards other guys from the Men's Group, but they were OK.

Michael continued. "I love David's honesty; it's changing my life. We share so many values. I know as sure as there is a God, we are right for each other."

People began to take out their mobiles. Michael's close friends paid attention to him, and they looked over at David. Michael continued. "I know people will have an issue with us but in a society of Equality and Human Rights, it matters that David saved my life and I love him." Michael's friends watched him with approbation.

"Michael, no one's homophobia is going to stop me loving you." The media staff started taking notes.

Ayodele Oladayo, a newspaper man from the *London Commuter,* who wanted to be a press officer for the Nigerian Embassy, said, "David, is this a publicity stunt?"

"I don't know any Black man who'd masquerade as gay; do you?"

Marcia Blackwood, a prominent voice in the Black media and local politics from London Live TV said, "But David, in the documentary you've presented yourself as a serious, intelligent businessman and a regular type of bloke. We all saw that you obviously like women; so how can you be gay?"

"Marcia, sexual preference does not define masculinity. On TV, Frasier is very camp, but he's not gay." She acknowledged the point.

Ciarán Mulroney, an Irishman with twenty-five years' experience of sports coverage and commentary turned to Solly because he'd help to make him a star and held his mobile up. "Solly how'd you feel about your brother's transformation?"

"Proud. Veronika went up to York at the crack of dawn, got my nephew out of bed and right on the doorstep she viciously said his dad's queer. Isn't it enough she killed David's other sons with drugs when she was pregnant, but then she does that. Adrian rushed home, but we're alright now. I don't care who David kisses, as long as he isn't a coward." Solly told Ciarán, and other reporters noted it.

"Are you really OK with your Dad being gay, Adrian?" a Black woman asked.

"We're *obsessed* with other people's sex lives. My dad believes in God and helps people. Everyone at his firm and millions of people on TV know he's no criminal. Stop asking me questions as if he's a Communist with a disease. He's a top bloke." Omar and Ahmed hoped their sons would be the same.

"We should talk," Maria told Adrian. "Even as grownups we want our parents to love each other and suddenly I realize Mum and Dad *really* do. I mean, divorce and hatred are as common as dirt. I just have to learn that your Dad and mine really love each other. We're the millennium generation, so this shouldn't be a big deal. It means..." She searched for an answer, and the monitors showed people in the house waiting and watching her anxiously and intensely.

"It means we have to change," Solomon replied. "We all have to get rid of the hate we cling to. His eyes which locked into David, were unflinching.

Britain's most famous Black actor asked Solomon. "Do you hate who David is?"

"No."

The other actors looked at David and their awarding winning pal. All four Black men exchanged tense glances. At the back of the room, Femi, an investment banker who could pass for ugly, scowled at David. He was a member of the Nigerian Business club who David casually knew. "You are disgusting; what you choose to be."

David yelled, "Shut your mouth before I come over there and smack you."

"So you've turned into a thug as well as a homosexual."

"If you don't like my life; then don't make it your business."

"I know back home people would spit on you." Femi declared with revulsion.

David pushed his way across the room, and people on the floor below came up to catch them live. They rushed up the stairs, and some girls got ahead and barged into the room.

David came face to face with Femi and then smacked him. Solly was close behind with Adrian watching fascinated by the confrontation. Femi threw a punch but missed so David grabbed his wrist and twisted his arm up his back and people wanted a fight.

Femi contemptuously yelled, "Poof!"

"If your mother charged less for taking it up the arse, I wouldn't have to deal with you!" Grace's brother, Erwin, yelled 'Yeah!' as he moved out from the crowd. No one in the room had ever heard an insult of that kind, and they were all caught in shock.

Angus said to Barry. "Black men are the best, aren't they?" His flirtatious tone excited Barry. Even though Barry preferred white men, but the corporeal and intellectual flash that distilled David's persona aroused him as no one else had.

David eye-balled Femi and pushed his chin out gritting his teeth daring Femi to hit him. Michael proudly watched, and his sons and daughter were forced to reconsider everything they thought they knew about gays' timidity.

"You antiseptic bloodless eunuch!"

"Yes Daddy! Lash him again!!" Adrian screamed poking a hole in the air.

David stepped back and spat on Femi's flies. The white mess in front of his privates looked obscene.

Angus said, "You're a malignant bigot, but I can help you with that."

Tony said, "Get this savage bitch out of my face."

"Mate, in his own way he may be trying to tell David he wants him."

"I'm a man!" Femi yelled.

"I'm a doctor, and I'm telling you, you're not."

Tony twisted his face filled with bitter revulsion, and glared at Femi. The guests and the media zoomed in with intrusive scrutiny. Tony said, "My wife and I work with fantastic gays in our salon, *Fabuloso*, and they're great."

"You don't understand mate. This person is male, he's not a man." Clad in gold as he was, Angus' words and presence seemed omnipotent, but Femi protested bitterly.

Amy leaned in and said to Grace. "Good God, that doctor must read from the same book of curses as David." Grace nodded, and the look in her eyes told Amy something more. Amy looked at David and back at Angus and then at Grace.

Her blue eyes and ginger hair was filled with energy. She had no secrets from Grace because she loved her as only decent people can, so she clenched Grace's hand and looked at Angus and David and back at Grace again. "Were they, are they?"

"David is the love of his life." Amy looked at Angus, shocked.

"Don't stare, there are cameras all around," Grace whispered. "I'll tell you everything when we get home." Amy eyed her closely and nodded her head.

Solly suddenly stepped in, and people were pulled in by his stardom. "You two," he said to Angus and Tony, "shut it." Pointing at Femi, he said, "You, spunk face, fuck off!" Every woman in sight remembered his Brazilian underwear Ad showing him race across the pitch to score a goal with the tagline: 'nothing to hide'. All the men loved him for his amazing skill, and the fact he was bought by the Brazilian club. Britain lost him, and Solly told aspiring boys, it didn't matter because the world was theirs.

Femi left as fast as he could, and Erwin followed him out and downstairs pass people. "I know you Nigerians have your ways, but I'm from Hackney so let me run it down for you. "If you trouble David again; I'll take a hammer and break every bone in your foot." Erwin stepped back, and Femi went out the front door with all due haste. Erwin turned around and saw countless people on the stairs and hallway watching him. He fixed his jacket and went looking for David.

Upstairs, Michael was on his mobile telling the caterers to serve. He looked at the crowd in the room and told them. "I have Champagne, hors d'oeuvres, canapés, Bruschetta, moi-moi, jollof rice, ackee and saltfish. Also Indian, Italian and a few Greek dishes." Adrian and Michael's sons dashed for the food. "In the kitchen, there's beer, wine, cocktails, waters, and freshly prepared fruit juices. In a minute, the music will start, and David and I are here all night to meet you and talk about things; be my guests." The catering staff entered the room carrying platters of food and disposable napkins.

Erwin took David by the arm and led him away from people, into the hall. "You handle yourself good but like I said years ago; makes no difference you're gay, you done right by my sister, she still loves you, and that goes for me. Anybody trouble you, threaten you because you're gay; come to me, and I'll put them in the hospital." David nodded, and Erwin patted his face and then walked away to get some food.

Angus told Grace. "My work's going great; now all I need is a man?"

"Me too: it's weird, now David not afraid anymore, I'm not either." She leaned in and quietly told him. "We chose the wrong man to love, didn't we?" Her words cut through him and she felt the pain in him, so she led him out the room quickly.

CHAPTER THIRTY-TWO

Grace escorted Angus through the congestion hall, pulled a door open and they were in a utility room with a new washing machine, brooms, and a vacuum cleaner. The smell of paint and adhesive filled their nostrils as music and voices filled the room. "I'll never tell, sweetheart, talk to me," she said holding his face in her hands. His pain appeared to break his face and she thought he was going to scream so he covered his mouth and he sobbed with convulsions. She hushed and patted him comfortingly as she had comforted David and Adrian in the past.

Through his tears he said, "In a way I always knew he'd never be mine but I hoped…"

"I know. I've felt so bad for you because even though he moved out, he never left me. We've always had Adrian and that's kept us nice." She forced all her emotions back down to prevent herself from crying. "Here's what you do to get over this…" She tilted his head up, took a hankie from the inside of her black wool dress at her shoulder and dried his eyes. "I've read your work; your dignity will help lift you up. Your ideas can save lives. When our sons fall into misery because of how they're treated and talked about, your work is out there to save them. God is proud of us; your mother told me you *really* believe." She kissed him on his eyebrow. "Life changes, so we have to. He has!" She smiled compassionately and confessed.

"I'm going to let somebody else love me. Are you?" He thought about.

"I spent all day with Amy, you remember her? My Irish friend…" He nodded. "She's my soul sister. Her skin color makes no difference. Amy and my brother, Erwin. We talked about my life and my future: what's right for me. Gus, everything changes. Even with a man you love the most, like my own child, who's now a man. Men leave to start their lives. Marriage, kids, jobs, health; so many things change us. Look how nice you look tonight. There are guys out there who want you, I can sense it. There are men out there for me too. Erwin told me my beauty is immortal. Isn't it great that a brother can say that? I have to learn not to let rage scare me. You know how much I hated that cunt."

He smiled and their past lifted him. "I fuckin' hated her more."

"No you didn't. She's the only white person I've *ever* hated." He looked at her deeply, pulled her to his chest and kissed her head.

"If you allow someone else to love you, I promise you, darling, you'll heal."

"You reckon?"

"I've come through everything a woman suffers when she feels unloved. Last night I cried and said to Erwin, I want something for myself and he told me. 'You've got it'. People in my life love me, especially David's family... even yours."

Angus pulled himself together. "They christened you with the right name – you know that? Thanks love." He kissed her forehead.

"Wipe your face," she told him as though he was family. "Do I look alright?" His smile was truly reassuring and her heart went out to him again. They had shared so much pain and loss together it was a story in itself; however they kept a low profile even though they had shared over 20,000 words in text messages and hours of telephone conversation.

****

Surrounded by Ignacio, his former academic colleague, a gender scholar of distinction, as well as Omar, Ahmed, and three patrons, Michael asked. "What do you think of David?" Isabel, a wealthy patron who considered herself avant-garde in every way threw her arms around him, as only Brit's who adore Margot Fonteyn can, and exclaimed her approval. As a group, they tried to be fashionable and 'hip', as their clothes and manner indicated, but they had no luster because years of government regulation of their professional conduct left them desiccated. Michael shone among them because he was saturated with valiant love.

"I love his rakish style," Isabel declared; "his eloquence, and...passion,"

Omar said, "Bring him to my villa in Saint-Tropez. All this must be taxing,"

"It has been. I'm a bit worried for him." Michael told them.

"Why?" Michael excused himself and Omar and Ahmed followed him.

"David's built a great company, but the homophobia in his heritage is lethal. He could lose his business. I'd back him myself, but this house has swallowed up a lot of my money."

"There is another way?" Michael looked puzzled. "I could lend you the money, with an interest fee or I could give you the money under certain circumstances."

"What circumstances?"

Omar turned to Ahmed and they exchanged some words in Arabic and nodded.

"We'd give two million pounds each to watch you both together."

Michael walked them away from people towards the landing and up the stairs. "Haven't you dropped that sum of money at the tables in Cannes?"

Ahmed nodded. "Then I'll tell you this." Michael came face to face with Bruno and he gave him a high five and went into the emerald room and then gestured for the nine people in there to give him some privacy. They left and he closed the door.

'You fucking bastards with all your money! Michele calm yourself so they don't know'.

"I buy Fine Art and deliver it to clients around the world; clients and friends like you." He took hold of the cross hanging from his neck. "Yes, I sat in and watched the two of you. I told you then I wouldn't join in…"

Ahmed interrupted. "You wouldn't risk it because you're… intact. Are you still the same?" His arrogance and body language suggest he always got his own way.

Anger rose in Michael and forced a sour taste into his mouth. "The men in the Group and the doctors working with us mean nothing to you?"

"Would ten million dollars get you over the hump?" Ahmed asked sarcastically.

'You vulgar Godless swine. You cannot fuck us for money. Heartless liars'.

"We are speaking of pleasures," Omar added.

"I will share this pleasure with you. One morning after praying, David kissed me and his face was a miracle of love. No work of art or ten million ever had more beauty." Ahmed felt his judgment but he'd bargained with CEOs, governments, and Kings. "Would David turn down ten million dollars?" Ahmed asked challenging.

Omar pressed himself flush against Ahmed, put his hands inside Ahmed's pockets and played with him. Both of them clearly looked like they enjoyed being 'naughty' but Michael watched them with the knowledge of art histories depiction of male lovers carved and painted from ancient Greece up to the 21st century so he felt nothing.

"You have wives, sons, and daughters, and you earn millions of dollars every week. Isn't *this* too much?"

"You're a big man; I want to know if you're a great man in bed: ten million?"

"Keep your ten million, and I'll keep my ten inches." Michael walked away. "Don't be so proud!" Omar said. Michael turned to them blazing with Italian beauty and glory. Only Sophia Loren and Paolo Maldini could have shown more Italian pride. Michael idolized both of them and that made the power in him fierce.

'Both of you are not men. No heart, no love; no honor – animals'.

"My family, everything in my pants, my work and my man, David, I'm proud of them. I'm only ashamed of you. So leave my home or I'll have you thrown out."

Downstairs in the dining room, Lola, Cynthia, and Grace were deep in conversation. "Cynthia, you must come over to me and we can talk. I think it's amazing that we've never met properly. And then it takes your son and my ex-husband to bring us together. How can I run from this?"

"You don't have to Lola. I'm in De Beauvoir Town, Hackney. Come over."

"Nice: we're in Muswell Hill, but I'd love a house in your neighborhood."

"We do have one of the best houses there. Can we meet over the weekend, Lola? My husband's away on business and we can have the day to ourselves."

"I'd love that! I don't go out enough," Grace told them. "I've been afraid to go out on dates because Adrian gets so stroppy when I see someone. So I haven't..."

Michael walked passed them but he didn't hear them and they were so engrossed they didn't pay attention to him. He was singularly focused, but only he knew his goal. He was moving as if he was programmed, repeating: *'David, David, find David'.*

In the kitchen, Michael's sons and Adrian were grouped together. It looked like they were hatching a plot, but they were all scanning their mobiles and checking social media. Cesare said, "This one says; it's a hoax because any bloke who shags like David can't be queer." All of them looked at Adrian then each other for a moment.

Adrian added, "This one says if women like anal with Dad why'd he need a bloke?"

285

Roberto said, "According to the Tweets, Black men aren't gay, it's a white thing."

Fabio looked disturbed. "What?" Cesare asked. Impatiently he grabbed the mobile.

"'I pity the bitch that gets that Zulu dick up the arse'." Cesare cursed in Italian.

Michael entered the room but left because he couldn't see David.

Upstairs Angus stood in front of Barry's mixing deck, eyeballing him. It excited Barry because Angus had the kind of sexual magnetism Barry liked in white men.

"…tell the truth," Angus said; "or you'll miss the best performance by a Greek fuck-master in a romantic thriller." His closing comment made Barry hard and sticky.

"Since when's a Scotsman a Greek?"

"Since I got my big fat Greek love sack, age fourteen." Barry wanted to jump on him right then and there, but Angus turned to leave and bumped into Bruno and the other decorators.

Angus flicked his eyebrows and one of the pretty boys saw him as he buttoned his jacket to cover himself. Jose, the fabulous 'man tart' licked his lips and said. "Yeah Papi, I can help you unload that fuck-truck." Angus fingered his jeans and then shook his head.

Tony witnessed everything, and as Angus came closer, he said, "I'm married."

Angus looked him up and down as though he were deciding. "I'm all over you guys."

"Really, in bed or in life?" Tony wore a suit better than any Favela guy could.

Angus laughed. "Not bad. So many married men are hopeless, at everything."

"I'm married to Lola, so I'm good at everything." Angus realized who he was. Without thinking, he took out his worry beads. "Did you save her or did she save you?"

"You're the psychiatrist." Angus didn't expect him to be playful. "Tony Ramires," he shook Angus' hand and stared at the scarlet worry beads in his left hand.

"I think you're dying of heartache. I suffered with it." Angus really gave him a close look even as they walked past everyone. Tony was smarter than just his clothes and Angus got no sense of heterosexist judgment from him.

"Since I'm the psychiatrist, why don't you tell me, what *you* think?"

"Irony; the true mark of a gay man. I can tell plenty, I'm a hairdresser." For the first time all night Angus felt like laughing. They took drinks and walked upstairs.

Michael's friends found the atmosphere to their liking because in their elite academic environment, theories proliferated based on their reading rather than actual contact with people of different race and class backgrounds so they enjoyed the milieu.

Downstairs, David's friends thought the Event and the vibe were stranger than any film or play they'd ever been in. A famous actor said to another. "I've seen David out with incredible girls: did you twig?" The TV star said no. The media people asked their opinions on David and Michael. "I've known David and Solly since we were kids. I'm surprised he didn't tell me before, were like family so I love him." On the monitors around the room, people saw Michael walk into the frame which showed him staring. David was talking to a smooth thirty-year-old from the Caribbean press, as Michael edged him out of the way and David was face to face with him.

"Why must I beg people to accept me? Every one of us has seen how they twist our love into their hatred. It's simple; I love you." He grabbed David and kissed him. Their faces filled the screen in a loving embrace and they appeared on all twenty monitors throughout the house as everyone watched. Cameras and mobiles flashed and David and Michael's faces burst into light time and time again. No matter what people told the media about their acceptance, everything they felt was registered on their faces watching both of them. Michael's friends loved what they saw because this was the first time they were able to feel his soul. They'd heard him on the subject of everything but as he was drawn into their kiss, his face showed them the man they hardly knew.

Cesare put his arms around the twins and held them closely and Roberto pat Adrian's his back they watched their fathers. Solly saw the turmoil like storm cloud moving across his father's face and he went to him and hugged his shoulder. Barry played Donna Summer's *I Feel Love* and joyful screams broke out in the house. It took Barry eight seconds to cue it because he knew when a moment was right and he started his light show. Barry brought the house lights down and Michael and David's cinematic kiss lit the faces of everyone in the house. No live show by any pop star on the planet packs the punch of fact and fantasy as David and Michael's reciprocal kiss because the truth lifted their spirit. There was nothing more profound they could have said to their families and as a result, Tony and Lola, Grace, and Adrian, as well as Cynthia, and Solomon were no longer shocked. Solly yelled, "Testify my brother!" as he grooved to the music. Because he sounded the cry, everyone else in the house whistled and hollered and Solly's fans took his lead. When David looked out, his smiling eyes met the crowd with humble pride and Michael looked out at people with heroic modesty.

****

Michael was in session with his analyst Dr. Nasir, the North African Muslim, who specialized in bisexual carnal duality in Afro-Asian men. Nasir's work was greatly influenced by his Civil Partnership with Dr. Claude. His modern office had eight giant posters of the planets on his walls. This made the room strangely vacant. However, the planets imbued the room with mystery and the atmosphere of his patients' psychological and spiritual catharsis lingered.

"Now you've told your family about your *true* love, what if anything has changed? Have you learned anything more about yourself?" He asked sincerely.

"I've past two levels of fear. Telling my children and my best friends, I'm no longer a typical man with orthodox desires like pussy, money and football. And then consenting to anal and enjoying it. David doesn't fuck me in that *Fifty Shades of Gray* or *9½ Weeks* vile manner. I've discovered how to accept sexual pleasure as a homoerotic experience of love. There is such a taboo in accepting another man as a lover. Also, for me, it's fused with my love of Black's humanity."

"Talk me through that."

"The humanity of Black people reminds me that every psychotic regime, whether it's Imperial or Communist hasn't crushed them. When I allowed David in my flesh, I felt humble. I wanted to give him my flesh and soul." He took a minute.

"As a father, husband and professor; after a football game, in the locker room men saw me as a 'real man' because I've got the cock and brains to prove it. I intend to keep every merit I've earned, and still have David's beautiful cock in me. Because I am a man, it felt sublime to give another man the power to change me."

"Do you reject the active/passive binary? The transition from women to men often establishes who'll be dominant?"

288

"I've *never* wanted a man to ride me. With David, he has such sexual mystique I love it. When I first met Lola she also had that kind of mystique; her innocence and the promise of spiritual and sexual love. I love that unique Afro sexuality." Michael stood up and walked over to the far side of the room.

He looked at the spellbinding image of Saturn in the glass frame and took a moment to study it before he said anymore. Dr. Nasir quickly took shorthand notes observing him.

"The day I put the rope around my neck one of the things that stopped me hanging myself was admitting I wanted love and sex with a man. I abstained and I never touched another woman; I had a wank watching Hallie Berry but for God's sake she is fucking gorgeous. During the yearlong depression, the truth disgraced me. Watching the line-up of Black athletes on television...I wanted to fuck all of them! I was shocked at myself, then the disgust if my kids knew my mind... and betraying Lola." Michael placed his hand on the plant and gazed into the sphere. "I'm sick of living by rules I didn't invent." He walked toward Mercury. "I'm deeply drawn to the forbidden."

"How so Michael?"

"I come from a humble background; very Italian, really Roman and Catholic. I've broken all the family rules: Jamaican wife, mixed race kids, my attraction to a guy as a teenager and now loving David… in the flesh. When we're apart, I can't stand it."

"You're a successful independent businessman; surely you haven't become dependent on him?"

"Does your husband still fuck you properly?" Dr. Nasir wouldn't answer, but Michael's stare was confrontational and insistent.

"Alright, yes he does." Michael nodded his head deliberately.

"And you fuck him right?" Nasir nodded. "So you understand the need. David has all the qualities that inspire love, a body and soul filled with God's creation. My brother-in-law sees only sin. *Deficient*! Let him live with his hatred and suffer."

Dr. Nasir was surprised by his words and he pursed his lips together.

"Excuse me; I listened to his rants about 'queers' who don't deserve to live."

"When you're deeply in love, Michael, you'll forgive him."

"I am deeply in love."

"Not yet; you've told your sons and daughter, but you haven't said anything to indicate they've accepted your love and desire for a man. Nor have they affirmed they are proud or happy about your transfer of love from Lola and them to David."

"I haven't stopped loving them."

"You know that, but that's not the conversation they're having about you."

"They have to show me consideration because I've always put them first. They won't allow me to dictate their lives so they must allow me my rights," Michael replied pounding his chest.

"Michael, like all my patients you still hurt at the thought of losing your kids' love. David means a great deal to you, and so does your children's acceptance."

"What must I do?" Michael moved across the room to the planet Earth.

"They are probably preoccupied with what role you play with David. They'll discuss how religious practice and the rules governing masculinity has been thrown out the window now you're with a man."

"We're not a devout Catholic family."

"When it comes to a father choosing a man rather than a woman as a lover, kids turn to fundamental traditions for 'legitimate' answers. Very few of them rationalize your motives and psychology: they analyze you based on their own psyche. Namely do *you* fulfill their self-image? Your children want to be as good as if not better than you. When they base their values on the 'symbolic order', they have to reject their imaginary 'ideals', for imperfect truth."

Michael thought that through for a couple of minutes, moved away from the planets and sat in the Chesterfield sofa in front of Dr. Nasir and told him. "I know how to reach them. They hate injustice; I'm going to teach them a life lesson about it."

CHAPTER THIRTY-THREE

Michael laughed and shouted at the other driver in Italian. He wound down the window and the Neapolitan younger driver told him to kiss his mother's ass and Michael told him. "Go to your mother's house, find her panties and sniff them!" He told David what he said and he laughed heavily struggling to breathe. The road zigzagged through the Siena Mountains with its dazzling gold light and rustic landscape.

The man in the other car screamed, "*Tua Mamma bocchinara.*"

Michael told David. "He says my mother is a fluffer." David tried to shake off the laughter but couldn't. Michael yelled, "*Brutto figlio di puttana bastardo... Mangia merde e morte.*" Michael explained that he called him an ugly son of a whore, so he should eat shit and die.

"*Ce un cibirut*!!" the man cried out and Michael laughed very loudly.

"What did he say?"

"He says I have a small dick." Michael and David laughed hysterically.

Sitting in Michael's American cream and gold 1958 Plymouth Fury, David felt wonderful. Michael was tousled much to David's liking and he gestured for David to move closer which he did. Michael's open white shirt, Mediterranean tan skin with a crucifix against the short hairs on his chest gleamed in the light. David eyed the light gray and black stubble on his chin and clearly he needed a shave and a haircut. David placed his hand on his lap and squeezed knowingly and Michael blew his horn and it sounded be-bar-daar-daar!

"I love this car!" David told him.

"He's wonderful no? I bought him in California and I keep him here, because in London he would get nicked. Since I have a garage now, I really had to get him out of my sister's place." Michael navigated the winding roads of Siena extremely well and David settled comfortably next to him for three minutes. Suddenly he remembered the death of James Bond's wife, the car chase in *Quantum of Solace* as well as the cars that were destroyed in the *Italian Job* along with the film's cliffhanger ending and he pulled back and gasped.

Michael felt him flinch and David cried, "Stop the car!" Michael checked the road and did so. David unbuckled and got out of the car and caught his breath and tried to steady his nerves. The view around them at that height was spectacular due to the color of the land and sky. Michael approached him with a loving embrace to calm him.

"I just had the strangest feeling. There are so many death scenes shot on roads like this. We have to be careful I can't lose you," he concluded panting.

Michael kissed him and he could feel it all over.

"We must get you to my old home before I fuck you here in the car."

"You wouldn't dare," David replied with a glorious smile. Michael sat him down on the hood of the car and gazed at him. In his T-shirt, jeans and trainers he was everything Michael liked and he loved David even more. David sensed he had affected him.

****

In David's office later that day Sophia and Willy were in the board room with several of David's key clients. Mr. Man signaled to Willy for a private conversation and he ushered him out of the room and into David's office. Willy sat in David's seat and indicated to Winston to be forthcoming.

"Willy, I can work with you, and I want to work with you." Willy fixed his suit and tie. "But a contract is a contract and I don't understand how I can break it without David sue me and fuck up my business."

"Me and Sophia have spoken to lawyers, there's a get-out clause David didn't consider. You can come and work for me and I'll manage all of you."

"David and that Italian guy will pressure…"

"Fuck David!"

"It was me they threatened to cut up, not you."

"His Nigerian bullshit is something I'm done with."

"It's the Italian who tell me that. Me-no-know what kind of Mafia connection he have, but me-no-want Mafia bad man come for me."

"Is pure terror tactic David's using." Winston lunged across the desk. "And when they cut me up or David and use his father's legal dealings to take my career from me what happen then?" Sophia came in and asked what was happening.

"Big men talking, go outside," Winston told her.

292

"Save that shit for your bitches and Baby-Mama."

"Girl, step outside, Black man talking!" He was dead serious and she couldn't fight him because Willy took sides against her. She left and Winston pointed at Willy and his face and gesture told Willy to keep his woman in check.

Ten minutes later Willy led Winston through David's office, and he pointed at a blown up photo of Mr. Man. "You see you up there Winston, bigger things coming."

Willy let Mr. Man head into the board room and for the ten seconds that Willy was alone he eyed David's office. His look of avaricious envy was naked and vain. He had no chance of owning the company because he wanted the return of revenue David had with is clients and employees. He walked into the plush boardroom to take command.

Without hesitation, Willy walked to the head of the table and spoke to David's clients full of confidence. "David Bankole wrote a morality clause into your contracts." The groups, solo acts, and two DJs knew about it. They were all Asian, African, Caribbean, and mixed-race young contenders. Their dress styles stated they weren't ever hoping for mainstream chart pop stardom, especially not the youngest, a Black female who David discovered through his young apprentices. Nikki was a Gospel singer. Terry eyed Willy unsettled by the secrecy of the meeting, therefore, he slipped his mobile out of his pocket surreptitiously and turned on the recording App.

"David says you can't engage in homophobic, sexist, racist behavior in public, but he's done that shit. He disrespected his ex-wife, set himself up as a martyr of Black suffering at the hands of a white woman he's branded a drug fiend who killed their kids." A shock wave went across the room as each client exchanged looks.

"His immoral conduct entitles you to leave him if you want. I know most of you have strong feelings about gays and their lifestyle in the Black community. I have backing for a new company and if you want, I can start you at the beginning of the year in a new kind of management with Sophia and me. Also I…"

"You've got your nerve," Terry said. "David signed me to DJ his events and built me up with the understanding that my life will be honored by him."

"His homosexuality doesn't bother you?" Willy asked.

Terry got to his feet and pointed at Willy and Sophia. "What is that your damn business! I've watched you since last year when he signed me.

I've seen you sniff around this woman!" Sophia looked startled and the other clients remained silent and transfixed by Terry's confrontation. He looked down at the table for a moment and saw that his mobile was recording, but no one else saw him checking. "Let me tell you, guy, I knew you were a pussy but I didn't know you were a cunt!"

"Don't talk to Willy like that," Sophia warned him.

"Listen you lot, as David has said to me, if you make deals with cut throats you must expect to get your throat cut! You're stealing a man's business... Willy. He built this and us!" Terry walked out.

****

That same night, in her nicely furnished Bayswater flat in West London, Maria was in her kitchen making dinner for her brothers and their girlfriends with Fabio passing food he'd washed and chopped to her along with plates, bowls and taking everything from her after she'd finished dressing the food. They were all speaking in whispers because their partners were in the other room and periodically they called out through the doors to set the table, find music and DVDs for after dinner.

Her brothers were conservatively dressed, but her skimpy top bothered Cesare because her apron top made her looked like she was topless. Everybody was gesturing and the body language of each of them revealed who had the greatest strength and power. As Maria made the assorted Spanish dishes Cesare pointed at her. "You're going out with that fool in there and playing mother and vamp to fulfill his adolescent English ideas of a hot Mama. And while you do this you dare call Papa a... '*un homo feticistico invecchiamento*'. Is this the only Italian you learned?"

"What does it mean?" Fabio asked. Cesare looked at him angrily.

"Imbecile! She called my father an aging fetishistic homo."

"She's entitled to her opinion." Cesare slapped Fabio in the face with the back of his hand. "You're just too white, you know that," Cesare said through his teeth. "Since when did your little dick get big enough to act like the man of the house? If anyone could be homo it would be you because you two are like a fag and a hag."

Roberto gripped Cesare and told him face to face, *"Mi piacciono Ha anche detto che sono geloso del fatto che Papa' attrae sia donne che uomini di colore di bella presenza, quando io attraggo soltanto spazzatura bianca. Odia il fatto che lei è nero."*

294

"How dare you!" Maria threw the platter of food onto the floor and it smashed. Fabio was lost, so Maria told him, Roberto accused her of hating the fact she is Black. "He also said I'm jealous Papa attracts beautiful Black woman and men; when I only attract white trash."

Fabio said, "Who the fuck gave you permission to talk about her, you little git."

"Oh, I thought you were gonna say little prick because you're the only one with that problem." Fabio lunged to hit Roberto and Maria held him back. Her boyfriend and Cesare's girlfriend came in to see what smashed.

"Maria is everything alright?" Jamie asked. He was a Stocks Trader with a soft Cockney accent who was upwardly mobile in his £35K job at one of the firms in the City. On any Friday night, he was high on lager and bravado. Zara, Cesare's African Italian voluptuous girlfriend eyed them and she knew something was wrong.

Just then Ilona, a very pretty Croatian girl came in with a carrot and breadstick in her hand and looked at all of them. "Sounds like a mini-drama in here."

Maria forced a smile and said, "Please go back in, I'm nearly finished." They all looked at each other, awkwardly, and then left the kitchen.

When they were gone, Maria pointed at the door. "Roberto, don't start up with me. And for your information, I don't have those horrible thoughts against Papa. I can't believe he left Mama to..." she whispered, "to fuck a man."

"Maybe they love both ways," Roberto said and Fabio slammed him in the chest.

"The idea of Papa being David's bitch... *E'orribile!*"

Maria said, "What confuses me is that for a year he was so dull, just caught up in his head. Then he gets a body like a gladiator, a guy like Bankole, a house like a palazzo, his toffee-nosed friends, and rich clients praise him and our mother acts like its fine."

Cesare said, "One of the things I like about my mother is that nobody rules her. I think we're talking about his sex life and ignoring who Papa is."

Roberto asked Maria and Fabio, "Would it make you happy if Papa was killed or died tomorrow?" Fabio made the sign of the cross and deeply protested anything of the kind. Roberto said, "If he could hear this, this... judgment of our father... it would make him so desperate. He was suicidal because we ignored him. Maria, *perché non puoi essere felice per*

295

Papà? Fabio, I'm sorry I… I'm sorry for insulting you." Roberto started crying. "Papa has never done one thing to me, or any of us that's unkind or shitty. Don't hate him." And then Roberto couldn't stop crying. "Please Fabio; Mama and Papa are entitled to their life. They love different people now. Papa is nice."

Cesare said, "Look the baby is crying because you upset him, Fabio."

Fabio held the back of Roberto's neck. "*Ascoltami fratello. Onoro il Padre mio.*" Maria kissed Fabio's shoulder and Cesare touched his face, kindly.

Cesare told Fabio, "You see, you remember we're Italian. Honor our father is the right words for you to remember Fabio. And don't forget the pride of our mother." As brothers and sister, they all put their heads together in a head-on huddle. "Now make your mother happy and find a nice Black guy Maria." She screamed with a glorious smile on her face. "I saw you looking at Adrian," Cesare concluded.

"Oh come on, he's so young." They placed their heads in a circle and laughed.

"No, she likes Solly. He's a star, a hero and sooooo handsome…" Roberto said.

"*Vaffanculo!*" Cesare and Fabio smacked him on the head and laughed. Maria laughed too because they were her best friends, not just her brothers.

CHAPTER THIRTY-FOUR

The following morning David squeezed orange juice and prepared coffee, toast, and ham. Outside the sounds of the Roman streets were unmistakable. Michael stood in the doorway of the humble working class kitchen, without a top but in his pajama trousers, watching David barefoot in just his shirt until he turned around startled. "Don't do that!"

"*Cara dispiace*, I mean sorry darling." Michael's body filled most of the door frame leaning on his shoulder. "I should have got up earlier to do this."

"You were exhausted from driving, besides, I like being in your childhood home and taking care of you."

"In this apartment as a boy, my sister Angelina and I were spoiled. Mama and Papa gave us everything underprivileged parents could."

"This isn't a poor house."

"Believe me we were poor." Michael took the coffee David held out to him. "Last night we put the bags down and fell into bed. Let me show you the mansion. Bring your coffee." He led David through the narrow brown and cream hallway into the living room. It was filled with brocade furniture, floral wallpaper, and patterned carpet. He whistled through his teeth. "I fucking hate chintz! This decoration is done by my sister. All this kitsch – it's her life. What did you think of her?" David didn't answer, but Michael's stare pushed him to respond, so he finally did.

"I think she was tolerating me. The 'black queer' whose seduce you, a family…"

"Stop, she has issues. A more self-absorbed and neurotic woman is hard to find. She was cold to Lola, but Lola told her 'fuck you if you don't like me'." David laughed at that. "My sister would protest forever if you call her a bigot, but she doesn't like the 'black blood' in our family. But my parents adored Lola because she is fabulous, and our kids have so much personality. Anyway, I have no interest in my sister. And her kids are so insolent; the boy especially. One time Cesare slapped his face, like he was a bitch, for a remark the fool uttered."

"Cesare looks like the kind of man who talks with his fists. Solly is like that."

Michael nodded in agreement. "Anyway – look the photos." David studied the pictures. "This is me and my sister, Mama and Papa at the church around the corner. This is here, outside this apartment building. I'm three, Angelina is two."

"Even then you were so cute, look at your curly brown hair like a cherub."

"*Basta*!" David laughed and Michael took him through the family drama. "If my parents were alive I know they'd be ok with me, us…"

"Really?"

"They adored Angelina and me. Love was all they had. We had no money." He looked at his parents wedding photo. They were two beautiful Italians aged twenty.

"What did your father do?"

"A mechanic, he worked for Fiat many years and then Alfa Romeo. There are no pictures of him in the last five years of his life. He became fat and hated having his picture taken but then two days before he died… he and my mother had this photo taken." Michael pointed to it. They were still clearly in love as his father's gaze at his mother, and hers at the camera showed. "They were good people. No violence… just shouting, like opera types." Michael's heart still spoke of them through his eyes.

"How did they pass? Years apart or…"

"They were staying at a friend's summer place in Naples. Junky criminals broke in to steal, but my parents were there and they killed them." Michael's face went tight with grief. "Those shits were caught and convicted." He took a second. "Just one time I nearly beat Fabio and Maria. I discover they were doing drugs at University: weed, ecstasy – pill popping." Michael sounded off in Italian. "Those twins…" His gesture was unmistakably Roman. "They share something strange. Anyway, I got them medical help. Lola spent four months with them and they are now completely clean. The doctors were good, but Lola did an amazing job; I will love her forever for that."

The door knocked and Michael gestured which indicated he was expecting company. "Ah here is Luca. I know him for years and I want him to meet us."

Michael went down the hall to let him and escorted him into the kitchen. David followed and Luca bowed at both of them. He could have been seventy David thought or possibly older. His complexion was buttery, his brown eyes were very alert and his aging face held two creases at the corner of his mouth. He had a full head of hair, but it was ash gray. In his dark suit and polo neck jumper he looked solemn but once he began talking he was completely animated and lively.

Listening to him David thought he asked ten questions in Italian, but he only asked two. Michael pointed at the chairs in the kitchen and he sat.

"It's very good to see you again Michele. You see my English is more better?"

"Father it's important I talk to you. It's about my man and me. This is David." Luca reached out to him.

"Hello."

"I am Luca; don't be confused that Michele called me Father. I was his priest once, but since I'm gay I left the Church before they accuse me of being a child molester, it's become an obsession. I'm just an aging queen," he confessed with a wonderful flourish and a toss of his hair.

"Oh right…well… that clarifies that."

"Don't be sarcastic David." He turned to Luca. "David mistrusts priests. We both share that and many more things. David is very religious."

"What faith?"

"Baptist; my faith in the Holy Trinity and the Virgin Mary has never wavered. I despise the Catholic Church for its bigotry – anyway before I start preaching. I do pray every morning when I head out to work for my life and my salvation."

"Do you believe yourself to be a sinner?" he asked with all intent.

"No, I believe God loves me."

Luca turned to Michael. "He has no crisis or conflict, what do you want of me?"

"We are like-minded and our meeting feels destined," Michael told him, impassioned, with sparkling bright eyes. "There are incidental things and coincidental things that bind us. But we share the same philosophy on fidelity. As my former priest, you know me. I consider men that cannot live faithfully to be rapacious quasi-rapists!"

"Always with you, it's absolutes."

"Do you forget how well I understood the Seven Deadly Sins?" he turned to David. "I was obsessed with the subject as a child. It led me to study art. People who hate us the most are usually guilty of all those sins. Avoiding these sins has been my guiding light." Michael grabbed Luca by the jacket. "I won't be judged by prurient bigots!"

Luca responded as passionately as Michael. "English, Luca, I want my man to hear."

"I left the Church to avoid such discussions," he answered with a tortured look on his face. David saw the grip he had on Michael's arms and he recalled the level of anguish in his own father's eyes. "Hypocrisy and weakness are failings we all share. You made your life from this house. Continue to define your own destiny." He turned to David. "Do you want to share all you have with Michele?" David said yes. "Then you both have my blessing as gay men who honor love." Luca's brown eyes softened knowing he'd done all he could for them.

"Thank you, I wasn't asking for the sanctity of the Church, I wanted your blessing, father," Michael told him and David studied the two of them.

"Now Michele..." Luca pointed at him. "Take me to someplace gay and chic!"

Michael pinched his cheek. Luca raised his hands to the heavens and said, "He no longer lives in Rome, but he knows all the fabulous places. I am single and I am sadly seventy-two which means, as a gay man I ought to be dead! But these little divas who have their own language, fashion, affiliations, internet dating and peep shows; I am not going to kill myself to make them think they own the city." Michael kissed him on the top of his head, smiling.

Luca said, "*Mi piacciono I bei le belle uomini con cazzi favolosi e culo troppo.*"

Michael laughed so hard he staggered away from the table and had to lean on the wall. From the vivid expression on his face, David wanted to know what was said but Luca wouldn't translate and Michael couldn't speak. David eyed the forced innocent look on Luca's face and he knew it was sexual, but he also knew *he* wasn't the butt of the joke.

"Are you going to tell me what he said?" David asked Michael.

"Darling, I am going to teach you Italian..."

"I have an Italian speaking language course online App on my iPad and I'm going to learn it with or without you."

Luca said, "Please David, don't come upset with Michele, I say to him. *I like beautiful men with fantastic cocks and ass too.*" And Michael went into another fit. Sputtering with laughter like a WW11 airplane coming down.

"I used to tell this man my confession and just like that, seventy-two years of age, he tells me he likes cocks and ass! Life is a circle! You guys wait I get dressed and take you out to a private place one of my clients recommend to me." Michael kissed David passionately and afterward placed the palm of his hand on Luca's face.

****

Michael walked through the streets of Rome wearing Armani casuals as if he owned the city because he had David's hand in his. David looked younger in a white T-shirt, blue jeans and red sneakers. Michael felt carefree, and that was a totally new sensation because as a husband he felt greatly protective towards Lola after he came out of the Army. When he became a father, he felt a greater responsibility to his children.

David wore a smile that felt new because he was conscious of feeling in love. Only his mother and father held his hand; and when Solomon stopped holding his hand when he was ten and a half years of age, Michael always yearned for it. It was the main reason why he held Solly's hand or his shoulder until he was thirteen because as his big brother it wasn't seen as strange at all. David felt so alive he took out his mobile and called Adrian. "Hi, it's Daddy, I'm blazing happy right now I couldn't keep it to myself. Michael is showing me Rome. There's so much of everything. The autumn light and the city is fantastic! Are you alright? University good, is your girlfriend happy?"

People and traffic came from all directions. He swung Michael's hand high in the air as he listened. "Great! I'll keep in touch." Michael gestured for the mobile.

"Adrian, morning! Everything is beautiful here. No drama, Daddy and I have set up an online space to share pictures of the trip with you. I emailed you the link. I wanted to do this because he never shuts up about you and your life so I hope it's ok I share him with you?" They walked around people and out of the way of traffic, but the noise level rose as the neared St Peter's Square and Luca pointed out several things to David. "Thank you son: I know if I don't talk to Roberto in a week it makes me anxious. God bless, I'll send you the pictures, but your Dad is the techno wizard; bye." He slipped the mobile into David's back pocket and pinched his arse. David choked and laughed.

For the remainder of the day, Michael became a tour guide and show-off. He explained the history of Rome from St Catherine, the Borges, Popes, the Renaissance, the Protestant 'threat' to the Church, Baroque and Bernini, the Sack of Rome and Counter-Reformation, the Vatican City

301

and the Republic. Luca added necessary commentary just to shut him up but as Michael pointed and gestured at the city keeping David engrossed, Luca realized how deeply in love they were. Even strangers saw it when the three of them sat down for a coffee, a cold drink, and when David and Michael shared an ice-cream together, passing it to and from each other.

Luca didn't fancy Black men, even as a youth when Rock and Roll and R&B brought countless African Americans into popular culture and the press. However Luca admitted the color of David's skin, that glowed like chocolate, his adoring eyes at Michael, and David's physique, charged with muscular life and energy made him more striking than anything Luca had read as a priest or a painter. He took photos of Michael and David throughout the course of the day and by the time Michael took him to an exclusive café club, Luca was worn out.

It was only when Michael told him, "this is a 'Silver Daddies' club;" that Luca found his second breath. Luca saw men in their sixties with men in their thirties and that rejuvenated him. As soon as a handsome man came to Luca and asked him to dance, David ached to be alone with Michael and he saw it. They stayed thirty minutes and then left, raced home as quickly as they could and then made love like fallen angels throughout the night.

CHAPTER THIRTY-FIVE

In London the following day, Cynthia walked Lola through her home. It was decorated in a distinctive Caribbean Colonial style interior right through to the veranda that led into her colorful garden of wildflowers and potted plants. Cynthia looked lovely in a full-length garment of free moving materials in Indian and Caribbean prints.

Lola moved confidently in a beige trouser suit and maroon silk blouse, her makeup was perfect, and her loose curled hair swung around her neck. The house smelt fresh and the hallways and rooms they walked through were all bold, bright primary colors with cream, tan, brown or green silks and fine cotton. It was the first time Lola could see how 'old country' Cynthia was because her preference for the colonial was very telling. She knew women like her back in Jamaica.

As they entered the 30x30ft living room, a young woman came in and asked. "Would you like the drinks served now ma'am?" She was a shy nineteen-year-old with an unmistakable Jamaican accent.

Lola quietly said, "Please tell me that is your live-in servant girl."

"Yes, she is." Lola laughed out loud, and Grace came into the room wearing strappy sandals, a tight pair of jeans and a white T-shirt. Her locks were twisted and turned into a high top leaving her long neck uncluttered.

"I would say let your hair down, but look at you! Girl, you're looking good," Lola told her happily. They all settled into different single sofa side chairs packed with big cushions. "Miss Cynthia! I love this place. And wait…" the sound of 1940s Calypso music came on. "Lord have mercy!" she screamed and flopped around in her chair. "Not since I was a child I hear this!" The sound of St Andrews in the Parish of Jamaica echoed in Lola's voice.

"You know since when, nobody call me Miss Cynthia. I choose Calypso because apart from Marley and 'lovers rock' I don't like vulgar tunes or those ugly boys who can't shut their mouth – chat shit about batty and t'ing." Grace kissed her teeth.

"You know Miss Cynthia, any chef as good as you, must have back home in her British life," Lola said with her hands up, gesturing gracefully.

Cynthia exclaimed. "For true! I have to fly the flag for Jamaica in my family because the boys are more Nigerian than Jamaican."

"I see Jamaica in them, especially Solly. I use to love his after game comments. He switches the Nigerian, to Jamaican and 'British bloke' t'ing well, but I always hear his English grammar and Black savvy; it's very becoming." Cynthia couldn't have been more proud and retiring, which was distinctly her truth.

"But their father has a big influence on them."

"That's saying plenty," Grace remarked. The servant girl brought them drinks.

"Lola, try this, it's ginger made into tea, muscovado sugar, pimento and two kinds of rum." Lola took the crystal glass and took a sip. The taste hit her immediately.

Lola said, "Now that is a back-home medicine!" They all laughed and Lola move to the Calypso beat and smiled. She had another mouthful and eased back.

Cynthia said, "I called my sister to tell them how great it is to meet a lady from back home and discover our families. But your family has such a reputation in education back home."

"So Miss Teen Jamaica, here I am with you in your home." Lola enjoyed playing the part of a mock hoity-toity lady. "My family looked up to yours and how you set yourselves up in Mandeville."

"You know I was formally Miss Teen Jamaica!" Lola nodded. "I know your business is one of the top 10 salons in the country. I'd have come there before but I can't get over to Hammersmith in West London and come back to work in any kind of time. I read the special they did on you in Black Londoner's newspaper and you did the hair for that musical…"

"Yes, it's weird we haven't talked."

Grace said, "Well, we've got plenty to talk about since our men are dating." Each woman eyed on another for close to a minute.

Lola said, "I haven't come here because of them. I'm here to meet you and put some good people in my life. We spend our lives talking about men. You'd think we hand nothing to share as women. Particularly considering we all have kids and in this era of PC, drugs and inequity we

304

still have to look out for our men, and ourselves. Women need mental, physical and spiritual support networks."

"But would we need those if we didn't spend so much time dealing with men?" Grace insisted.

Lola took a breath and leaned over to Grace. "What can I do to help you, Grace?"

"Tell me about Michael. I'm still trying to figure out why David fell for him."

"Oh, that's easy. Michael is the most charming, smart and sexy man I've ever met. And until I married Tony; I thought Michael was *it*."

"What do you mean?" Cynthia asked.

"My family thought I was... out of my mind. They didn't hate Michael because he's white. They went nuts because I fell for a 'poor white man'." That fact fascinated Cynthia and Lola saw it.

"Oh yes! But when a man never hits you, or belittles you, and gives you all his earnings; and presents you to people like you're royalty... trust me, you keep that kind of guy. I'll bet David responds to Michael's dignity and kindness, everyone does."

"We're talking two men here," Grace added.

Lola tossed her hand to the side and said, "Michael is touched by an ancient spirit: Eros. He's also something of a peacock, go online and check out the symbolism. Michael transformed himself from an overweight suicidal recluse; into a fit, dynamic entrepreneur who jets around like a CEO. Everybody used to flirt with him: male and female staff and students; flight staff, women at traffic lights; the bank manager."

"The bank manager?" Cynthia asked stunned.

Lola put on a husky voice, acted manly and said: "Oh Dr. De Farenzino, can I get you anything. Do be sure to call me if you need loans, insurance or anything!"

Cynthia screamed with laughter! "Was he psyching Michael or something?"

"No, he simply fancied him. Interesting thing: I knew I was safe against Michael cheating because he isn't attracted to white women at all, and it turned out he didn't fancy the men either. With Black women, that was something else. But I started Pilates, invested in Yoga, a godsend for me; went to Women's groups studying social history, literature, handicrafts and world cooking. I kept myself interesting to fuel Michael's passion for Black Culture and everyday life." Grace and Cynthia listened intently.

"Women caught his eye; he wouldn't be normal if they didn't, and Hallie Berry used to stiffen his resolve." The look on her face made them gasp.

"And then… gay?" Grace replied totally baffled.

"David's interesting because he's an intellectual with sex appeal. I can see why Michael is interested in him because David's a 'class act' which comes from you and his father I'm sure. Why a man and not a woman?" She threw her hands up. "But Michael doesn't do anything half-way. One day he came home sick and tired of the student's greed – they want a degree, but they don't want to work for it. He said 'I'm going to run my own business; I hate the students' laziness. He'd written books, done the lecture circuit for years. Next thing, he's happy and making money. And that's when his passion came back: we were so happy for five years. My forties were my happiest years because he adored me and I had everything some Black women ignore: freedom."

Grace moved forward to study Lola. There were questions she wanted to ask, but she was aware that having spent most of her life with her Pentecostal Congregation and friends she lacked Lola's worldview. Grace felt she knew all she needed to know and that is why she and Amy were the greatest of friends.

"Testify Sista!" Grace told Lola because she felt a great affinity to her.

"I have my kids, my business, reputation, brains, *and* wardrobe. Because I didn't depend on Michael; he depended on me, but not as a 'high hopes' broke, poseur. Michael's given lecturers at the ICA with his reading of *The Labyrinth of the Postmodern Romance with Black Urban Culture*, and stopped the show when he came down from the stage, kissed me and went back up on stage to finish his thesis on multiculturalism. At the end, my eldest, Cesare yelled 'bravo Papa bravo'!"

Grace was moved because nothing in her life was like that even though she and Amy could do a double act on life as lived by British women of Jamaican and Irish heritage. "Seriously Grace, all kinds of people asked me questions about Michael's reading and understanding of mixed race life! One woman, with a toffee-nosed accent, asked me – 'does your husband get his ideas from you?'" Lola said filled with contempt for the woman. "I told the wretch: NO, he gets his ideas from people like *you* who still look down on us. The bitch mash-up!" Cynthia and Grace rocked back in their seats. Cynthia clapped her hands, smiling beautifully.

"Obviously, you can handle yourself," Grace said. "I hope things go well because David has to deal with a shit storm. *The Black Press* newspaper didn't have anything kind to say about him, the event or the online sex tape, documentary, call it what you will. They said exposing himself was stupid."

"Fuck them!" Cynthia replied. The servant girl turned round at the door and didn't enter because Cynthia seldom swore so she took that as a sign that private talks were in progress. It also silenced Grace and left Lola acutely aware of the fact that Cynthia was a mother exasperated by convention. "They're against him ever since his call for less homophobia in 'Grime' and hip-hop, but they like Solly." She paused. "What gets me about those journalists is that they're stupid. My sons are two archetypes: Solly is a James Brown while David is a Sly Stone."

Lola nodded to herself. "Oh, that's fantastic Miss Cynthia. Solly is straight-on Black power in his rhetoric and David is more racially diverse: men and women united."

"Those amateurs think all Blacks must share one mind; damn fools. They better leave my child alone!" She called for more drinks, and her servant came quickly.

Cynthia started a different cocktail and tried to calm herself. "Back home, my family lived through colonialism, national upheavals and American infiltration of the worst kind and we still triumphed."

Lola told her. "Very few people are in your class, Miss Cynthia. If you didn't do anything else, your restaurant would still speak for you."

"Mum's something else, isn't she?" Grace proudly stated.

Lola sat forward and reached for Cynthia's hand. "You've established the Caribbean Cuisine Quality Federation. Everybody else is judged by your standard, my God! And if that wasn't enough your Weight Watchers cookbook is a bestseller."

"Those people at *The Black Press* newspaper have called me a snob because I won't agree to an interview. Until they respect my family's World War II service record to Britain, Solomon's family title and their dedicated service to Britain during World War II, David's work and not just Solly's football stardom, they can piss off."

"They do refer to Solomon's oil money and profile cases a lot," Grace added. "But they don't know him. Solomon's pride is being African, not being rich."

"How did you and your husband meet Miss Cynthia?"

"Our families arranged our marriage. And it worked out well, if not perfectly. But certainly good for me." She got up and ushered them into the dining room which was exquisitely decorated. A broad range of foods were laid out and waiting.

****

Later that Sunday afternoon, Solomon was in session with Dr. Claude at his office because Solomon refused to go to a clinic even though Dr. Claude told him the meetings weren't held at clinics. In his office, Solomon felt in control of things sitting behind his desk. Although he was dressed casually, no man looks informal in Aquascutum menswear.

"Alright, what do you want from me?" Solomon said in a condescending manner.

Dr. Claude told him in Yoruba. "Watch yourself, or you will lose your son!" Solomon fell silent and contrite. "Come out from behind that desk," Dr. Claude added and stood up. Solomon took 30 seconds to move but eventually he did.

"Let us sit here." Claude pointed at the sofas in the office next to the windows looking out into Cavendish Square. "Why is there no tea? Next time have that ready. I like lapsang souchong, no milk, and one sugar." Solomon was amazed by his conceit. "You attempted to kill your own son and that needs examination because that is a dreadful, indefensible type of homicide." Solomon buckled under those words.

"What age are you?"

"Almost sixty-five," Solomon mumbled.

"Are you proud of your family?" He said yes. "Do you love your wife?"

Smiling, he replied, "Deeply!"

"Why?"

Solomon was taken aback. "She's only been with me and wants no one else. She's a wonderful mother and a woman that likes peace and calm. Our marriage was arranged by our parents who served Britain in World War II. Our fathers had great fellowship as Pan-Africans. Cynthia's family was one of the best in Jamaica and mine are one of the highest in Nigeria. Sometimes marriages don't work out, but ours has. She has instilled honor in the boys, and calm… mostly. David dramatizes things to get my attention."

"Is that because you don't pay attention to him?"

"I pay attention!! I spent more than £90,000 on his education start to finish! I attended all his school sports and music achievements, and I invested in his business."

"He's in serious trouble. Michael believes his clients will turn on him because David's has the guts to defy the laws of Black manhood."

"What does Michael know about it?"

"Mr. Bankole, Fundamentalists, make death threats and kill 'infidels' by honor killings; you know this all too well: you're a criminal defense QC. Your son is in danger if you do not help."

"Who has threatened him?"

"Michael told me one of his clients has. Suppose there are others. Or people in the communities that feel heterosexuality is a mandatory requirement of masculinity?"

"I cannot control what people think or believe."

"No, but you can ensure justice to shield your son." Solomon thought about it.

"Yes, I would, and I will do that."

Dr. Claude reached out and took both of Solomon's hands in his. "When did your father stop beating you? What age were you? Tell me what it was like for a war hero like him to spend time with you and what you talked about?"

"What has David told you about that?" he lashed out.

"Not as much as you just have."

Solomon got to his feet and pointed down at Dr. Claude. "Do not toy with me!"

Dr. Claude yanked his hand and pulled him stumbling awkwardly into the sofa.

"Repeating your father's propensity for domestic violence will not help you. He was strict and drove you to succeed. I'm talking about his pride in your name, his War record and what men in our country must demonstrate to fulfill the rites-of-passage to manhood. Your devotion to power has made you evil."

"You fucking dog! I am David Solomon Bankole!"

"I'm sure that offers your wife no comfort. You say your marriage is good but would your wife say the same? Your brutality to David; hasn't it distressed her and now, when your compassion and tenderness is required to support David, you play mind games with me, trying to conceal your ingrained bigotry."

"I am not a bigot."

"Prove it. Show your son you love him. Protect him against the vicious words and actions of people who'll attack him. If you speak up for David's human rights that will prove you're a bigger man than your title. I

309

know your family's history back home. Show me if you're bigger than your profession." Claude had Solomon's fullest attention, so he got up and stood over Solomon.

"Men like you are a disgrace. You inherit power from your Yoruba ancestors, and you think it gives you the right to belittle ambitious men."

"You don't know me."

"You think not? I know your loving sons are the product of their mother. I have seen and heard both of your sons. Their praise of you is their mother's work." Solomon was about to protest. "Or perhaps you'd like me to expose you to your evil." Solomon stood up, and Dr. Claude shoved him back into the sofa.

"How do you call yourself a doctor with the care and welfare of patients?"

"I am going to cleanse you of the bile that pollutes your blood and soul." Solomon stopped cowering defensively in the leather sofa and gazed at him.

"Through Buddhist hypnosis, I'll help you find Kamara, so you'll willingly reject brutality. Solomon, your humanity is in peril because you practice Black sexual oppression. It lies at the root of social agony due to rigid family practices. Free yourself and be loved instead of respected. Shall we start the hypnosis now?" Solomon couldn't remember the last time he was scared of anything which is why he knew he was afraid. He believed Dr. Claude had the power to see into him and destroy him.

Solomon said "yes" as if he were pleading guilty and hoping for mercy.

CHAPTER THIRTY-SIX

In Rome an hour later, Michael guided David through the back streets and alleyways. The sunlight trapped in the distance captured David's attention. Most people were in Church, and the smells and bells of Catholicism were familiar to Michael.

"Here is where I saw my first film. *Cleopatra* with Elizabeth Taylor, my mother idolized her. She thought the Taylor-Burton love story of scandal, passion and jewels was the height of glamor. When it started here in back in 1962, Mama read everything about the scandal and saw the film fifteen times."

David said, "First film I saw by myself was *Big* with Tom Hanks. No glamor, just great. I liked it because he wanted to be someone else in a way. I wanted to be me, but lighter, I felt I was too dark. It's one of the things that drew me to Michael Jackson."

"But you are incredibly handsome and truly sexy."

David burst out laughing.

Michael was stunned by the realization. "You don't know you're beautiful?"

David blushed and turned away, but Michael turned him back to face him. "You are *so* beautiful. It's innocent, erotic, and even spiritual."

"What… there aren't Black Saints and virginal heroines that shape our culture."

"Have you never heard of the Black Madonna and St. Maurice?" David said no. "We are in the right city for this; I'll show you something later. What is your favorite subject in the world?"

"Music; working on something great like *Fear of a Black Planet, Innervisions, Kind of Blue* or *Thriller*! Those albums changed the landscape of popular culture. I think musicians from Louie Armstrong and Duke Ellington to Michael and Ice Cube have changed the sound and identity of modern life: linguistics, fashion, Black political pride. Aretha and Mary J can tell you more about Black womanhood than anything written about us in colonial literature. And the Bible has nothing to tell me about being an intellectual with Black sexual dignity. So much of our greatest comes out of music. And we're seeing new perceptions of intellectual artistry in this era with Black actors."

"This is one of the reasons why I love you. Eloquence is one of your skills."

"Any other skills?"

"Yes, I feel my soul and God's presence when you make love to me." David stopped walking and scrutinized Michael because his statement resonated in David's soul. Standing there in the streets of Rome, there wasn't any monument or icon that Michael could think of more sublime than David.

Michael put his arm around David's shoulder and led him. In the throng of European faces; David stood out in the crowd.

They walked on for a time and soon came to the middle of the Via della Stamperia at the back of the Trivi Fountain. Tourists and locals were everywhere. Michael rested his arm on David's shoulder and pointed out notable things. "My God," he said to David. "We are coming to the fountain. When I was a teenager, one night I walked into the fountain, remembering *La Dolce Vita*, but thinking of my boyfriend and I had a wank." Michael walked him to the Trevi Fountain, but it was fenced off under restoration.

"Fucking typical!" Michael said. The sunny area was filled with tourist and all the shops, ice cream parlors and cafés were bursting with customers. The streets were literally congested with foot traffic as they were pushed and shoved about, with ten different languages going in one ear and out the other. Michael saw a cab, flagged it and bundled David inside. The sunlit streets, flat fronted shops, and countless people flashed passed as they made their way to the other side of the city.

When they got out of the cab at the Appian Way, David recognized it. Michael took a good look and remembered everything important. "I used to play here as a boy. Sometimes my father would bring me, sit down over there and explain history to me of the Roman Empire. The wars, neo-realism; and after that he'd take me to the movies." He moved in close to David. "Is your father going to give us a headache? I ask because Maria is giving me a headache. She is like my sister: good intentions but brittle."

"Dad's contemptuous of anything he doesn't value. With Dr. Claude's help, I'm going to make him discover the better part of himself." Michael realized there was still so much more to David he still didn't know.

Later that evening Michael and David sat in the kitchen and ate couscous with figs and fish for dinner. The old fashion kitchen with its out of date fittings and utensils were a stark backdrop. Outside on the streets the air was bursting with Italian; also the aroma of food, the constant traffic, and sounds of music filled the kitchen as they occasionally looked at each other. David had on football shorts and a vest. Michael had on dungarees and nothing else: they were both barefoot.

Michael filled their glasses with beer and they emptied their glasses gulp after gulp. When they put the glasses down, they kept eyeing each other which made them both sweat.

"I love the fact that you can fix your car and explain the history of Saints."

Michael tried to belch but didn't make it. "What do you mean?"

"It's unusual to find the professor and the proletariat in one man."

Delighted by him, Michael said, "Come, sit on my lap."

"Captain Hornblower, that's just too dangerous."

"How is it dangerous?" Michael saw that David was brimming with mischief.

Upstairs a family started arguing, and so they looked up at the ceiling. The speed of insults and denials were accompanied with stomping about.

"Will that be us in ten years' time?" David asked him.

"First I have to teach you Italian. Will you teach me how to scream and moan?"

David could see the lust in Michael's eyes. "Just you understand this David Bankole. If you fuck me, I'll scream." Michael joyfully smiled. "I promise." David caressed Michael's face.

Michael started to respond in Italian and David stood up. The table separated them so David darted left to right but didn't know which way Michael would come at him. This thrilled Michael to bursting and David kept his eye on him.

Michael put his big hand inside his baggy dungarees and David couldn't take his eyes off him. "Are you hurting him?"

David looked like a transgressive youth who couldn't have been more excited if he was about to get laid for the first time. He slowly removed his vest. At the sight of his patterned brown sugar chest, and muscular limbs Michael's mouth went dry. When David pulled off his shorts and threw it at Michael, who rose up with sexual energy. "Get in the bed."

David exited, Michael picked up David's shorts and followed him into the bedroom with its ugly drapes, lovely wooden shutters, and low-lit bedside lamp throwing shadows around. Standing on the flokati rug drew Michael's attention away momentarily. Michael tossed the shorts on the bed, unhooked his dungarees and walked around David. The sight and vision of his fully aroused naked body gave Michael a hot flash. David pushed him onto the bed, and they made love.

****

At the same time in London Sophia and Willy rolled over in bed and grabbed smokes. She sat up and her body was magnificent. Willy looked at her totally satisfied and said, "How long will it take? We can't work out of this flat for long; it's a dump. I want offices ten times better than David's. I want to make fifty times more money than he did. He thinks he can beat me. Despite the rant from Terry, all of them are willing to come with us."

"Money settles all disputes, their 'serious Black agenda' for political whatever is total bullshit!" Sophia stated. "They want to earn more. And they want fame. I have to admit I didn't expect to hear anything out of that Terry guy. I thought he'd come quietly. But we have Mr. Man; the DJs and the rest of the crew. We can replace Terry. I like the idea of the apprentices' talent scouting. We should keep that."

"We'll have to dump the apprentices. Our backers aren't looking for me to run a training academy they expect a return on investment."

"What do you think he'll do when he finds out?"

"I don't give a shit. This is business. His moral stance was his undoing. You can't tell people how to act."

"Especially when you're a queer," she casually remarked. "He's most probably up to his arse with that Italian," she concluded as she finished smoking.

****

Michael and David lay on the bed almost steaming hot, dripping with sweat, breathless trying to recover. They were strained, but due to their diet and exercise regime, they still had spunk. In the shadowy room, they looked at the cracks in the ceiling unable to speak. Their legs and arms hung off the bed. David's veins were jittering under his skin. Michael glanced over and caught sight of David's pouting lips, so he eased in and

314

kissed him with laughter in his lungs. It seemed to give David a virtual transfusion because almost immediately David started laughing.

Michael rose up to look at him. "*Bellissima.*" He climbed onto David and began licking his skin. That tipped David back into a newly inflamed state. "You know I watched porno but nothing in them is like you in me. You kiss my heart the way you fuck." *'Keep talking Michael; tell me again I really am beautiful and lovely'.*

Michael got out of bed and dragged him into the darken living room. Michael put on an old album: *Nat King Cole sings George Shearing plays* and the scratchy track *Let There Be Love* came on. Naked, they danced happily and in tune. The kitsch room was virtually transformed by their devotion; especially since a free-standing lamp lit only their loving faces and pulled them out of the darkness in the room.

Shortly afterward, they were in the small shower together and barely able to move. "There might have been a time when all I could offer you was this. A place I grew up. I'm glad I left and made a family and money. Now my new home is worth five million pounds. Money and work are important. I stopped teaching to make more money. Here is a question for you. Suppose you can't get any more clients?"

"I'll work harder for the ones I've got," David said with the water beating down

"What happens if you lose one. That Winston character is already a lost cause."

David washed his armpits and chest while thinking. "I can't lose all my clients. And I still know how to run events. I know lots of actors, media business people. TV people. I can drum up business. I started with nothing and built the business." Michael turned him around and washed his back.

"Who are your best bets in the entertainment/media communities?"

David thought about it. "I'm friends with loads of Black actors in London. And I know lots of DJs who gig the holiday hot spots from Ibiza to Mykonos, Stockholm. I also know TV producers who like me and invite me back for shows."

"Have you ever thought about becoming an agent for actors? I know people in America looking for actors in England. I could introduce you to a guy. He's a casting director and he hates most of the agents in London. You could fill that slot."

"As an agent or casting director?" David asked cynically. Michael nodded.

"Those Black fundamentalist hate-crime advocates can't be trusted. I'm talking about *your* clients. I think they'd stab you in the back. Do not be passive. Be prepared for trouble and have a backup plan if it turns to shit."

"I just came out. No one can blackmail me. You heard my clients in the film."

"That was before you said you love men. You need to do business with more enlightened people. Your father is an anomaly when it comes to that."

"Michael don't. I can't throw my father away, I've told you; I can't!"

"I'm going to say this and then shut up. Your 'Urban Grime' clients don't read. You shouldn't beg them for acceptance. I brought you here to get a rest from all of last week's commotions. I can help you build an agency; casting or as an agent."

"I'd never asked for money."

"You're not asking. I'm offering to back you."

"But I still have a business turning over a million in profits."

Michael gave him the soap and pointed at his back and David washed him.

"David, how rich would you like to be?"

"I have no complaints earning over a million."

"I earned that four years ago. I had three great deals that put me in big. That year I earned a million I took Lola to New Zealand, first class luxury; people had to treat her like a great lady, whites had to *serve* my wife; no Māori treatment. You want power; let me help you get the money."

"You sound like you're going to switch to a Tony Montana routine."

Michael turned around and grabbed him. "With you, I'm afraid of nothing because I love you." David shook! "Tell me you love me."

"Yes Michele Giancarlo De Farenzino, I love you." Those spoken words impacted on their bodies, but eye to eye they didn't look away and the joy of that truth eased forward slowly and David caressed Michael unshaven face and Michael reached between him and moved in for the kiss they'd remember for the rest of their lives.

****

Later that Sunday night, Cynthia, Grace, and Lola were in Cynthia's pastel lemon and white bedroom and there were several dresses were on

316

the bed. They were all quality garments, but Lola diplomatically told Cynthia. "Except this one, I think you should change your wardrobe. All of these lovely dresses are too old for you. You're sixty-one, which makes you by my calculations forty-nine, so you should celebrate your fifties!" They all liked that. "Excuse me!" Lola continued. "Michael re-made himself when he was fifty. Of course, he does have other things gifts going for him, but you have the right to customize yourself."

"How should I customize…"

"What gifts has Michael got?" Lola looked at Grace and she shook her head in a funny manner which made Cynthia slightly nervous. Lola intuitively picked up on it.

"In the elegance and beauty of this lovely bedroom I dare not speak of it."

Cynthia said, "Go on, we're talking."

"No, this is not my house; I'm in Miss Cynthia's bedroom."

"You have my permission. Tell us everything."

"I'm not some drunken Trench Town tramp. My father is a professor a Mona."

"Excuse me Miss Lola, but your father is one of the greatest Caribbean historians of our generation. I made my children read his books."

"As you say Miss Cynthia: he and my mother raised a lady. I shouldn't have said anything. We've been talking about us and our lives today. Besides, my husband Tony is very loving, so these days I have nothing to complain about."

Lola looked at Grace. "Also, we mustn't dwell on their sex life because from what you've both said; David is no single-minded sex maniac. Companionship is vital to Michael. So on that subject let me tell you something, Miss Grace. I have a guy working for me who's perfect for you. He's also dedicated to his Church, but he knows life is real, and not scripture. I'm going to invite the both of you to dinner."

Lola got up from the king size bed and looked around the muslin and silk decorated bedroom, with its scent of perfume and freshness. "This has been the best day of the year and I'm so glad we're going to make something of our lives as friends."

"Let me get Noel to drive you home."

"Noel?"

"He and his sister work for me; you've seen her all day. Noel looks after the wear and tear in the house and he supervises David's house. David hasn't got time to clean up. He's too busy running the firm, Noel looks after that; watches over the cleaners, everything. Let me call him." When Cynthia left, Grace slipped her hand into Lola's.

"You really think this guy is going to be interested in me?"

"Definitely, you've got yourself into a rut and you need someone to appreciate your femininity, your worldly view of life. How long has it been?"

Grace took a second before she decided to simply tell the truth. "Years."

Lola gasped. "Leave this to me. His name is Clive, he's forty, Jamaican, with some Indian blood like me; red skin, six foot, clean shaven, about a 44 suit size."

"You've sized him up all right."

"Just in case that has connotations that bother you, I've only ever had two men in my life, Michael and now Tony." Lola looked around to check if Cynthia was coming back.

"Clive was previously married, but sickle cell anemia took her. No children, lives alone and dying little by the day." Grace looked interested and touched. "Girl, the man is choice; but instead of him looking for another woman, he stays at the salon or works for the Church. He gets on fine with the gay boys at work so you don't have to worry about that. Ok, let's stop talking before Miss Cynthia comes back. Do you think she likes me really? I can be a bit free with my mouth." Grace locked her fingers between Lola's and embraced her.

CHAPTER THIRTY-SEVEN

The following Friday at 11.30p.m. Michael walked David through the famous Via Veneto and showed off his friend and lover to the rich and greedy. In his oyster colored Armani best suit, black silk shirt, and Loriblu shoes Michael felt good. Dressed in his best emerald green Ozwald Boateng mohair suit, red shirt, and red colored shoes, David swaggered and their *bella figura* impressed onlookers. Not even at the age of thirty-five did Michael look as good as he did that night.

Michael took David to the plaque dedicated to Federico Fellini, and after that he took him to the *Café Extravaganza* for champagne cocktails and to be seen. The place was alive, like an architectural organism packed with wannabe stars from 'great' families and fashion: footballers and their 'girls', models and their photographers, as well as international celebrities from classical and popular music. The sound of glasses and gossip in five languages caught Michael's ear as he told David. "Do you realize that the clothes and jewels people are wearing in here are probably worth millions?"

"Yes," David casually answered.

"Oh I forget; you come from a family of dignitaries and money. I didn't but I learned more than these people. So now I have more love, sex and money than them." David tried not to laugh. "It fascinates me that your father took you to Austin Reed for everyday clothes and Savile Row for specials. What's fantastic is that you look better than the hip-hop fellas and you could entice a Machiavellian playboy."

"Shut up," David replied besotted and thrilled by Michael's love.

They were sized up and judged by the patrons because unknown to them, strangers knew who they were because of the online clamor that had been trending. "The contrast between your place and this is quite something Michele."

"I love that: this fake glamor and the beauty of you in my home." Michael gazed at David and couldn't look away. In spite of the wealth and style of the place 'Michael and David radiated God's grace through their devotion', a tabloid writer would report hours later. He'd go on to say:

'Dressed in everything you'd expect from the gay fashionistas they were splendid; David with Black beauty and Michael with Italian sexual charisma'. Even though the years of homophobia in Roma had changed; the notion of 'Mother plus Father Equals a Normal Family' still underlined the mass populous perception of 'normal'. What beguiled the crowd was Michael and David's gay pride. True spiritual, mental and sexual love made Michael and David psychologically invincible; so appeared to be untouchable regardless of anyone's hate.

From the back of the club several men rushed in and circled them, taking pictures. David was startled.

"Michele! What does it feel like to win this man who left his wife for you?"

Michael replied in Italian. "He did not leave his wife for me. We are both divorced. His Ex is a cunt; my Ex-wife is an angel." Cameras flashed and mobiles recorded him.

In English, a tabloid writer asked David. "How did you fall in love with an Italian and not a black man or woman?"

David scanned around the club and saw men with mobiles and cameras coming at him.

"Why shouldn't I fall in love with an Italian, he's beautiful and sexy as only romantic Italians can be. I'm not the first person from the African Continent to win the heart and soul of a great Roman. Michele is a Godsend after the Jezebel I was married to."

Michael said, "*Senti, mi rendo conto che si metterà le immagini a mezzo stampa...* so write your stories and take photos, but write this. Love changes us all." They were bombarded with more questions and Michael told them in Italian to stop.

A Frenchman said, "The hottest topic online is about you two and 'Gay Dads'. David's clients say he's immoral and his British TV fans say he's lovely. Some football players and actors say David's wife is a nasty bitch out to destroy a black man's reputation."

Michael told them. "She's an adulteress and a junky. What she doesn't invent she imagines. David was a faithful husband and continues to be a loyal father. This is why I love him because only a father knows the true meaning of devotion."

"Why should I be condemned because I love Michele?" David held Michael's hand aloft and then kissed his fist. Mobiles and camera flashed around them. David took a note from Solly's media savvy and stood and posed knowing he looked great and Michael posed showing off his pride and sex appeal without even a hint of shame.

Walking along the Via Veneto past people dining to the sound of Italian music, David took it all in and said, "Solly would love this. He's such a star. When the media turn to him he has star quality that just comes alive! The women that used to call and send pictures of themselves – some of those pictures were X-rated. When he married you could hear hearts breaking, even more than when he left the club and went to Nigeria. Oh yes, he's invited me to a charity match for sickle cell anemia soon. Do you want to come and watch a brunch of Black guys play footie?"

"Anytime!" he yelled out loud.

David asked him, "Just how much of an exhibitionist are you?"

"You ask *me* this with your film online."

"Alright, score one for your side." David took his hand and pulled him to a stop outside one of the many restaurants. He yanked Michael in close and embraced him. Tourist and locals looked up from their drinks and David kissed Michael's lips, his neck, and caressed his hard-on then kissed his throat. Some people coming past them stopped and bellowed, stunned by the outrageous kiss.

Michael turned to the onlookers and said, "What can I do, he's an African Prince, and I'm a poor Italian." Michael yelled: *"Kiss Me Honey Honey Kiss Me,"* and started doing the Cha-Cha up the Via Veneto. He continued singing as he tossed his hips and wiggled his bottom. He changed a line in the song and said: "don't care honey if you suck me off…" and David let go the loudest and most vulgar laugh some people had ever heard. The lights in the streets, the scooters, cars, and people out strolling all lit up as Michael caught their attention. David dash and got him and they ran down the Via Veneto away from everyone.

Michael and David were in the back seat of the darken 1958 Plymouth Fury with their mouths full in a giddy sexual frenzy. Michael pulled back and tried to calm down. "I said we should christen the car but this isn't good enough. I want to go back to the bed my father made love in and my mother gave birth in."

Reeling, David said, "You stopped sucking my cock to fuck in your parents' bed; this must be a legacy of Roman decadence." He settled down momentarily then told Michael when the reality came back to him. "Listen, I have to go online and check us out; those tabloids can't know more about us than we do."

"Ok because tonight I'm going to drink from the pump." He pulled his pants up and drove off with lust and love in his blood.

Back at Michael's home, the two of them scanned their iPads and mobiles and found the Tweets launched by Roberto, Adrian and Solly. They had hashtag threads in support of David and Michael as gay fathers. They both read them with stunned surprise and pride in their sons. David said, "They're totally driving and creating support for us. Adrian posted this picture of us here in Rome. Look at Solly's Followers and the messages we're getting. The boys are amazing to back us like this." Michael continued searching and reading.

"Look here, these threads from Lola and the staff at her salon."

"Bloody hell! There's a whole thread leading to Gus' website connecting gay dad's in Amsterdam and London. That man has never wronged me."

"Never mind him, love me." Michael pulled him up and stripped him.

The night revealed their repressed cravings and as a consequence, they went at each other voraciously. In the erotic chaos, Michael was haunted by a soliloquy coming out of everything he believed in. '*Take my blood and sperm and possess my flesh. Hurt me and love me because I'm yours. No drugs, no sadomasochism can absolve us from slavery: only your heart, cock, and spirit*'. Astride David, Michael was conscious of heroes due to his Art history; so Alexander the Great and Achilles riding into battle filled his mind, and he rode David and went beyond himself, knowing his father conceived him and his mother gave birth to him in that room. Seldom do men see each other's glory but their flesh and acumen was more than myth. The power of their bodies and soul compelled Michael to proclaim the truth that homoerotic history demands of all lovers. He said: "Fuck me, darling! I... Kiss me since you love me."

Secure in this knowledge David was astonishingly tender in every respect. Michael had David pulsating through him and he remembered his orgasm with Lola and the birth of his children. He'd seen them all come out of her and into the world and now he felt David enter him. The pain was real and the ecstasy pierced the bones holding him together. David looked up at Michael and his stiff flesh and wet skin urged him on. David had him as if he was transcending the ecclesiastical boundaries of morality that excommunicated both of them.

Then through a traverse David gave himself to Michael and the lexicon of gay ideals were overshadowed by David's subconscious. He intermittently kissed Michael all over his skin in between utterances... "I

won't scream, I won't say stop; just… swear to me you won't vanish."
When Michael moved into him, David did scream and Michael said,
"Shall I pray to you as I make your flesh my body?" He pulled David
closer and chanted Indian, Japanese, Hebrew, Polynesian, Navajo, and
Aborigine mantras. He took hold of David's shaft and declared.

"On the splendor and power of this cock…" and then he gave praise to
it in nine languages. Michael trembled at the sight of David's heroic, strong
body. If the planets were in kissing distance, they couldn't have created a
greater Supernova than the bright darkness that entered and left Michael and
David's Being, which altered their vision.

****

They lie in each other's arms for an unmeasured period of time, but it
was long enough for both of them to know they needed each other. "You
know darling, this poor apartment has seen my birth and the conception of
Roberto. Lola and I were here: now you and I. Do you see now why you
mustn't worry about me vanishing?"

"My Dad loved me very much when I was a boy and when I became a
man he vanished. That's why I'm paying for him to see Dr. Claude to
cleanse him of the brainwashing. If one day you vanished from my
heart…" David turned away from him, and Michael looked at his spinal
cord for longer than he realized. For no reason, he could explain Michael
became tearful and pulled David close.

"This room and this City are sacred to me. I gave birth to Roberto in
this room. Tonight you and me – we put life back into our bodies. Not
fertilization but we're carrying each other's DNA."

David had to think about the full meaning of that. "Why didn't you
tell me about the significance of this room? Earlier in the week, you were
teaching me how to curse in Italian."

"This isn't a Church. My father took his belt to me in here when I was
fourteen. Mama came in here to curse him when he said she spent too
much money on movies. My grandfather came in here to fart after a good
meal. This place, like my love, is real."

"Do you think they're watching us in here?"

"No, but I know people who'd pay fabulous money to watch us make
love."

"What? I'd never let someone into our bedroom."

"Not even for ten million?"

David took a moment. "Who has that kind of money to throw away?"

"Omar and Ahmed. They said they'd pay ten million to watch us."

David smacked him, and Michael was startled. "Don't say filth like that to me again."

"Sorry, forgive me." David nodded his head. "What I'd like is for you to set up this meeting in LA. Please call soon and we'll…" Michael went and got his mobile and dialed. As he got back into the bed, David was surprised as they waited for an answer.

"Hello J.J, it's Michael, I'm in Rome with my fella. How's Carlos and Bryan?" Michael listened and caressed David overjoyed to have him in his arms.

"It's good to hear the family is well. Listen my fella wants a meeting to discuss what we've talked about with your son." He listened and kissed David.

"We can fly out later today. He wants to hear the ideas." He listened. "No, strictly actors, he knows that." He listened again. "That's great I'll get tickets and call you back." Michael hung up and gave David the eye.

"You're so beautiful!" David said joyously.

"I mentioned Ahmed and Omar because I wanted to know you're above them."

"They're not my friends. They're yours."

"No, they're not. They're strictly business. My friends are not immoral. They don't fuck their women and screw men on the side. People that use the money to grease their sexual cogs… that's depraved."

"Are you sure you're not Catholic?"

"Pantheist more like. If you give me a day, I'll tell you about my first reading of Spinoza, but not now. Today I believe in you." Michael backed into him, they settled down, entwined naked and fell asleep.

BOOK FOUR

Commitment

Winter–Spring 2016

CHAPTER THIRTY-EIGHT

A week later in London David's staff sat in the boardroom giving testimony as if it were an inquest concerning Willy and Sophia. David listened to the staff closely as they recounted what they'd been told and their fears about being out of work.

Barrington the St Lucian guy who was delighted with his Christmas bonus told David. "Sophia said we should keep working until you got back and you'd tell us what to do. But the thing is, David, all the clients have left and gone with her and Willy. How can they just do that?"

Jennifer, his best online saleswoman said, "Terry's the only one who didn't go. He texted us all on Sunday, and we met that night. I got a train back from Brighton that afternoon, and Terry played us a recording of the secret meeting Willy and Sophia called in here. They promised the clients' money, and they went for it, so they've left us. Willy said since you're... gay and weird... shagging your ex-wife online and..." She couldn't go on. The staff was embarrassed.

David told them. "Come on, say it."

Barrington eyed David with the tenacity of a bold salesman. "Willy and Sophia told the clients you've violated the morality clause in their contract, so they have the right to leave you rather than you dropping them. Willy said you've slandered Veronika."

David's was so angry his gut felt like it turned. "I have evidence of everything I said concerning my ex-wife's addiction and the death of both of my kids. Anyway, before this becomes an emotional mess, I ask you to give me the rest of this week to sort things out. Even though Willy and Sophia's conduct has placed your jobs at risk, I will not be making anyone redundant or firing any of you." David could see that all of his staff were relieved.

"Madeleine you're the new office manager." She was a beautiful person from the Seychelles, even though her looks didn't match her spirit. David met her on the Tube as he 'clocked' her eying a woman. When their eyes met with knowing laughter, he liked her immediately because she was a Revisionist 'lipstick lesbian'. No one knew, but she and her girlfriend wrote all of Mr. Man's material. As 'butch' and 'fem' friends, she and David spent many hours talking about the pleasures of masquerade.

"Jill, please assist Madeleine." Jill, a hungry English girl from an upper-class background, was an excellent online sales optimization web consultant. Three years earlier she came into David's office and sold him her professional services for a one year contract, and she proved to be so valuable he gave her a permanent job.

At his home, David walked through the hallway from the kitchen into the living room as Terry brought him up to speed. "…so I'm the only client who didn't leave. I was really glad I recorded Willy and Sophia so you could hear for yourself."

"I won't forget this kindness and your loyalty Terry."

"How are you going to handle it?"

"Sophia's forgotten there are rules and laws concerning employment contracts, client confidentiality, data protection and bribery. I'll remind her."

"You're relaxed about this. I'd be fighting mad. I mean they're both shit."

"I am very angry, and I'm going to make Willy and Sophia regret this."

"That ministerial voice of yours sounds so cool. I can't believe you're gonna get down on them with the beating they deserve."

"I'm furious, but going off on them isn't the way." He thought for almost a minute, and Terry watched closely. David took out his mobile and dialed Erwin.

"Good! I thought you might be out. I need you to help me fix something. Call me back in fifteen, and I'll update you." He ended the call and turned to Terry.

"Why didn't you go with them? He offered you the prospect of great money…"

"I don't spit in someone's face when they help me. Besides, we're more than that, aren't we?" He held up his right hand and Terry gave him a high five.

David got in his car and drove over to De Beauvior Town, one of the most exclusive parts of Hackney where his parents lived. Historically Hackney was a poor Borough of working class immigrants, but there were parts of the Borough where houses could rival any in the London's high-class areas like Knightsbridge, Hampstead, and Chelsea. David called

Erwin and told him what had happened and asked him to get over to his parents' house immediately. He drove down Camden Road getting angrier by the minute. The street lights and shops showed the first lights of Christmas.

Solomon came to the door and took a look at him. His casual tailored elegance was impeccable. He eyed his son, and he knew something serious had happened.

"What it is, Tunji?" David went in and entered the study. It was a beautifully furnished room also decorated in the Colonial style, but it had no soft fabric, it had elegant wood carved furniture and wooden shutters.

"Willy and Sophia have stolen all of my clients. They're setting up business. Willy said the morality clause in my client's contract enable them to hold me to the same standards which he claims I've violated by coming out as gay."

"Your contract does not state that your clients have to live by your standards. It states they should refer to the 2010 Equality Act and abide by those regulations and refrain from racist and defamatory statements. That is not a legal issue he can use to impeach your conduct."

"I called Erwin, so they'll be here soon."

"Good, we're going to teach them a legal lesson they'll live to regret." Cynthia came in and saw them in deep conversation. She had on a black trouser suit with a red silk blouse and red shoes. Her hair was perfectly styled by Lola. She looked better now than when ten years younger.

"David, what is it?" He briefed his mother. What David outlined infuriated her. Cynthia stepped into the hallway. "Solly, Alice come down here now!"

A while later, Solly, David, Erwin, Solomon, Alice, and Grace were gathered in the study. Cynthia walked around the room as everyone eyed and listened to her. "Solomon, leave the room. You're a QC, you cannot hear this." Solomon watched his wife, and a smile lit his belly eying her. He stepped outside. "I expect you, men, to punish Willy with the full might of our family's name!" Grace forgot that Cynthia had a temper, but she felt it at the end of Cynthia's sentence.

"My hard earned money and your father's resources, and money are invested in David's business. I've watched you work and sweat and sacrifice to build the firm and make it a success!" Cynthia crossed the room to David and placed her hand on his shoulder. "You are all my men; you have balls!!" Erwin looked at Solly and David eyed both of them.

"Go to that son of a whore and bring him down!" David looked at Erwin, who wore the same smile. "Don't utter a word to that illegitimate …dog. The day will come when I'll speak to him!" Cynthia crossed the room. "Erwin hurt him. Mark him and cripple him so badly he won't recover."

"Yes, Mum!" She turned around, and her eyes reached David before she did. "David, he's very proud of his collection." She stood still. "Smash it!" He nodded. "You don't have all night so Solly, go with your brother and speed things up."

"Yes, Mummy." She walked over to the door and called Solomon back in.

"There's something I need you to do for me."

Solomon happily gave her his full attention. "Of course, honey."

"What is the family motto?" she asked them all.

They all said as one voice in total. "If you can't hear you must feel!"

"David, if I know you, and I do; you're thinking of all kind of crazy shit to get back at Sophia." She walked right up to him. "Wait because I can see you in trouble if you're left on your own. Sophia is white. You cannot go after her without someone saying you hate white gals." Alice elbowed Grace, and she indicated for her to pay attention.

"Only a woman can truly punish another woman. Men use sexual humiliation." Solomon loved the way his wife's intelligence served her. "Let's see how she copes with me. Solomon, I want your legal counsel. I want her to suffer every day of her miserable life for years to come."

"As you wish." Solomon agreed.

"Mum, I'm gonna introduce Willy to grief he'll mourn for the rest of his days."

"Ladies, go home and cook, your men will be hungry after they come back from Tottenham later. This is an Arsenal house, but since you're going over to Tottenham later tonight, take that rage with you." The two football teams' hatred was notorious.

Solomon began singing "Tottenham fuckspurs…" and the other men joined in.

Coming from Tanzania, Alice might have been confused by their singing chants, but after all her years of marriage to Solly she understood everything.

"I have not finished talking to you." All the men shut up.

"That son of a whore, Willy, and that bitch think they can mess with David because they believe, as 'right thinking' Black folks, we think

David is a disgrace!" Cynthia pointed at everyone in the study. "Do you?" she asked Erwin.

"After he's looked after my sister and respected me, no way."

She nodded.

"You?" she asked Solomon. Everyone looked at him. He said no. "Are you lying to me?" He repeated no. One hand was in a fist, and the other made a claw with her finger pointing at him. "I have grounds for divorce and if you hate our son…"

"Honey, I swear on the soul of our daughter."

"Then you are allowed to come to my bed." He looked relieved. "David, send Michael my love. And come for dinner on Sunday. I want to know what kind of retribution you have for that mongrel bastard and his nasty bitch." He nodded. "I'm going to rip his brains out when you're done with him." Cynthia's words struck fear in Alice and passion in Solomon because he was aroused by the fire and strength that made her the woman she was. When Cynthia left the room, it was filled with the spirit of Jamaica that attested to the Marrons she descended from.

****

When everyone had gone home, and Solomon and Cynthia were in bed, he said to her.

"You're fantastic you know."

"I live with extraordinary men, that's why."

"I think David can keep the firm together. He didn't come to me tonight like a lost and weak boy. He arrived full of fire. I think Michael has something to do with his increase in confidence."

"I'm glad you can speak of Michael without the hate and rage."

"I don't have any hate in me tonight." She looked at him and knew that she still loved him and would continue to until she died. She pulled back her nightdress, and he took off his pajama top, and they made love for the best part of the night. She was pleased he could still make her happy and feel loved and sexually fulfilled. Solomon was psychologically and physically aroused. At the age sixty-five, he was proud that he didn't need Viagra. He was full of himself and filled with love for his wife.

****

At two o'clock in the morning, Erwin broke into Willy's house wearing a balaclava. He waited to adjust his eyesight to the darkness, and then Erwin wrapped the rope around his leather covered hands and he made his way up the dark stairs towards the bedroom. He didn't stumble about because he'd been there hundreds of times before over twelve years and soon he reached out for the bedroom door.

He crept in and head toward the bed where Willy was sound asleep in the overheated room. Erwin felt for his ankles and feet and then looped the noose around his ankles and then went to the top of the bed to see his face. He reached down, slipped the rope under his head and then yanked it over his head and pulled tight. Willy woke up choking, and Erwin sat on him and snapped his little finger. Willy couldn't scream, but Erwin shoved his face into the pillow until he was suffocating. When he yanked the rope to pull his head up, Willy gasped for air.

Erwin kept hold of the rope, reached for his underpants on the floor and stuff it into Willy's mouth. Erwin took out his knife and stabbed him in the knees and ankles. The pain was utterly dreadful but it was intensified when Erwin punched him in the pubic hairs, and that was so excruciating he shit the bed. Downstairs, David and Solly were destroying his prized Ska blue-beat vinyl collection along with his Reggae and 1970s Soul albums. Solly removed records from their sleeves and took a knife to them.

CHAPTER THIRTY-NINE

In Michael's new home, David was in bed making love to him. The new king size bed was covered with brown satin sheets and the bed was on a beach wood platform raised it off the ground. Across the room, there was a grand white leather sofa and a giant Samsung interactive television that sat on the far side of the room. The walls were covered with gold colored mosaic tiles and golden silk material from the Far East: with a texture of luster and sheen which made the walls at a high-level gleam. Highlighting all this was the size of the room itself which created its own grandeur.

Writhing across the bed, David was almost out of his mind in ecstasy as Michael made love to him. Pure love and sexually explicit sentiments came out of his mouth as David caressed his skin and flesh inside out. Michael was captured by the sight of David's glistening hot brown skin that showed all his muscles. For a moment, Michael thought of other visually beautiful things but the true meaning of exquisite at a visceral and primal level impacted on him. As a result, David absorbed the mental and physical power of Michael, and eventually Michael fell into rhapsodic splendor when he reached the height and fell into the abyss as David swallowed his screams in kisses.

Michael could barely regain his senses. He floated through time where iconic scenes in Art's history virtually pulled him in. The sight of the *Death of Sardanapalus* by Delacroix with its luxurious excess filled his head. When he recovered, David kissed him again and got up and head out of the room, glistening brown, with sweat on his hot skin. Michael wanted to speak, but he was self-conscious of making a fool of himself telling David his body was greater than anything in art's history. So he lay back and tried to regain his balance.

When David returned minutes later with a bottle of Bollinger and two glasses, Michael watched him approach. "Does anyone look better in their birthday suit?" David gave him the eye and Michael sat up. "Every time with you, it's different. Is your cock, sex mad all the time?"

"He's up against big competition."

Michael flippantly replied, "Yeah, Rocco Siffredi is a runner up, but I haven't mastered my understanding of your body as yet. It took me a year to learn Lola's body. For us, the more I learn about you is the better I'll get. Are you ok with that?"

"Yes, and besides… the way you respond; I don't know if I'm getting better, but the way we make love *and* fuck is epic."

David poured them champagne. "Here's to your new house and bed, and to us." They drank, and David began thinking about everything. "We shouldn't have any secrets about things that have happened since we've been together."

Michael felt as if his heart skipped a beat and he found it difficult to swallow. "What?"

David looked at him and then looked away. "Solly, me and Erwin broke into Willy's house. We beat him up and trashed the place to make it look like a burglary."

Michael punched him in the shoulder. "I'm sorry. I know you have your thing with the 'Seven Deadly Sins' and I must seem like a wicked…"

"Shut up!" Michael got to his feet and he looked like a monument standing on the bed over David, and his sexual anatomy became a threatening trifecta. "He stole my clients, put the staff on the brink of redundancy, I might go out of business."

"My mistake with the children was loving them so much I was afraid to impose my will or tell them what to do to ensure they came to me for advice. I will not make that mistake twice." He jumped off the bed and crossed the room. "Those grimy people you represent use their Black fundamentalism to bash you. The filth in their head is online! You've lost this battle even if you win them back legally." Michael took his mobile off the white sofa and dialed. Standing there in the sunlight with his arm up, the phone to his ear and his fist in his waist he looked like a contrapposto sculpted hero. "J.J and Carlos need an answer. Shall I tell him yes?"

David thought about his family and he looked at Michael standing before him naked.

"Yes, say to J.J and Carlos I'm in."

"You can establish yourself as an actor's agent or set up a casting agency. I will share my contacts with you and you can turn your firm around."

"I'm not in business by myself; I'm backed by my family."

"Who owns most of the firm, you or them?"

333

"Me but Mum's money started me up, and Dad's legal knowledge and the family money went into the second year of salaries, equipment, marketing, and taxes."

Michael got J.J at his home in Arizona. "I hope all is well with you. J.J we have decided to go ahead. Will you come to London and we'll show you the business, introduce you to some of David's potential clients and take care of you. My house will have more furniture…" David told him to invite J.J to his house. "David wants you to stay at his house, it's beautiful." He listened and then handed the mobile to David.

"Hi! I'll contact the actors." He listened. "I'll get back to you ASAP, J.J."

Michael said, "Don't work behind my back. Come to me." He smacked him lightly.

****

Solomon was sitting in the back of his car stuck in traffic, and his driver strummed his fingers on the steering wheel and exhaled through his teeth. Solomon looked at the back of his head and then looked out the car and saw they were barely moving. He grabbed his briefcase. "I'll take the bloody Underground!" He opened the door and got out in the middle of the street, and another driver called him a 'fucking bastard'. Solomon looked at the twenty-something-year-old Brit in a transit van. "Brainless peasant!" In the congested road with red buses, black cabs, and cars as far as the eye could see crammed into an enormous colorful street pizza landscape he crossed Islington's Green and Upper Street to head for the Underground up ahead.

Solomon walked like a royal in his Prince of Wales gray suit and stood out in the crowd. When he got to the Angel station, a scruffy man in a yellow and red anorak shoved one of the free papers at him and Solomon took it. Heading down the escalator Solomon began reading the paper and he saw a story about David and his clients' accusations about him. Entitled, 'Man and the Hood' the story concerned David as a married man who declares he's gay and shameless, and the Urban Black men calling for punishment against him because he's turned on them. When Solomon read some of the quotes from his clients about David as a pervert, he was so furious he rushed down the escalator and back up the other side, out into the street and called his driver.

Two hours later Solomon was in his office with Dr. Claude and he couldn't keep still. He paced in every direction and read quotes out loud as Dr. Claude observed him. "This one!" He stood still for a time. "When a Black man chooses to be a bitch to any white man, how can he expect to be trusted?" He stared at Dr. Claude hoping for an answer, but he said nothing. "That doesn't offend you? What about this. 'All homosexuals are an abomination in the eyes of God and deserve crucifixion'. Or how about this. 'Vote whether you think he was queer before or after he married'. This online trail has over 5,000 responses. What about…"

"This hatred is circulating in the Black underground mainly." Dr. Claude said, "There are more than 45,000 Tweets and online calls for David's clients to shut up. David has told me Dr. King and Gandhi's approach for non-violence will win out."

"You cannot know this but he's soft I tell you. He isn't a tough bastard like me. These statements, claiming Veronika killed the kids to prevent him molesting them. Or as an African, with a son and marriage, Michael is just his white bitch. David is a humane person. He's none of these things. Being gay doesn't make him less of a man."

Solomon tried to calm down. "I'm going to prosecute them!" Solomon started pacing frantically. "If anyone in government made statements like this, they'd be out of office and in court. That man who said women scientists cry and fall in love too easily. He had to resign because his statement was sexist and…" Solomon stood still, and Dr. Claude could see the idea fill his mind and pull him up, so he stood even taller.

"Tell me, come on Solomon."

"To degrade and continually humiliate someone for their gender or sexual identity, that is Sexual Harassment! It's law! I am going to sue those ghetto scumbags for sexual harassment against David because no one has the right to degrade him."

"What about you?"

"Are you joking? I have spoken to Lola and Tony. Michael is a highly decorated Academic and a wonderful father. His sons said so. Michael and David aren't a couple of cocksuckers cruising Hampstead Heath. They love each other, and I never understood that until I saw them together. My son has put himself in the firing line, and that is the kind of courage in the fight for a man's civil rights and human rights I know all about. Akoni Akoni!!"

Seconds later his Akoni came into the office. "Yes sir!"

"Bring me everything we have on Equality Rights and Sexual Harassment. Also call David and tell him to come in immediately. I want him and Michael in here because I'm going to save them from the shitstorm that's brewing." Akoni left.

"Doctor, isn't there medical or psychological explanation we can use in court. The Tweets and ravings must indicate a profile; the way someone's behavior constitutes a racist pathology?"

Smiling Dr. Claude said, "I will be very happy to help you with this."

"This isn't a joke."

"I know. I'm smiling because every time I help a patient, I feel pleased. Don't you realize you've changed?

"This isn't post-war Nigeria with the inherited dogma of our post-colonial or tribal experience. My friends have told me that David has re-defined fatherhood. It's interesting that because they've seen him fuck his wife, it's blurred the lines of his sexual identity."

Dr. Claude nodded. "You told me in the second session David's sexuality reflected on you and that distressed you. I told you sexual preference does not define masculinity despite the myth that it does. What are your thought about that now?"

"Cynthia and I have been close and passionate since David come out. It's interesting that David came to me when he learned about Willy and Sophia's takeover."

"He trusts you because he always wants you to be his protector. Every man needs a protector. It's why we form bonds with other men. They're our heroes."

"You've presented a convincing case. I never thought a homosexual could be a heroic, strong man. How long did it take to put the dossier of evidence together?"

"I add to it. The facts about gay and bisexual men have a long history."

"I double checked all the evidence you cited."

"I knew you would."

"Kinsey, Olivier, Malcolm X, Brando, and Billy Preston, CEOs in technology, in football, Thomas Hitzlsperger, Robbie Rogers; Art, Basquiat, Music, Bernstein. Don Lemon! You've taught me a lot." Solomon took the time to think. "One doesn't have to be heterosexual to be a 'man'. This is a life lesson."

Dr. Claude asked him to reflect on the day he assaulted David.

"I was out of my mind with tribal pride. These sessions have dismantled things. If you weren't Nigerian, I would never have listened to you. But you and David understood my psychosis. I'm telling you, doctor, it's amazing how quickly someone can change; if they want to."

"There are people that would prefer to kill their sons and brothers rather that have homosexuality disgrace the family name…"

"Knowing the kind of neurosis I was living with gives me a great preparation for prosecuting his clients."

****

David walked into his father's office with Michael and saw Dr. Claude. Michael and David were in sloppy T-shirts, jeans, and trainers. "Pardon my appearance; I've been over at Michael's decorating." The receptionist closed the door and they sat down.

"These vile statements against you online; you haven't defended yourselves against any of them. I am going to take legal action against them, and so I needed to meet urgently. I want us to come up with a plan."

"Why is Dr. Claude here?"

"Because I want you all to know I've learned certain things. We're going to stay here until we come up with a plan." They all looked at each other and settled into their seats.

Four hours later when the table was packed with takeaway boxes of lunch, they all looked tired and wound up. David said, "I have it!" They looked at him. He walked over to a whiteboard. At the top of a hierarchy chart, he put Willy's picture up and wrote. "He's been inciting people to attack me, calling be a walking abomination that should be killed as a homo, etc. We have his written statements as evidence. Then there's this bastard."

David scrambled for a photo of Evadney and put it up below Frank. "She blogs I've made up stories against Veronika. She blogs like she's an addict saying Michael and I are dirty homos who deserve death." He placed several other pictures on the board until he came to Sophia and Frank.

"Set a trap. Get apologies from the clients about me mistreating Veronika. She'll confirm I haven't made up lies. We pay her something. The clients will realize Sophia and Willy had no grounds for impeaching me as their manager. So we win." Solomon liked that. "Dad, get your staff to write an apology statement and we'll insist on it being signed." Dr.

Claude and Michael looked more closely at him. "When we have their apologies, you can use their signed statements as an admission of guilt."

"Very nice. This trap must be tighter. I will have each statement written to fit the level of active stalking and harassment of each of your clients."

"The 2010 Equality Act provides grounds to win this case for sexual harassment. In one of the blogs I've read, they're asking people to assault me because I'm gay. Charging them will send a message about stalking and hate against gays.

"I like it," Solomon said. "Let them think this is only about an apology and a case about their contract and then spring the *coup de grâce*!" He laughed!

"Why are you prepared to act now?" Michael asked. Solomon moved from behind his desk and went to Michael. "I had no respect for you before. Your wife, ex-wife, and sons have told me what kind of man you are when I invited Lola to dinner. I've read your work on Pan-Africans' post-colonial struggle, it's outstanding. In my mind homosexual meant weak and blasphemous. Millions of Black people suffer the same inculcation as I did. It's incredible Dr. Claude cured me of this. And it's all because of you David." He didn't know what else to say. "I know the two of you are in love. I'm sorry I couldn't see the reality of what it means." Dr. Claude watched the three of them. They were tentative about what to do, but Solomon wanted to move so Michael stepped in and moved them both together, and then Solomon broke out in a smile David loved. Dr. Claude felt good as Michael watched them closely.

CHAPTER FORTY

Cesare drove up to the University Student Union entrance past countless people going in and out of buildings. The area around the Union was typical of hundreds of new buildings on campuses nationwide. He honked his horn when he saw Adrian and his girlfriend; Ivy came out of the building. Ivy screamed and clutched her neck when Cesare honked at them. Adrian looked at her and then eyed Roberto, who was hanging out of the white 1976, Rover P6 2000 like a rascal, waving at them.

Ivy Wilson was a British-born Caribbean shy girl. Adrian liked that about her a lot because he did fancy urban ghetto babes with fake hair, nails, implants or the speech and attitude that pointed toward a 'street credibility'. Even though Ivy wore a T-shirt, denim jacket, jeans and white sneakers; her body indicated why men frequently whistled at her. Her cinnamon brown complexion, hourglass figure, and voluptuous breasts grabbed people's attention, but more than anything else, what people liked about her most was her big fluffy afro hair. She sometimes wore lipstick but no other makeup. She was simply an athletic young woman who strode through the street without a handbag but always with a brown leather satchel.

"Hey, brother where are you going?" Roberto asked, and Adrian gave him the finger. Roberto opened the door, got out, grabbed him and quickly kissed his face. Even though the University was packed with international students; onlookers were a bit startled by the sound of aggression and the gesture of affection. Adrian patted his face. "This is my girl, Ivy. She is a Church raised debutant, so watch your manners." Roberto took her hand and kissed it. He then told her in Italian he was pleased to me her. "Oy!" Adrian said watching him work his charm.

Cesare yelled, "Come on you bitches, get in the fuckin' car!"

"Forgive my brother Cesare; he's in sales, so he isn't very refined."

Cesare said, "You better get in the car before I smack the piss out of you, you prick."

They all got in, and Cesare turned around to greet them. "Hey people, let's go party."

At a party, packed with students in an array of street fashions and bad taste, Cesare periodically eyed a girl who was trying hard not to look over at him while talking to another girl. Ivy asked lots of questions and people passed her from every direction and tapped her shoulder or nodded at her. In his upmarket sports casuals, Cesare clearly did not resemble the other students. "What makes you so popular, Ivy?" She leaned on Adrian, glanced at him quickly, and he winked at her.

"I write stories about the students' achievement in the College newspaper. People are always coming to me." Adrian put his arm around her and tucked his thumbs into the waist of her jeans. "What do you do Cesare?"

"I'm an agent. I sell new writer's books to publishers."

"That sounds fascinating." Cesare noticed how naturally glossy Ivy's skin was.

"Actually, it really is. I meet hundreds of writers and talented people every year. What are you studying?"

"Management, my heart is set on Human Resources. This is where my vocation really lies." She took Adrian's hand. "So how did you get started in your profession?"

"I did a joint in Literature and Visual Art, at UCL mostly because of my father. He taught me a lot as a boy. I loved listening to Dad read me stories about art's history and paintings. But even with a 1st Class degree, I couldn't find a well-paid job in galleries or museums. So I went into recruitment sales and discovered how to analyze people's vocation and creativity. Two years later I got into a literary agency, and that combined my best talent."

"Is your dad an artist?"

"No, he's part agent but mostly a buyer. A couple of years ago, he made a great sale and took us to America to meet his main supplier. The man owns a museum in Arizona – has hundreds of paintings. Dad's a major dealer for him. Anyway, I saw how Dad ran his business, and that inspired me to nurture talent."

"It's interesting that your dad does that and Adrian's dad runs an agency managing singers and musicians, they should talk…" She stopped, realizing her gaffe and tried to smooth herself out of the bind before she got twisted.

Cesare saw her floundering and said, "I know; it's awkward because it isn't farfetched, but it's happening."

Roberto smiled too broadly. "Yep, life and love know no boundaries." Cesare knocked him on the head with his knuckles. "Aoow!"

Ivy said, "You'll get used to it in time." She leaned in and they came closer. "Today gays are everywhere, and nobody's bothered. Well, not women. The 2010 Equality Act is a real learning curve. I studied it for a coursework project I had to do. I've been telling Adrian, love is love; if your fathers are in love, you'll all lose a piece of your mind if you drop them."

All three guys eyed each other, and it made Ivy uncomfortable. "Please don't say you've all agreed to throw your father's lives away?" She was deeply distressed.

"Baby no," Adrian told her. "How could I?"

She held up her hands and pushed them back a little. "That's alright. I couldn't go out with you if you were that kind of person."

"Really?" Roberto asked her. "You'd dump him for that?"

"Yes," she replied in a matter of fact calm tone.

"But if you were raised by a Church going family…"

"This is 2015. My parents are very proud of me for staying out of trouble and being here. But I don't like them because they want me to be a good Jehovah Witness."

Cesare said, "This is why I love Papa; he's never forced me to do anything, although he has persuaded me to do things."

Roberto said, "It would be interesting to do a documentary about you and the Jehovah life you rejected particularly in this religious climate."

Adrian told him, "No Roberto, the best story for your graduation film would be a documentary on your dad and mine. You could call it *Our Fathers*."

The thought took shape in Roberto's mind. "Fuck me sideways! That's it!"

The girl who conspicuously avoided Cesare came over quickly. "Have I just missed a Eureka moment?" Her voice was characteristically English. Standing close to him Cesare then saw that she had tattoos on various parts of her body.

Fifteen minutes later, Cesare and the English girl, Roberto, Adrian and Ivy were all in the main room dancing to Pharrell Williams' *Happy*. Each of them knew they could dance, but as they danced alone and with the girls, they discovered their own happiness. By the middle of the song, they combusted into a dance frenzy with the two girls in front. A third girl came to join them because she was overjoyed and the three men showed

341

how a great groove got under their skin The girls showed the boys what female excitement meant for them dancing with guys they found exciting. The other fifty-three people in the room crowded around to clap them onto the finale.

Two hours later Cesare was on the pile of coats shagging the tattooed girl, and on the other side of the room, Roberto was shagging the girl who took a fancy to him on the dancefloor. Even though they didn't know it, the drink's punch was spiked with ecstasy. They were not alone in the darkened room lit with a single ultraviolet light propped up by the side of the door; several other couples were making out, and the room was filled with the smell of sex. The girls having sex with Cesare and Roberto had a hard time muffling their cries.

When Roberto and Cesare drove back to London at two-thirty in the morning, they were still happy, laughing and telling dirty jokes. When they finally got back to Cesare's flat at Drayton Park, near Arsenal's home ground in Islington at five in the morning, Cesare was bursting and so like a drunken football lout he stopped in the middle of the deserted street and pissed off a pint of beer. It felt so good he started laughing out loud.

At the flat, Cesare made a Spanish omelet of chicken, sausages, ham, potatoes, and pumpkin, all of which were left over meals he'd had throughout the week. He made a pot of honey and vanilla tea which Lola bought him and they sat down and ate. Halfway through, Cesare said to Roberto. "We should do this more often. I really miss meals at home. Sometimes I get home after ten hours' work, knackered with a takeaway dinner or I bung it in the microwave and I sit here alone, eat, drink, fart, watch some TV, read a manuscript and off to bed. That's unless I have to go to a promotions thing where I usually get hooked up. Sometimes it's a few dates and then back here or it's back here right off because the she's felt the snake and can't help herself."

Roberto laughed unashamedly because he had been drinking in the car and now he was at the tipping point. "You get that too?"

"I've been using this dick when you were stilling pissing your pants."

"You're fucking twenty-eight, and I'm twenty-two so shut up. You might have had more girls than me but I've been in love and you haven't." Cesare conceded that.

"In some ways I wished I could have studied in Italy but I've done alright. Granted I have to bring in writers and novels that don't meet my taste but suit the times because Umberto Eco's *The Name of the Rose* remains my favorite novel of all time. But Steven King's *The Shining*, Ellison's *Invisible Man*, Camus' *The Outsider*, and Genet's *The Thief's Journal*, are strong contenders. Today I don't think these great novels could be marketed for attention deficit online consumers. I miss the days when Papa took us to museums, exhibitions, and events and asked our opinions; or Mama taking us to the Commonwealth Institute and all of us learning history."

"When I'm trying to relax, I see Mama accepting awards and prizes for her work on the health and beauty of Black hair or all of us in the kitchen listening to her. Dad with his new book projects, Mama with her TV appearances. It inspired me to be a filmmaker. Our childhood was so mixed and crazy: Greek grandma and Jamaican grandpa."

Cesare gestured to confirm how loopy they were. "The house was filled with painters, teachers, dressmakers, factory workers."

Roberto reminisced. "All of them coming to the house and telling stories about life! Aunt Daisy cooking 'soul food' because she could include the American dishes with all the Caribbean ones." They stopped eating and reminisced personally.

Cesare said, "Uncle Cleavon ranting on about 'queers' and perverts; telling stories about being a big shot at work. Bragging about how much pussy he got."

"The I-Js made our family unique," Cesare agreed. "Our Italian-Jamaican families inspire me as a filmmaker because everybody who came to the house and Mama and especially Papa could tell great life stories." Cesare gave him a high-five.

"What I really miss are the Friday night movies Papa showed us," Cesare confessed. "I love cinema because of all those wonderful weekends and all of us in the living room with the light low watching films from all over the world. The smell of fish and veal, red wine, and fresh cake." Both of them ate for a couple of minutes and Cesare said, "Remember watching *Rome Open City, Paisa* and *Germany Year Zero*?"

"Are you kidding me? That's when Papa broke down in tears and left the room. We all went after him. He was sitting on the stairs, and he told us about our grandma and grandpa living through occupation and poverty. Mama said 'now tell them why life is good'. Papa picked up Maria and said: 'Your mother and I fell in love, and I left the Army, married Mama and we came here, had you and built this'."

Cesare put his fork down and contemplated. "I'm living like I lost my dad. We're thinking about him and the family as though we've lost them.

Right now my life is made up of work, shagging, drunken nights out with my work mates, football when I can, takeaway food, stress and mild depression. I want my dad. Papa isn't gone! Mama and Tony see him. Adrian sees him, and I don't see my own father? What kind of dysfunctional mess have I gotten myself into?" he asked Roberto, distraught and helpless.

Roberto asked him, "Can you think of a time when Papa neglected us?"

Cesare thought about it and said, "No".

"Papa isn't fucking about. He adores David. He won't humble himself to any of us. I won't deny my father... and you'd be crazy to. Remember in *Tokyo Story* when the sons and daughter neglected their parents, and only the daughter-in-law was honored with the father's love. Or in *Bicycle Thieves* when the boy's dad is ridiculed by the other men and his son takes his hand. I've always been guided by that and *Rocco and His Brothers*." Reference to that film moved Cesare. Roberto held his hands out across the table and Cesare took it agonized by his pride.

CHAPTER FORTY-ONE

Tony watched Michael punch and beat the heavy bag until his muscles were bulging and the sweat began pouring off his face and down his neck to his chest. There was no stopping him, he kept going until he looked vicious and then Tony had to stop him. Michael buried himself into Tony's well-worn tight body. He felt Michael convulsing and led him off into a dark corner of a corridor to the side of a changing room. It was an old-fashioned laborer's gym in Hackney that made no attempt to be trendy and attract 'Hackney Hipsters'. Tony liked that about the place.

Michael looked Tony in the eyes and told him. "Those fucking ghetto boys; they called me a white plantation master and David, my nigger slave."

"Disgusting! That sounds more like that fucking American filmmaker, not you. But they don't even know you. Why do you read that shit?"

"David and his father are making a case against them, but I tell you… I want to show them how an Italian deals with enemies. I love David, I give him my body. How can I be some white plantation racist when I would die if he left me?" Tony pulled him into a sauna away from the Caribbean and Jewish guys walking toward them.

In the wooden cabin, the two of them sat facing each other. "Why are you upset by such ridiculous slander?"

"The online millennium morons they talk to don't know me. Intelligent people who read books might. Love is not about master slave anything! That's a psychotic mess that damage people suffer from. David's studied the Classics; he's instinctually gifted. He'd never say, take me, rape me call me your 'nigga'."

"Sometimes your sarcasm makes me laugh!"

"No really, I told you before – I love Black pride and beauty in the heart of existential men and women." He grabbed Tony's wrist. "You must know what I'm talking about, you married my wife. Tell me how she's changed you?"

"I don't know how to tell you this." A flabby, aging man entered and they exit and headed for the changing room which was empty. They got undressed. "You're telling me you've been married to Lola this time and you feel no change in your life?"

"Oh sure! She is lovely and practical. She feels a bit guilty about everything she does. I think I love this about her the most. They made their way into the showers with ease because almost fifteen years of brotherly friendship left no mysteries between them. They showered quickly, went back into the changing room and got dressed.

Forty minutes later they walked down Broadway Market; a street crowded with artisan's handmade goods specially cooked world cuisine and macrobiotic dishes. Although no one would admit it, the entire five-block area was shabby-chic; and that's what made it so attractive, but the house hunting opportunists who aspired beyond their means were allergic to the truth, unlike London's East Enders, who been there since the 1800s. In the past five years, Broadway Market had become the hippest pocket of Hackney, and it was littered with poseurs in self-conscious 1980s retro punk-romantic clobber. Tony and Michael, who were both in their fifties, walked down the street in boots, jeans, and plain T-shirts and they looked classless because they both grew up in Italian and Brazilian poverty, full of pride without self-delusion.

They went into the only regular pub in the market and ordered two pints of beer from the ruddy face publican. *We Won't Get Fooled Again* by The Who was playing. Locals filled the pub, and they were happy to avoid the twenty or thirty café bars in the market. They hated what their area had been turned into, and they didn't welcome the millennium hipsters or their values.

Michael picked up his pint and slowly and quietly gulped and swallowed until he emptied the jug and ordered another. Five seconds afterward Tony finished his pint and Michael told the barman same again. When the next round came, they moved away from the bar into a corner of the cluttered pub, shielded by the people. Tony told Michael he had the answer to his earlier question as to how he's changed.

"Since I've been married I'm not anxious anymore. I used to be uptight so I'd just meet women and fuck them." Michael choked. "They wanted me to," Tony stated. Michael laughed freely and patted Tony's face.

"But I wasn't happy, especially when I saw no way of being with Lola. Now we're married I haven't had a bad day. When I saw her slap her father's face! I knew she was no diva who ran her mouth; she fights for her love ones and herself. It really put a fire in me. Today's 'bitch and

346

moan' drama that some women buy into, as they check a man's every move and run him around; I couldn't marry that. I hate if a woman tries to control me. Lola is a humanitarian – beautiful heart. Since we've been married I feel so peaceful but sexy…" he concluded to indicate and avoid the subject.

Michael grabbed Tony and pulled him closer. "Yes, that's it, that's real. Tony, I need you." Michael scanned around him quickly to see if he was making a scene. He spoke into Tony's ear. "I can't allow myself to be powerless."

"Michele, calm."

"I won't let it happen again. I had to stand back so my kids could own their lives. I no longer had the right to tell them what to do because today, 'PC' in their mind means entitlement. Anyway, David and his father have plans to legally penalize his clients. David's overthrown his father with a strange Greco-Roman mythic similarity."

"Michele…"

"Listen, 'the Greek' taught him philosophy, love, and psychology. I did an online search of his work, its brilliant! David is bound to the Greek and now with the aid of his father, David has less need of me. I was not born a Roman to capitulate to Greece or any man. David is mine: which is why I give myself to him."

Tony stopped drinking. "You mean you let…"

"Yes…" Michael smiled and took a breath that left him smiling. "Yes."

"It doesn't…"

"There are no limits with us. So *I* want to protect David from those degenerates because that's what a man is. His family comes first."

"You're not who they say you are. You've written books and have very important friends in the academic world and with art collectors."

"I don't know. I think once again I have to live with the loss of power." Michael reflected. "I grieve, and I have to keep it to myself because I don't want David thinking I'm weak and at the mercy of my children. But as there's a God in heaven, I miss my kids so much, some days I wake up and stuff the towel in my mouth and scream – 'I'm your father and I need you'."

Tony told him in Italian to ensure he wasn't overheard. "You have made yourself bold; rebuilt your body, overcome depression and everything else. I see Maria, Fabio, and Cesare very often; I'll speak to them."

"Oh yes, please." They drank up, and Tony went to buy another round. Michael stood alone tense but glad he could talk to Tony since he trusted him deeply.

'David, darling, I'm strong, I can help you. I understand you need your father, but I am your man. I want to live and die with you. I'm physically yours. Need me!'

Seven minutes later Tony came back with the drinks and kicked Michael's boot to get his attention. "You look so worried. Where are you?"

Michael took the pint. "I was just thinking. I'm going to ask David to marry me."

Tony was elated so he held his fist out and Michael punched it. "Congratulations!"

"Ah but first I must show David what he's getting."

Tony whispered in his hear. "You have equal sex, a high IQ, and money."

"David has to know I'm fearless. My publishers have offered me a contract for a collection of my essays on sexual politics and Black culture. I'm going to write about what we're living with, going through – and I want the essay to speak volumes."

"What you really need for today's youth and culture to 'get it' is an image. I did your hair after you lost weight and…" Tony stared at him and then looked up and closed his eyes. He reached up and snatched the oxygen out of the air. "Greco-Roman, I have it! Stylists come to me because Lola and I have the best people for Black hair and beauty. There're hundreds of images of our work at *Salon Fabuloso* all over Europe. I am going to create a look…no an icon of you. I'll get you married and finally happy. I'm going to use my brother Giovanni for this. He understands irony as all gays really do. But he'll give us something more. Call this my wedding present, but for fuck sake, no more depression! Look at you, you've got a beautiful man, perfect health, and publishers offering you contracts!" Tony brought a smile to Michael's face at last.

****

In York, Adrian rushed down the stairs ten days later to get to the front door as quickly as he could. The delivery man made him sign for a large package, and he quickly did so and stood there in his sloppy T-shirt and shorts. Adrian ran back upstairs shouting, 'it's here' and began tearing open the wrapping. He went into the bedroom, and Ivy sat up and he jumped onto the bed and joined her. Her bedroom was the warmest shade of pink with hanging chimes and papier-mâché decorations that she made whenever she was happy or sad. Her black duvet with silver patterns and the stuffed toys on and around the bed linked back to her childhood. Adrian got through the packing and took out a 12x12 photo of David and Michael.

Ivy said, "Bloody hell! That is fantastic." She gazed at it and started unplaiting her cornrow hair. A smile spread across Adrian's face as he looked at his father.

It was a shot of David and Michael in white athletes' singlets, standing on heavenward steps with blue sky and clouds over their heads. The gay rainbow colored interlocking rings hung around their necks as medals and lay beside their muscled chest and abdomen. They look like Olympians in love with each other. Grace and Lola stood beside them as classical Goddesses in white, standing on steps just below them. Both women tossed gold dust, and their hair was streaming with gold ribbons blowing into the breeze. Michael and David's uplifted faces; triumphant and glorious was filled with strength. Their muscular hands were clasped, and their arms are filled with power.

Since they were ascending heavenward, they looked caught in action and their arms and legs indicated that. The back pages of most newspapers captured that kind of action, but the adoration in their eyes made a distinct difference. The smiling love in Grace's eyes as she stood beside David was exemplified in her hand that sprinkled his hair with gold dust. Lola's outstretched hand and fist threw the gold dust above Michael's head and it fell into a Roman military helmet's arched plum directly over his imperial styled hair. Behind all four of them, the ribbons spell out: *No Limits.*

"Your dad looks so sexy." Adrian struck the same pose as David, and Ivy laughed out loud. "Try it again in twenty years."

"Dad's only seventeen years older than me. He's not some superman."

"Come here you idiot!" She joshed him lovingly. He kissed her and made a move to make love to her. "Excuse me, I haven't done my hair!"

"I plan to mess it up. Besides, you no need any extras... so fucking gorgeous."

"Hold that thought. She got up and headed for the bathroom on tip-toe with the perfect wiggle in her hips and bounce in her breasts under her black baby doll nighty that gave him a lift which she saw.

"Morning glory; nice! Put on something to showcase 'big daddy and the twins.' I've told you I hate those shorts. They do *not* excite me; so get to it mister; showcase that talent." He stood in limbo. "I'll bet your Dad has great bedroom manners, there's an awful lot you guys can learn from gay men."

"Yeah, like what?"

"Style and finesse, there's a reason Michael adores him, can't you see it? And let's not forget Veronika on her knees begging him for more." He looked her up and down and saw her naked underneath her nighty, which increased the pulse in his pants.

"With your potential and my enthusiasm do you think we'll end up screaming?"

Thrilled by her Adrian said, "Come on woman…" Like a man twice his age.

"In case you need some inspiration, take another look at your mother and father: I expect nothing less." The smile on her face could have launched a thousand children into the world from men desperate to unload.

In London later that day, Tony kept looking at the photo of Michael and David that was enlarged into a billboard in the studio. His younger brother Giovanni was intensely looking at the photo in a magazine layout that read Hair and Style by Tony at *Salon Fabuloso* and photography by Giovanni Ribeior.

He leaned on Tony as if he were a pedestal. Giovanni had a rugby player's build with a hard face and beautiful whiskey brown eyes and thick eyelashes. "I could fuck him," he confessed and trailed off back into his conscious fantasy, clad in a workmen's khaki overall but with a red scarf around his neck. The studio walls were filled with shelves that had a vast range of cameras dating back to the 1930s and all the equipment that had historically documented the moments that changed the world we live in. Only one blow up image was on a wall and it was Pierre Verger's *Bonfim* image taken in Brazil. Verger was the subject of his dissertation and his inspiration in photography.

"Is that all you have to say?" Tony asked him bemused.

"Of course, the hair is fantastic; you'll set the trend with that style among men of all ages. I see David's hair on Black sportsmen all across South America, but it won't look so good on them, as it is on him. Fuck he's so sexy."

"I thought you were talking about Michele."

"No, I prefer Black men."

"But most of your boyfriends have been white."

"I know," he said sighing. "But I have to eat." Tony laughed harder and louder than he had in a month. "It's no joke. There is such a taboo with Black men on the gay scene, and there is the racism!"

"What do you mean?"

"Ok, so I look as if I might be Black and the rejection for that is so shit."

Tony didn't understand. "It's horrible when you get turned down because they think you're some thug. Anyway," he said pointing at David, "that guy's one hell of a man!"

"It was Michele and I came up with the Greco-Roman concept!"

"Yeah and David took to the role perfectly."

Accusingly, Tony said: "If it's wood you need, Michele is packing timber."

"Yeah I remember when Lola got drunk and said on their honeymoon she thought she was giving birth when he had her! If he had me, I'd have to walk on a zimmer-frame." Tony laughed violently.

"You don't have to use all of it, you know."

With casual pragmatism, Giovanni said, "But that's like having a car that can do 150mph and you only go at 40." Tony kissed the top of his brother's head.

"How can a brother of mine be so funny, and so disgusting?"

"Because we have different fathers." Tony felt oddly very branco Portuguese Brazilian because Giovanni was really preto Black Brazilian.

"Anyway, back to the point: I love the finished product! When this goes into the Trades, we're going to get so many new clients!" Giovanni stopped talking and looked at the billboard again. Tony felt Giovanni's mood swing as he became reflective.

"What?" Tony asked him.

"They're so beautiful; I think it's great what you've done for your friend. I tell you, when this hits the streets, London will be talking about them as if they're vogue. Look at them, they're irresistible! It's so gay and yet simple. That is a real trick, because everyone expects gay to be camp, and it's not."

"We're saving that for the video YouTube Ad!"

"*That* isn't camp, how long do I have to teach you?"

"It's a bitch slap!"

Giovanni pointed at him and said, "Yes, it is! And his son filmed it. Another one who's beautiful!"

"You fancy him? He's straight!"

"So?"

"Stop talking before I slap you." Giovanni laughed and couldn't stop. Tony watched him, and he realized even though he seldom mentioned it, he loved his brother.

"You know, I might know someone you'd like." Giovanni stopped and moved closer, keen to know more. "According to Michele, he's some kind of psychological genius when it comes to Black men's fears and fancies."

"Where's he from; is he a Black?"

"No..." Giovanni's shoulders slumped, and the look of cynical disappointment washed over him as it did so many other times. "Listen to me G, we both know kidding aside that your affairs with Black guys don't last because you don't trust them. You think they'll run off like Papi and leave you miserable like Mama. She lived in misery, and it drove her insane. We witnessed it."

"You think I'm turning into a tragedy like Mama?"

"Not yet but watch yourself. I thought I was becoming a tragedy until I married Lola." Giovanni rubbed his shoulder.

"This guy Michele told me about. He's Greek, David's first; taught him love and courage: the ancient Greek way," Tony said with a vibrato that echoed a 'taboo'.

"How old is he?" Giovanni asked, excited by his brother's provocation.

"Forty-something, I met him at the Media Event when Michele and David came out. Dressed to the nines in a gold suit, and a brave face but I suspect he's very lonely. I recognized some of my demons in him." Giovanni listened more attentively. "When I was out with Michele a couple of weeks ago, we talked, and I realized he doesn't want the Greek near David. At the Event, the Greek, Gus is his name, was in mourning about David. His heartache was so severe. Gus wants to meet someone to bring him to a new reality." Giovanni smiled and took hold of Tony's arm.

"Nothing is going to break these two apart," he said pointing at the billboard. "I don't have gaydar, and I know that! Now, you my brother could..." Tony continued with an innocent arabesque that exposed his cunning. "You could get this Greek Gus."

"What does he do?"

"He's a psychiatrist and professor at a Dutch University. I asked him about it and he couldn't keep his mind off David and Michele. No man happy in his work is not gonna brag about his accomplishments."

"Yes, look at you," Giovanni said pointing at the wicked smile on Tony's lips.

"Shut the fuck up and pay attention. Gus totally goes for Black guys, and according to Michele, he fucks like a Titan. Michele's DJ had some of him and told Michele everything down to the last stroke." Giovanni thrilled at the thought and came over all camp. Tony watched him and delighted in his transformation.

In their native language, Giovanni said, "Could I be devious and do it?"

Tony burst into their dialect, "I've been listening to you bitch and moan for five years! I've gathered this intel so don't tell me you're gonna sit on your ass instead of use your ass to get what you want. He's there for the taking. You don't have to con the guy. You just have to trust yourself. I spoke to Gus for a couple of hours that night and drove him back. The man is crying out for love and so are you!"

Giovanni leaped in the air and said, "Ok! When do we meet?"

"Tricky, he's in Rotterdam." Giovanni began cursing and wagging his finger. "We could go and show him these photos and stay a weekend. You could be fabulous and get Gus tuned up, yes?" Giovanni rattled his tongue like a whistle. "Ok, I'll take you to meet him. We've been blogging about Michele and David, so we've made a friendship. When you meet, reveal your knowledge about social policy as we saw it growing up in Brazil. He will be fascinated by your intellect. He isn't interested in a prick. On the drive back I remember his contempt for slutty boys." Giovanni nodded.

****

In the lecture theater at the Film School, Roberto felt slightly nervous as he previewed the introduction to his MA graduate film for his peers. They were the unusual crowd of privileged egocentric rich kids that gave a damn about what they could say in film at this point in time. The technical lectern in front of Roberto posed no problem, and his peers watch and waited. Among the under the thirties, no one there had any unkind feelings towards him, but he still felt nervous.

The lights went down in the high-tech auditorium and the seventy-seven students waited for him. "If you want to Tweet anything about this, just go ahead." Roberto's faculty tutors were seated in an area away from the students at the front of the lecture theater. Roberto felt sorry he didn't dress up for the presentation, but Michael asked him to underplay everything.

The image came on screen and counted off from five to one, and then Roberto was on screen in beautiful rich color. In the living room of Michael's new house, he sat in front of his birthday cake and blew out the 22 candles. Roberto wore in a crisp white shirt and jeans. Michael walked into the frame and sat beside him. He wore a red shirt and tan corduroy trousers. On the black leather sofa, they seemed strangely lifeless because Roberto was remote and withdrawn and he soon started crying.

"What is it son, Roberto talk to me. Baby, tell me why you're like this on your birthday. You ought to be happy?"

"Everybody hates you. They write all those dreadful things online." Roberto wiped his face. "You're a plantation slave fucker, an old queer. Gay slang I don't understand. These people don't know you how can they say this?"

"Listen to me…" Lola came and sat next to them. She took Roberto's hand. "I love your mother and I always will. The two of us have changed is all it is. These people who talk all this shit, they know nothing about us."

"Darling, you know what it is." Lola cut in. "They suffer from a kind of disease that seem so rife in your generation. They have an opinion, and they think that's a fact."

"Lola it's because they consume each other insolent stupidity online. They can't hold a debate or conversation, most of them. They have a point they want to make and that's it. They never seem to ask where the evidence for these ideas come from. Do they know you and I were devoted and faithfully married parents – no!"

"Why weren't you sneaking out and going after guys?" Michael was about to speak, and Roberto turned to Lola. "Why didn't you find another man since Dad wasn't what a husband ought to be? Did you take solace in someone else?"

"Don't be disgusting," Lola said. "Your father and I had no one else except each other. People who love each other don't take comfort in someone else's bed."

"Lola this is 2015," Michael said, "and today some people love the thrill of sin! My God how difficult is it to be faithful when you love each other? Until I changed, I never wanted anyone else besides you. Did you darling?"

"I'm not a thrill seeking slut. I'm a wife and mother who believe in God."

"Those boys who blog and Tweet about me, they've never even met me."

Roberto embraced his mother and father and soon began breathing audibly.

The scene cut to Roberto and Adrian driving down a motorway. "Too bloody right I'll do the documentary with you." They were on their way to an Arsenal match dressed to support their team. Ivy was in the back talking with Roberto's girlfriend.

"Dad's clients are a bunch of out of this world cunts!" Ivy leaned in and hit him on the head. "I'm not talking about flesh and beauty life supporting vaginas here. Not even the succulent pussy that drives men crazy!" Roberto's girlfriend whistled! "I'm talking about a bunch of diseased creatures that suck the life out of decent people like my dad, who made something of them."

Roberto replied, "They say it's your dad who's diseased and un-natural."

"They had me, that's natural. He's in love with Michael, that's also natural."

"But that's their point; loving another man is unnatural."

"What do they know about it? They can't even love a woman. Every female they've had has dumped them. Do you think it's because they can't fuck or can't love?"

"Both!" Ivy said.

Roberto said, "No mek me get Black in here or I'll answer this issue for real."

"But see yea," his Cuban girlfriend said. "Are you passing for white?"

"I'm Italian Jamaican, and that means no ignorant ghetto trash fucks my family."

Ivy sat forward, and Adrian moved aside to give her room. "Forget your art film, just ask your fathers and our families how they feel about everything and put it online. The public has a right to an answer to Tweets

355

like 'who'll be the first to cut off David's dick to stop the white disease from spreading."

Furious, Adrian said, "Clamp your mouth, please!" Adrian sat still, Ivy sat back, and Roberto saw he was close to tears, so he reached out and rubbed his shoulder.

Days later, Cesare was on his lunch break at work in his overcrowded office filled with books and manuscripts watching the online video. His professional stoicism faded away watching Michael and David. His laptop showed Michael in a talking heads video with a black background. "Dad, how is it that you love David?" Michael looked joyful and very well groomed sporting the hairstyle Tony created for him, and he was wearing the white sports gear from the poster. He smiled without even thinking.

"I love him because he needs me." The image cut to David.

"Why do you love my Dad?" David was wearing the same white sports gear, and he glowed especially with the gold dust in his hair.

"Because he's a cultural genius and he's so kind." The video cut to Grace looking super with her funky dreads tied with the gold ribbon.

Adrian asked her. "Mum, why do you love Dad?"

"Your father has always taken care of us."

Lola came and sat beside Grace and Roberto asked her. "Mum shouldn't the two of you curse and damn Dad and David for what they are?"

"Those clients that David helped, they didn't write the Bible, and neither did God Almighty. The Ten Commandments which are the words of God has no condemnation for them so why am I going to listen to a bunch of brutes who'd sell your father for thirty pieces of silver. God has brought them together, and no one is going to tear them apart."

Grace looked up into the eye of the camera. "I don't live in the Old Testament; I live in Hackney." Laughter echoed into the frame and Cynthia came and sat beside Grace. She was also dressed as an older Goddess and her hair was beautifully styled with her bun at the back of her head tied with a long gold scarf. She sat between them and took their hands and held it. She looked left and right at Lola and Grace.

"Hatred is a terrible disease." The video ended reading: A film by Roberto De Farenzino. Cesare was totally engrossed as Roberto came to him and gestured for an opinion. He looked at the laptop and the poster image of Michael and David faded in over the wives and mother's faces until it slowly vanished.

356

"I think it's good. It's direct, but I want to know the story behind those words and images. You've gone to a lot of trouble to send a message. Document this struggle."

As the film ended Roberto came up on the stage beside the screen. "The racist, homophobic and inciting call for violence against our fathers has been horrid." He looked at all of them. "Do you think there's a feature film to be made?" Adrian and Ivy stood up and then Roberto's tutor, an aging cinéma-vérité veteran, stood up and turned to new filmmakers in the lecture theater.

****

Michael was reticent when he entered Solly's office and kept giving himself a pep talk as he approached. The view of the Canary Wharf city with all its steel and glass towers and the high-tech gadgets, futuristic furniture designed to support the body, in addition to the display screens loop playing famous moments from football's history looked like a cross between an exhibition center and a sci-fi movie. In his silver-gray suit and fire engine red shirt and blue suede boots, Solly looked unapproachable, especially with three PA's, a secretary and a colossal Black guy who was his minder, watching him.

'He's a world-famous football star, not God. You've met Sophia Loren! Come on!!'

"Solly, I have to speak with you. It's very important and confidential."

"Everybody, please leave." The well-dressed staff exit and they were alone in the 50x50 foot office. "Yes?" Michael watched him and Solly seem to become the perfect male Cyborg created by sports scientists and his OWN self-determination.

"My ex-wife's husband is helping me with an ad campaign. I have..."

"I've seen the clip on YouTube." Solly began texting as he spoke.

"I know your work. And launching the African Boys Football team to compete in your newly created Continent's tournament is..."

"I'm familiar with my work. What do *you* want?" Solly sounded imperious.

Michael mumbled in Italian and then he said, "I want to marry David!" Solly put down his mobile and walked toward him and very slowly he broke into a warmhearted smile.

"That is so wonderful, congratulations! David is gonna piss himself."

"You are not against me marrying your brother?"

357

"Of course not you, doughnut," Solly replied in typical London banter.

"But this cold reception…"

"I have sponsorships, millions, a business to run; I have to exercise my power." Solly laughed like a maniac and stroked an invisible cat as if he were a Bond villain."

"*Rompere le palle, merda*!" He complained about Solly breaking his balls.

"What do you need?"

"I have a book of essays coming out soon. I need a cover. I want you, David and I to be on the cover. Something that challenges David's clients…"

"Those bastards David worked so hard for; they're *man*strating every time they Tweet and blog. Their *man*stration proves to me they're not men." Michael was amused by his turn of phrase. "I like what you've done so far. That poster is fantastic Michel! But it's not enough. You have enemies, and you've failed to deal with them."

"What would you do?"

"Shame them! Humiliate them. Let them hope for forgiveness and offer none! Your classical heroic ad and the video is good. You've got over a million views on YouTube." Solly picked up four steel balls, tossed and caught them effortlessly.

"How do you know about…"

"I'm following you guys online. People keep asking me to comment on David. He's planning something; isn't he?" Solly rolled the balls in his hands, and he walked in and out of the sunshine, lighting his steel and glass office, with the financial wealth of the city behind him. Michael noted the change in his voice. "David is a master of deception. He isn't a liar, but he's great at hiding things. He gets that from Mum. They can kill you slowly, and you won't even know it's happening."

Solly took great pleasure in unfolding a story. "Dad was spunking happy like I've never seen him when David got an offer from Cambridge to study the Classics. David threw it away and went to Manchester. Dad was crushed. When Dad suspected David might fancy the male of our species… Has David mentioned a trip to Nigeria when he was…" Michael said yes. "With the help of Gus, David, flushed away the Nigerian 'cure'; had a son and then came home to be a father. Dad was relieved because he adores Grace. Living his double life, David left Grace for Gus. But terrified of losing Adrian, he left Gus and married Veronika." Solly walked back into the light and said, "David is tormented because he is *tormented* – understand." Michael nodded.

"David used to kiss and caress Veronika, which drove Dad into a dribbling, spitting rage because he hated her. I could go on forever. My brother and my father have battled all my life. Their ego and should I say 'tism' undermines their lives." Solly tapped Michael on the chest. "I was hoping you could control David."

"It sounds like you resent David."

"I love him. He taught me all the mistake not to be made with my father and so I had a very happy and loving life with my Dad. David has come a long way; he's come right out and told everybody he loves you. He didn't do that with Angus. Gus never fought back to claim David. You're making the *same* mistake. David is caught up with his clients and all that. He wants their heads on the chopping block, right?"

"Your father is working on it with him."

"Are they helping you to manage your kids? When Dad invited Lola to dinner, she said only one of your kids is totally on your side. Why isn't David planning how to help you overturn that: because the honor of the Bankole's is at stake? Bollocks!"

"His clients have wronged him; he has a right to go after them."

"Since you're going to marry into this family I'm trying to help you. After all, you love David and that's the real start of healing for him." Michael was totally baffled now. "Be, his, Guru! Offer him loving sex, approval, wisdom and restraint. Make him look up to you so he will yield to you without you dominating him."

"How can you say this? Are you jealous of him or…"

"Why would I be jealous of him, I'm Solomon Bankole Jr. I have twelve million, a wife, three kids, and presidents and two kings love me." He turned around and walked back to his desk and sat down.

"I want you to stop being so gay. Crush your enemies! Those boys who blog online, *man*strating about 'normality': I'd come right out and call them sons of whores and criminals. I'd tell them to their face, 'your nothing but an ignorant eunuch!' If they tried to take a punch at me, I'd drop them, then shove their head into a blocked toilet."

"I'd like to do that but…"

"You're gay and defensive. An intellectual… Your ad campaign says all that. You're brilliant and those scumbags are brainless! If I were you, I'd create an iconic image to show the world what I think of them. Wanna hear it?" Michael nodded. "I'd have a body shot of David tearing up photos of those slags with them in pieces at his feet," Solly declared standing up. Michael thought about it and it was clear he liked it.

"That's a great image of power and it's not even bloody violent – Brilliant!"

"If you've been paying attention, Professor, *you* should also be in that photo. I'm looking to you to be an inspiration to David and hopefully all our family. Put yourself in the picture. Make David understand he cannot spend his life plotting. He did that with Veronika and he got her and that criminal, real good. He and Dad will bond and heal some old wounds working together on the '*Bankole Stratagem*'. But he has to put *you* in the premiere league, not at the top of the second division." Solly went to a cabinet and took out a leather bullwhip. It uncoiled and touched the floor. He cracked it with villainous pleasure. "I love this! In the States, they go to shooting ranges. I just get this out – it's better than having a wank at work to boost your performance."

"I had no idea you were this gregarious."

"I'm Solomon Bankole Jr. Haven't you heard." Michael laughed. "Remember, Professor, a Guru, a lover, and Augustus. I read online he is your hero. I'm expecting you to bring peace to the warring factions in both our families." Poised like an action man with the whip and the power of London behind him; Michael felt they'd finally met.

Michael opened the front door and let David in. The interior decorations made the hall look more homely. "When I got your invitation by messenger I opened the black box and came over as invited." David was well dressed and looked excited.

"This is as important as our first date. Please come to the living room." David watched Michael's body in motion since he was dressed in cutoff jeans, a vest, and trainers. Michael went and brought him a brandy 'old fashion' cocktail. David was about to propose a toast when Michael stopped him. "Meeting you has changed my life. Now we're done I want to thank you." David was struck dumb and motionless.

He stared at Michael, but he couldn't speak. The pain began to rip through him and eventually, panic tore through David's guts and brought him to tears. He spoke but no words sounded in his mouth and he had to force himself to speak up. "Why?"

"I have learned how bad neglect is. My kids are putting me through that right now. Not Roberto or Cesare. He came to me yesterday and asked to take care for me. Cesare missed the happiest years of his life with us as a family. I'm relieved to have him back. You and your father – I don't get it, and I no longer want to figure it out. He has changed, he asked for your forgiveness, and right in front of me, the two of you showed no heart. Now both of you are caught up in your plots, and I must sit quietly somewhere." David tried to cut it. "Silenzio. I am not prepared to suffer neglect again! As much as I feel for you, I won't become nothing. My love doesn't matter to you because you prefer to battle with your father and waste time on those Grime bastards."

"*Michele per favore, ho bisogno di te e giuro sulla vita di mio figlio ti amo.*"

"You really swear on Adrian's life you need me and love me as you say?"

Crying, he replied, "Yes, yes I do. Believe me! I have no plans that don't include you."

"I will not be the understudy to any man you become fixated with."

"There's no one else, there couldn't be." He frantically searched for words. "Please, darling please don't leave me."

"Will you stop wasting your energy on those scum boys and feeding off the anguish between you and your father?" He put the drink down and embraced Michael.

"Then we'll go upstairs, and in that bedroom, I will show you what loving means. I will show you what a man is and teach you to honor the claims you make. I don't want to punish you. I want you to learn the difference between devoting yourself to a faithful man and wasting your life on worthless men." David took his hand and pulled at him.

"Take me, *Insegnami*, teach me, *io ti amo*; I love you." David led him upstairs.

The following evening David got into a black cab, used his mobile to call his brother and put his iPad and wallet down. London flashed past through the windows.

"Solly, hey guy; listen this is an emergency, can you get in your fucking Ferrari and get your world famous arse over to my place. I'm fucking… messed up."

He listened and lay back on the seat and soon the cab just seemed to take him away.

David walked into his home and began peeling off his clothes and staggered up the stairs until he got to his bedroom. He pulled off everything until he was in his pants, and staggered over to his Hi-Fi and sorted through disks. He played the last movement of Tchaikovsky's *4th Symphony* and then he made his way over to the chaise lounge and rest there until Solly came into the room and found him sprawled out. Solly dashed over to him and yelled, "David, David! Dave – Tunji!! Are you alright?"

David caught his breath and focused. "Oh, hi, hey – yeah. I am so fucked… it's amazing." He tried to form his next sentence, but he got lost as Solly watched him.

"Have you taken something? David look at me!" David looked at him and laughed. "Yes, I've taken something. We shared a love injection!" He laughed and couldn't stop laughing.

"Have you taken drugs … what am I saying? You know Daddy would beat you into the hospital. What happened? Where've you been?" David could see Solly looked as worried as he was concerned.

"Let's go to my studio. I'm gonna take my guitar and pay homage to the reality of love. You wanna lay down a few tracks because I am gonna record a club classic in praise of the orgasmic mystique." David got up, headed over to a wall and he leaned on it, and it opened. He turned on the light, and all £4,000 of his Fender Stratocaster guitar shone in red and white. In the closet were also several other guitars and a gold trumpet. "Hey Solly, I have your trumpet in here. Come to the studio with me, and we'll snatch back the teenage years." David turned around, and he saw a glint in his brother's eyes.

"Right now I totally get Veronika. She used to film me making love to her, and I told her to study Marianne Faithfull's *Broken English*, listen to Patti Smith's *Horses*. Learn from Nico. We'd fuck and go to the studio, me on booze and her on coke. But she wouldn't learn; she wanted to be a pop star instead of a Rock Goddess, I recorded her that way and she destroyed the demos. So she got mad and fucked me crazy." He laughed knowing their secrets and games which he learned to love for seven years.

"What have you been doing? What happened to you, Dave?"

"Michael gave me a fucking lesson!" David took out the guitar and the trumpet and walked back to Solly.

"What happened?" David put the instruments on the bed, sat on the floor and took a breath. Solly got up, moved near to him and waited.

"He scared the hell out of me and then… blew my mind." Solly looked puzzled.

"I thought he was going to leave me. Do you know how many blokes and babes have offered me their Oushty-Bushty?" David asked with an elusive smile.

"I've shown you my fan mail. And *everyone* knows I'm married. After the Brazilian underwear ad campaign, I was offered everything perverse."

362

"Right, you got me there. Anyway, people don't dump me. He took me to his bedroom and put on Hendrix. Then he yanked off his clothes as though he was getting ready for a street fight. He had this basket of freesias, all kinds of colors and he pulled off the petals and threw them on the bed. He came at me like he was going to beat the crap out of me, muscles bulging, pecks pushed out and tight. He pushed me backward, bit by bit until I fell on the bed and he launched into a spoken word recitation in Italian and climbed onto me, and the smell of the freesias started to cloud my head." Solly sat closer, and David sat upright and began describing things using his hands and face.

"Hendrix's *Voodoo Chile* was playing, and Michael kissed me, and engulfed me like an angel taking over my body. After a while, he had me."

Alarmed, Solly asked him. "He didn't grudge fuck you or anything like that?"

"No… It's on my iPad. He said look at what I'll be missing. And those flowers."

David lay back and tried to recall everything, but he couldn't because he didn't know he was allergic to the freesias pollen, which deeply affected his metabolism and respiratory tract. "He recorded me and then he told me to record him. Afterward, he told me to leave and think about my 'sins'. Solly got up and went into the bathroom.

Five minutes later, Solly came back and saw David still 'out of his mind', so he yanked him up and marched him into the bathroom. He stepped into the tub and helped David in and then he turned on the water. David yelled and cried out as he swallowed hot water. Solly reached for a washcloth and forcefully began washing his face and neck.

"Clean your fucking self up. Come on! Get on with it." David was topsy-turvy, so Solly smacked him all over with the washcloth. "You're a fucking hazard ready to drag us all over the place, and I will not tolerate it." He shoved David about, splashing water in every direction.

Solly took down the hose and David fought off the jet powered water until Solly threw it at him and growled, got out of the bath in his button up shirt and wet trousers. "Where's the iPad?!!" David told him. Solly looked like a drenched rugby player heading off at half time as he left to get the iPad. Solly found it in the bedroom and watched it. What he saw stunned him; and sank deep in his mind and body.

Half an hour later in the kitchen, Solly took three minutes for the cold Guinness to settle. David entered in black pajamas. Solly wet clothes was damp and creased stuck to his body. He lifted the glass and gave David a dirty look.

"Sober now?" David's gesture was vague. "Alright then; I tell you this as a man with four kids, an amazing wife, great parents, and fans worldwide. It's over!!" David flinched, startled by his brother's voice. "I've seen it all. The visceral fight between you and Dad and this *man-fatale* seduction you've got, plus your Dark-Facer *Star Wars* power over adversaries with Dad as an Imperial ally." Solly gestured to follow him to another room and he made his way to the games room that was decorated in art deco which provided a calm interior.

"Solly I'm not in the mood to be lectured by you."

"Don't take that tone with me or I'll take this belt off and explain things to you. Do you know what you've done? You have shamed our father. He told me that he flew into a rage and strangled you, nearly killed you. He is so ashamed of that he cried from the heart to me. You drive him crazy because your defiance emasculates him. I've told Dad, and I'm telling you. This Chief and Prince Bankole battle is over." David walked around the snooker table and touched and fidgeted with board games, chess, Monopoly, scramble, the train set, and darts, along with other toys from the pre-digital age.

"You have won! Dad is a mess who runs to me for comfort. His physical abuse against you is no joke; I remember your tears and pain." Solly followed behind David and spoke into his ear in a chastising provoking tone. "But after you married Veronika and kissed and touched her up in front of him that was a beating. And all the lies you told to hide Gus: hid you from all of us." David turned and stared at him. "But with Michael, you've really beat Dad because he has no power over either of you. If that wasn't enough, I saw on the iPad you've got Michael loved-up and crazy. Adrian told me Gus is broken hearted because you always sacrificed him for women. I've seen you flirt with hundreds of girls, obviously to masquerade, and you left them wanting. I can imagine, you've broken the balls of a fair number of blokes who didn't stand a chance. You're a *man-fatale,* and it's no wonder you and Veronika really hit it off." David tried to speak.

"Shut it!!! You've beaten our father. Now let Dad recover. Dad is even seeing a shrink. Do you think he'd confess that to anyone if there was no change in him? Mum doesn't know about it." Solly kept his eye on David as he went and got his drink.

"Adrian told me Michael's twins are sticking the pins in him. How long do you think your love will last with you doing that to our father, and forcing Michael to watch it? Real love, my brother, is compassion." David stopped in stride and eyed Solly with the realization of why Solly was so loved in Britain, across Africa, and in Brazil.

"You're so great with Adrian and lovely to Grace. With Mummy, you're a total human being, and with Dad, you're a fucking idiot!"

"Before you give me another lash, can I remind you I've tried to reach the man."

"Collaborating with him to tear those ungrateful double-crossing niggers apart is not a loving connection. Dad said you offered him your hand in his office the day you two conjured up some new plot. You're not a couple of Mafioso Heads," Solly proclaimed pointing at him. "Now Dad needs *you* more than you need him, let him champion your cause in court. Let him protect you from their evil because their posts stink like shit on a barbecue! My friends and a prime minister from back home called *me* and said take immediate action against them."

"Solly, I'm no longer angry at Dad. I know Mummy loves him and needs him. I've told Michael I won't turn against him even though he and Gus hate Dad."

"Michael is a father suffering... oh, what you call it..." Solly thought about it. "Yeah! Alienation of affection. Lola explained some things to Mum," Solly told David with a true heart. "Michael's kids neglect is the source of his grief. Are you helping Michael to get his kids back? When Dad withheld his love, look what that did to you. Do your man right. You're not even a two-timer, so assure him of your love, he needs that."

"We're very happy."

"Shut up! I've seen the iPad recording. Dorian Gray, OO7, and Dracula could learn from you. The 'fucking banquet' you had with Michael couldn't hide how much he loves you. I've deleted the recording. You and Veronika use sex for power and dominance. Michael said you're his, as Alice once told me I'm hers. Let him be a hero to you. Without Alice and the kids I'd only have money. Without our father, I'd be a punk." Solly's hands pleaded. "Dad loves opera and musicals. He sang to Mum at breakfasts on Sundays. He appreciates the arts. He took us to embassy parties, and he lost our sister, and loves us even more now." Solly's eyes shone with tears and David grabbed him and comforted him, holding on tight with all his love.

CHAPTER FORTY-TWO

David stood in front of his guests formally dressed and asked if any of them required drinks. Nine Black British actors and one actress were all seated in his living room. J.J, an African American, and Carlos, a Puerto Rican, were sitting side by side. None of the actors knew it, but J.J and Carlos had a fascinating history of survival under life threatening circumstance, which is why after forty years together they were deeply in love. Even though Natasha wasn't certain, she was pretty sure they rated the millionaire's club because J.J had a diamond ring that was so big anyone could see it from a distance, and Carlos had diamond earrings Elizabeth Taylor would have loved.

Carlos put his iPad to one side and studied all of the talent in the room, and J.J gave Michael the nod, and he went over to David and stood in front of everyone in the decadent living room. David glanced over at Michael, and then he began.

"I've invited one of Michael's closest friends over to London to meet you because I am going to start a new agency for Black British actors. The men and women I want to represent not only include you but newcomers who don't want to play the black beast in anything on offer in Britain."

Michael said, "From the online scandal, you might know I am David's partner. Over the years, I've seen talent like yours neglected. My ex-wife had a lot to say on the subject as a Jamaican who'd lived through Thatcher's Britain to Blair's Britannia. For myself, I've seen my favorite actors from Colin Salmon to Marianne Jean-Baptiste vanish from British screens. I am now in the position to do something about it. My business friends, J.J and Carlos, are collaborating with us."

J.J said, "Our son, Bryan, runs the Actors & Casting Agency side of our business. We run the museum and gallery. Our business turns over minimum $70 million a year after taxes. Our ambition is to find a partner to open an Agency in the UK managing Black British talent."

Carlos said, "We've been thinking about a London office for years, Jeff and I spent some of the happiest years of our lives here in the 1970s and 80s. We wanted the right kind of man to go into business with. David's media 'coming out' bravura is the stuff of legends. He's got the blood and guts we like."

Michael said, "Let me show you Carlos' and J.J's assets." Michael turned on the TV and a promotional film about their Arts Foundation and the awards and prestige it had gathered since 1992 played. The first fifteen minutes focused on the fine arts, it shift to an agency casting and management for another fifteen minutes, and then presented their seventy clients working in theater, TV and film for the last fifteen minutes. The fact that a lot of the clients were gay and the majority of them were happy was underlined but the statements that the actors and actresses made about Afro and Hispanic cultural trust, and integrity. When the actors' credits in theater, TV and film productions rolled by at the end, the actors in David's living room were impressed. Michael stopped the DVD.

David said, "Today's also important for us because Michael's son has decided to support our business."

"The media scandal has brought him back to me." Michael started running off in Italian and J.J expressed his friendship and compassion in Italian.

David told the actors. "J.J's son Bryan knows the film business and lots of producers."

Michael said to David. "Here's the good news." David took his hand, and everyone could feel it. Each of the nine actors that knew David could tell he was devoted to Michael. They knew each other from TV and from years past when they went to his mother's house for parties and protests, as well as the Hackney Riots of 2011, which brought them together speaking to the Black community in news programs and at churches.

"My eldest son, Cesare, he is here with David's son. He wants to explain some things we discussed. Let me bring him." Michael was slightly nervous. David gave him a kiss and Michael felt better. "I bring him, please wait."

David said, "Michael's sons and daughter have been going through their issues about us."

J.J asked the actors, "You guys don't have problems with Michael and David being in love do you?"

The most famous actor currently working in Britain said, "Those of us that aren't gay are the minorities in film and theater."

Natasha said, "Word honey! All of us love men, and the rest of us are just camp!"

Carlos enjoyed her quip and shared something with J.J in Spanish.

Michael returned with Cesare, and he introduced the actors to him. "Papa I go to the cinema and watch television, I know who they are."

"You know them, but you don't *know* them. Shut up and pay attention." Something about his scolding touched Natasha, and she felt empathetic trust toward Michael right at that moment. She was instantly attracted to Cesare, so she tried not to stare. His Italian-Jamaican looks appealed to her greatly and tingled a down her back.

Michael said to Cesare. "Tell them."

"I work for one of the big Agencies in London," Kwame asked which one, Cesare told him and he was impressed. "I could run my own business with what I know regarding client management, contracts, sales, PR and marketing, and who to talk to when it comes to manuscripts. I don't handle actors, but I want to. David's very experienced with artists in the music business and we are going to America to do some knowledge transfer and training. So at Christmas, I'm going to resign my post and work with David at this new agency." Overcome, Michael nodded and kept nodding his head.

"I've spent too much time away from you, Papa, and I don't like it. This will be great for me because, I want more in my life. Since *you* can change, I can too."

David said, "I want to offer you a three-year contract. If I fail to get you work in the first year, you can drop me. There are amazing Cable TV drama productions and films in the States. I know I can deliver. I'll never offer you anything like *Bullet Boy* or *Top Boy*…"

"Fuck that shit!" Paul said violently. "That is my bottom line. My agent was pushing me into those roles, and once you get that label, you're blacklisted."

Julius, one of the biggest TV stars, replied, "Yeah, and I need to look at my daughter and not be ashamed of what I'm doing to earn money."

"Have you noticed the way mothers' look at you?" Lee a RADA trained classical actor asked. "They look like they want to spit on you for representing the nastiest drug fiend, who morphs beyond fiction, to damage their kid's psyche and fuck up in life."

Another actor said, "I don't mind playing a villain because the can be interesting. But how many writers come up with a Stringer Bell character? *The Wire* was ace because those characters had psychological complexities, and suffered from deprivation, plus ignorance."

"I'd do the Denzel role in *American Gangster* because that villain was complex,"

J.J told them. "There's all kind of roles written by new writers, but they're not produced. I want to change that. Ever seen a great film called, *Deep Cover* 1992?" The actors jumped in with joy at the memory of it. "David is going to get you the best work and you guys are so good you could give the stars at home a run for their money with the kind of talent you have. Sweetheart, how do you feel about working in TV?" J.J asked Natasha.

"No problem," Natasha happily replied.

"So will you sign with me in the New Year?" David asked.

Harry, a lesser known star asked. "David what are you going to do about your clients who've left? Their tweets are so hateful." Harry was only less known because he worked in the theater rather than film and television.

"I've organized a legal response to that," David replied quietly.

Isaac said, "David I've known you for twelve years. That is not an honest response."

"Alright, you're my friends, so I'll tell you. Think back to John Galliano and multiple that with vengeance."

Cesare said, "Their rants are not about your dignity, Papa; they're vermin."

J.J said, "Back home, guns and violence would have shut them down already."

"No lie!" Carlos concurred.

"Anyway, we have a future; they don't. So, Natasha, guys, will you sign?"

Michael left the room and took Cesare with him. He walked into the hallway, across to the media recreation room and closed the door. "Listen to me, no matter what their decision there is something more important than that."

"What is it, Papa?"

Michael took him by the shoulders. "You've come back to me." Cesare felt the depth of emotion rise standing face to face with his father.

"I had to. You and Mama are what I want to be: honest and kind. Most blokes today they live for work, they don't have any character. Their ego is the pride they live for. Their women and children and job titles are the extension of their vacant soul. I was living this…" As Cesare search for the word his eyes filled. "…executive pride, that is all blah and no blood or honor."

"Don't be so dramatic." Michael's devotion and love shone in his face because he felt grateful for his children. Smiling at his father, Cesare's tears fell.

"Papa, will you help me to get back the happiness I felt growing up because this emptiness I'm living with is killing me. It started when I stopped caring about things." Adrian came in and saw them, so Cesare tried to pull himself together.

"Is everything alright? Why aren't you in here?"

"Your Dad's working the room. Papa needed me in here." Adrian could feel the strength between them. "Cesare, your mother and I have changed the dynamic of the family, but we are still a family. Only now there is more to us. I intend to marry again. Very soon I will ask David. Adrian, my love for your father, is equal to my love for the rest of my family. To think of you as a son through marriage, what are your thoughts about that – both of you?" Cesare looked at Adrian with the greatest warmth.

"You love Dad that much?" Michael said yes. "Good." The reality started to shake him. "Uncle Solly keeps texting me to say, back you." Michael embraced both of them, and Adrian searched their faces and saw nothing but genuine love which made him happy.

CHAPTER FORTY-THREE

Solomon stepped out of the hallway as some staff went back and forth and into Akoni's office. "The minute Veronika arrives, let her wait five minutes and then call me. Give me the cheque for £150,000." He took the cheque out of the drawer and gave it to Solomon. As he signed it, he said, "David and I know the measure of this woman; she will reject my first offer for this. It's so stupid really because the monthly deal would help her, but she's a grasping creature, so she'll take this and probably destroy herself."

"One can only hope. I am really happy that no Nigerians were harmed during the execution of this plan."

"Akoni!" Solomon laughed so loud, men and women came out of their offices to look and see. They were all Nigerians.

"Get back to work we have punishment to deliver!" They went back to work.

"Do you think my son is entangled with 'the great white master'?"

Solomon made his way into his adjacent office. He went to the mirror first to double check his appearance, but dressed in a Savile Row suit, Foster & Sons Jermyn Street handmade shirt and shoes he had nothing to worry about. He went to his desk, sat down and took fifteen minutes to look over all the files he had on each one of David's clients. "I'll deal with you bastards later."

His phone rang, and he picked up. Give me one minute and then show her in. He picked up the files and locked them into his drawer and placed the key in his waistcoat pocket. He stood up and adopted an imposing stance and waited.

Akoni brought Veronika in, and Solomon stood there like Nelson's column. "Veronika, good morning, sit please. Can I get you anything, vodka, gin, sherry?"

"Mint tea thank you, it's eleven o'clock in the morning."

"One never knows: mint tea and an espresso for me, thank you Akoni." He left and she sat down gracefully. She wore the best suit she had even though it was four years old. "Now I don't like you and I never will," Solomon told her and that unsettled her. "However, I understand you've fallen on hard times." The little smile that turned his mouth was slight but discernable. "I am going to help you. I advised you to get a lawyer why haven't you come with one?"

"I can't afford to split the money you've promised me."

He gestured to indicate the choice was hers. "Alright, let's talk about a settlement that will help you."

"My doctor says I suffer depression and dependency syndrome."

"I don't care." She was stunned by his bluntness. "Don't be worried. My offer is a five-year salary of £30,000 which comes to £150,000. For this settlement, you will present yourself at a meeting in David's office later today and confirm that nothing he has said about your marriage is untrue. His clients will be there. I'm suing each of them for everything they've got."

"Why are you so wicked?"

"Why are *you* so disgusting?"

"Your son hates you, you bastard!"

"No, he doesn't."

She stood up and told him. "Many nights we got drunk and fucked cursing your name."

"How immature of you both, but he's grown up now he's recovered from you."

"It must be terrible for you to know your son is homosexual. Maybe if you didn't beat him as often as you did, he wouldn't have looked for comfort in another man's arms." That hit Solomon squarely. "Love is a funny thing, isn't it. You rob a child of love and then they regress back to their childhood to find comfort." Solomon had to give her words consideration. She knew that she had his attention, so she stood up and forced him to back away from her. "What did you do to David when you abducted him from school and flew him out to Nigeria?"

"Nothing that compares to killing his sons." He stood up. "You lost him then. If he became disinterested in women after that, you can take the credit because nobody has ever hurt him as much as you have." She backed down, a little. "It's good you remember the past so vividly. It will confirm facts his clients think he's invented about you and your marriage."

"What do you want from me?"

"The truth and nothing but the truth. I'm going to put certain questions to you before his clients and you'll answer truthfully."

"Pay me first, and maybe I'll do it."

"The settlement is £2,500 every month as employees would be paid."

"Fuck you I want it all now!"

"No."

"You want to verify David's heroism and masculinity to the black mob who Tweet about his disgusting preference and suffering at my hands."

"You have cost him a lot."

"It isn't me who takes it up the ass."

"Yes, you do. You beg and plead for it."

Petulantly, she folded her arms and looked sullen. "Give me all of the money today and I will say what you want." Solomon spun around in his chair and looked out the window. Veronika sneered delighted with herself. She couldn't see the triumphant look on Solomon's face; she only saw him reach for the phone and speak to Akoni.

"Tear up the cheque and write a new one for £150,000. I'll be out to get it shortly." Solomon adjusted his triumphant expression and turned around to face her.

"Alright, you win." She stared at him smugly.

Solomon looked vexed, and Veronika took great pleasure in the sight of him.

At David's office, his clients were assembled in the boardroom and his staff walked around the room handing out folders to the clients. Michael sat in a corner. Sophia was there, and Willy was also there still suffering from the beating. They had all seen better days which is why no one smiled. The office staff sat on the chairs against the wall and watched the clients sitting at the oval boardroom table. Each member of staff had worked very hard for each and every client at the table. In one corner of the room, a video camera was on, and a stenographer on the opposite side in a different corner.

Cynthia entered in a full-length black silk robe, a long gold colored scarf tied around her waist with a colorful belladonna corsage attached. She had on scarlet lace gloves. Solly walked ahead and pulled out a chair for her. One of David's clients noticed how thrilled Solomon was just watching her and Michael thought she possessed mythical Greek presence like a new age Lysistrata, David's favorite heroine.

"I don't have all day, and so we'll come to order immediately," Solomon told them. "You people have been making slanderous statements against David and that is going to stop as of today."

Mr. Man stated. "He is queer; that ain't slander."

"I'd advise you to speak when spoken to or I will have you prosecuted."

"For what?" he replied as if his words were profanities thrown at Solomon.

"Breach of contract you recalcitrant upstart." None of David's clients liked the sound of that even though they didn't know what the word meant. "I have every intention of prosecuting *all* of you. I have all the facts I need from David, and I'm ready to speak to your lawyers." David eyed them all as the stenographer did her job.

"First matters. It has been suggested by William Grant and Sophia Van Dyke that David invented stories and issues related to his marriage that are mendacious, fictitious and defamatory to his ex-wife. I intend to call her to answer to these questions." Willy and Sophia felt uncomfortable, so she got up to leave.

"Walk out that door, and I will have the police arrest you immediately," Solomon stated. "They are here." She turned her head around instantly.

"On what charge?"

"You're a thief. You have stolen company property worth over £4,000. Furthermore, you have also stolen intellectual property from this company. You have accessed files from this company. Moreover, you misinformed the clients who are managed by this company that you have the authority and freedom to manage their business and finances when you do not. Similar charges apply to that man there." Solomon said pointing at Willy. "Leave if you want. The other charges will be read to you at the police station." She looked at Willy, but he was helpless.

"Do stay," Solomon said playfully. "There may be a way out for you." Everyone watched to see her next move. She went back and sat down.

"Call Veronika Lupei." One of David's staff exit and then brought her in. She didn't look at all nervous; she walked in defiant and unapologetic. What she lacked in class and chic she made up for in sexual power. She called on her heroine, Catherine Tramell from *Basic Instinct* to psychologically empower her, and her dress and coat was reminiscent of the iconic white suit, even though her suit was pink. Her blond hair swayed like barley in the breeze. Cynthia hated her even more than Grace could.

Solomon moved toward Veronika. "Will you please raise your hand?" He gave her a bible and swore her to Oath, and then she sat near the stenographer. He asked her a series of questions that had been publicly stated by David and rewarded and Tweeted by his clients. After she had answered all of them, he said to the clients. "You are free to ask her anything."

Evadney, a young gospel singer, asked her. "Weren't you humiliated by David secretly filming you when you had sex? Or the things he said about you in his film?"

"No, we had filmed our sexual exploits many times. My humiliation came from the shame I felt after my second miscarriage. I felt fat, horrible and fated to stay home like my mother and do nothing with my life. I came to England for more than that."

Evadney asked out of curiosity rather than care. "How'd things go so bad for you?"

Solomon said, "We do not need to hear about her failed career as a pop singer again."

Evadney yelled, "Can you let this woman have a voice Mr. Solomon Bankole."

Cynthia quietly stated, "That is her failing. She doesn't have a voice." Evadney was infuriated by Cynthia's remark.

Cynthia said, "I have a question for you, Veronika. Did David ever abuse you or deny you security? Or did this family ever mistreat you prior to your divorce?"

"No, you made me feel like I was your daughter: teaching me about your life, cooking together; buying me clothes and helping me with my… dependency. I felt like your daughter especially after she left for Africa and you were lonely," Veronika earnestly told her. "I cried when I heard she died. The two of you…" Veronika remembered the great times they had and the help they provided. "I'm honestly sorry for her passing." David saw Cynthia was moved by her words.

Frank was one of the founding members of the 'Grime' movement and one of the toughest Black men in Harlesden, with a devoted underground following. He kissed his teeth, eyed Michael and yelled, "Can we get back to this blasted queer!"

"I did not give you permission to talk to me; you ugly moron."

No one had ever talked to Frank in that manner, or he would have beaten them senseless.

"I'll fucking kill you!" he yelled with spit in the corner of his mouth.

Solomon said, "There is a stenographer and a video recording you young man: I will use them to have you incarcerated,"

Veronika said, "Being married to a Black man, I understand Frank; we used to be friends. Frank tried to flatter me on a few occasions, but I couldn't make him understand. All of you men here who are shocked at David; you have so much anger. I had more anger than you..."

"Yeah after the stuff he said about you in the documentary..." Evadney replied.

Veronika turned in the swivel chair and crossed her ankles. "No, the sex tape is real. His judgment of me in the documentary is not lies. My head was so mixed up because he loved me and I was guilt stricken for miscarrying. You guys don't have any power; David has." She looked right at him and took a moment.

"I could fuck every man in this office within an hour and leave you dry. David had me over and over again and left me... wet, baptized in sperm as if I was born again," she confessed with open hands reaching out to them. "When he took his pulă out of my mouth I cried like a baby," she told them putting her index figure between her lips sideways with her red nail perfectly painted. Michael found her fascinating.

"You men like to look at beautiful women and please yourself, buried inside her," she said sticking her neck out, eying them. Every man except Solly was drawn in by her.

"When I couldn't have children I had to make it up to him. He forgave me. So I did anything he wanted." She cast her head down, and clients watched and waited. "A man's orgasm means nothing to a woman who cannot bear him children. It's only when we don't want your children because we only want you; that's when everything comes together. You think that your size and strength is what pleases a woman? No, it's the *knowledge* a man like David brought to my pussy that made me give him my ass. He filled me with... oh, you say it in English..." She sat as 'The Thinker' and after a time she flung her head back and her hair splashed across her face. "*Jouissance!*" She looked at all the men knowingly. David remembered some of the times they were equally naughty and daring in the privacy of their home and sometimes in public.

"What the fuck does that mean?" One of the musicians asked her.

"*Jouissance*, a women's pleasure, her sexual rapture." Her fingers opened like a Venus flytrap, and soon the guys were in the palm of her hand. "It combines physical and spiritual aspects of female experience. Between my breasts, in my ass, pussy or my mouth; David made me feel mystical eroticism." Veronika took off her jacket. Her lips were open and she placed her hands together as people do when they pray, and then put her two index fingers to her lips. Now her bare arms and log legs were the focus of their attention.

"What you know about being men rests on violence and your pulă... your dick. David read poetry to me and between the verses, he kissed my pussy. He taught me how to eat caviar, enjoy the Riviera, understand classical music, and out of that he conducted a symphony in my vulva!" A bomb blast outside couldn't have distracted the men from her. "He's a cock tease and a lover." Michael admired her because art's history taught him about her kind of women represented by Delilah with Samson and Judith and Holofernes.

"Sounds like you're still in love with him," one of the other musicians said.

"He despises me, so I don't love him. I regret the blindness I walked into after we married. I wanted everything a woman from poverty yearns for: fame and money. I thought that was security. My security would have been my children and his fidelity…"

"He isn't all that!" Sophia interrupted. "You called him queer online!"

Cynthia and Solly eyed Veronika.

"Yes, but not in the way you guys have. David is queer because he has the capacity to love women the way you don't: he knows what a feminist is looking for. That comes from the teaching of your sister and your Mum, no? Because he can love women romantically, emotionally and sexually, I don't understand how he's with Michael. That's what I find 'queer' about him."

Frank said, "How you turn batty man?" Solly got up violently, and Frank flinched. Solomon's force of will stopped Solly from attacking Frank, but Solly wanted to punch Frank in the throat.

Solomon said, "Now you know David invented nothing about his marriage I want a public apology from each of you. Considering the defamatory lies you've told about him you've created a great case for slander and I will gladly prosecute you." Solomon walked up to Willy. "Your Tweets are the worst, so I'll start with you."

"Don't ride me or I'll fucking kill you, understand!" Willy snapped.

Solomon looked him straight in the eyes. "Please read that back."

The stenographer read it, and Cynthia said, "This is why you can't manage people because you're inferior. But that's to be expected considering your mother."

"What?"

377

"Your mother wasn't married to a white Jamaican, who died as she claimed. She was going out with a policeman. He was a very nice man, but she didn't have the courage to marry him when he proposed because it would take a brave Black woman to marry a policeman after the Tottenham riots. So she threw him away and kept you. Obviously, you didn't inherit his pride because he was as Black as any white man could be. I knew him! White people aren't all evil, William. That comes out of…"

"Liar! Fucking lying bitch!" He tried to stand above her but stumbled because Erwin had disabled him.

Cynthia looked him in the eyes and said, "If you saw your father's face, you'd know that white policeman is your father. I've called him to bail you out, so he'll be waiting for you at the police station you're going to."

"I can't be white. I'm not white."

Cynthia nodded yes as he said no repeatedly.

Cynthia's blinding eyes reached into him and tore at his mind and vitals. She knew his hysteria against the police and his desperate need to be Black when his peers saw him as almost white, and she watched as the truth ate through him. Solly thought Willy was going to implode and David's passive aggression bordered on imperial dominance.

One of the clients said, "Fucking bitch." Veronika got up, went to him and swung her arm up and scratched him across the face leaving four bloodlines.

"Do not take their mother's name in vain you heartless nigger!" She stood motionless breathing heavily. Not even Pandora could have looked more willful.

Everyone except David and Solly was stunned, and Solomon tapped on the table and said, "Order!" Cynthia glanced at him, conscious of her love for him. Michael also realized how David became the man he was watching this family's drama.

"Now we come to a more serious crime, your attempt to steal David's clients." Willy looked anxious. Solomon exit and the room went deathly quiet. David eyed each of them and felt pure hatred. Veronika took her seat and relaxed. Michael sensed there was something still at work between David and Veronika.

Solomon re-entered with a policeman. "There he is. This man stole confidential files from this company with the help of this woman. She has also stolen a company iPad, Apple MacBook Pro 13, and an iPhone all worth over £4,000.00. Her clear intent to steal the devices is evidenced by the fact all of the devices are at this man's house."

"Pure lies." Willy yelled, and Solomon ignored him.

"Furthermore on the iPad and MacBook, Willy and Sophia have letters they're sending out using this company's files and records. Our device track and trace security have verified this as you've seen in the papers I've submitted to you."

"I'm pressing charges, Officer," David said. The police tried to arrest Willy, but he flew into a rage, but he couldn't walk or run because of Erwin's Achilles cut.

"All you white bastards live for the day you can put your hands on a Black man and charge him with something: please David!"

Cynthia confronted him. "I comforted your mother. We fed you and gave you employment. Then you steal from my son! Go to jail, and I hope they tear you up."

David told the clients. "He nearly ruined all my employee's lives. They've worked hard for you. I have five charges of Intellectual Property theft against you. Take him. I'll be at the station later." The police took him as Willy resisted arrest.

Cynthia moved to Sophia. "My son gave you position and trust in his company, and you tried to steal his work." Cynthia placed her hand on Sophia's stomach. "I curse your womb! No child will live inside you." The clients were so shocked they looked scared and felt afraid. Veronika physically ached with grief. The stenographer's pale Welsh face lost color as she put her hand to her mouth.

Sophia said, "Don't give me that black voodoo obeah shit like I'm an idiot."

Solomon told her. "I have something tangible for you. We're suing you for ten million. The letters you and William have written and signed to your new financial backers. I have those letters!" She tried to speak. "They're saved on this company's laptop!"

"I have full access to the content locker of the Mac Pros you both stole," David added. "Both William and your letter letters are now in my possession: so nice of you to sign, scan them and store the letters on the iPads and laptops."

"The house that you live in," Cynthia said. "That will soon belong to us."

"That's my family's house…"

379

Cynthia said, "Your family, who are also backing this take-over, are going to pay."

"You Bankole's," Mr. Man said, "are just fucking Nigerian Babylon."

Solly told him, "We are and always will be 100 times better than you."

Sophia tried to dash out, but David said, "Stop her. The police will be back in a minute." His staff blocked Sophia's exit and restrained her when she tried to leave, and she started yelling. A police officer re-entered and the staff handed her over.

"The charge is intellectual property theft, company property theft. Dad…"

"The issue of loss of income to this firm is another matter I'll discuss with her counsel." Sophia tugged her arm away from Jennifer and left escorted by the police.

The clients were seriously anxious. "Now for the rest of you," Solomon stated.

Knowing the trap lay in what he said, David told them. "I don't want you as clients any longer. I'm terminating your contacts on the grounds set out in the 2010 Equality Act based on discrimination. That clause in your contract applied to equal rights and the dignity of people you engaged with as a client of mine. Of course, all of your Tweets against me violate those principles, so you're all fired."

Solomon told them. "You have no rights to the videos or songs that this company has written, filmed and created. They remain the property of Bankole multimedia production & management. Any use of Bankole audio and visual material must be paid for; all royalties belong to this firm as you did not write your own material. To the DJs. All logos and visual material may not be use by you publicly at any time without the written consent of this company. Violation of this copyright will lead to prosecution."

One of the core 'Grime' revisionist artists, Mellow; an extremely successful performer who could well be described as the best looking operator in Lambeth, stared at David and said, "What about my studio sessions. I'm halfway through…"

"The project is canceled, and of course since my money and resources paid for those tracks, they're mine," David stated.

"And my album due this Christmas?" Mr. Man asked.

"I own every aspect of that. The writers of that material are going to record it. I've had your voice removed, so you needn't worry that I'm stealing your voice."

"How come you're so wicked?" Mr. Man asked.

"Winston pay attention," Solomon told him. "I want a public apology posted in all your Tweets by this time tomorrow. Failure to do so will result in us holding you to the time remaining on your contract." They didn't understand. "That will mean you cannot get new management. This firm will keep you inactive for the time left on your contract. That's three years with some of you. I have an apology written for each one of you. Post it on your web page and Tweet it also. Then you'll be free to go."

"When the industry hears what you've done…" Mellow began.

"We're willing to suffer the backlash. We just want you gone." David told them.

Cynthia said, "I've haven't seen this kind of rubbish in one room since the 2011 Riots!" Solomon locked eyes with her in agreement.

Solomon told them, "In the folders is your public apology, read it and post it. The list of sites where they are to be posted has been selected by the Bankole staff knowing your fan-base and blogs. They are going to monitor you. They'll feedback, and if they don't see your apology, you won't be working for some time to come. But your solicitors will confirm that. My firm has the resources to do this. Ask yourself if you can afford the costs that I'll insist you pay," Solomon told them.

"Dad, thank you," David said formally. "I want this lot out of my office now."

"Naturally," Solomon replied and Veronika burst out laughing. "'Naturally'; oh, I love this word."

Evadney hated her so much that she could hardly swallow; her body became so tight.

Jennifer told the ten clients at the conference table, "If this is your idea of Black pride, you guys have got a lot to learn." That stuck in the flesh of all the Black men.

"It is approaching four o'clock," Solomon casually remarked. "I expect to see the first posts this evening and up to the deadline of 16:00 hours tomorrow, otherwise you'll being paying legal costs for the next five years."

Mellow asked, "I just have to sign this and I free to take my business elsewhere?"

"Yes, that's right," David replied.

"So the apology means that much to you?" Mr. Man asked.

"Yes, it does," Solomon replied. "David doesn't want to face other clients with the same attitude."

Frank aggressively cut in, "Even if we say sorry on the internet that doesn't mean all of we don't thi'k you're a dirty homo." David and Michael flinched. "I don't have to pay no solicitor money to sign nothing. I will done with you and move past this shit."

"Since your vanity is precious to you, look forward to the apology. But I tell you to your face a nasty bitch like you should suffer AIDS and die." Frank smiled. "Come let we go to a computer and done with this woman." The clients sneered and laughed as they exit. Veronika walked over to David and Cynthia watched her.

Veronika told David. "They looked as smug as I once felt before you made a *cause célèbre* of me."

"Knowing your love of infamy I used the videos. Have you found the right man as yet?" She ushered him outside and then walked him out of the building into Hoxton Square in the heart of Techno London City packed with agnostic 'media' junkies. The neophytes of technical business were all good looking and fashionable, but Veronika believed they had traded their soul for a career in cyber technology no aging person would thank them for.

"Lots of media contact me because of the tape and documentary. Also, hundreds of guys emailed my website, but the men were fakes. Thrill seekers you know."

"You never asked me for the videos back or hassled me…"

"I posted my videos of us, but it just made you look more like a fucking love God and me a tantric sex addict. What was so clever about your defense is that if you are gay then how are you so majestic in bed with me. I would have told some of the media anything to defend myself, but I think your mother would have killed me if I made you out to be a black rapist beast. Your Mum is very scary sometimes. Back there with the belladonna flowers. You know I use sex as a weapon, you do too."

"Me…"

"Oh fuck off. When we were together the number of women you attracted and scared off, from the way you think, and dress and dance then turn the evil eye on if they get too close. I learned seduction from you."

"You've got the honey pot, not me, all men want some of that."

"Yes, people offer me their sympathy and a better life. Only thing is they have no love for me. Out of all the guys who contacted me, only one could name his obsession as a philanthropic martyr with me as his Magdalene, who he could rescue from sin."

"What didn't you like about him?"

"He thinks he's a saint. He's so…blank. But he's very rich and obsessed with me. If I get tired of trying to be normal and independent, I'll marry him."

David looked into her eyes. "You made me crazy when you went after Adrian."

"It was a mistake. I was fucked up and really… Oh, mother of God how many mistakes have I made in my life. Unlike the Polish immigrants we come here, and we want everything, but we haven't got the East-West balance right yet. I *was* so sorry to hear about your sister." He attempted to speak. "No listen, please tell you mother I can imagine her grief and I understand her protection of the rest of you. She looks incredible these days. How has she changed?"

"We've all changed, especially Dad," he said and took her hand and rubbed her wedding finger. "I forgive you. You have your excess; we all do. I just went nuts when Adrian came home after you went up to him. You can call me anything dreadful, but you shouldn't have gone after him."

She caressed his face and looked deeply at him. Her hair blew in the breeze, and there was no denying her change. They had once loved each other and traces of it were clear in their faces. A window across the square opened, and someone snapped them together.

"You've changed. You don't hate me anymore." He acknowledged it. "You hate those clients of yours. I know you; you're not going to let them off. You're going to shit on them, aren't you?" She smiled at him. "I remember when you were wicked; the night you beat that guy who called me a vampire cunt. You rip off his T-shirt, shit on him and wipe your ass. Does Michael know you are that crazy sometimes?" He shook his head no, and she smiled.

"I loved that photo image, and the publicity of the two of you with your mother and the mothers of your kids, very classical."

"It was Michael's idea. Everything about him is beautiful."

"I didn't speak up for you today just for the money. You loved me." He nodded.

She was so pleased he could look her in the face and acknowledge it.

David said, "If you have any chance for happiness, take it. It works wonders."

"I'm clean now so, I'll consider it. I have the money your father offered. I can't build my independence on it, but how would you feel if I sold my story?"

383

"Embellish all you want but Dad will rip you apart if you lie about us. I'll make sure of it." She embraced him, and he kissed her goodbye.

"I underestimated you before, I won't do that again. God bless darling." David watched her walk through the square in between people and she still had more elegance and self-possession than half the population. They had shared so much together, and he no longer felt rage toward her.

CHAPTER FORTY-FOUR

In Cynthia's restaurant a day later the heads of the three families occupied a round table. David casually spoke to Solly, who sat on his left and his father who sat on his right. Michael seemed to still reign over his sons, Roberto and Cesare on either side of him. J.J shared secrets with Carlos on his right and their son Bryan who sat on his left.

The restaurant was closed to the public for the night and seated around them were friends of the families. All nine actors with their wives and girlfriends, and Natasha, who was regally solo. On the next tablet besides theirs were David's employees with seemingly one odd man out, Terry. He had no idea how much money the families had, but he was certain they were all millionaires. He was intrigued by Carlos and J.J because even though he placed them in their late sixties and early seventies, which was correct, they were so financially healthy they looked years younger than their age.

David had kept Terry on salary, but he had nothing to do, and he saw no place for himself in the future with David. He'd spent £300 on a suit, something he'd never done before, but he still felt like the cheapest man in the room. He couldn't help but study David, and he was acutely aware how much he'd changed. The most colorful and aromatic dishes were brought out by waiters. Terry's thoughts were so occupied with David he didn't notice he'd left the table and come over to him. When he saw David had gone he was startled to turn to his right and see him standing next to him.

"Can you give me a minute?" David asked. Terry nodded, and David led him to a table in the corner away from everyone. Terry watched David pull up the seams of his trousers to sit by the side of him. "I don't want you to worry. I'm not going to have any more business with clubs and venues needing a DJ, but I have an offer for you. Will you be my PA, train and work alongside me?"

"You're gonna be busy with everything you have to do. I don't want to mess that up by doing the wrong thing."

"Don't worry about strategy and policy, ethics and contracts; we're all going to be trained and re-trained in those areas. I'll employ a good secretary to work under you, excuse the expression. I want you to work with me." David's face was confident.

"Why?"

"I trust you 100%, and you and I have the right background to work well."

"Because I'm the only Black man you've ever had sex with?"

"You'll never betray me." There was warning that rung in Terry's head, but David's steady affectionate look wasn't conspiratorial.

"You're so different now. You love him; I know that. What's it based on?"

"I trust him, he's smart, he adores me… He has the most perfect cock imaginable, and he could give classes on fucking satisfaction. With everything we do we're equals."

David looked over at Michael and sighed. "His kindness restores my faith every day. He earns over a million and dresses like a prince; what's not to love." Terry could see in his gaze at Michael the love he'd never had. Michael looked away from J.J and locked eyes with David on the other side of the restaurant. Their eyes spoke to each other, and that made Michael's heart smile across his face. David's euphoria was so great he began to breathe unevenly.

Solomon watched the exchange between them and noted the delight on David's face. People around the table peripherally caught sight of David and Michael, but all of the actors had a clear view, and they studied the men. The stage star Taio and film star Isaac eventually turned to each other and lowered their voices to exchange a private thought. "If a woman looked at me the way David is looking at Michael, I'd be carrying timber in my pants." Both men were in their late-thirties, and they had been with enough women to know passion in all its variations.

Isaac said, "Chekov and Stoppard couldn't write that look for Black men."

"Face it," Taio said quietly and then checked around him before he spoke. "There's queer, and then there's love. These two aren't queer." He settled back assertively and took his pretty Dominican wife's hand, and she leaned into him happy because she was a woman who was at peace in life.

Terry tried to be casual but he now deeply regretted his notion of independence. "I remember when we dreaded how people would slam us for being gay and now…"

"Now I don't care. I won't ask for permission to love."

Terry took his hand and said, "I'm really happy for you. It will be great to work with you since I'm gonna be trained…"

Grace and Alice arrived. Grace was accompanied by Clive. David's employees gossiped with each other when Clive led her over to Cynthia, and Lola moved around to make way at the table.

"Terry we'll talk more about it. I'm glad you believe in yourself now. Only losers think they can go it alone." David went back to the banquet table, and Terry recalled the dates and nights they spent together. David always wanted to introduce Terry to his family, but he didn't want to. Now Terry wanted to be at the family table.

****

David stood in front of everyone, and they all looked at him. "Ladies and gentlemen it gives me great pleasure to announce my new firm: The Black Actors Agency. I signed our first ten clients who met the staff who'll work on their behalf. Please let's have quick word from our American partners."

J.J got to his feet and his six foot seven frame made him seem larger than life. He cracked his knuckles, and his 25.5 carat diamond ring caught the light.

"Where'd you get that rock man?" Tony cried out, and much to everyone's delight J.J laughed. Lola elbowed Tony, and he kissed her and stared at J.J waiting for an answer.

"My husband gave it to me for our 25th anniversary." Tony whistled and clapped and other people joined in.

"How big is it?" Tony asked. Michael laughed and laughed loudly. Cesare and Grace got a big kick out of watching Tony. Natasha and all of the actors loved it.

"Dad, don't answer that!" Bryan said loudly. He was a smooth looking dude who resembled a stately Hip-Hop mogul with a touch of the porn star about him. At his age, there were signs that he was a street smart dude who'd hit the big time. The employees watched him and wanted to work with him without hesitation even though not all of them would be staying in the firm since they were no longer in the music business.

"So anyway, if you smutty Brit's can keep it down. My son has the American office, and since we have no intention of telling you guys what to do, David will own and run his office here in London. We offered to put up the money, even though we'd never ordinarily do that; but David turned us down. He is setting up this office independently."

David said, "Cesare and I are going to change the relationship with client representation. Cesare recommended we find scripts and package the material and stars to sell. They do this in America but not for theater. I have apprentices who I'll keep on and they'll scout for talent as we're going to launch a Youth Theatre casting department.

I believe in our future so strongly I'm selling my house and using the capital to rebuild the agency next year." All of the actors applauded him.

Carlos got up and pointed at David. "You got guts and heart to go with those balls man." In his off white bespoke Valentino suit and black shirt, Carlos looked good.

"I wanted this gig in London for my son because America must look outward. My family is going to protect your business," Carlos continued and held his hand up. His heavy bracelet encrusted with diamond slipped down his wrist a little way and his 25th-anniversary ruby and diamond ring stunned Cesare.

"Michael's made some good money for my family. I'm talking over 30 million in the sale of art for our artists. I believe in you David and your clients. I've seen their work on film and TV and David I've seen you work in bringing law and order to those worthless pricks who tried to malign you." Tony positively bonded with Carlos as he took Lola's hand.

"My father and I exterminated the vermin in the company, and I thank him for steadying me because there were days I wanted to hear they all died in a plane crash." David got to his feet. "Carlos, I welcome your family into a partnership with my family. Most of all I thank Cesare for coming back to his father and offering to work with us."

Cesare said, "We're Black Italians. That's true strength! On the streets, in the bedroom and in business!"

Lola stood up and cried, "Child of mine you got that right!!"

Grace leaned over to Clive and said, "I wish I was more like her."

"I don't. I like you the way you are." She was touched by that.

Michael walked around the table and stood face to face with David. "I'm glad David wants J.J's family to join him in business. David, I want you to marry me." He got on his knee and held up a wide gold ring with a 10 carat stone that J.J helped him to find.

All of his employees were flabbergasted. From the other side of the room, they got up and moved closer. The actors were stunned, and Natasha was overjoyed. Cynthia was dumbfounded and Lola smiled knowingly. Cesare was in shock and Solly, and Roberto were truly happy. Carlos and J.J knew Michael was going to ask so they stood there as cool as fearless moguls. Grace looked over at Solomon, and he was pensive.

David said, "Oh my God! *Certo che ti sposo tesoro sei incredibile e ti amo!*"

Michael yelled, "My God you're speaking Italian!"

Terry asked Erwin, "What did he said?"

"I don't know."

Michael got up and put the ring on his hand. "Oh wow! You honestly love me. Dad!"

Solomon moved forward and pulled him close to his chest. "He really loves me!"

"I know he does." Solomon said and looked over at Cynthia, who had tears coming down her face. David grabbed onto him tightly.

Grace pushed her way forward and looked him in the eyes and then kissed him. "Finally, someone has made an honest man of you. Bless you darling. God bless you."

His smile to her was heartfelt. Clive moved closer and held Grace's shoulders and smiled at David. David looked at her and Grace nodded at him. He kissed her face.

Lola took Tony's hand and he pulled her in and kissed her. Solly crushed himself next to his brother and put his arms around him and his father. Cesare turned to Roberto and pinched his cheek. He then looked over and saw Natasha with tears in her eyes so he went right over to her and kissed her. She didn't pull back so he leaned in and she felt him rise up on her so she stepped back stunned.

"If you're not involved with anyone or going through anything that requires... 'Closure'; can I take you to out someplace you'd like. Do something you'd like?" The shy look on her face delighted him when she nodded her head.

Michael pulled David out of his father's arms and led him out of the crowded restaurant onto the street. "You always make me happy, since the first day we met." David kissed him in the cold night air, and his family inside pulled back the curtain and their faces filled the window. Solomon was tearful because he couldn't stop himself. When David and Michael broke their kiss, they moved away from the restaurant, and David took his mobile and called Adrian. "Hi! Michael and I have agreed to marry. It just happened. Son, so happy – I miss you!" Michael yelled 'see you at the wedding'.

"Dad, that's amazing! Have you told Mum?"

"Yes, she was there!" Michael led him up the street to his car. "Later!!"

Dashing up Great Portland Street, David said, "Tomorrow, I get you a ring as well."

"What I want is to take you to bed. With everything going on we haven't run amok in ages. Tonight we'll put love into every fucking kiss we share."

"I hear you; with all the legal and psychological talk about gays' rights, the ins and outs of our lies got lost."

"I'll give you in and out when we get back." Michael declared.

"Me first."

"No, me."

"If you dare try to fuck me, I'll scream." David ran a yard away and Michael caught up with him. He watched him mouth something, and then he eventually heard him whispering, 'help'. Michael smiled.

"I don't think I'll ever stop loving you, David." He put his arm around Michael, and they walked away.

CHAPTER FORTY-FIVE

Lola and Tony's upmarket hair salon status was evident by the number of awards on display. The news coverage pictures of Black women at fashion shows in London, Brazil, the Caribbean, and the States clearly looked like African beauty pageants. Maria was seated, and Lola was combing out her hair and styling it. The salon was full and her eight members of staff were busy working around her doing scalp treatments, dreads, relaxing and cut and style. She had five men and three women because she could not work in an all-female environment. She preferred the company of men, and she could manage them far better. When she previously had only women as her entire staff, the level of disharmony between them was a complaint her clients feedback to her. So Tony suggested bringing men onto the staff.

Every member of staff was very well dressed; there was no sense of a fly by night business that stayed open until ten at night because the staff ran late on each appointment. She had a booking agreement with clients, that Tony wrote, which stated: clients who were thirty minutes late would have to pay a £20 cancellation fee which resulted in almost all the clients keeping to time. Tony also built in one dummy appointment into each member of staff's calendar to make sure they had lunch and time to team manage people running later by ten to twenty minutes. Due to the time keeping regime, the salon ran well. Clients could book an appointment and know they'd be in and out in ninety minutes.

The other distinctive feature of the salon was that there wasn't background music, which was almost a standard feature of every salon in the country. The three female members of staff were Caribbean and Ghanaian, two of the men were Black British, and favorites with the clients and the other three men were all Latin American gay men. On Lola's side of the salon, she worked with the men and on the other side Tony worked with the women. This meant they could manage directly and sustain great client focus. Lola looked to her left and right and saw that every one of the clients looked very relaxed and happy; except for her daughter Maria.

Lola leaned down and quietly said, "You're getting on my fucking nerves." Maria blanked her expression, and Lola said... "Come to the office with me." Lola's eyes were unrelentingly insistent; so Maria got up and followed her mother with half of her hair styled and shaped and the other half ruffled and wild. They went into the comfortable office with a two-way mirror that showed everything in the salon.

All the staff knew they could be monitored from the office. Lola pulled herself uptight and tense. "I'd like you to explain why you're acting as though you've been hard-done-by."

"You tell me Dad's going to marry David like it's normal."

"You and I could sit and chat about the facts of life, women's needs, men's passions, but honestly darling I think we're passed that. I want you to consider a few things your father's done for you. He got you your job. He paid for your degree studies and student living costs. He gave you every kind of love a girl needs growing up, and he's protected you. He's reached a time in *his* life when he needs a soulmate and happiness. Why do you begrudge him, love?"

"He's never come to me to explain why he rejected the family for a flashy man. He's totally changed. Once he used to look like my Dad. Now he's all Mr. Hunk with his gladiator body and young man: I mean where does all this come from?"

"Believe it or not; Michael and I have earned the right to our privacy as your parents. He hasn't abandoned you. You're casting him as *strange* purely because he's found another aspect to his capacity for love. What stands out in your father's character is that he always put us first. Unlike the cheating boyfriends you've had, Michael never cheated on me or you kids. He's protected us from discrimination when people treated us funny. He's one in a few great white men."

Lola sat down warily and upset. "I'm the one who ought to be mad at him...."

"Why aren't you?" Maria asked perplexed and irritated.

"Because he hasn't done anything unkind to me, he was suicidal, and that terrified me. Every day I lived in fear. Tony helped your father and I through that. It's one of the reasons why we fell in love. We're supposed to give you unconditional love but what you're doing is horrid. Papa's on the verge of disliking you."

"I haven't done anything wrong."

"Yes, you have. You're condemning your father when he's given you a lifetime of devotion." Lola's accusation pushed Maria into a plaintive state of mind.

"He's…" Lola began crying and Maria watched as sadness consumed her mother. In her state of sorrow, she looked at Maria with accusing eyes and it made Maria feel shameful that she'd upset Lola like that.

"Mama stop – please."

Lola jabbed her finger in Maria's direction. "You stop. Are you going to hound your father to death? Beauty isn't simply about looking pretty; you need compassion." She began speaking in Italian asking God where she went wrong with her daughter.

"Sorry Mama." But Lola was overwhelmed with tears. "When you hurt your father you're hurting me. And for what: because you're selfish."

Maria watched, but she couldn't remember when she'd ever seen her mother cry like that. What she didn't understand was the devotion instilled within Lola's soul for Michael. "My father wasn't half the man Papa is to all of you. Papa never put his needs before you kids or me." Lola's tummy tightened as she tried to continue. "But you think you have the right to hurt him. How dear you treat him like that. As rich as my family was, they were never emotionally generous to my brothers or me."

"Mama, Dad, betrayed my trust," she declared. Lola got to her feet and walked in a circle. She stopped to look at her staff, and she was momentarily heartened that she had Tony and all of them. She believed her life and reputation depended on them.

"You think he betrayed you. Alright, now I'm going to tell you something…" Lola braced herself, and Maria grew deeply anxious just by the sight of her mother's stance. "Papa became suicidal when he saw how little you, Fabio and Cesare seemed to care about him after you graduated. Your busy life and neglect ate him up, and he became increasingly depressed. At least with the boys they'd all go to football matches. He was so lifted after that, but with you… he asked me in tears why he didn't matter to you anymore. He lost his trust in you."

Tony came in, and he felt the tension at once. "What's going on?"

"Maria said she can't trust Michael because he wants to marry David and he's rejected the family."

Tony studied her before he spoke. "Some people would call you a stupid bitch, but I'm not gonna do that. "Your father loves you like no other woman because you're his only daughter. You've emotionally switched off, Maria, so it's hard for him to reach you, to understand your heart; but since you were a girl he told me he owes it to you to try harder because he doesn't want things to end up the way they are with his sister. From what I know she's a pious uppity bigot, and yet you and your brother spent two weeks with her and missed your Dad's engagement dinner. Two weeks with a bitch who…"

"Hates me, but I don't care," Lola said.

"Except for Roberto, you've all taken a lot from him. Think about him now." Tony approached Maria and gently put his hand on her shoulder.

"I'm not your father, I can't tell you what to do, but I can give you some advice. You kids seriously neglected Mike, and he wanted to die, he felt so useless and unloved. Haven't you violated his trust by withholding your love? Mike's never lied to you. He's devoted to all of us."

"Even though he's shagging some bloke?"

Tony turned to Lola and rolled his eyes. "If Mike was out there laying the pipe to teenage boys I would be the first to kick his ass. Your father is in love and about to be married. Married… now that might not be your dish, but David comes from a high and mighty family, and he's no slut! Get your mind out of your father's sex life and see the man, and while you're at it, take an inventory of everything he's given you."

"I've told her that darling."

"If you spit on your father…" Tony reflected on his bond with Michael. "You'll live in misery." Tony was about to walk out and go back to his client when he stopped and looked a Maria. "Love is so much better than failed ideals. An act of kindness will make you feel so much more powerful. You pick your boyfriends by your ideals," he said factually rather than judgmentally. "Let heart govern your intelligence. Lola, darling," he kissed Lola. "Mrs. Malwa is waiting for you. Maria, ideals are for educated fools, be smarter than that." He left them alone. Lola watched him go back out to the clients and put on his happy face. He directed the staff and went back to finish Ms. Tara's funky dreads. No sooner had he started he looked up and blew a kiss at the mirror in the salon through which Lola could see him.

****

Solly and David were playing on a charity football team in Manchester for sickle cell anemia within the Black communities nationwide. Each team was made up of former Black professional players and stars that love football. The event was covered by a local station and several independent sports media channels, including three from Nigeria were also there.

The event was set up by Solly back in Nigeria and people were only too glad to volunteer earlier in the year. Out on the pitch in the second half Solly's team were getting very good support and so were the other team. The teams were made up of media 'guys', CEOs of major yet unheard of Black business' nationwide, actors, athletes, Black 'City boys' in the financial sector, construction blokes who were active in communities across Britain, and a Black-Welsh rugby player who also liked football. Solly darted and zigzagged about the pitch like a man of twenty. It was totally clear why he was a star striker because he was bold and took every opportunity to score. The fact was he was a natural player that still had tremendous tackling skill and ball control.

Right alongside him David played like a man who loved the game. He didn't have Solly's skills but he did have great defensive skills. Surrounded by the other twenty Black men they all played to look good and win. The crowd was made up of directors of companies and heads of organizations, along with the ten thousand spectators. Two-thirds of the crowd was African Caribbean, and throughout the match African High-Life music was piped into the stadium, and he kept the crowd and players happy. They shouted for Solly, and he found their love helped him to seize the moment and break free to score a goal which involved him taking four players. The screams and cheer for him were magnificent as players from both sides rushed to lift him. In his white shorts and shirt with red piping, he looked as vital as he did in his glory years from 1999-2012.

When the men finally put him down they resumed playing, and nine minutes later David scored a goal, and Michael and Roberto leaped to their feet and cheered madly, joined a moment later by the crowd. As David sat on the shoulder of one of England's new famed actors he felt truly happy. They soon went back to the game, and before long the other side scored and the crowd was delighted by the fact the match was full of action and excitement. Everybody was playing not simply for themselves, or the charity but they all knew as African Caribbean's they didn't want to be afflicted with sickle cell.

In the changing room after the match, both teams were dirty, sweaty full of joy and cheer. Michael came in and looked among the smiling African and Caribbean faces until he spotted David and then went over and shook his hand. Without a word he stared at David and he couldn't hide his love. Solly watched them, and he looked uneasy, but no one noticed it except David.

"Michael, give us a minute. We need to talk to Solly; after all, he arranged this." He nodded and went out of the locker room. Some of the men felt a bit awkward. An East African guy said, "If you two are about to marry, don't treat him like a WAG." David went to Solly as the men continued talking.

"I didn't want this to turn into another moment about Michael and me."

"I appreciate that. Since I've come back to protect the kids and the missus from Ebola, the two of you have taken over the family's time."

"Even though you've said nothing I knew we must be getting on your nerves. Dad has been so busy with the lawsuits; he hasn't helped me to get you settled back." The rowdy men were getting louder and more animated as they undressed. Solomon came in and made his way through until he found his sons sitting together.

"What wrong?" He knew his sons even better than Cynthia did.

"Nothing but the 'David and Michael show' is getting in Solly's way."

"I never said that. I said I brought Alice and the kids back for their safety and you're not the only one with plans." David was contrite. "I have to re-settle here, and Alice and I have talked about it. I want to help you, and you can help me too."

"What, anything." Solomon watched his sons. "I've got more football money than I'll rationally spend. Why haven't you come to me for the agency launch money?"

"How could I take your money when you have a wife and kids?"

"I've got sponsorship money, millions. Sell me your house, and I'll give you a wedding present of the capital to launch your agency. You can give me a piece back later." David thought through the impact and consequences and then he agreed. "You need me. Fuck the hoopla, come to me." At that moment, they felt muddy and beautiful.

They got undressed and went into the shower to clean up. The men in there showed no aversion to David or exhibited any signs of panic. Nor did a single man in the shower make a joke or pass a remark that could possibly be considered homophobic. They spoke about their moves on the pitch and how well the teams played. Some men shouted over to Solly in Nigerian and asked him about Alice and his kids. A few other men commented on his decision to return to England due to the Ebola outbreak.

Solomon sat down and watched the men in the changing room dress to leave, and he listened to the banter coming out of the shower. When everyone came back from the showers, Solomon was aware that, of all the men in there, his sons looked the fittest even though David was older than some of the other guys. For half a minute when he observed his sons undressed, he felt confident about himself, particularly since he and Cynthia had started making love more frequently and they wanted for nothing sexually. He was especially pleased David body showed no signs of effeminacy.

A Barbadian bus driver well known for 'Black boys mentoring support' shouted over to Solomon. "Man I like how those nasty bitches apologized on Tweeter. David, one of the kids in my group, said you didn't deserve the slagging Mellow gave you."

"All of your clients, have apologized isn't it David," another asked.

David continued to get dressed as he replied, "Yes, all of them."

Solomon told them, "Keep paying attention to that story."

"Those boys completely out of order!" a friend of David's stated. He was a Jamaican-born senior account for a huge corporation in the City who hated bullies.

Solly told his friends, "The part I like is that all of David's clients chat so much shit they landed in their own mess. Nine local councils have canceled their gigs at the music festival because they won't condone homophobic acts of oppression."

A doctor at Hackney's local hospital said to David. "Nobody here has that corrupt mind, to think, much less say that nasty shit about you David. You and your parents have given a lot of time and money to the borough so get on with our life, man." David stuck his fingers in his mouth and whistled thanks to all the men.

"This is why we are survivors," David told them. "Common trash is not the voice of Black Britain. I won't forget your consideration." They were all sloppily half-dressed but grand. Solomon stood between his sons and pulled them in by the shoulders, and their friends were happy to see them like that.

"Solomon, I like that picture of you in your legal outfit standing beside David. The headline, 'The Rights of Men' champion. I understand no one ever bring a case like this to court before. You think you going to win."

"It helps that they confessed to lying about him and their statements online are distinctly homophobic, designed to stalk and degrade David and Michael. What has surprised me is the number of important people

397

who sent David Tweets, emails and messages of support. Our case is looking good." Solomon was proud of protecting David especially since he had overcome his own prejudice.

CHAPTER FORTY-SIX

The Registrar was a solemn looking Englishman in his early fifties. He glanced around Michael's beautifully decorated sapphire reception room with cream and white drapery, chairs covered in white linen on one side of the room and cream linen on the other side. There was a plinth in front of the window standing four foot high and a grand bouquet of white roses and cream orchards. His Canonbury house was dressed for the occasion by Bruno, who knew some of the best gay men in wedding and ceremonial designs. Claude and Nasir, J.J, Carlos and their son; all of his new clients, and their families filled the house which looked like a little villa due to the sapphire, emerald and ruby titling, the marble and the newness of the re-decoration.

David and Michael were dressed in silver gray suits, violet shirts, and white bowties. "Good morning ladies and gentleman and welcome to *the little palace*, the home of Michael and David. My name is William Lynch and we are joined by Arthur Nobbs who will be registering this ceremony for the future." Arthur sat off to one side. He was an animated fellow in his forties who looked like he'd lived a world of sin marked by his expression and truly naughty eyes, which didn't escape Angus' detection.

"We are all here today for the marriage of Michael and David. I must, first of all, tell you that this room has been duly sanctioned according to the law for the celebration of marriage; you're here to witness the joining in matrimony of David and Michael. If any person present knows of any lawful impediment to this marriage, you should declare it now."

"None," Solly stated loudly. "They had a Civil Partnership ceremony at the registry office on Friday." People throughout the room chuckled happily.

"Thank you, but no other outbursts please." Cynthia smacked Solly and Lola laughed from her side of the room.

Michael and David stood up. "Before you are joined together in marriage it is my duty to remind you of the solemn and binding character

399

of the vows you are about to make. Marriage in this country is the union of two people, voluntarily entered into for life, to the exclusions of all others." David's smile lifted Michael's heart, and Maria took her mother's hand.

"I am going to ask you each, in turn, to declare that you know of no legal reason why you may not be joined in marriage." They both nodded to him.

Michael said, "I do solemnly declare that I know not of any lawful impediment why I, Michael Giancarlo De Farenzino, may not be joined in matrimony to David Tunji Bankole." Carlos and J.J looked at each other remembering their other wedding.

David said, "I do solemnly declare that I know not of any lawful impediment why I, David Tunji Bankole, may not be joined in matrimony to Michael Giancarlo De Farenzino."

"We will now have a reading," William told them.

Adrian came up to the front, and he looked very smart in his purple suit, white shirt and burgundy bowtie. "Every boy needs his father for protection, football and dealing with the world that beats us down. Daddy, my favorite memory of you, is the day you took me to University and waved goodbye. Mum started bawling her eyes out. You kissed her, told her something I didn't hear but the way she stood upright and held you I knew we'd always need you. In my room that night, I cried because there's nothing like Hackney in York." Michael's sons smiled and nodded to themselves. "Then later you called me and started reading jokes from some book and one by one I began laughing until I was in a state: really drunk on your jokes. Not a day passes when I don't think of you; that's how I know there's big love in my heart for you." was choked up, but David was emotionally steady.

Adrian stepped back and Roberto, Fabio, and Cesare got up and moved to the piano, and picked up a clarinet and a violin. They prepared themselves and Maria rose in her lovely fitted satin cream dress and stood in front of her brothers. She looked at Lola and Tony and then shifted her gaze to Michael. "Papa, it's been a long time since I've sung for you, so here's your favorite. I sing this as an 'act of contrition'. Hear this not for my forbidden love, but for yours." Her brothers began playing and then she opened her mouth and sang *O Mio Babbino Caro*. The most heavenly sound came out of her, and each person listened to her agog. She was transformed while she sang and her skin, and her eyes glowed. Her gestures enacted her emotional plea to her father as expressed in the song;

as the girl pleads for the love, she feels toward a boy her father does not like: however, something much more ironic was underlined as Maria sang.

When she finished; everyone got up and cheered! Michael rushed over to her. He attempted to grab her, but her perfect dress and ribbons stopped him. She held up her finger and said wait. "One more." Michael stood back and William and Arthur waited for them. Roberto played the clarinet opening to *Send in the Clowns* and Cesare on piano led the way for his sister to begin.

Maria understood the song well so she could express the misunderstandings she and Michael had gone through. Michael understood every nuance because he had so many regrets with her all tied to his love for her. When she finished, she knelt before him and looked into his eyes. "Papa, forgive me." He took her hand and pulled her up. He kissed her briefly and lightly on the lips, so she broke into a smile that had been hidden for too long. She stepped back and went to her brothers who kissed her also and then led her back to her seat. Lola was intensely proud of all of them, and suddenly for whatever reason, she could smell orange and cherry blossoms in the room very strongly.

William told them all to stand. "Now we shall move to the exchange of rings." Tony and Solly came forward and stood behind David and Michael. "Repeat after me: I call upon these persons here present, to witness that..." Solly and Tony gave them the rings. Angus watched, and he felt lost but happy for the love of his life.

David began. "I call upon these persons here present, to witness that..."

"I, David Tunji Bankole," William stated.

"I, David Tunji Bankole."

"Do take you, Michael Giancarlo De Farenzino, to be my lawful wedded husband." David gleefully pulled a face smiling broadly.

"Do take you, Michael Giancarlo De Farenzino, to be my lawful wedded husband."

William looked at Michael. "Repeat after me. I, Michael Giancarlo De Farenzino."

Michael held his head up high. "I, Michael Giancarlo De Farenzino."

"Do take you, David Tunji Bankole, to be my lawful wedded husband."

"Do take you, David Tunji Bankole, to be my lawful wedded husband."

"You have vows to express," William stated.

"David," Michael began solemnly. "Love is the only salvation we have here on earth. I promise to protect and care for you. I vow to no other man or woman from this day forward. Previously, Lola Millicent Wallace married me, and our four children and her life will always be sacred to me. Knowing this love with her and my children, I promise to love you no less. Nothing and no one can ever stop me from loving you." David gave him his hand and Tony passed the ring to Michael, and he put it on David's finger. Carlos took J.J's hand, and they shared an intimate smile.

David turned to his mother smiling joyfully. He looked back at Michael and said, "I will be faithful and devote my life to our wellbeing. I vow to honor our marriage, learn from your wisdom and share my hopes and fears with you. All my life I wanted to be free: marrying you has made this possible."

Michael gave him his hand, Solly passed the ring to David and put it on Michael's finger.

William looked at both of them. "Now David and Michael have both made the declarations required by the law of this country and have made a solemn and binding contract with each other in the presence of your witnesses, friends and family and on behalf of Arthur Nobbs and myself, I am happy to pronounce you husband and husband. Congratulations. Ladies and Gentlemen this is the conclusion of the marriage ceremony. Will you please be seated for the signing of the Register."

Michael and David followed William over to Arthur, and they went through the formality of signing the Register as photographer and videographers moved in to capture everything. Roberto's cameramen had been unobtrusive during the reading and recitals, but now they were on full alert.

Dr. Claude and Dr. Nasir stood up and cheered as they signed the documents. Angus stood up and whistled and Giovanni tugged his kilt. Not to be outdone, the three brothers cheered on and Adrian crossed the room to join them.

Lola went and kissed them all while Cynthia went to Maria and showered her with praise which she gladly accepted. The change in season had helped her a lot but most of all she and Adrian had become text pals. He told her about his studies and Ivy took a genuine interest in her work. She now felt stronger about everything that mattered to her and so she went over to David and took him to one side.

"Your son is really fantastic. I was in a panic at one point, and Roberto gave me his number because I had to ask him something. Since then he's been a real help I've never made friends with Caribbean men." David heard a great deal more than she said. "You've both made me question myself. And your father's landmark case of sexual harassment. We usually think that only women can be sexually harassed. Your father's changed that; well all of you of course. There are crazy people out here who do shit because they don't care about others. Adrian and Ivy have been great."

"There's a lot I have to learn about my son."

"I went up to York and Ivy was so cool, and when we talked, I learned things. Is it alright if I come over a lot because Papa and I are very close?"

"Come and see him whenever you like."

She made a jaunty gesture and held her neck. "Great! I mean the wicked step parent would be such a cliché." She kissed him and dashed off. Lola came to him immediately.

Lola said to David. "Finally, she's settled. She and Michael were so close once. Lola watched Maria snuggle her way into her father's embrace. "I love the dressing of the house for the wedding." He walked her over to Adrian. "I'm so glad Cesare has joined the firm."

"He and I worked well during the training sessions with the Americans. We had so much to learn about the legal process on contracts. He has a lot of client management ideas I like a lot." Lola was about to answer, but the cameramen intruded and so she gave them the finger and then blew a kiss.

"Sorry, that's rude," she told the cameraman. "I'll talk to you soon. We're having a confidential powwow right now." They backed away.

David said, "Roberto is excited about his film. I've tried to be as supportive..."

"If he's crowding you, tell him to back off." David shook his head.

In a corner, Adrian and Fabio appeared to have forced smiles on their faces.

Adrian said, "I'm not fucking kidding mate, I will go ghetto fucking crazy and knock your arse out if you say anything. You're here, and I'm here to respect our fathers. I know I'm not over the moon about him being gay, and neither are you, but if you out me or mess up this day for them, I will fucking tear you apart." Adrian forced a smile.

"When we spoke you agreed with me." Adrian led him away from the family and guests toward a room, but people were everywhere, and so he saw the bathroom was empty and ushered him in. J.J saw them go in and he was baffled. Bryan also saw them enter and turned to his father.

"You know what Dad, I don't think there's any love going on in there."

"I don't know the middle son very well. But I know Black folks and that face was cop hostile, and Fabio ain't no cop so what's he mad about?"

"What is it you say, Dad… 'don't busy yourself, with what's not your business'."

J.J gave him the nod. "Ok." He adjusted Bryan's bowtie and led his son back to Carlos.

Inside the bathroom, Adrian had Fabio flat against a wall with his hands around his throat. "You gotta learn to shut your fucking mouth." Adrian looked so violent his face was changed. He looked older and scary. "I don't like to think your father is fucking my Dad!"

"According to Roberto, it's your father who's riding my Dad."

Adrian punched him in the stomach. "I've been talking to your sister, and my girl to deal with this. My issues are my shit. I don't wanna be like the pricks who posted that filth online about my own father. He's a great bloke. Ok you and me both have issues about the shagging and blow jobs; but didn't you see them when they exchanged their vows. There's love there, and you and your sister can help me realize the true depth of what it means for two fathers to be in love." Adrian let him go.

"Doesn't that make us hypocrites?"

"You're evil twins; you've got me twisted with your shit. I wanna be like Cesare and Roberto. Not a fucking adolescent bigot who can only relate to his father on a level of who he's shagging. That's fuckin' sick. I'm bigger than that, I am!"

"If you're having all these issues maybe you're not." Adrian punched him hard in the chest, and it pushed Fabio back, so Fabio came back at him with a punch him in the gut. It took a minute for them to settle themselves.

"I can't live without my Dad," Adrian said frightened and distraught. "I'm going out there, and I'm gonna smile, dance and be nice. Ivy told me if I started some Black man moralistic rant or judgment she'd leave me. I'm not losing that woman."

"You're entitled to your feelings even if your girlfriend doesn't like it."

"What are you talking about? A man is nothing without a woman."

404

"That's my point! That's why I don't like my Dad being gay."

"Fabio, they've both got women in their lives – our mothers." Adrian backed away and wrestled his thoughts. "I don't like you. You and your sister spread your germs on me. "I love my Dad. *Your* bullshit almost drove your father to hang himself." That statement hit Fabio far worse than a punch. Adrian eased back.

"Yeah, sometimes I struggle coming to terms sexuality, but he isn't evil: he loves me, and I love him." Adrian had to fight back the tears. "Rot in your own Godless thoughts about your father; that's your sin, not mine," Adrian declared pointing at him. "You and your sister can go to hell."

Adrian unlocked the door and left him in there. He walked through the house and found David in the Ruby room and embraced him. J.J and Carlos stopped outside the door. They heard Adrian speaking Yoruba, and they felt his intensity with his father.

In the library, the walls were packed with books on History, Post-Colonialism, War, Culture and Art. The colors of the book spines made an unusual rainbow throughout the room. Lola and Tony looked around. "He has all this knowledge in his head, it's impressive."

Lola said, "Have I told you how much and how happy I am because of you."

He shook his head no, and Lola leaned in and kissed him with all her heart. Tony could feel her smile come through him and he felt wonderful knowing their love life and their everyday life satisfied both of them.

Forty minutes later, Michael and David's family and friends stood around the sides of the living room as the sound of *When I Fall in Love* sung by Nat King Cole filled the air. David and Michael moved to the center and began dancing. All the faces of their closest friends swirled past them as they danced and applause slowly rose up.

You Are the Sunshine of My Life by Stevie Wonder began, and Grace led Clive onto the dancefloor. He was really happy. He liked Grace much more than she knew. Lola and Tony went out and danced and then Solomon and Cynthia came to the dancefloor. People watched and then the music changed to Shirley Bassey and Groove Armada's remix of *Never, Never, Never*. Lola screamed, turned and grabbed Michael and danced with him. It was clear they had danced together hundreds of times before.

Lola's gestures were dramatic and as she waved and swayed, she curled her hands and moved her fingers. Their sons cheered them on, and Michael moved around her in semi-circles taking her by the waist and the wrist and David were reminded the first time he ever laid eyes on Michael at the Notting Hill Carnival in 2014 dancing with a Black woman on the street. Cynthia admired Lola so much she felt and wished their sisterhood would bring them even closer now. J.J looked at Carlos, and he deeply regretted that he was too old to dance as he used to up until he was sixty-five. That didn't stop Carlos from standing behind him and swaying him left and right.

Ivy got Adrian out on the dancefloor, and they showed the 'grown-ups' they could dance as only millennium mash-up mates can. Cesare led Natasha into a dance, and she moved like a gypsy seductress with swerves and curves.

The afternoon brought more music, dancing, joy, and happiness. Toward four o'clock, the food continued to be served. Michael walked David into the garden and said to David. "Just two more hours."

"Then Roma for honeymoon sex with my husband." They didn't see Solomon behind them, so Michael was startled. Solomon looked younger and very happy."

"Solomon I have to ask you. The sexual harassment case is looking good. What will the win decision bring?"

"No one has brought such a case to court. If we win, a lot depends on the judge. This case does mean homophobic bigots will think before they preach. People understand what it means to be branded a racist. If someone's a convicted homophobic bigot, they'd become a pariah. It could affect their employability, their social position. I'm hoping it will bring a prison sentence. David, those morons are now a national scandal, they're virtually outcasts."

"This is my wedding..." Adrian and Roberto came into the garden arguing. "I don't want to hear about those bastards."

Roberto told Adrian. "It would be really powerful to start the film with you and me commenting on our fathers considering that's the title of the film. Don't be a shit; that's the only thing left to do. My brothers and sister are at the end of the film. I want you to kick it off with me."

Adrian sighed and threw his hands up. "Alright, you certainly win points for persistence." Roberto punched the air and dashed back inside but turned back.

"There's no docudrama out there like this!"

Lola, Cynthia, and Grace came into the garden laughing their heads off with their arms around each other. "Oh here's where the men are," Grace said looking at them. "You lot are nice, but I got my own business now." She laughed so richly Clive came into the garden to see what was happening to her." His gaze at her was telling.

"That answers that question," Solomon said, and all the women laughed. Clive realized they knew all about them and Michael could see he was bashful but pleased.

Solly and Alice came into the garden with their kids. Solly clapped his hand and told them. "Now my further duties." He led David and Michael away.

David and Michael moved through the crowd to find Angus. He was talking to Adrian in the kitchen. "We're ready." Adrian pulled David away and walked him into a cleared area of the hall.

"I want to be as loving as I can, Dad. I... you've forced me to grow and change. Give me time. I'm sure every guy has to adjust to a new father with a re-marriage."

"Are people being horrible to you because of me?" Adrian didn't answer. "At University has the sexual harassment case caused..."

"No, actually the faculty is really nice to me. I didn't know Michael was so well known. Most of all, Ivy is fantastic. She always talks sense. Rome awaits; go on your honeymoon."

Angus tried to lead David away so he could change for their flight to Rome. "Gus, will you look out for him?" David asked.

"No he's a grown up, you know... a man," Angus replied looking heavenward.

Solly, Angus, and Tony as Best men and Ushers led them out. They all went upstairs to the master bedroom. "Please Gus, explain to him. He just worries about Adrian like he's a baby," Michael said sarcastically.

Downstairs, Cynthia said to Lola, watching other guests, "This is one hell of a beautiful house; the mosaic titles and the silk walls, these floors, the designer furniture, art objects and... everything!"

"Michael always had taste, even when he didn't have any money. His parent's apartment in Rome is poor, and I think it inspired him to want more. I think he wants to spend some of his honeymoon there because deep down, I mean at the root of the man's psyche; all this," she gestured at the house and family: "is what's proved he's no poor fool without the brains to improve himself."

Cynthia said, "On that first day when the case hit the headlines about gay sexual harassment I remember Michael told me at dinner, 'they don't know what kind of up from poverty white nigga I am. I'm gonna give

407

them a Rap they didn't learn from Michael Franti'. I looked up Franti and discovered his race and political identity in hip-hop."

Lola said, "Anyone stupid enough to play a race card on Michael will learn how Jamaican he's become." Clive came and took Grace away, and Lola and Cynthia joined Carlos and J.J.

Upstairs, Michael asked Adrian. "Is something troubling about our wedding? Your father's still worried for you. He's neurotic but not crazy. Do you have issues with us?" he asked anxiously.

"No Papa; Dad's projecting, He has a guilt complex because he doubts he's a great father," he replied in a haughty manner. "Until he recognizes I'm a happy pussy, money and football kind of bloke he won't be convinced. Help him grow up... please." Solly laughed heartily and turned to David accusingly.

"That's a real man talking," Michael said pointing at Adrian. "So hurry up and pack!"

Angus said, "Michael, do not nurture his paranoia. Trust me, it's epic!"

"Gus, don't say my concerns for him as a child were neurotic."

Gus lifted his kilt and flashed him. Adrian was standing beside him so he could see. All the men laughed so loudly they made the blinds shake.

Tony said, "I hope Roberto has captured some of this in his film because you gays are funnier than the Marx Brothers."

"Tony, *vivrai molto più di una vita tranquilla con questa Diva!*"

"*Ascoltami tu, cazzo, morirebbe di noia con un ragazzo timido. Sono il tuo cazzo di marito favoloso!*" Michael replied.

"What are they saying?" Adrian asked.

"Never mind that!" Solly replied. "You bum-shaggers need to get on the plane."

Adrian laughed so heavily he looked fit to burst. In his gray, skinny suit, he tightened into a gray human ball, doubled over, punched his knee and then flung his body wide open.

"Uncle Solly..." he pointed at him. Solly loved the expression on Adrian's face. "Listen, Papa, take care of Dad. Daddy, have a great honeymoon and don't give Papa a headache worrying about me. I'm no over privileged weakling who can't cope." He went and kissed Michael's face.

Angus told Adrian, "Considering the crazies and dumb bastards I have to deal with at University; you should stay in touch because thinking back on our online campaign in Amsterdam and London, for your dads, you three are the only decent straight blokes I can call my friends. Apart from my dad, you lot are blokes I can learn a lot from you."

"Daddy and Papa both have vision, so no worries. I'd love to take Ivy to Amsterdam. I can just imagine a shagfest with her, an Ajax game; they're a good team, plus the Rijksmuseum and Amstel beer would make for a great long weekend."

"Aye, but you gotta go to the Bijlmermeer it's the Black neighborhood."

"We'll talk." Adrian pointed at David and Michael. "Love's on the rise."

"Adrian called us Daddy and Papa," Michael said. "Oh God, that's amazing!"

"We love both ways, amazing things are bound to happen."

A smile played around Michael's face and David caught it from him and they looked great.

finale

Rachmaninov's Rhapsody on a Theme of Paganini played loudly in their heads because Michael and David were listening to it on their flight to Rome. They looked up as the plane entered the clouds and Michael kissed David as they sped through the vapor.

A handsome steward came to them, tapped Michael on the shoulder and told him a passenger complained about their kiss. David took the Marriage Certificate out of his pocket, and Michael handed it to the steward who read it. The thirty-two-year old's Italian face lit up, and he looked even more handsome than he already was when he told First Class. "Today's their wedding day; they just got married!!" The other three gay men serving screamed with joy, and within the elite compartment, the staff rushed about and brought them champagne. For the passengers that didn't like it, they had to live with it because the gay men were beside themselves, and so were most of the others.

David kissed Michael and the gay 'fly boyz' just loved what they saw; it gave them hope of love. An elderly English couple held each other, and when David opened his eyes, all he could see wish Michael's love in his face.

Later they were both in matching white see-thru pajamas that Angus gave them as a wedding present. The sublime passage of the *18th Variation* began playing, and both of their hands reached out to each other's face. They felt euphoric but looked enchanted. Michael unbuttoned his gossamer jacket and with the music playing David was guided by its waltz and half turned and left his jacket in Michael's hands. He reached out and pulled the silk tie, and Michael's flimsy pajama pants were suspended by the sash in David's hands. Michael rose to the occasion and David eyes were filled with magic and mischief. The music was positively alive in one of the greatest recordings ever captured.

Under the silk, David began throbbing, and Michael lost all rational thinking. David had planned the night for weeks, right down to the music and so he engaged in honeymoon love and sex with Michael that ran the gamut from exquisite love to the erotic heights that inspired Michael to give and take everything that was now his. When Michael's spirit informed his soul there was nowhere else to go; he fulfilled everything he'd ever dreamed of. When they were still, Michael was in tears. David asked. *"Che cosa è cara?"* Michael embraced him lightly.

"Twenty, thirty years from now I'll love you even more." David smiled as he never did in his entire life.

The following morning, they heard the bells of the city and dashed to the window and Rome spread out before them. A knock at the door of their luxury suite forced them to turn around and a handsome waiter wheeled their breakfast in and left them. It was everything a wedding breakfast should be.

Michael said, "You look beautiful, even more than over the weekend during the Civil Partnership ceremony and yesterday at the wedding." Michael took a good look at him and his shining white smile and sunlit brown face matched Michael's eyes gleaming topaz brown, and his tan Mediterranean skin."

"It must be the honeymoon sex."

"It's because you have no fear in you anymore. Naturally, my astounding carnal knowledge has filled in the blanks."

"Testa di cazzo!" Michael opened the bottle of champagne and poured them two glasses.

David watched him and said, "We are so lucky. People are starving, dying, living in fear and destroyed because of sickness. We have money, a beautiful home and amazing children." Michael handled him a glass. "I mean I'm starting a new business with clients who respect and trust me."

"What you did for your father is the heart of you, so don't put a 'but' into that sentence."

"Definitely not: I know where my butt belongs." Michael gazed at him with the rarest love because he looked adorable in his white pajamas when he stood up to toast.

"To this life and the next."

****

Out on the golden hot streets of Rome, they put on their sunglasses. In their cutoff jeans, sandals and white shirts they were totally at ease and so Michael kissed David. A lanky white American college boy with a snooty face shouted "faggots!" out loud.

David replied, *"E'terribile che si merda dalla vostra bocca."*

411

The college boy stopped and turned back. "How's that, nigger?"

Michael replied, "He said it's awful that you shit out of your mouth." The American's lips peeled away from his teeth to verbally retaliate, but Michael pulled a long flick knife out of his pocket, and the twenty-two-year-old college boy backed off.

"Go back to Wyoming where you belong." The threatening look on Michael's face was menacing, so the American gave them the finger, and they gave him two different rude Italian gestures. The student darted into the crowd, and they walked on.

David looked at Michael knowing he was safe and would always be protected.

"Marriage is going to take some getting used to. You appear to be the jealous kind, Michele: are you?" They walked in the sun as a smile tore through Michael's chest and turned his mouth into a half moonshine, drunk with love and passion.

"I'm Italian, what do you think?"

David took his right hand bearing Michael's eternity engagement ring and their fingers locked the wedding band and eternity ring into a large brown and tan fist.

Two kilometers on, they came to Ponte Sant'Angelo and walked up to Castel Sant'Angelo. Michael said, "Listen carefully. Can you hear him?"

"Who, what?"

"Think opera!" David thought carefully and told Michael.

"Pavarotti, *E lucevan le stele* from *Tosca*." Michael took his hand and he looked over the bridge and up at the Castle. Spring cast a golden light upon Rome. "We're legally married, I think my parents would approve."

"We can see Luca today instead of mid-week if it would make you feel better."

"It's alright. Lola and the children gave us their blessing. It's true, poverty and sickness ruin life today; but when I was a boy that was Italy too. It didn't destroy my parents, and it won't break us. Tomorrow, I want to go and see my mother and father?"

David nodded. "After that, the evening will be fantastic because we have the tickets to see *Most Happy Fella*: great score!! After that – there's honeymoon sex!"

"This show better not be anything like a Lloyd Webber musical because I'd hate that. I'd never force Grime or hip-hop on you," he said probing Michael's principles.

"Marriage is all about compromise," he stated, to explore David's expectations.

"Ok but a Webber musical… Yuck!" He shuddered. "As you get to know me you'll find I'm very flexible." The playful tone of his voice and the promise of their undiscovered life delighted Michael. "But *that* music, no way! Luckily Dad taught us a lot about opera, and I like it, especially *La Bohème*."

"I think the greatest rap album is Public Enemy's *Fear Of A Black Planet*."

David was surprised and delighted. Their discovery of more shared interests lit their hearts. Michael took David's hand and then hummed an aria as they happily moved on.

CLA

9|17